ON A RISING TIDE

A Novel
by
Richard H. Triebe

authorHOUSE™

1663 LIBERTY DRIVE, SUITE 200
BLOOMINGTON, INDIANA 47403
(800) 839-8640
WWW.AUTHORHOUSE.COM

First published by AuthorHouse 12/21/05

ISBN: 1-4208-7849-2 (sc)
ISBN: 1-4259-1077-7 (e)

Library of Congress Control Number: 2005907508

Printed in the United States of America
Bloomington, Indiana

This book is printed on acid-free paper.

Artwork based on that by Tony Bryan from NVG 92 *"Confederate Blockade Runner 1861-1865"* Courtesy Osprey Publishing

Maps Courtesy Rod Gragg, author of *"Confederate Goliath"*.

.

Dedication

This book would not have been possible without the help and support of my lovely wife Barbara Triebe. I love you Barbara for making me feel special everyday of my life. Without your encouragement <u>On A Rising Tide</u> would still be a dream.

ACKNOWLEDGMENTS

There are many people I would like to thank for editing my manuscript. Everyone had something unique to offer and you all helped make my story exceptional. I want to thank Carol Barry, Carol Blake, Michael Budziszewski, Wanda Canada, Ken Denne, Anne Godfrey, Nan Graham, Jean Nance, John Peckham, Ellen Rickert, Roberta Sell, Kay Schaal, Melissa Spell, Barbara Triebe, Linda Triebe and Carol Weinhammer.

Most of the events in this story actually happened, such as running the blockade, and the battles of Fort Fisher. They are as true to history as the author could write them. The characters such as Colonel William Lamb, Daisy Lamb, Confederate Generals William Whiting, Major General Braxton Bragg, Union Generals Butler and Alfred Terry and Union Captain John Thomas are real and accurately portrayed. All the rest of the characters and situations are fictional and a figment of the author's imagination.

PREFACE

"The importance of closing Wilmington and cutting off Rebel communication is paramount to all other questions-more important, practically, than the capture of Richmond." Gideon Wells, United States Secretary of the Navy, September 15, 1864.

Due to the Northern blockade, the port city of Wilmington, North Carolina, fell on difficult times during the last year of the War Between the States. Inflation skyrocketed and many necessities were unobtainable at any price. General Sherman's army had burned a path of destruction through Georgia and South Carolina and was threatening to invade North Carolina. Although the Confederate army had tried to stop the Federal advance numerous times, its efforts were ineffective due to a lack of men and provisions. The Confederacy was slowly losing the war through attrition. Running the blockade in fast, unarmed ships was the South's only hope to obtain the supplies needed to lift this terrible siege.

The port of Wilmington, North Carolina, was ideally suited for blockade-running. It was only a two-day sail from Bermuda and the Bahamas, and it had an excellent rail system to transport the desperately needed supplies to the Virginia battlefields. This in itself was reason enough to choose Wilmington as the port of entry. Equally important was the protection Fort Fisher afforded the ships running the blockade. It was the largest and most powerful seacoast fortification in the Confederacy and guarded the approaches to the last open port. If the Federal army were to capture the fort and cut this vital supply line, the Army of Northern Virginia would be forced to surrender and the South would lose the war.

In December 1864, and again in January 1865, President Lincoln launched an invasion force to capture the fort and close the port of Wilmington. It was the largest combined Army and Navy assault until World War II.

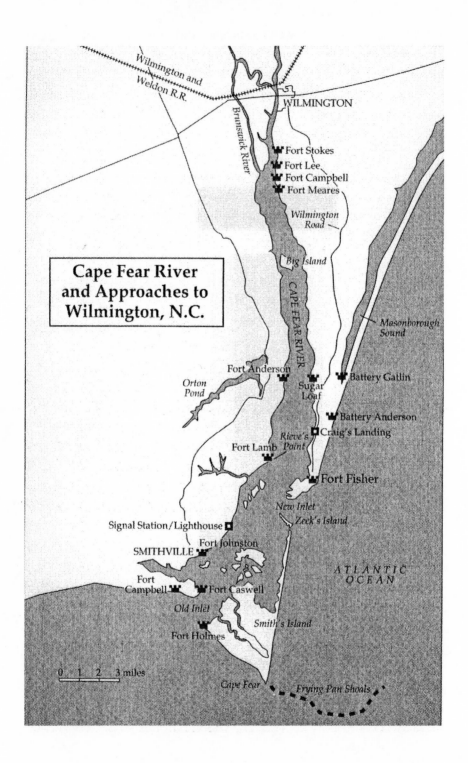

Cape Fear River and Approaches to Wilmington, N.C.

Wilmington and Weldon R.R.

WILMINGTON

Brunswick River

Fort Stokes
Fort Lee
Fort Campbell
Fort Meares

Wilmington Road

Big Island

CAPE FEAR RIVER

Masonborough Sound

Fort Anderson

Orton Pond

Sugar Loaf

Battery Gallin

Battery Anderson

Craig's Landing

Rieve's Point

Fort Lamb

Fort Fisher

New Inlet

Zeek's Island

Signal Station/Lighthouse

SMITHVILLE   Fort Johnston

ATLANTIC OCEAN

Fort Campbell   Fort Caswell

Old Inlet

Smith's Island

Fort Holmes

0 1 2 3 miles

Cape Fear   Frying Pan Shoals

CHAPTER 1

June 25, 1864

Captain Wade McKay braced himself against the freshening breeze on the starboard paddle wheel box and peered through a telescope into the black void of the moonless night. As his darkened ship sped toward shore and the shallow water which could spell its doom, he watched and listened for the crash of the surf against the North Carolina coastline that would tell him when to turn south.

The *Atlantis*, which had recently been built on the Clyde River in Scotland, was the newest of the sleek blockade-runners that had evolved during the war. Although this was her maiden voyage, McKay had every confidence in the side-wheel steamer's ability to outrun the Union gunboats.

Since the beginning of the War Between the States, the Federal naval blockade had forced the Confederate blockade-runners to take risky precautions to avoid capture. By June 1864 the blockade, like a vile snake, had tightened its grip on every southern port, strangling them one by one until only the North Carolina port of Wilmington was left.

When the *Atlantis* neared the coast, the captain ordered the paddle wheels disengaged and the working canvas hauled up the short fore-and-aft masts. This not only silenced the slap of the paddle wheels as they churned the water, but it also allowed McKay to hear the pounding surf several hundred yards away. To that end, he had placed a lookout in the forward crows-nest and had posted additional observers around the ship. Since the Federal warships needed to stay at least a half-mile offshore because of their deep drafts, McKay knew there was just enough room for his unarmed blockade-runner to slip by. Also, he had carefully calculated his ship's approach to Wilmington so it would arrive twelve miles north of New Inlet during a high tide on a moonless night.

The low, 225 foot hull of the *Atlantis* was lead-gray, and blended perfectly with the horizon and the sand dunes on shore. In the event they were discovered, her engines could deliver enough horsepower to quickly elude any pursuers. Every precaution to prevent capture was taken because each precious cargo brought through the blockade gave the South new life and meant it could fight a little longer.

McKay pulled his short-brimmed naval cap tighter against the brisk swirling wind and leaned into the railing to help steady the telescope. His black bush of a mustache all but covered his mouth and his strong angular features were tense as he scanned the North Carolina coastline. After many long minutes of nothing but darkness, he saw the faint gray surf line and heard the unmistakable roar of the breakers crashing against the shore.

"Mr. Hunter, hard aport!"

"Aye-aye, Capt'n!" the quartermaster sang out, then spun the wooden-spoked wheel to his left.

The twenty-eight-year-old sea captain, his face and hands weathered by the wind and sun, grabbed the railing and called to the deck hand below. "Mr. Taylor, move out smartly with that lead line. I want to know the depth every five minutes."

"Yes, sir!" the mate called, tossing the line out in front of the bow, then walking the length of the foredeck while hoisting the line to read the fathom marks.

McKay hurried down the steps to the bridge and opened the speaking tube to the engine room. "Mr. Reichman, raise steam, but keep the wheels on standby. We may be needing them soon."

The knife-edged bow swung around to port and sliced through the waves, spraying foam high into the air.

"Steady as she goes, quartermaster."

McKay scanned the horizon again and noticed several flashes of lightning off the forward port quarter, signaling a storm out to sea. He spotted the lights of a distant warship blinking in the swell about two points off the port bow. Judging by her running lights and smoke trail, she was traveling in the opposite direction on a course which would pass within a hundred yards of the *Atlantis*.

McKay was faced with a difficult decision. He could not go any closer to land because of the shallow water, so he had only three options. He could turn out to sea, but he would be presenting the warship with his beam and plenty of sea room for the Yankees to give chase. He could turn around, but he would lose valuable time and maybe the cloak of darkness when the sun rose in a couple of hours. The last choice Mckay had was to sail dead ahead and hope they weren't detected. The *Atlantis* was rigged to be silent, and with her speed she could easily outdistance her pursuer. This knowledge allowed McKay to stand confidently by the helm and attempt to maneuver his ship through the blockade.

The Federal cruiser was between McKay and the storm, and occasional flashes of lightning backlit the warship's upper works perfectly. She was a three-masted ship of war with a funnel amidships and two high side-wheels.

The distance between the two ships diminished rapidly, until they were within a half mile of each other. Thunder rumbled across the sky and the lightning gave the ships an eerie, specter-like quality.

The boatswain rushed into the bridge. "Sir, the engineer has a full head of steam. He's waiting for your orders."

"Thank you, Mr. Gallagher." McKay motioned to the forward port quarter, handing his boatswain the telescope. "It appears we have company."

The mate raised the glass. "Yes, sir, she's a Federal gunboat, all right. Twenty-two guns by the looks of her."

McKay nodded agreement and glanced at the junior officer he was training to run the blockade. John Gallagher had bushy side-whiskers which extended down to his jaw, then came up again to form a mustache while leaving his chin bare. He wore the usual naval dress currently in fashion: a blue coat with plenty of gold buttons and a short brimmed, peaked cap cocked jauntily to the side.

Through his glass McKay could make out the warship's gleaming bow wave and judged her speed to be about five knots. He was relieved she was going about her normal patrol and hoped this meant her lookout had not spotted the *Atlantis*. He knew it would take her a while to raise steam, and by then the blockade-runner would have a comfortable lead.

McKay was close enough now to make out the naked spars on the warship's shroud-covered masts. Her deck appeared deserted. Most of her crew, he suspected, was lulled into complacency because of many tedious hours of inactivity. This was an excellent sign. It meant the Federal cruiser could not fire her guns for another five to ten minutes--critical minutes which he needed to get out of range of the deadly cannon.

As the ghostly blockade-runner drew abeam of the Federal gunboat, a mighty bolt of lightning split the sky and spilled its brilliance to the sea below. McKay stood frozen on the bridge, disbelieving the terrible timing of the lightning burst.

A loud steam-whistle pierced the night with a continuous wail, calling the Federal sailors to their battle stations.

"Damn it!" McKay rushed to the speaking tube and snatched it open. "Mr. Reichman, all ahead full!"

The deck on the *Atlantis* shuddered as the paddle wheels came to life. The blockade-runner rapidly picked up speed and soon left the Federal gunboat a quarter-mile behind.

The boatswain rushed out on deck, training his telescope on the warship. "She's coming about, sir!"

McKay nodded, glancing at his pocket watch. He estimated the *Atlantis* would have another five minutes clear sailing before the warship opened up with her guns.

A rocket zoomed high into the night sky behind them, then flew over the blockade-runner trailing a golden shower of sparks.

"What a glorious welcome," the boatswain remarked with sarcasm, watching the missile high above them.

4

"Never mind. Keep a sharp eye out for any other Federal ships."

"Yes, sir," the boatswain replied, leveling his glass again and scanning the sea.

"Ship one point forward of the port beam," the lookout called from aloft.

The second warship's bow gun split the darkness with an orange tongue of flame which was followed closely by a distant rumble of cannon fire. The warning shot arced across the *Atlantis'* bow, sending a towering geyser of water into the air.

"Quartermaster, hard aport!"

The boatswain stared at Captain McKay. "Sir, we'll be turning right into them."

"I'm well aware of that, Mr. Gallagher. Hopefully the next salvo will hit where we were and not where we're going. Also we'll be presenting him with our bow, a smaller target."

By the time the warship's cannon flickered again, the blockade-runner's bow had swung to port. The shot whistled above the *Atlantis,* falling seventy yards behind them. The small ship continued to zigzag while cannonballs exploded all about her, sending huge spumes of water high into the air, which then fell back to sea like the rain from the coming squall.

McKay opened the speaking tube to the engine room. "Mr. Reichman, can we raise any more steam?"

The engineer's voice came back sounding tinny and faraway. "I don't know, Capt'n. The boilers already have five pounds more pressure than they were designed to hold."

"Well, if we could have another ten pounds, it might make all the difference in the world."

"Aye-aye, sir. Ten more pounds it is!"

Just then, the sea ahead of the blockade-runner erupted into a foaming spout of water.

"Hard to starboard!" McKay barked at the quartermaster, as the spray crashed onto the bridge.

5

McKay brushed past boatswain Gallagher, shouting to the mate on the foredeck, "Mr. Taylor, keep me informed of our depth! I don't want it to go below fifteen feet!"

The young man, still gazing in fear at the frothy water where the cannonballs had fallen, glanced nervously at the bridge. "Aye-aye, sir!"

Gallagher shook his head in amazement as Captain McKay coolly went about issuing orders while his world was exploding all about him.

The next spread of shots burst in the water where the ship would have been if she hadn't turned.

The warship continued to swing around, exposing her cannon, which gleamed in the night like formidable teeth.

"Quartermaster, I want you to turn hard to port when I give the signal."

McKay leveled his telescope, studying the Federal gun crews as they loaded their cannon for another broadside. The men ran out the carronades, then awaited the gunnery officer's command to fire. This was the signal McKay was waiting for.

"Now! Hard aport!" McKay shouted, motioning quickly with his arm.

The quartermaster spun the spoked wheel until it became a blur, causing the ship to lean sharply into the turn.

The warship's thunderous broadside illuminated a rolling cloud of gun smoke. Cannonballs arced toward the *Atlantis*, one cutting some cordage aloft, while the others splashed into the sea around them.

Every gun on the Federal warship's port side fired but one. The crew of a rifled pivot gun near the bow watched to see where the shots fell, then rushed to turn the elevation screw to adjust the range. These men were crack shots and worked independent of the other cannons. The gunner yanked the lanyard and the friction primer ignited the cannon's black gunpowder with a deafening roar, hurling its deadly missile toward the *Atlantis*.

The exploding shell tore away most of the blockade-runner's paddle wheel box. Despite the tangle of wreckage, the paddles continued to churn the water, thumping into loose boards and knocking them out of the way.

Off the *Atlantis'* forward port quarter, the Federal warship turned again to expose her starboard cannons. They belched smoke and flame, and several seconds later the balls whistled through the rigging, splashing into the sea just beyond the blockade-runner. The warship continued to tack, bringing her port cannons to bear.

"Hard to starboard, Mr. Hunter."

The *Atlantis* turned away from the warship, again presenting as small a target as possible. Like a gift from heaven, a torrential downpour began and spoiled the aim of the Federal gunboat before she could fire. The crew aboard the *Atlantis* whooped for joy as a shimmering curtain of rain erased any trace of the menacing vessel.

Captain McKay grinned, slapping the quartermaster on the back. "Steer two-one-zero and head for home, Mr. Hunter."

"Aye-aye, sir! It'll be a pleasure."

The blockade-runner turned south-southwest, making a dash for New Inlet and the Cape Fear River. Their speed was such the *Atlantis* burst clear of the squall line in a matter of minutes exposing the warship, less than half a mile away and closing fast. This gave the Federal cannoneers in the bow an excellent shot. They fired their pivot gun, and the exploding shell shrieked toward the *Atlantis'* bridge.

The blockade-runner's roof exploded into a thousand splinters, hurling McKay against the starboard bulkhead. When the captain regained his senses, he glanced around the smoke-filled room. The quartermaster lay at the base of the helm with a fist-sized piece of his skull missing. McKay felt something warm on his cheek. He wiped it with his hand. To his horror, he discovered the man's blood and brains had spattered all over him.

The boatswain saw blood everywhere and rushed to the captain's side, fearing he was mortally wounded. "Sir, are you all right?"

A sea captain's cardinal rule is to never show fear to his crew. Although shaken by the gore around him, McKay hid his emotions the only way he knew how--by being aggressive. "Damn it, Mr.

Gallagher! Can't you see I am?" he snapped, motioning to the quartermaster laying on the deck. "Mr. Hunter's dead. Take the helm!"

The boatswain shoved the dead man out of the way, then grabbed the wheel, waiting for an order from the captain.

"All right, Mr. Gallagher, let's turn to port before we get hit again."

The boatswain's hands slipped on the blood spattered wheel, causing him to grab the spokes as he turned the wheel to port. The vessel's quick response to the helm told McKay she was still sound. He snatched open the speaking tube to the engine room. "Mr. Reichman, do you have any damage?"

"No, sir. Some coal spilled out of the bunker and went all over the floor. How about you?"

"A Yankee ball exploded above the bridge and took most of the roof with it."

"My, God! Is everyone all right?"

"We lost Mr. Hunter."

"That's a damn shame."

"Oh, Mr. Reichman, did we ever get that ten pounds of steam?"

"Twenty, sir, would you believe twenty?"

"Wonderful! You keep up the pressure, and we'll be in Wilmington before you know it."

"Yes, sir. Those Yankee cannonballs are all the encouragement I need."

"I'm sure they are." McKay closed the speaking tube and returned to the helm.

As the sky began to lighten in the east, it revealed two more Union blockaders. One gunboat bearing down on the *Atlantis* turned into the wind to fire a broadside at close range.

"Hard a-port, Mr. Gallagher! Let's show him our stern."

McKay realized they were in serious trouble the second the broadside thundered across the water. One ball shattered the foredeck into kindling and another toppled one of the funnels. It clattered to the deck, just missing the bridge, and rolled partially into the water. Since the funnel was dragging alongside, it acted like a second rudder, turning the ship and slowing it. A deck hand grabbed an axe, chopping at the cables which kept the smokestack from going over the side. In a few moments, it fell free and the blockade-runner resumed her south-southwesterly course. Without the funnel in place, the furnace did not have the draft it needed, and the paddle wheels began to slow.

While the warship prepared to rake her again with its cannons, heavy gunfire rumbled across the water from another direction. These guns had the booming resonance of huge shore batteries.

McKay squinted toward the southern coastline and saw the enormous mounds of Fort Fisher in the distance. Ragged puffs of smoke rose from those earthworks as the Confederate artillery grumbled at the Union warships.

Again the Federal gunboat tacked to bring her starboard cannons to bear, while the water around her boiled with countless shell splashes. One cannonball struck the base of her foremast, and it crashed on top of the deadly forward pivot gun. In the confusion that followed, the Federal ship never got the intended broadside off. Instead she continued with her turn, sailing out of range of the fort's guns.

Seeing both warships sail away from them, the crew on the *Atlantis* whooped and jeered the retreating vessels.

While the men were tossing their hats into the air and cheering the boatswain noticed a plume of black smoke to the east.

"Sir, you'd better have a look at this," he said in a grave voice, handing his superior the telescope.

McKay fixed the glass on the small ungainly craft coming toward them. It had none of the graceful lines he had always associated with ships. "It appears the Yankees aren't letting us go without a fight. They're sending a monitor to intercept us."

The appearance of the new ship was even more threatening since its iron sides were impervious to cannon fire, and the blockade-runner's speed had dropped to six knots.

McKay calculated the distance to the inlet. The *Atlantis* was coming abreast of the fort's mile-long sea-face and would need another ten minutes to be in the clear.

9

Like an impregnable metal fortress, the monitor steamed ahead, spitting fire from her two guns. The shots fell well short, but the balls continued to skip across the water for another hundred yards. One cannonball bounded over the shattered foredeck and splashed into the ocean beyond. Four of the crew were using a mattress and some blankets to repair a leak in a few loosened hull plates when the shell whistled over their heads. They continued their work, little disturbed, until the leak was fixed.

When the gunners from the fort saw the puffs of smoke from the monitor, they quickly adjusted their cannons and opened fire. The most impressive fire came from the Mound Battery at the south end of the fort. This battery had a tremendous range because it was perched on a sixty-foot mound of sand.

"It's reassuring to see the guns from the fort fire in our defense, but I'm afraid they're wasting their ammunition," the boatswain remarked with a halfhearted smile.

"Yes, but it does lift one's spirits."

McKay grew concerned when he noticed a cloud of heavy smoke billowing from somewhere near the Mound Battery. Soon his fears turned to shouts of joy when he saw the Confederate ironclad *CSS Raleigh* steam out of the inlet from behind the mound of sand. "Yes! That's the stuff!"

"Sir?" the boatswain asked.

"Look!" McKay pointed toward New Inlet. "The fort's sending out its own ironclad to do battle."

Boatswain Gallagher gazed in awe as the guns on the *CSS Raleigh* thundered across the water at the Union monitor. Between the guns on the Confederate ironclad and Fort Fisher, a maelstrom of cannon fire kicked up the sea all around the Federal ship. The monitor steamed on, but as the storm of shells became thicker and a few bounced off her turret, she retreated to safer waters.

The men on the *Atlantis* shouted, shaking their fists at the Union ironclad to show their contempt, while the *CSS Raleigh* steamed protectively between them and the blockading fleet.

Tom Burriss, the Cape Fear River pilot, had come to the bridge to see what all the excitement was about. River pilots were known for their flamboyant dress, and Burriss was no different. He cut a dashing figure in his wide-brimmed hat, ruffled shirt, a long black coat and tight fitting boots. The pilot looked out to sea, smiling beneath his flowing mustache. "Splendid! Now the Yankees are showing their true colors. Don't they look grand when they turn and sail away?"

"They do indeed," McKay replied with enthusiasm. He faced the Mound Battery as the *Atlantis* passed, removing his cap, and bending at the waist to show his admiration.

"Hear--hear!" the pilot shouted, bowing low and sweeping the deck with his wide-brimmed hat.

The men in the battery returned the salute by waving their hats in the air and cheering the blockade-runner's arrival.

McKay faced the pilot and said, "Mr. Burriss, I turn over command of this ship to you."

"Thank you, Captain. Do you have any immediate orders?"

"Yes. I would like to give Colonel Lamb my compliments. Is there a wharf near the fort we can use?"

The pilot spat his cigar's tip out the door, then nodded. "That would be Craig's Landing. It's about a mile north of the fort. His cottage is near there."

"Very good. See to it," McKay said, then went forward to check the damage to the bow.

The pilot scratched a match alight on the wheelhouse bulkhead and lit his cigar before issuing orders to the boatswain at the helm. Every ship entering the Cape Fear River required the guidance of a skilled pilot to safely navigate the inlet's treacherous shoals.

Two crewmen entered the bridge, removing their shabby straw hats and bowing their heads in prayer when they saw the quartermaster's bloody remains. After a moment of silence, they carried off the body while other crewmen began clearing the debris from the recent shelling.

When the *Atlantis* docked at Craig's landing, Captain McKay and the boatswain walked the sandy quarter mile path to Colonel Lamb's cottage. As they approached, they saw a soldier in a short gray jacket, talking to a woman by a picket fence. The soldier respectfully held his red artillery kepi in his left hand and the horse's reins in the other. In a moment, he replaced his cap and rode off in the direction of the fort, nodding to the two men as he passed.

Daisy Lamb noticed the men walking toward her and waited at the gate. Her silky brown hair, parted in the middle, framed an angelic, childlike face.

"Mrs. Lamb?" McKay inquired, removing his navy-blue cap.

She nodded.

"Ma'am, I'm Wade McKay, captain of the blockade-runner *Atlantis* and this is my boatswain, Mr. John Gallagher."

"Was it your ship the Yankees were shooting at, Captain?"

"Yes, ma'am. Seems they don't take kindly to our running their blockade."

Daisy's face showed her concern. "I hope no one was hurt."

"I reckon we're all right, Mrs. Lamb. One man was killed, and they damaged our ship a mite."

Daisy Lamb gasped softly. "Oh, dear! Is there anything I can do?"

"Yes, ma'am. We came to see your husband. Is he about?"

"No, Captain, he's not. He rushed to the fort when he heard the guns."

McKay frowned, shaking his head. "That's too bad. I wanted to thank him. Would you tell him Captain McKay was here and sends his compliments?"

"Of course I will, Captain, but why don't you stay for breakfast and tell him yourself? A courier told me he'll be along soon, and I know he will want to hear all about your escape."

"Thank you, ma'am. I'd like that."

Mrs. Lamb led them inside the whitewashed three-room cottage. The low-beamed room contained a cast-iron stove, a rough sawbuck table with six chairs, a ballast stone fireplace and an old cabinet which was stacked with blue and white plates, cups, and bowls.

"Would you gentlemen like some coffee?"

"Yes, ma'am," McKay said, while the boatswain nodded eagerly.

The men sat at the kitchen table while Mrs. Lamb went to the cabinet. She set two cups before them and was carrying a pot of coffee from the stove, when the sound of a rider made her pause and gaze at the door.

Hurried boots clumped onto the porch, and a slim, bearded man in Confederate gray opened the door. His broad forehead and nose were shiny with sweat from the day's heat, and his cotton shirt hung open at the collar.

"Captain, this is indeed a pleasure," Colonel Lamb said, crossing the room. "I was hoping to meet you."

McKay rose to meet him and they shook hands. "Thank you, Colonel. I'm Captain Wade McKay and this is my boatswain, John Gallagher. We came to thank you for your fine defense of our ship. We wouldn't be here without it."

Lamb waved a hand in dismissal. "No thanks are needed, Captain. Fort Fisher was built for your protection."

"I'm glad it was, because we certainly needed it today."

Lamb smiled and nodded. He had heard the same story from countless other grateful seamen. "Gentlemen, please do me the honor of having breakfast with us."

"We would consider it an pleasure, Sir."

Colonel Lamb regarded the seaman for a moment. "Forgive me for staring, Captain, but I was wondering why we haven't met until now. Most of the captains stop at Fort Fisher before they run the blockade. Why haven't you?"

McKay nodded, "Well, sir, I'm new to the area. I sailed out of Charleston until the Federal Navy closed that port last March."

"I see. But if you couldn't leave Charleston, how did you get to Bermuda?"

McKay was not offended by the questions Colonel Lamb was asking him. He suspected the fort's commander was merely doing his job, watching for spies. "I traveled to Wilmington by train. Then I sailed to Bermuda on the *Will of the Wisp* to pick up my new ship, the *Atlantis*."

"So that was the *Atlantis* I saw."

McKay nodded.

The men sat down while Daisy Lamb poured a cup of coffee for her husband. Lamb smiled at her, then said, "She's a fine ship. The South could use more like her."

"Only the most modern ideas were used in her construction," McKay said with a hint of pride. "She's built of iron and designed specifically for blockade-running. She's fast, with a narrow beam and a large stowage capacity, yet she still sits low in the water. Her paddlewheel housings are covered with canvas, and she can blow off steam underwater to reduce noise."

Colonel Lamb stirred his coffee, then set the spoon down. "What's her speed?"

"She averages sixteen knots, but when the conditions are favorable she can make eighteen."

Lamb raised his eyebrows, impressed.

The boatswain, keeping his fingers around the warm cup he had just set down, broke in. "Colonel, I must tell you how amazed I am by Fort Fisher. I had no idea it was so enormous."

"It wasn't always that way," Lamb said with a shake of his head. "When I was assigned to defend Confederate Point in 1862, it was nothing more than a few earthworks with seventeen guns. I saw how important it was and decided I would build a fort strong enough to withstand the heaviest fire of any guns in the American Navy." Lamb lifted his cup and smiled. "Now it mounts forty-four heavy artillery pieces and is the largest fort in the Confederacy."

"Wouldn't a masonry fort be better?" Boatswain Gallagher asked.

"Quite the contrary. Since it is an earthwork, the sand will absorb the impact of the largest shells and will not shatter like a masonry fort."

"Most impressive, Colonel," McKay said, then added, "I can see a lot of thought went into Fort Fisher's construction, but will this be enough to keep the port of Wilmington open? The people in Charleston also thought their city was well protected by the forts in the harbor. The Federal Army and Navy assaulted it many times before finally realizing they did not have to capture Charleston to close the port. They merely tightened the blockade and halted all traffic going in and out. Aren't you afraid of them doing the same thing here?"

"Yes, I am, but I don't believe the Federal Navy has the resources to do so. Fortunately the Cape Fear River has two inlets which are separated by Smith's Island and Frying Pan Shoals. Geographically, the inlets are only three miles apart, but because the shoals jut so far out into the Atlantic, that distance has been expanded to forty miles."

"It amazes me why the Federals would even attempt such an impossible feat," Daisy Lamb said, as she stoked the fire in the stove with more wood, then slammed the door shut with an angry clang. "Don't they know Wilmington can never be closed?"

"I wish that were true," her husband said with a frown. "According to the latest intelligence, President Lincoln is considering an invasion before the end of the year."

"Are you certain?" McKay asked him with concern.

"Yes, I am. I haven't heard anything definite yet, but it's only a question of time."

"Why doesn't the North just leave us alone?" Daisy asked, wiping her hands on her apron.

"President Lincoln has no choice," her husband told her. "He's under great pressure to end this terrible war and to save the Union. Wilmington has become a major obstacle because it provides the Confederacy with the means to resist. Therefore, it must be eliminated."

Colonel Lamb fell silent for a moment, then added, "I received a letter last month from General Lee urging me to keep Wilmington open at all costs. He said he could not continue to defend Richmond if Wilmington fell. As you know, gentlemen, if the Army of Northern Virginia evacuates Richmond, then there is no hope for the Confederacy."

While the men nodded in agreement and sipped their coffee, Daisy fried country ham to serve with the biscuits she had made that morning. The thought of war coming to Wilmington upset her so, she needed to stay busy to keep from thinking about it.

*   *   *   *

While McKay was visiting Colonel Lamb at his cottage, deck hand Judson Bates concealed a bottle of whiskey under his shirt and crept down to the coal bunker near the *Atlantis'* engine room. Most of the coal was used during the blockade-runner's voyage from Nassau, but there was still enough to conceal him. The bearded man with the bowler hat climbed over the mounds and made himself as comfortable as he could in the hot bunker. Weak light from the engine room illuminated Judson's reflection on the dark bottle as he slipped it from his shirt. Licking his lips in anticipation, he pulled the cork from the bottle, then swallowed eagerly. The satisfying warmth of the liquor soothed his nerves and helped him to forget.

Bates pulled a thin cigar from one of his shabby pockets, then scratched a lucifer match alight on the sole of his boot. With a trembling hand, he held the flame to his cigar. It wasn't the years of hard drinking that made Judson's hand shake so, but an old injury to his right wrist.

When the cigar was drawing properly, Judson blew a plume of smoke across the dim bunker and wondered how he came to be in such a hazardous place--a place where Yankees lurked around every corner, just waiting to blow your ship out from under you. He took another swallow of whiskey and thought about when his troubles began.

The only pleasant memory he had was when he worked in the fish market, but Ashley ruined that for him. She had made a laughingstock of him, but he showed her. Still, that's where his troubles began. It was *women.* Ashley was just the first.

*   *   *   *

Earlier that night, at the Deering Plantation, across the Cape Fear River, Reuben Thomas stumbled to the door of the darkened slave's quarters and opened it, lifting his glistening, ebony face to the sky. Although there was no moon, he could see the storm clouds roll in off the ocean illuminated by occasional flashes of lightning. A soft female voice called behind him. "Close that door, Reuben, an' com'on to bed."

He turned, pointing outside. "Them's cannons, Cally! Mizta Lincoln's soldiers done come to set us free."

She sat up, waving a sleepy hand. "No, it ain't. That's thunder. Now com'on back to bed before we got to git up."

Reuben stayed where he was, listening to the regular booming that came from the direction of Fort Fisher. He said quietly to himself, "Them's guns. Big guns. I know it."

Cally's voice grew angry now. "Reuben, com'on back to bed! Massa Deering don't want no tired niggers on dis plantation."

Reuben looked out the door again. "No! I ain't tired. Not yet, I ain't. I hear de glorious sounds of freedom ringin' in de heavens!"

Cally rubbed the sleep from her eyes, then shook her head. "More'n likely it's another blockade-runner gone aground, an' bein' shot full of holes."

Reuben smiled, turning his face to the coming storm. "No, it ain't! Dat's de sound of freedom!"

CHAPTER 2

The war changed Wilmington dramatically. The city's population swelled from ten thousand people to more than fifty thousand in a few years. The lucrative trade involved in blockade-running filled the town with speculators from all over the world, and quite often the crews from the ships themselves were from other countries. They were young and reckless, and because running the blockade paid so well, they had plenty of money to spend. These men demanded a good time, and certain people in Wilmington were willing to provide it for them. An incredible amount of money changed hands wherever this trade flourished, and this attracted all sorts of unsavory characters. Crime was epidemic, and robbery and murder had become commonplace.

Due to greedy speculation and the tightening of the naval blockade, food had become scarce and the necessities of everyday life were priced so high as to be unobtainable by the average person. Persuaded by their husbands and sweethearts, and with the constant threat of Wilmington being attacked by Union forces, most women left town. Many of the large, beautiful homes belonging to the best families were vacant or rented to blockade-running companies to house their crews.

* * * *

The workmen on Craig's Landing tossed the *Atlantis'* mooring lines into the Cape Fear River's tea-colored water while deck hands hauled the lines aboard the blockade-runner. The ship signaled her departure with a three-second blast from her brass steam whistle, setting the port side-wheel into motion and moving the ship slowly away from the wharf.

McKay took his place next to the pilot at the helm. The bloodstained shambles of the bridge reminded him of the horror a few hours before. The roof, what was left of it, had been blown to bits sending deadly missiles everywhere. One of those missiles had found the quartermaster and killed him. The seaman had left his family in Charleston with plans for them to join him in Wilmington when he found a place to live. Hunter had even invited McKay to dinner once they were settled. Now there would be no move or dinner--only a letter McKay must write telling Hunter's wife how he had died.

McKay examined the wreckage again, then dug a two-inch iron splinter from the paneling behind him with his pocket knife.

The pilot glanced over his shoulder, and said, "That there's Billy Yank's callin' card, sir. This bridge only got a few small pieces of an explodin' shell. If it was a mite closer, there'd a been no bridge left at all."

"Or me, either," McKay observed, fingering the shrapnel thoughtfully.

"Reckon so," the pilot said, casting an experienced eye at the swirling water and the shoreline. The bend in the river they were approaching had treacherous currents, and a pilot needed to stay alert.

Several rusting shipwrecks along the water's edge made McKay increasingly uneasy. Each time the blockade-runner steamed past the corroding hulk of another unfortunate vessel, his stomach tightened up a notch. He found himself examining the pilot's every move and wondering if the man had sailed any of these ships to their destruction. Doing nothing while his ship was in danger was foreign to McKay. Finally, he could sit still no longer.

"Mr. Gallagher," McKay blurted.

The boatswain was making an entry in a small notebook and looked up. "Sir?"

"Go below and inspect the patch in the forward hull. The mattresses we used to plug that leak will have become soaked and may allow some seepage. Check the bilge and see if the pumps can handle the water."

While the boatswain went to the forward hatch, McKay stepped outside to watch for hazards. He paced the deck, looking this way and that, calculating where a safe channel might be. Before long, the warm marsh-scented breeze and the unique shoreline caught his attention. The maritime forest of live oak, stunted in size and sculpted by the wind and sea, gradually straightened to become tall longleaf pines fringed by the ever-present marsh grasses at the river's edge. White herons stalked the shallows for fish, then froze to watch the strange, smoking craft cut a widening vee in the turbulent waters. McKay could picture himself in a small boat, fishing the Cape Fear with only the herons and the osprey for neighbors. He treasured the idyllic youth he'd had fishing and exploring the rivers and creeks around Charleston. McKay wondered if young boys still fished this river because of all the hardships war brings. It was sad to think these simple pleasures might be lost to the next generation.

As the *Atlantis* rounded a bend, a clearing with tall marsh grasses came into view. A little farther on, the grasses gave way to lush green rice swaying in the breeze before a white mansion with six Corinthian columns. Long mounds of sand separated the rice paddies from the river. An overseer wearing a broad-brimmed planter's hat stood on the highest embankment, watching several dozen Negroes wade through the rice paddies, weeding them. He turned and nodded to the ship as it passed.

McKay waved in recognition. "Mr. Burriss, what plantation is that?"

"That would be Deering Plantation, sir," the pilot said, adjusting the wheel so the ship stayed in the main channel. "Been there since the 1700's, so I hear. Ain't nothing like it used to be, though. What

20

you see now is just a skeleton. Mr. Deering had to cut back because of the war, you know."

"Why's that?"

The pilot shrugged his shoulders. "Weren't nobody left to tend the fields. Most of the menfolk are gone. Seems the war and yellow fever have taken so many."

McKay left the railing and returned to the wheelhouse. "I recall reading about the fever in the Charleston papers. The editors said the sickness was brought in on a blockade-runner and used the epidemic in Wilmington as an example. They warned the same thing could happen to our city if we weren't careful."

The pilot nodded, then paused to light a long black cheroot. He spat the cigar's tip out the door and scratched a match head alight with his thumbnail. "The fever came aboard the steamer *Kate* during the summer of '62," he said when his cigar was drawing properly. "People burned barrels of rosin to purify the air, but it didn't do nothin' 'cept put a cloud of black smoke over the city. I remember, it appeared the way you would imagine hell to be. Come to think of it, it was."

"How did the city get rid of the fever?"

The pilot puffed on his cigar, deep in thought. "Don't rightly know. Some say the cool fall temperatures chased it away. All I know is when the fever left, it took over eight hundred souls with it."

As the *Atlantis* steamed around the next bend, the imposing earthen ramparts of Fort Anderson came into view. A large three-sided wharf extended into the river from the western bank. Three men were on the wharf and one was motioning the ship to dock.

"That'd be Doc Sutton, the health officer," the pilot explained, taking the cigar out of his mouth and flicking the ashes onto the deck. "He'll want to inspect the crew for any signs of sickness. The city don't want another plague."

"What happens if he finds someone with yellow fever?" McKay asked.

"They keep the ship in quarantine for thirty days. The crew goes to Mount Tirzah Hospital, while they fumigate the blockade-runner." The pilot stuffed his cigar back under his flowing moustache.

McKay's brow furrowed in agitation. "Thirty days! Don't they realize I have desperately needed medical supplies aboard?"

"Yes, sir," the pilot said, steadily turning the wheel toward the dock. "The army is s'posed to unload the cargo with barges, but it ain't easy findin' somebody who ain't afraid of a boat with yellow fever aboard."

McKay called down to the engine room to slow the engines, and the *Atlantis* glided to a stop alongside the wharf. Several deck hands threw lines ashore, which were quickly fastened to four bollards. When the gangplank was in place, a gentleman with an imperial beard and carrying a black bag stepped aboard. Two young soldiers carrying muskets followed him.

McKay assembled the crew on the foredeck. The physician examined the men for any signs of headache, fever, unusual rash or aching joints. When his inspection was through, the doctor gave the ship a clean bill of health and permission to go on to Wilmington.

After the pilot had told him how the war and yellow fever had ravaged the area, McKay expected the port city to be a mere shadow of what it had once been, so he wasn't prepared for the flurry of activity which greeted him on that sunny June day.

The half mile wide river was filled with watercraft of every description. Three sleek blockade-runners, several stern-wheel paddle boats and numerous barks and sloops were huddled against the wharves, loading or unloading their cargos on both sides of the waterway. To the west, on Eagle's Island, was a shipyard with a boat under construction. The hull was on blocks, surrounded by scaffold, and workers were hammering broad, oaken planks onto massive ribs. To the north, a turpentine distillery was circled with hundreds of barrels, and beyond that was a wooden three-story cotton press and several large warehouses. Banded cotton bales lined the wharf and were being loaded onto the deck of a blockade-runner.

Across the river, white church steeples stabbed at the skyline, heralding the town of Wilmington. Stylish brick buildings dominated the busy waterfront while blockade-runners lined the wharf, discharging their cargos. With its massive pillars and pilaster corners, the venerable three-story Customs House rose above the collection of smaller structures. To its south stood the Market House with its peddlers hawking their wares in the humid air beneath the column supported roof. North of the Customs House was the sprawling Cotton Exchange, a maze of warehouses where cotton and rice were brought for auction. A procession of wagons, piled high with bales of cotton, made their way to the dock and traded their loads for barrels of merchandise which the ships had brought through the blockade. The streets of Wilmington also bustled with activity as men in beaver hats, frock coats and beautiful women in fancy gowns and plumed hats strolled by to pursue their various interests.

The *Atlantis* found an open berth at the foot of Chestnut Street, just ahead of the side-wheel blockade-runner *Lynx*. While the mooring lines were made fast, dozens of spectators gathered to congratulate the captain for running the blockade and to view the cargo as it was unloaded and put onto horse drawn carts.

As Curtis Snow walked to the waterfront to greet the blockade-runner which had just arrived, he worried about the dinner party that evening. He'd been a shipping agent with Burgess & Linden for a little over a year now, and his finances were barely keeping pace with inflation. He could not afford to lose this job. A chill swept through him as he recalled those dark days in 1863 when he had lost his employment as a clerk in a dry-goods store. The Yankee blockade had slowed the flow of goods into Wilmington, and there was no longer any use for a clerk with nothing to sell. He was let go with a promise the store owner would rehire him when things returned to normal. Curtis doubted if they would ever be normal again. As his savings disappeared, his worries soon overwhelmed him. His despair was so deep Curtis had even contemplated suicide until this job came along. Through his work as a shipping agent, Mr. Snow became aware of the money that could be made by investing in the cotton exported to England. It was possible to buy a bale of cotton for twelve cents in Wilmington, then sell it for at least a dollar in England. In order to take advantage of this profitable business, he had taken out a mortgage on his house, then bought eight hundred bales and had them loaded on the blockade-runner *Osprey*. With a little luck, Curtis would pay off the bank and deposit a handsome profit.

Because Curtis had never dealt with Captain McKay before, he felt it was extremely important to start off on the right foot. Therefore, he decided to show the captain he was in charge now that the cargo had reached port. After all, Curtis was Burgess & Linden's agent in Wilmington, and it was his responsibility to determine what was best for the company.

Four deck hands aboard the *Atlantis* unleashed the gangplank from alongside the forward gunnel, extending it to the wharf. The first man to board the blockade-runner wore a brown, low-crowned top hat and a frock coat of blue-gray while carrying a walking stick in his left hand. The agent for the British shipping company found McKay on the deck, outside the bridge. "My compliments, Captain, on running the blockade. I'm Curtis Snow, Burgess & Linden's agent here in Wilmington."

McKay shook hands with the man. "Thank you, Mr. Snow. I'm Captain Wade McKay, master of the *Atlantis*."

"I see you've had a rough time of it," Curtis said, nodding to the damaged bridge.

"Yes, we have," McKay said, his mind flashing back to the scene of horror in the wheelhouse. "My ship suffered three hits. One man was killed."

"I'm terribly sorry. Is there anything I can do?"

"Yes, could you tell me where I can have my ship repaired?"

"Of course, Captain. Wilmington has several shipyards, but Cassidey's is one of the finest. The government built the *CSS Raleigh* there, you know," Curtis said with a hint of pride.

McKay nodded with approval. "If they're good enough for the Confederacy, then they're good enough for me. I'll take the *Atlantis* there after we've unloaded."

24

"Excellent, Captain. We need to get this ship repaired and loaded as soon as possible. I've arranged for Wilkes Morris to auction the cargo out of his warehouse on Granite Row this Tuesday. I would like you to be on hand. It's good for business when people can meet the captain who braved the cannons of the blockade."

With all that had happened this morning McKay had no desire to be charming. Although his eyes flashed his displeasure, he knew the man was correct. McKay had promised the owners he would cooperate with their agent. "I don't think you'll need me there."

"It's your duty to attend, Captain," Mr. Snow reminded him, arching a stern eyebrow. "Besides, we want to keep the owners happy by fetching a splendid price for their goods. You have to admit, when the captain's present it builds a certain excitement."

The agent paused, then added, "By the way, Captain, you're invited to a dinner party at my home at seven o'clock. Speculators from all over the South will be there. I want you to meet them."

"You mean entertain them, don't you?"

Mr. Snow smiled wearily, folding his hands over the head of his walking stick. "In a manner of speaking. I'm certain these men would love to hear some of your sea stories."

McKay nodded. "May I bring one of my crew?" He briefly considered dumping the quartermaster's bloody corpse in his agent's parlor, in front of his appalled guests.

"Of course you can," Mr. Snow answered, then looked the captain over and saw his clothes were torn and spattered with blood. "You do have something else to wear, don't you?"

"Yes," McKay replied through tense lips. "I'm sorry I didn't have time to change, but I was busy dodging Yankee cannonballs."

"Very amusing, Captain." Mr. Snow was entirely unamused. "Save the humor for our guests this evening."

"Yes, sir. I'll try to remember that."

"See that you do. Good day to you, Captain," Curtis said, touching his gold-headed cane to the brim of his hat.

McKay watched his agent leave the ship, then called to the boatswain. "Mr. Gallagher, will you join me for dinner tonight?"

25

The junior officer peered out of a broken window in the bridge. "Is that an order, sir?"

McKay nodded. "Yes, I guess it is. We're going to a dinner party at our shipping agent's house. I don't want to go alone."

The boatswain grinned and said, "You can count on me, Captain."

"Thank you. Oh and, Mr. Gallagher, please wear something presentable."

Agitated, Boatswain Gallagher walked over to Captain McKay while the crew was unloading the *Atlantis*. "Sir, Bates has been at it again. Somehow he managed to sneak a bottle of whiskey aboard, probably at Nassau, and ever since we got through the blockade he's been having himself a grand time."

"Is he drunk?"

"Yes, sir, he is," the boatswain said. "But that's not all Bates did. He hid in the coal bunker, then lit a cigar and nearly started the ship on fire. A stoker found him passed out behind a pile of coal with his cigar still burning. The coal dust might have exploded. He's a danger to have aboard, sir."

Folding his hands, McKay asked, "Is that all?"

"Yes, sir, but I wish you'd have a talk with him. He won't listen to me."

"I intend to. Where is he?"

"He's passed out on his bunk, sir."

McKay was on his way to the crew's quarters, when he heard the Chief Engineer call after him.

"Oh, Captain," a short, balding man in blue trousers and a grimy undershirt shouted as he scurried across the deck.

"Yes, Mr. Reichman?"

"Since we're gonna be laid up for repairs, I'd like to get the boilers checked out, sir. I know I shouldn't have done it, but I tied the safety valves down so they'd hold more pressure. Those high pressure boilers were designed to hold thirty pounds of steam, but for a while we had as much as fifty."

"You do whatever you feel is necessary, Mr. Reichman. By the way, you did a wonderful job outrunning that ironclad."

Smiling nervously, the Chief Engineer said, "Thank you, Captain. But I have a little secret to confess."

"Oh? What's that?"

"Well, sir, I threw your breakfast into the furnace," he admitted, then lowered his gaze self-consciously.

"You did what?"

"You said we had to have more steam," he explained quickly, "so I took two sides of bacon from the cook and threw 'em in the furnace. That bacon grease makes a lovely fire, sir."

McKay chuckled. "Well, I'm sure bacon never saw better service."

The engineer laughed when he saw the captain was not upset. "No, sir. It was just what the fire needed."

"Well, chief, you keep doing that and there's no way the Yankees can catch us."

Reichman grinned. "We'll show 'em, won't we Captain?"

"You bet we will."

McKay went to the crew's quarters below and found Bates snoring loudly on his bunk, and shook him awake.

Squinting at the officer, the groggy man asked, "That you, Capt'n?"

"Yeah, it's me, Bates. What's this I hear about you hiding in the bunker with a bottle of whiskey?"

Bates propped himself up on a bony elbow. His face and clothing were grimy with a mixture of coal dust and sweat. "Well, I figgered runnin' thru alla them Yankees an' stayin' in one piece a man has a right to a drink."

McKay nodded. "I can't argue with that. The trouble is, you drank the whole bottle, then had a cigar while you were on duty."

"Yes, sir, I did," Bates said, then shook his head. "Man can't have whiskey without a seegar."

"Well, Bates, your cigar nearly set the coal bunker on fire. One more incident like that, and I'll leave you in Wilmington." McKay gazed at the sailor for a moment, and added, "You know I've got to punish you for being drunk, don't you?"

"I surely do, Capt'n."

"All right then, no shore leave for forty-eight hours. Stay in your bunk and sober up. You'll stand watch on deck tonight."

Bates stiffened and gave the Captain a crooked salute. "Aye-aye, sir, full speed ahead."

As McKay turned to use the ladder, a crewman scrambled down almost on top of him. The deck hand became embarassed when he saw who it was. "Sorry, sir. I didn't see you."

"What's the hurry, sailor?"

The man gave McKay a sly grin. "Well, Captain, there's a cathouse across the street that has two of the sweetest little ladies standing in front. Bates here owes me two dollars, and I intend to get my money and enjoy their hospitality before the rest of the crew does."

"Are you finished with all your work?" McKay asked in a stern voice.

"Yes, sir. Doc put me on light duty since I hurt my wrist in that gale."

"All right, but take it easy on Wilmington. We'll probably be here for a few weeks while the ship is being repaired, and I'm not bailing you or anyone else out of jail."

McKay climbed the ladder up to the main deck and went to his quarters. The bill of lading needed to be checked against the auctioneer's statement to see if they tallied. When McKay had the necessary papers, he opened the door to his cabin and went to the gangplank. Across the street he saw the crewman he had just spoken with reach into his pocket and hand money to an attractive woman with auburn hair. McKay shook his head in dismay at the thought of so many young women being forced into a life of prostitution by these difficult times.

A little after seven P.M., Captain McKay and Boatswain Gallagher walked the few blocks from the riverfront to Curtis Snow's house. Wispy Spanish moss hung down like an old man's gray beard from the massive branches of six live oaks which helped to shelter the stone path leading to the two-story Georgian home. The men climbed the wooden stairs to the wide front porch and pulled the brass bell handle.

A Negro servant girl opened the door and ushered them into a high-ceilinged parlor where dozens of elegantly attired guests milled about, chatting. Mr. Snow was surrounded by a group of men debating whether England and France would declare the blockade illegal and recognize the Confederate States of America as an independent country. When Mr. Snow saw the captain and his guest enter, he went to greet them. "Ladies and gentlemen, may I please have your attention?" he announced, facing the crowd with raised hands.

The voices grew silent and all eyes turned to him.

"We would not be celebrating tonight if it wasn't for the courage of these men. I give you the master of the *Atlantis*, Captain Wade McKay, and his boatswain, Mr. John Gallagher."

Excited applause filled the room, and several men came over and shook their hands.

An overweight man in a black frock coat with a gold waistcoat said, "Most impressive, Captain! I saw the damage to your ship, and it's a compliment to your skill as a sea captain you were able to bring her in at all."

McKay smiled politely. "Thank you, sir. However, when you have a fine ship and crew, such as I have, it makes one's job much easier."

"Spoken like a true gentleman, Captain," the man said, nodding agreement.

McKay noticed a woman across the room he had seen in front of the brothel on Water Street that afternoon. The woman's gown of blue satin was cut in a daring décolletage that exposed her shoulders and the creamy tops of her breasts. Tall and slender, she had a wealth of glorious auburn hair curled into fashionable ringlets which cascaded down her graceful neck. Her blue eyes were large and expressive and seemed to linger on his a moment before she glanced away. No matter where this fascinating beauty went his gaze would follow.

"Don't you agree, Captain?" a voice asked, suddenly interrupting his thoughts.

The woman was so distracting McKay hadn't heard a word that was said. "I'm sorry. Could you repeat the question?" he asked, embarrassed.

"Of course, Captain. It is my feeling England and France will recognize the Confederacy and intercede on our behalf. Don't you agree?"

"That was a distinct possibility at one time," he said, while his eyes followed the young woman around the room. "However, I think the defeat at Gettysburg determined they will remain neutral." McKay admonished himself for being so attracted to a woman who was a common whore, a woman whom any man could have for a price.

There was an audible murmur and the men nodded in agreement.

"Nevertheless, Captain, don't you think our glorious victories will prove to President Lincoln that we are a force to be reckoned with?"

"What victories have we had lately?" McKay asked, then noticed the woman coming toward them. *What business could she have here? Was she with someone he was talking to?*

"Why, Fredericksburg. . ."

She was coming closer. . .

"First and Second Manassas. . ."

She came toward him.

"Chancellorsville, those are just a few."

The woman joined them, and to McKay's dismay, she took his agent's arm, then smiled. "Father, why don't you introduce me to the captain?"

"Certainly, dear," Snow said, patting his daughter's slender hand. "Captain McKay, this is my daughter, Brooke."

"I--I am honored, Miss Snow," he said in a voice which could barely contain his surprise. This newest revelation, that she was Mr. Snow's daughter, bewildered him even more. *Why had she been in front of that brothel?*

30

"Thank you, Captain," Brooke said, then eyed him curiously. "I saw your ship unloading at the dock this morning. I'm sure you brought many luxuries, such as wine and cigars, but did you bring anything to ease the suffering in Wilmington?"

"Yes, I did, Miss Snow. I also brought food and medicine."

She smiled, impressed. "A blockade-runner with a conscience. How novel. I imagine you thought food and medicine would fetch a higher price than wine."

"No, ma'am. I always include such things in my cargo."

Snow glared at Brooke, then turned to Captain McKay. "I must apologize for my daughter, Captain. She can be very blunt, just like her mother, when it comes to how the war is affecting the people."

McKay smiled. Knowing Brooke was not afraid to express her opinion about the war and blockade-running made her even more attractive. "I see. If Mrs. Snow is half as beautiful as her daughter, I can hardly wait to meet her."

Curtis became troubled. "My wife was not feeling well and retired early. She contracted yellow fever during the epidemic, and it left her very weak."

McKay nodded understanding, then turned to Brooke. "Miss Snow, you said you saw my ship unloading this morning. Do you work downtown?"

"No, Captain. I was collecting donations near the waterfront for the Ladies Soldiers Aid Society," she answered proudly.

Suddenly it all made sense to him. She was collecting money for charity when he saw her. "The Soldiers Aid Society is most fortunate to have someone so lovely work for them."

Brooke smiled graciously. "How very kind, Captain. It seems your skill as a blockade-runner is only exceeded by your charm as a gentleman."

The rest of the evening was a blur for McKay. His eyes could see only Brooke. His mind could think only of her. Even when he was led away to discuss business with the other men, his thoughts kept returning to the beauty he had just met. At his first opportunity, he went looking for her. He found Brooke on a green velvet settee, politely listening to an elderly woman talk about her rheumatism.

During a lull in the conversation, McKay leaned toward her and softly asked, "Would you like to go outside for a breath of fresh air?"

Brooke smiled up at him, relieved at being rescued from this boring conversation. "Yes, Captain. I'd love to," she replied, then took his arm.

As they opened the front door, Willie Mae, the Negro house servant, thrust out her lower lip and scowled at the couple. "Where you goin', Miz Brooke?"

"Captain McKay and I are just going on the porch for some air," she said.

Willie Mae crossed her big arms and said, "Not without me you ain't. A proper lady don't go nowhere with a gentleman 'lessin' she got a chaperone. You knows that."

"Yes, Willie Mae, I do. Come along if you must."

The couple walked across the wide porch to the railing while Willie Mae plopped down in a corner chair, grumbling to herself. The night was hot and a few moths fluttered around the brass kerosene lamps on either side of the entryway.

While Brooke disliked the men who brought the cargos through the blockade and helped fuel the fires of inflation, she could not deny she was intrigued by the handsome blockade-runner captain beside her. She secretly admired blockade-runner captains. They were dashing and had an attractive air of confidence about them. There was something special about a man who defied death and the Yankee blockade. "I'm glad you got me out of there before I said something rude to one of daddy's guests," Brooke confessed.

McKay glanced at her, puzzled. "Why would you do that?"

"Captain, are you aware of what happens to your cargo after you bring it through the blockade?"

McKay was well aware what happened to his cargos once he reached port, but he was so fascinated by Brooke that he let her go on anyway. "I believe so. Any supplies which don't belong to the military are sold at auction."

"Are you familiar with speculation?"

McKay shrugged, suggesting he knew very little. "Well, I know speculators buy cargos at wholesale hoping the prices will rise."

"Yes, but that isn't all they do. Speculators purchase all of the essential products to keep them off the street, then wait for the prices to rise before releasing them."

"I've heard something to that effect, but I thought it was just good business sense."

"Good business sense nothing!" she said. "Those men my daddy has invited to our house are the biggest speculators in the country. They contribute nothing to the war effort, only to the suffering of the average citizen who can't afford to buy a loaf of bread."

"How bad have the prices become?"

"You don't know?" she asked, astounded.

"No. I don't."

"Bacon and sugar are over a dollar a pound, coffee is five dollars and flour is twelve and a half cents. And that's just for starters. The prices seem to be rising every day," Brooke said, shaking her head in disgust.

"I was aware of some shortages, particularly in medical supplies, but I had no idea things had become so critical."

McKay saw the skepticism on her face and explained, "You'll have to excuse my ignorance, but living on a ship insulates a seaman somewhat. We hardly ever have to pay for anything. The men eat their meals aboard, and the ship's stores are purchased in the islands because everything is cheaper there."

"So you weren't aware of the runaway inflation?" she asked, still unconvinced.

"Well, I knew prices were high, due to the blockade, but I didn't realize they had become that bad. Why doesn't the government do something?"

"I don't know. They probably tolerate it to some extent," she said with dismay, then explained, "There are very few government owned blockade-runners, so privately owned vessels are extremely important. Maybe the government is afraid if they start telling companies what they can and cannot do, they won't receive the military supplies they need."

"That makes sense, but I thought the high prices were due to speculation."

"They are," Brooke assured him. "But since speculators are willing to buy in volume, and pay higher prices than the average citizen, the blockade-running companies would rather deal with them."

McKay nodded, then smiled at her. "I see. I also see that you're a very sharp lady. How did you become so knowledgeable about speculation?"

"Well," Brooke said, "being the daughter of one of the biggest shipping agents in the state didn't hurt. However, I believe my work with the Society helped the most. I could see people were having a difficult time and decided to get some answers."

McKay looked out at the night, thinking about what she had said and listening to the faint clip-clop of a horse pulling a carriage down Third Street. The ornate kerosene lamps glowed softly yellow as a man and woman strolled from one pool of light to the next. Suddenly he turned to Brooke and asked, "Why don't I tell the speculators at the party the auction won't be until later? That way the citizens can buy goods at lower prices because there won't be anyone to outbid them."

"That would be wonderful!" Brooke said, her face flushed with excitement.

McKay smiled. He did not see how Brooke could become more beautiful, but she did. "I saw you this morning, you know."

"You did?"

"Yes. I was leaving the *Atlantis*, and I saw you in front of that brothel across the street from the wharf," he said, smiling.

Brooke turned to him. "Oh my! What did you think?"

"Well, naturally I got the wrong impression. However, I thought to myself, what a striking woman."

"You did?" she asked.

"Yes. Then, when I saw you tonight, I was greatly relieved to find you're not that type of woman at all."

"I should hope so," she said.

"What puzzles me is, why were you collecting in front of the brothel?"

Brooke gave him a coy smile. "Because I've found that's the best place to fill my collection cup, Captain. You see, the men who frequent such an establishment always have plenty of money, and most of them feel so guilty about going inside they usually make a substantial contribution. You should see the look of surprise on their faces when I approach them," Brooke added with a grin.

McKay chuckled at the thought of men discreetly leaving the brothel, only to be ambushed by a righteous woman armed with a tin collection cup.

Brooke grew serious as she gazed at the magnificent homes across the street, their windows dimly lit with candlelight. "Wilmington is not what it seems, Captain. Just as you made a mistake about me this morning, please do not judge the city by what you have seen today. The war and blockade-running have changed things for the worse."

He nodded understanding. "I can imagine they have."

"This isn't the real Wilmington," Brooke went on. "Most of these people don't belong here. Our population was less than ten thousand before the war. It's nearly fifty thousand now. The only thing blockade-running has done for this city is to bring the worst it has to offer--greedy speculators, drunken sailors, disease and the crime which seems to follow these people wherever they go."

McKay was taken aback. "I always thought running the blockade was something positive. I never dreamed there was a downside to it."

"There is good and bad in everything," Brooke said. "Fortunately, the good is plain to see."

McKay frowned and was quiet. Brooke could see he was disturbed, so she changed the subject.

"So tell me, Captain. How did you become involved in blockade-running?"

"Well, being from Charleston and coming from a family who owned a shipping line dictated what sort of life I would lead. When the war began, I couldn't think of anything I'd rather do than to be a captain on a blockade-runner," McKay said, then added, "I became

35

painfully aware of the shortage in medicine when my mother died last year."

"Oh, I'm terribly sorry, Captain. What happened to her?" she asked, gazing up at him with concern.

"She suffered from consumption," McKay explained softly. "Finally the doctor explained to me since no medicine was available, he could do nothing more. She died shortly after."

"That must have been quite a blow."

"Yes, it was. However, it made me realize thousands of people were suffering because of the blockade. Since then I have insisted part of my cargo contain medical supplies."

Brooke turned in the darkness to look at him. "That's very noble."

McKay shook his head. "No it isn't. That's just being human."

Willie Mae saw how seriously the two were looking at each other and began grumbling loudly from her chair, making her presence known. Brooke lowered her eyes, blushing at the thought of what might have happened if the Negro maid had not been there. "I think it's time we rejoined the party, Captain," she said, taking his arm.

McKay nodded and led Brooke inside. The murmur of voices punctuated by bursts of laughter and clouds of white cigar smoke suggested the dinner party was a huge success.

Mr. Snow saw his daughter enter the parlor with Captain McKay and hurried over carrying a large snifter of brandy. "It looks as if you two are getting along."

"Yes, father, we are," Brooke said, her lips curving into a smile. "Captain McKay is quite charming."

"Excellent. I thought you'd see eye to eye when you got to know each other better. By the way, Captain, how long will it take to repair your ship?"

"The yard foreman at Cassidey's said it could take a month, sir."

"That will never do. I'll see what I can do to speed things along."

36

"Thank you, sir," McKay said, then remembered the plan he had discussed with Brooke. "Oh, I nearly forgot. Mr. Morris said he cannot hold the auction until one o'clock tomorrow."

"Why not?"

McKay shrugged his shoulders and thought of a reason his agent would accept. "He said there's another cargo ahead of us which needs to be inventoried and that was the best he could do."

Mr. Snow nodded, then remembered the notice he had placed in the paper announcing the auction would take place at nine the next morning. "Well, it's fortunate I have everyone here so I can tell them about the change."

"Yes, sir, mighty fortunate."

Mr. Snow turned to face the others. "Gentlemen, may I have your attention?"

The men lowered their brandy and cigars and turned expectantly to Mr. Snow.

"I have an announcement to make. Captain McKay has informed me the auction won't be at nine tomorrow morning as planned. It's been moved back until one o'clock in the afternoon."

McKay turned his head, then winked at Brooke.

Judson Bates leaned his shotgun against the starboard rail and watched his friends tramp noisily down the gangplank as they went ashore for the weekend. He was standing punishment watch and could not join them. The seamen were laughing and joked to Judson about how they were going to devour Wilmington and leave him with nothing but the scraps.

Judson threw his bowler hat to the deck in frustration and cursed. Sweat-dampened ringlets of his unruly brown hair sprang everywhere while his sideburns extended into a beard with no mustache. Irritated, he picked up a scrap of wood from the damaged deck to fling at the men going ashore. As he hefted the piece, he found it was the right size and shape for carving. Not wanting to waste a good piece of wood on the likes of them, Judson sat on a coil of rope, then unsheathed the bone-handled knife he kept on his belt and began to whittle. While Judson whittled, he thought of many things. How life was unfair to him. But most of all, he remembered how his troubles began when he met Ashley.

When Judson was fourteen, he went to work in a fishing shack. His job consisted of cleaning and gutting the catches of fish when they came in, then mopping the shop after closing.

Two years later, the filet knife Judson was using slipped and sliced his left wrist, severing a tendon. Although the wound received medical attention, the doctor could not re-attach the tendon and he lost some mobility in his hand. While Judson's arm was healing, the owner let him sell fish in the market next door.

This new job had changed Judson's whole outlook. For the first time in his life he enjoyed his work. He liked being in front of the store and socializing with the customers. He even dreamed of getting his own boat some day. Mr. Ingram, the owner, saw the fine job Judson was doing and agreed to sell him an old sloop he had.

Judson was thrilled. Every day he would stay after closing so he could work on the boat. One evening Ashley, Mr. Ingram's eighteen-year-old daughter, helped Judson caulk the planks in the hull. Ashley never went anywhere without her cat, and it curled up on the foredeck.

When it was quitting time, Ashley took two glasses and a bottle of whiskey from a cupboard next to the workbench. The two relaxed in the sloop's cabin, then drank a toast to the boat. After a few more drinks, they told each other about their dreams. Ashley said she wanted to live in Paris and paint. Judson told her he wanted to own a whole fleet of fishing boats.

When the mood seemed right, Ashley leaned over and kissed Judson. Judson was exhilarated, but embarrassed because he had never been with a woman before. He had heard stories from the other men at the fish house about how Ashley had pleasured them all, but he never thought she would have anything to do with him. The whiskey dulled his senses, and when the time came for him to make love to her, he couldn't perform. Ashley's pride was hurt. She ridiculed him as a Nancy-boy, saying he wasn't attracted to women.

Enraged, Judson grabbed the empty whiskey bottle and chased her from the boat. Ashley ran inside the fish market and bolted the door. Judson attacked the barrier between them, kicking at it and raving about how much of a man he was and what he would do to her.

As if suddenly coming to his senses, he stopped and looked around. The market was silent again except for the wind in the trees and the cry of the gulls from the dock. Somewhere in the distance a dog barked, then a man's voice hollered for him to be quiet. Fear of discovery caused Judson to drop the whiskey bottle and quietly leave before anyone noticed.

When Judson went to work the next day, the men snickered and made crude remarks about his manhood. Apparently Ashley had told everyone about the night before. Judson was so ashamed, he left the fish market and never came back.

One of Ashley's morning chores was to help load the fishing boats with bait. As she stooped to pick up a bucket, she screamed hysterically. There, resting on a bloody pile of fish guts, was her cat's head.

Judson's father had always belittled his son whenever he didn't live up to his expectations. When Halsey Bates heard about the incident with Ashley down at the fish market, he taunted Judson and asked his wife if she had a dress their son could wear.

Every Saturday morning Judson's mother went to visit her sister while his father stayed home usually sleeping off a drunk from the night before. Judson waited until she left, then got an ax from the wood shed and one of his mother's dresses. His father was snoring loudly in the darkened bedroom, so Judson jabbed him awake with the ax. The bleary-eyed man stared at his son for a moment, then made a clumsy grab for the ax. Judson jerked it out of his hand. But in doing so, he sliced his father's fingers. Seeing the blood running down Halsey's arm affected Judson strangely--made him feel more powerful.

"You cut me, you son of a bitch!" Mr. Bates screamed.

Judson's eyes shone with excitement as he held the ax. The iron blade gleamed in the dim light. "Yes, papa. And I'll cut you bad if you don't put on that dress."

"What? Get the hell out of here before I take that away from you and bust your head wide open."

"Why don't you try, papa?" Judson taunted, waving the ax in front of him. "Why don't you just try?"

"I will, you bastard!" Halsey promised, then swung his legs to the side of the bed. He started to get up when Judson slashed with the ax again. The blade ripped through the meat and bone of his father's wrist and sent him sprawling to the floor.

With fear widened eyes, Halsey clutched the bloody stump with his right hand. "You're crazy! That's what you are!"

"Yeah, I'm crazy. Crazy enough to hack you to pieces if you don't put on the damned dress."

Trembling, Halsey pulled his nightshirt over his head and awkwardly put on the flowered dress, all the time keeping an anxious eye on his son. His severed hand pumped a trail of blood on the dress.

"That's better," Judson said, smiling. "Now lay on the bed."

Halsey looked at his son like he was crazy and stayed where he was. "What is it you want from me? Do you want me to say I'm sorry? All right, I'm sorry I teased you. Now please fetch a doctor before I bleed to death."

"Uh-uh. Not until you get on the bed."

"I will not!"

Judson shook his head, dismayed. "Then you leave me no choice, Papa." He swung the blunt end of the ax blade at his father.

Halsey ducked, but the broad tip grazed the back of his head, and he slumped to the floor. Judson pulled the groaning man onto the bed, then raised the dress above his naked waist.

Judson grinned at the foot of the bed. He reared-back with the ax and hacked at his father's crotch until he was dead.

To hide any trace of the murder, Judson unscrewed the base of a kerosene lamp and doused the bed with the flammable liquid. He wanted the fire to look like an accident, so he smashed the lamp on the floor as if it had fallen from the nightstand. Now Judson placed his father's severed hand at the end of his arm so it would appear natural when the body was discovered. Satisfied he had taken care of every detail, Judson scratched a match on the doorframe, then set the room ablaze.

The death of Halsey Bates did not produce the results Judson had expected. As always Judson had thought only of himself and failed to realize how this would affect his mother. She seemed listless and seldom smiled anymore. Of course she grieved for her husband, but it was more than that. Everything they had worked so hard for was gone. Her house, what little possessions they had, all gone. She felt too old and tired to start again. That winter Elizabeth Bates developed a fever and died.

Judson was bitter ever since her death and began drinking to ease the pain. Because of his drinking, he could not keep a job.

Nine years later, the war provided a rare opportunity for Judson. Many jobs became available since most men were in the army, and new positions were created. One of these positions was running the blockade. Judson had traveled to the port of Wilmington and found an opening as a deck hand on a blockade-runner. Now, two months into this job, he was in trouble again.

Judson sat on a coil of rope and looked up from the boat he was carving. The shadows on the wharf were beginning to lengthen as the sun sank beneath the tree line on Eagles Island.

Suddenly a black man rose among the bales of cotton on the dock and called to Judson. "Mizta guard!"

When Judson saw the color of the man's skin, he picked up his shotgun and shouted gruffly, "Whadda you want?"

"I needs to speak with ya."

"You got me. So talk."

The black man glanced around nervously and crept from the shadows. "I don't wanna holler. Can you come heah?"

Judson had heard stories of runaway slaves butchering white folk. Although he held a shotgun, he wasn't going on the dock where a mob of blacks might ambush him. "I ain't leavin' this ship while on guard duty. Can't you come aboard?"

When the Negro rushed up the gangplank, and Judson saw how powerfully built the man was, he pointed his gun at him warily. "What's on your mind?"

"Can we go somewhere's an' talk? I's afeared. I ain't a freedman."

"I reckon you're takin' a powerful chance comin' on this ship, then," Judson said, eyeing him suspiciously. He waved his shotgun toward the riverside of the *Atlantis*. "We can talk over there. Ain't nobody gonna see us."

The men hid in the shadows behind the superstructure. Sweat glistened on the man's black face, while his eyes flitted around nervously. "I gotta git my family away from dis place. I wants to go to Nassau where a body can be free."

"An' you wanna stowaway aboard this ship. That right?"

"Yassuh."

Judson was going to tell him to go home, that he couldn't help him, but then he got a glimmer of an idea. Lots of people were profiting from this war. Why shouldn't he?

"I'd like to help you, but this here blockade-runner's gonna be laid up for a spell. You gotta come back when the ship has a deck load of cotton. I'll hollow out a space for you an' your family."

"Thankie, suh."

Judson lowered the shotgun and regarded the Negro thoughtfully. "I reckon I can sneak you some vittles when we sail, but it'll cost you."

The huge shoulders slumped in despair. "I ain't got no money."

Judson shook his head for being foolish enough to think a slave would have any money. "Then I can't help you."

The black man considered this for a moment. "I can git me some silver from de massa."

"All right, you bring me what you can, an' I'll let you an' yore family aboard."

"Yassuh! Thankie, suh!" The Negro smiled broadly and bobbed at the waist.

CHAPTER 3

Monday the women of the Soldier's Aid Society were scheduled to make canvas haversacks and woolen jackets for the men at Fort Fisher. The ladies had gathered in a large unoccupied room on the second floor of city hall. Brooke Snow was drawing a needle and heavy thread through two pieces of canvas while eighteen-year-old Virginia Drake sat at the long table opposite her, cutting a bit of cloth from a pattern. Virginia's blonde hair was pulled back from her face and terminated in large sausage curls which hung down to her shoulders.

"Captain McKay had dinner at our house last night," Brooke told Virginia, trying to sound casual but there was a hint of excitement in her voice. "He's captain of the blockade-runner that arrived yesterday, you know."

Virginia's eyes widened with surprise, and she put down the material she was cutting. "Tell me all about it."

Virginia and Brooke had grown up in the same rundown Wilmington neighborhood. They were best friends all through school and had shared their most private thoughts. All that had changed when Brooke's father became an agent for one of the largest blockade-running companies in the South. Now Brooke had wealthy new friends, and she attended wonderful parties where she met the most interesting and influential people. It was about this time Virginia became jealous of everything the other girl did.

"Well, daddy had a dinner party and invited everyone who will be at the auction today," Brooke told her. "When Captain McKay arrived, he brought one of the men from his ship. His name is John Gallagher. I think you'd like him. He's very handsome."

"I'm sure I would. Tell me about the captain," Virginia said, eagerly.

Brooke was pleased to see her news was having the desired effect. "Well, shortly after daddy introduced him, Captain McKay came over and asked me if I'd like to go on the porch."

"Did you?"

"Of course, silly," Brooke said, then began sewing again, waiting for her friend to ask for more details.

Virginia leaned forward. "So? What happened then?"

Brooke looked up from the haversack she was stitching. "Captain McKay told me he'd seen me earlier in the day and thought I was very striking."

"What else did he say?"

"Oh, we talked about so many things it's difficult to remember." Brooke recalled their plan from the night before and glanced at the clock on the fireplace mantel. It was after 1:00 o'clock. The auction would be over. "I guess it's safe to tell you about this now," Brooke dropped her voice to a whisper. "Captain McKay told the speculators the wrong time for the auction."

Virginia became confused. "Why did he do that?"

"He wanted to give other people a chance to bid, so the large speculators wouldn't be there to buy everything and drive the prices up."

Virginia was astounded. "But your daddy's firm will lose money."

"Yes, they will. But it's for a good cause. It's to help fight inflation."

Virginia shook her head. "Good heavens, girl! Your daddy's going to be angry with him."

"I hope not. The captain did it as a favor to me."

"He's trying to impress you," Virginia told Brooke with a confident nod.

"You think so?"

"Of course he is. Why would he want to make your father angry?"

"I don't know, but Wade is very sensitive," Brooke pointed out. "Maybe he did it because I told him how people were suffering because of speculation."

"Don't you know when a man is flirting with you?" Virginia asked amused, picking up the cloth and cutting some side panels for the haversacks Brooke was sewing.

"Of course, I do," Brooke said, then changed the subject. "Captain McKay asked me to go to Thalian Hall tonight. He's so refined. He just loves the theater."

"Does your daddy know about this?"

"Yes, I told him this morning, and he made his usual speech about staying away from men like him. But I don't care. Daddy's an old fuddy-duddy anyway."

Virginia frowned, then shook her head so the curls at the nape of her neck swung from side to side. "I declare this will be one of the shortest romances ever. Your daddy will never let you see that captain again once he finds out what happened."

Brooke gasped, dropping the material she was sewing. "Oh, no! He can't do that. He simply can't!"

The ladies in the room stopped what they were doing and glanced at the two young women to see what had happened. Intimidated by all the questioning stares, Virginia rushed over to console her friend.

"I'm sorry, Brooke. Don't pay any attention to me. Your daddy's probably very understanding about such things."

Brooke dug a handkerchief from her bag to dry her eyes. "Wh--what things are those?"

Virginia glanced up, as if searching the air around her for an answer. "Oh, romance. All men are ninnies when it comes to such things, so it is our responsibility as women to lead them in the right direction. You must tell your daddy Captain McKay was only trying to impress you. He'll understand. And if he doesn't, just cry. A father can't stand to see his daughter in tears."

Brooke nodded, encouraged. "I'll go to his office this afternoon to explain."

Virginia's mind raced to find a reason so she could leave early. She needed a chance to talk to Mr. Snow before Brooke did. "Oh, I almost forgot to tell you. My mother became ill last night, and I need to leave early."

"Oh no, Virginia. Is she all right?"

"I think so, but I have to check on her. Doctor McCutcheon gave her some laudanum and told her to get plenty of rest."

"Well, you go home and don't worry about a thing. I'll explain to Mrs. DeRosset what happened."

Virginia gave her friend a brave smile, but her eyes remained sad. "Thank you, Brooke. I knew I could count on you."

"What do you mean the auction was at nine this morning?" Curtis Snow roared at Mr. Morris.

"Yes, sir, it was. And I must say we didn't do very well."

"But Captain McKay said you had changed the time to one this afternoon."

The auctioneer stared at him. "I told him no such thing!"

"Good God! What will the speculators think?" Mr. Snow wondered aloud. "Quick, man! Tell me what happened."

"Well, sir. The bidders were buying small lots and, without competition from any of the big speculators, they were able to buy the whole cargo at discount rates."

Mr. Snow spread his arms and wailed, "I'm ruined! Absolutely ruined!"

"Oh, I wouldn't say that, sir," the auctioneer said, shaking his head.

Curtis Snow glared at Mr. Morris. "Burgess & Linden would. They will wonder what kind of fool they have in Wilmington."

Curtis paced around the room, shaking his head and tapping his cane on the wooden floor. Suddenly he stopped. "I know what I should do! I must write to them immediately and advise them of the situation. Tell them it wasn't my fault. That I had nothing to do with it," he exclaimed, then rushed out the door.

As Mr. Snow scurried down the planked walk, a boy burst through the door of the telegraph office and ran into him.

Curtis staggered back and glared at the boy. "Dear Lord! Watch where you're going, son."

"Sorry, sir. I have to bring this to the newspaper office right quick," he said, holding up a sheet of paper. "We just got word over the wire the Yankees have captured the blockade-runner *Osprey*."

Curtis Snow's face drained of color. He had seen how profitable speculation was so he had invested heavily in the *Osprey*'s load of cotton. He not only used what little savings he had, but he borrowed against his house to buy eight hundred bales of her cargo.

The boy looked at him curiously and asked, "Are you all right, Mister?"

"Yes--yes, I'm fine," Mr. Snow said, dismissing the delivery boy with a wave of his cane.

After the boy left, the agent took a handkerchief from his coat and patted his moist brow. *What would he do now? He had no money--maybe no job, for that matter.* Before Snow realized it, he stood in front of his office. As he unlocked the front door, he saw Virginia Drake coming down the sidewalk.

"Hello, Mr. Snow," she said with a wave.

He turned to the young woman and nodded. "Hello, Virginia. How are you?"

"I'm fine, sir. However, I'm terribly concerned about you."

"You are?"

"Yes, I am. Brooke told me all about the plan to stop the speculators from being at the auction. She said Captain McKay suggested it."

Curtis Snow's jaw dropped, his eyes widening in shock. He knew his daughter held a dark view of what he was doing, but he never suspected she would do anything like this. "I can't believe she would do that!"

Virginia shook her head. "I didn't think she was capable of doing it either, Mr. Snow. I was stunned when she told me."

Curtis stared at Virginia. "Brooke's your friend. Why are you telling me this?"

47

Virginia paused to consider the question. "Brooke is the sweetest girl I know, but Captain McKay seems to have a dreadful influence on her. I don't want your daughter's reputation ruined by associating with the likes of him."

"Thank you for telling me, Virginia. I'll make sure she doesn't see him anymore."

"You're welcome, Mr. Snow," she said, then added with concern. "Please don't tell Brooke I said anything."

"I won't, Virginia."

Curtis stepped inside his office, took off his high crowned hat and hung it on a coat tree. He sat at his desk and took a bottle of whiskey and a glass from the bottom left hand drawer and set them on top. It was the middle of the afternoon, too early to start drinking, but he didn't care. His whole world was crumbling around him, and that bastard Wade McKay was swinging the sledgehammer. In the middle drawer he found the Adams revolver he kept in case the office was robbed, then placed it next to the bottle. With trembling hands, Curtis Snow poured himself a drink and stared at the gun.

The next stop Virginia made was at the riverfront to see Captain McKay. The *Atlantis* was getting ready to leave the dock, and she hurried to catch the blockade-runner.

"Please, I must see the captain," she shouted to the deck hands who were about to remove the gangplank. One of them went to get Captain McKay, while the others invited her aboard.

When McKay was summoned from his cabin, he appeared perplexed and wondered what this woman could want.

"Hello, Captain. My name is Virginia Drake. I'm a friend of Brooke's," she explained. "I saw Mr. Snow this afternoon, and I thought I should warn you he's furious about what happened at the auction."

"I don't understand," McKay said, playing dumb. He wasn't sure if he should admit what he knew to this stranger.

Virginia smiled, then said with a wave of her hand, "Oh, it's okay, Brooke told me everything."

"She did?"

"Yes. You know. About the plan you had to keep the speculators from buying up everything."

"Oh, that plan," McKay said uneasily. "Well, thank you for the warning, Miss Drake. I'll apologize to him after I take the *Atlantis* to the shipyard."

Virginia hadn't expected he would do this, and quickly said, "I can take him a message. I'm going that way."

"No, ma'am. I need to see him myself, but thank you for your concern."

"You're welcome, Captain," she said, then paused, wondering how she might see this man again. "Since you're a stranger to Wilmington, maybe I could show you around."

McKay smiled. "I appreciate the offer, ma'am, but I need to get my ship repaired."

"Are you sure about that, Captain?" she asked with a suggestive smile. "I'll show you *everything* Wilmington has to offer."

"I'm certain you will, Miss Drake," McKay said. He took her arm and escorted her to the gangplank. "If I ever need a guide, I promise I will take you up on your generous offer."

She smiled as he helped her onto the wooden walkway.

When Boatswain Gallagher noticed Captain McKay talking to an attractive woman, he rushed over, hoping for an introduction. She was already leaving the ship by the time he got there, so he joined the captain at the railing.

"She's a fine woman, sir," the young seaman observed, watching the lady in the hoop skirt daintily step ashore. "I wouldn't let her out of my sight."

"She's yours if you want her, Mr. Gallagher. Tonight I have a date with an angel."

The boatswain gazed at him in surprise. "You met a girl even prettier than her?"

"Yes, I did. At the party last night. Remember Mr. Snow's daughter, Brooke?"

"I do indeed, sir. Another extraordinary woman."

McKay nodded in agreement. "I'm taking her to Thalian Hall tonight."

"Oh? What's playing?"

McKay paused, considering the question, then laughed. "I haven't the slightest idea."

When the *Atlantis* was docked at Cassidey's shipyard and McKay had issued instructions to the workers, he hired a carriage to take him to Mr. Snow's office. During the ride, McKay gazed out the carriage window at the scenery. Because the land sloped at a steep angle down to the river, the houses were terraced behind a series of masonry retaining walls. The various levels made the hillside appear like a giant set of stairs leading into the city. Elegant homes were nestled between huge magnolia and live oak trees and enclosed by black wrought iron fences.

As the carriage's iron-rimmed wheels clattered on the cobblestones beneath the leafy canopy, McKay noticed the streets were nearly deserted. Where were the residents of these splendid homes? On such a fine day McKay expected to see scores of ladies carrying pastel-colored parasols while being escorted by gentlemen in top hats. The faint sound of voices and banjo music drifted in the window, and McKay looked to see where it was coming from. Seamen, some in civilian clothes and some in uniforms, were lounging on a porch while a Negro minstrel played a lively tune. The men were smoking cigars and carrying on as if this beautiful building was some sort of bawdy house. McKay was reminded of the conversation he had with Brooke. She explained most of the inhabitants had moved away because of the crude element blockade-running brought to the city. Unfortunately, McKay saw evidence of that right here.

When the carriage stopped at his destination, the driver opened the door and folded down a set of steps. McKay emerged from the cab embarrassed because he had always considered such contraptions as unmanly. Opening the front door to his agent's office, McKay stared in disbelief. Curtis Snow was lying in a pool of blood on the floor next to his desk.

* * * * *

Brooke left City Hall earlier than usual. She needed to convince her father she was to blame for what happened at the auction, not Wade.

Brooke was considering what to say, when she saw a crowd in front of her father's office. Several policemen were keeping the people back while another was talking to Captain McKay and writing notes. Alarmed by all the commotion, Brooke pushed through the crowd. A policeman moved with hands outstretched to prevent her from getting any closer.

"I'm sorry, ma'am. You'll have to stay back."

Brooke looked at him with worried eyes. "But I need to find out what has happened. My daddy works here."

A heavyset police sergeant overheard the exchange and looked up from the report he was writing. "Let the lady through, Ed."

The man nodded, lowering his hands. Brooke swept past him and rushed over to the sergeant. "What happened? Did my daddy's office get robbed?"

"We're not sure, ma'am," the policeman said, touching the brim of his hat respectfully. He folded the report he was writing, then placed it inside his shirt pocket. "Have a seat, and we'll talk," he said, gesturing to a wooden bench alongside the building.

As Brooke walked to the bench, she noticed a grim-faced policeman was guarding the door to her father's office.

The sergeant pulled a red handkerchief from his back pocket, then sat heavily beside her, causing the wooden bench to creak and sag beneath his weight. He wiped the sweat from his brow, then frowned. "Hot today, ain't it?"

Brooke's eyes anxiously searched his face. "Yes, it is, Sergeant. You had something to tell me?" she reminded him.

"Yes, ma'am. I did." He sighed as if he were about to undertake some unpleasant task, which made Brooke all the more nervous. "Ma'am, your daddy's been shot."

A trembling hand flew to her heart. "Oh no! Is he all right?"

"No, ma'am, he isn't. He died before we got here. I'm terribly sorry."

Brooke's eyes widened in disbelief, and she shook her head, as if this motion could dispel what she had heard. "That can't be true. You must be mistaken."

"There's no mistake, ma'am. I've seen the body myself."

"Then it must be someone else. Somebody who had come to my father's office."

"I'd like to believe that, ma'am, but Captain McKay has identified the body. He's the one who discovered it, then notified us."

A tortured cry escaped Brooke's lips, and she averted her eyes to hide her pain. When she turned back to him, the police sergeant could see she was struggling to control her tears. "I want to see him. Maybe he's still alive."

The policeman shook his head, sadly. "A doctor has already pronounced him dead. I'm sorry, Miss Snow."

"I don't care what the doctor said. I want to see him anyway."

The police sergeant knew Mr. Snow was shot in the head, and the body was a bloody mess. "That wouldn't be wise, ma'am."

"Oh, Sergeant, please," Brooke protested. "He's my father."

"I understand, Miss Snow. However, seeing him now would only upset you more." The sergeant glanced around for assistance and saw the tall blockade-runner captain was waiting to speak with Brooke. "I gather Captain McKay is a friend of yours. Why don't you let him take you home, so you can be with your family? I'll let you know if anything develops."

Brooke removed a handkerchief from her small purse. "I must hurry and tell mother. I don't want her to hear about this from anyone else."

The big policeman nodded with a sigh, then placed his hands on his knees and struggled to his feet. He walked over to McKay, stuffing the red handkerchief into his back pocket.

As soon as the sergeant turned away, Brooke dashed for her father's office. The startled guard at the door tried to stop her, but she ducked below his arms and squeezed past him. Brooke froze in horror a few feet inside the door, burying her face in her hands.

Curtis Snow lay on his back with his one dead eye showing surprise, and his blood-filled mouth gaping wide open. A third of her father's head was missing, and the shattered flesh and bone were thick with flies.

In an instant, McKay gathered Brooke into his arms, then guided her outside to a waiting carriage.

CHAPTER 4

Two days after the dinner party people were again gathering at the Snow residence. A steady stream of friends and relatives came to the house to express their grief and to comfort Edith and Brooke Snow. The number of people present was a fitting tribute to how well respected the Snow family was.

The closed wooden casket was set up in the parlor along with thirty chairs for the mourners. Brooke and her mother sat in the front row, surrounded by close relatives. Every so often friends would come by to offer words of encouragement to the women.

Already physically and emotionally drained from the previous two days, Brooke began feeling faint in the hot, stuffy parlor. She was on her way to the front door for a breath of fresh air when she overheard Virginia talking to several other women.

"I'm friends with the police sergeant in charge of the investigation. According to him there are several theories about what might have happened. The first one suggests Mr. Snow committed suicide."

Gasps of shock filled the air.

"Virginia, how dare you say such a thing?" Brooke asked, appalled. She glared at Virginia, as if she were the source of her irritation, instead of the police.

The other woman lowered her eyes, ashamed. "I'm sorry, Brooke. I didn't mean for you to hear this. It's only a theory, you understand. One of many," she hastened to add.

Brooke's gaze softened. "I can appreciate that. I just find it difficult to believe someone would think such an awful thing. What proof do they have?"

Virginia glanced at the others, then back to Brooke. "Well, the sergeant said nothing was taken. Your father still had his wallet. They also found a gun in his hand and powder burns on his body, which means he was shot at close range."

"That means nothing. He might have been shot preventing a robbery."

"Perhaps. But the police also found an empty bottle of whiskey on your father's desk. Then later, they questioned a newspaper boy who had seen Mr. Snow right before the shooting. He said Mr. Snow appeared distressed about something. So distressed that he bumped into him in a daze."

Brooke knew her father had suffered bouts of depression from time to time--especially when he had lost his previous job as a clerk. He was thankful to have been hired by Burgess and Linden, and he took his new job seriously. Could the failure at the auction have affected him in ways she had not anticipated?

"The other theory is," Virginia continued, "Captain McKay went over to your father's office to apologize about the auction, but Mr. Snow had been drinking and threatened him with a gun. The two of them fought, and Mr. Snow was shot dead."

This made more sense to Brooke than suicide. Captain McKay did go over to her father's office, and he was the one who discovered the body. Anger and confusion prompted her to cross the room to where Wade was talking with three other men. They were smoking cigars and holding cups of coffee and speaking in hushed voices. Wade smiled when Brooke approached and the men fell silent.

"Is what I heard about my daddy's death true?" Brooke demanded.

McKay seemed surprised by her hostility. "I don't know, Brooke. What did you hear?"

"That you killed my father."

Although the men glanced at each other in disbelief, no one was more stunned than McKay.

"Of course I didn't. Who told you that?"

"Virginia. She said the police have reason to believe you're the murderer."

McKay was incredulous. "What sort of reasons could they possibly have?"

"They believe you went to my father's office to apologize, but he had been drinking and confronted you with a gun. The two of you fought, and my father was killed."

McKay shook his head. "That's ridiculous."

"It doesn't sound so ridiculous to me."

"Well, it is. I would never fight with your father."

"Even if he was drunk and had a gun?" she asked, glaring at him.

McKay shrugged. "Well, maybe out of self-defense. But I didn't kill him."

Brooke stared at Wade, weighing what he had told her. Suddenly it occurred to her that it didn't matter if he had pulled the trigger. The failure at the auction was all McKay's idea. Yes, she went along with it, but the idea was his. The conclusion she reached was simple. If it wasn't for him, none of this would have happened. Her father would still be alive.

"Please leave my house, Captain McKay. You are no longer welcome here," Brooke said in a stern voice.

"What?"

"You heard me. Get out," she spat, returning Wade's gaze with hatred in her eyes.

McKay saw Brooke stiffen with anger and realized trying to reason with her would be useless. He set his glass down on an end table, got his cap from the maid and left the house.

At eight o'clock that evening McKay wasn't at Brooke's side as he had expected. He was drinking a bottle of Irish whiskey in a tavern in Paddy's Hollow. The air was thick with smoke from countless pipes and cigars, and the laughter of dozens of men and women were accompanied by tinny music from a banjo and piano.

The noisy, smoke filled saloon seemed to be the perfect place for a man to forget his troubles.

A big busted woman in a low cut blue dress with mounds of curly reddish-brown hair sauntered up next to him. "Mind if I join you?" she asked in a sultry voice.

McKay tossed down a shot, then looked at her for a moment. "No. Not at all."

The woman slid onto the bar stool next to him and smiled. "My name's Amber. What's yours?"

"Wade. Wade McKay" he said, extending his hand. She slipped her hand into his. It was warm and slender.

"Pleased to meet you, Wade. So who is she?"

"What do you mean?"

"Sweetheart, there's only one reason a man drinks like that. And that reason has got to be a woman."

McKay poured himself another shot and motioned to her with the bottle.

"Sure, I'll have one," she said, then called to the bartender who was drawing a glass of beer. "Al, give me a shot glass."

The man looked their way, then nodded. He got a glass from the shelf behind him, then slid it down the bar.

"You were right about it being a woman. How did you know?" McKay asked, pouring them both a drink from the black bottle.

"Sugar, I've been working this tavern for fifteen years, and I've seen all types. You're not one of the regulars, and the way you're downing that whiskey means you're trying to forget something. That something is usually a female."

"You're a regular mind reader, that's what you are," McKay said with a grin. "This woman. Is she my wife?"

Amber drank her whiskey slowly, then shook her head. "Uh-uh. I figure it's your girlfriend."

"What makes you think that?"

"Well, you're wearing the clothes of a sailor, which tells me you're probably away from home," she said, appraising him. "You're neat, extremely good looking, and again, the way you're downing that whiskey says a lot."

"Oh?"

"Sure. If you were married, you'd drink it slow but steady because you've got a lot of time and anger to kill. If you're single, you'd drink as if there's no tomorrow. Like the whiskey can't numb the pain fast enough."

"You've got an extraordinary talent, Amber."

She shook her head. "No. I'm just observant. So this woman, what did she do?"

McKay was silent for a moment, thinking about his problem. "Well, I tried to help her, but things didn't turn out the way I had planned."

Amber laughed. "Do they ever? Look at me. Do you think I planned to be here?"

McKay didn't answer and took a sip of whiskey.

"See what just happened?"

"No. What?"

"Before I came over, you were tossing the drinks down," Amber pointed out. "Now you're sipping."

McKay shrugged his shoulders. "So? What does that mean?"

"That it helps to talk about your troubles."

"Yes," he admitted. "I guess it does."

"You were telling me about your problem, remember?" Amber prompted.

He hesitated, unsure of how to begin. "Have you heard about the shooting death on Water Street two days ago?"

"Yes. You were involved in that?" she asked, her eyes widening in surprise.

He nodded. "Yes. The man was her father."

"What happened?" Amber asked, leaning forward.

"Well, I thought I'd try to help, Brooke."

"Her name is Brooke?"

"Yes. Do you know her? She's Curtis Snow's daughter."

"Ladies of her breeding don't associate with common whores," she said with a hint of amusement.

McKay could tell her amusement was tempered with a bit of anger, so he changed the subject. "Anyway, she's concerned about inflation. The problem is, her father was a shipping agent who always tried to get the best price for his company's goods. Well, I attempted to help her out by telling her father the wrong time for the auction, so the big speculators wouldn't be there to drive up the prices."

"And?"

McKay fidgeted with his shot glass. His voice was sad. "Everything happened the way I had planned, except now her father's dead. The police have ruled out robbery because nothing was taken. That leaves only murder and suicide. Whichever it is makes no difference to Brooke, because she is convinced I was somehow involved in it."

Amber frowned. "Her reaction seems rather extreme, but she's probably distraught over her father's death." She paused, then added, "I suppose she might say anything if his death was a suicide. But why would she think that about murder? I mean it's something entirely different."

"That's because I haven't told you the whole story." He proceeded to tell Amber about how Brooke had heard he was under suspicion, then practically accused him of the crime.

"Have the police said anything to you about being a suspect?" Amber asked.

"No, they haven't. They're probably not saying anything because they don't have enough evidence to arrest me."

McKay poured himself another drink. "I just wanted to help, but I had no idea it would affect him the way it did."

"You can never tell what might set some people off," Amber observed, shrugging her shoulders. "Have you told Brooke what you just told me?"

"I tried, but she wouldn't listen. It's just as well, though. She's so upset I doubt anything I could say would help."

"Perhaps she'll be more reasonable if you wait a while."

"Maybe she would," McKay conceded. "How much time do you think I should give her?"

"Well, at least until after the funeral. Do you have any sort of plan?" she asked.

McKay shook his head.

"Come on, I'll help you think of one," Amber said, trying to cheer him. "What do you know about her?"

McKay swung around on the bar stool toward her. "She does volunteer work for the Soldier's Aid Society."

"What type of work?"

"Well, she collects donations and makes clothing for the soldiers. She also serves hot meals at the Waystation."

Amber fell silent for a moment, giving him a swift smile. "I've got it! Here's what you do."

*   *   *   *

The Snow funeral was held at Oakdale Cemetery amid the many live oak and dogwood trees whose branches intermingle to give the place its regal grace. Throngs of people crowded around the grave site to hear the pastor's service.

McKay wound his way through the mass of spectators so he could offer his condolences to the bereaved family. Brooke glared at him, then stalked away while he removed his cap, "I'm sorry for your loss, Mrs. Snow," he said inadequately. "Your husband was a fine man. We will all miss him."

The slight woman appeared frail in her black dress. She glanced up at him through her veil, and said, "Thank you, Captain. You are very kind." She paused, then added, "I'm sorry for Brooke's behavior, but her father's death has upset her greatly."

"Of course. I understand." McKay wondered how to begin--if there was a delicate way to say he may have caused her husband's death. "Ma'am, I owe you and your family an apology. I can't help feeling I may have had a part in what happened. You see, I changed the time of the auction which troubled your husband so."

She gave him a reassuring smile. "No, Captain. You had nothing to do with his death. Curtis was a gentleman. And Southern gentlemen do not take their own lives."

"Yes, ma'am." Still wanting to help, he added, "If you ever need anything, no matter what it might be, please feel free to ask."

Mrs. Snow looked up at him. "How kind of you to say that, Captain. I will always remember your generous offer."

"Thank you, Mrs. Snow. If you will excuse me, I'll offer my sympathies to your daughter."

Brooke stood among a crowd of guests wearing a simple black dress. McKay waited for the people to murmur their condolences, then leave. When the last mourner had drifted away, he approached her with hat in hand. "I'm terribly sorry, Brooke. Is there anything I can do?"

"Yes. You can leave me alone," she said, trembling with suppressed fury.

"I'm afraid that's impossible. I care about you too much."

Brooke spun on her heel and stormed away. Taking her mother by the arm, she led her to their waiting carriage and helped her inside. Brooke flashed a warning at McKay, then climbed in and the carriage drove off.

The next time Brooke Snow was collecting in front of Madam Sophia's Brothel, she saw McKay approach carrying a small leather bag.

"Hello, Brooke," he said, taking a half-dime from the bag and dropping it into her tin cup. "I would like to make a donation to the Ladies Soldier's Aid Society."

"Thank you, Captain," she replied through tight lips, then moved ten feet away, gazing in the other direction.

McKay took another half-dime from his bag and followed her. He dropped the coin into her cup, and said, "If this is the only way I can speak to you, I'm prepared to make donations all day."

Brooke's voice was steady, impersonal. "Since you're making contributions to the Society, I'll remain courteous, but that doesn't guarantee I'll listen."

"All right. I wanted to. . ."

She turned, walking away from him again.

He went after her, reaching into his bag for another coin. ". . . say I'm terribly sorry. . ."

She walked away again, and he rushed after her. He dropped the coin into her tin cup and continued, ". . . about your father. I. . ."

Brooke hurried away, and he followed her. "Look, if I put this whole bag in your cup right now, will you stop and talk to me?"

"You do what you want," Brooke said coldly, "but I'm not promising anything."

McKay was willing to take the chance. "All right then, put out your hand."

He placed the bag in her upraised palm. "Brooke, I had nothing to do with your father's death. You must believe me."

Her hard eyes seemed to bore right through him. "How can you say that?"

"I didn't kill him. The only thing I did was to change the time of the auction."

Brooke looked away and shook her head. "You still don't understand, do you?"

"Understand what?"

"That you're responsible for his death even if you didn't pull the trigger."

"How can that be?"

"My father was a weak man. Our savings were all gone, and he was afraid we might lose our house. He couldn't take another setback. Then you came along to make him look like a fool," she said, blinking back tears.

"I'm sorry. I didn't know. Is there something I can do?"

"Yes. Just leave me alone."

"Please, Brooke, I only want to help."

"No, you can't!" she returned with a flash of anger. "I'm having difficulty dealing with this because I feel guilty too. I keep telling myself I should have seen the signs. That I should have known he might do something stupid."

McKay could see she was hurting and touched her arm. Brooke quickly withdrew, turning away from him. The warmth of his touch awakened feelings Brooke had denied until now. She longed to be held and comforted by someone who was strong like her father used to be. Someone who could make the hurt go away. But this was the wrong man for that.

McKay took her shoulders in his hands, making her face him. "Brooke, we need to talk about this. Why don't I come by your house around twelve tomorrow?"

She tore herself free of his grasp, backing away from him. "No! Stay away from me, do you hear? Stay away or I'll call the police."

McKay shook his head sadly as he watched Brooke hurry down the planked walk.

"There you are!" McKay said, rushing into city hall where the ladies from the Society were waiting to turn in the money they had collected. He carried a small leather bag and halted in front of Brooke. All the ladies turned to look at the two. "I'm sorry I'm so late in getting back to you, Miss Snow, but some of the men were delayed in returning to the ship."

With everyone's eyes upon her, Brooke had no choice but to speak to Captain McKay. "That's quite all right, Captain," she said through tight, unsmiling lips. He handed her the bag, and it appeared heavier than before. "My, heavens, I had no idea the contribution would be so large."

He beamed with pride. "I'm glad you're pleased. The men may appear to be gruff, but they have a lot of charity in their hearts."

"They do indeed. You must remember to thank them for me."

"Yes, ma'am, I'll do that. And thank you for accepting my invitation for lunch tomorrow."

There was fire in Brooke's eyes. She did not appreciate being put on the spot like this in front of her friends. How could she refuse having lunch with this man without appearing ungrateful? She forced a smile. "It's the least I could do after you made such a generous contribution, Captain."

"That's very kind, ma'am. Where should I meet you?"

Brooke thought quickly. She wanted to meet him where the other women might see. Just in case there was any difficulty. "How about outside city hall, say around noon?"

McKay nodded. "Excellent. I'll look forward to seeing you then." He grinned, touching the brim of his cap. "Good day, Miss Snow. . . ladies."

The women smiled, murmuring their thanks.

When Brooke plopped the leather pouch onto the counting table, the ladies gathered around her, applauding. Although Virginia clapped like the others, her smile appeared strained.

The following morning a white-haired Negro house servant entered the dining room, and said, "Dis heah boy be from de shipyard, suh."

McKay patted his mouth with a napkin, then nodded. "Thank you, Grady." He was eating breakfast with five other men in the large house his company had rented for their blockade-running crews.

The youngster stood before him nervously clutching his green checked cap and announced, "Your ship is ready, Captain."

"So soon?" he asked, reaching for a crystal water goblet. "I was under the impression the repairs would take at least a month."

"Usually it would, sir. But Mr. Snow asked if we could hurry. Then when he died, everyone at the yard felt so bad that we wanted to do this for him."

McKay nodded. "I'm sure he would have been pleased."

The boy broke into a wide grin. "Thank you, sir."

"You can tell the yard master I'll pick up the *Atlantis* this morning and move her across the river to the cotton press."

"Yes, sir. I'll tell him right away."

"Here, this is for you." McKay stood, reached into his pocket and gave the boy a dime.

No sooner had the messenger gone than Grady came into the dining room again. "Miz Drake's waitin' to see you in de parlor, suh."

Curious why she wanted to see him, McKay excused himself. When he entered the parlor, Virginia was trying to close her yellow parasol, but the clasp appeared to be stuck and the canopy kept popping open.

"Here, Virginia, let me help you with that," he said, crossing the room.

Virginia stopped fussing with the parasol and smiled. "Thank you, Captain. I'm afraid I'm helpless around anything mechanical," she said with a wave of her hand.

He took the parasol, then slipped the spreader ribs down past the retaining ring and closed it.

"There you are. Good as new," he said handing it back to her. For the first time he had a good look at Virginia. Her matching yellow gown, trimmed in white lace and decorated with gaily colored azaleas exposed her shoulders and the inviting swell of her breasts. The neckline was so low, he quickly looked away embarrassed.

"Thank you, Captain McKay. I hope you don't mind me dropping by, but I thought today might be an excellent time to show you the city. It's such a lovely day."

"I'd love to, Virginia, but I'm afraid this isn't a good time. I have to take my ship across the river to be loaded, and then I'm meeting Brooke at city hall at twelve."

"Can I come with you? I've always wanted to see a blockade-runner sail. It simply amazes me how you men can handle such a big, powerful ship," she said.

"It's a tremendous responsibility," McKay admitted, trying to keep his eyes on Virginia's face and not her bosom. "However, it's like anything else. Ability comes with experience."

Virginia thought for a moment, then brightened with an idea. "I know what we can do. If you take me along, I could walk with you to city hall and point out the sights along the way."

A smile spread over McKay's face. "Sure, I'd like that."

Virginia offered her arm to him. He took it, then got his blue naval cap from the coat tree in the hall.

The couple walked to Third and Market where they found a carriage to take them to Cassidey's Shipyard. While McKay went inside the yard office, Virginia opened her yellow parasol and walked over to the wharf where several ships were docked. A crewman was hurrying to board a ship, and she asked, "Sir, is this the *Atlantis*?"

Judson Bates took off his bowler hat and placed it in front of him, concealing the bulge in his shirt. "Yes, ma'am." He hoped he was successful in hiding the bottle of whiskey. "We're due to leave here any minute now."

"My, she is a fine ship," Virginia observed with awe.

"That she is, ma'am," he said, then added, "If you'll excuse me, I've gotta make sure everything's ready to load our cargo."

"Of course."

"Thank you, ma'am," he said, bending from the waist, and turning around quickly before he put the hat back on his head. He scurried up the gangplank, disappearing down a hatch before anyone noticed.

Boatswain John Gallagher strolled out of the bridge, checking the time on his pocket watch. When he glanced up, he saw the woman from the day before gazing at the ship. "Good morning, ma'am!"

Startled someone was watching her, Virginia stammered, "Good--good morning, Captain."

Gallagher nodded a greeting and took off his cap. "I'm just a boatswain, ma'am. If you're looking for Captain McKay, he's not here."

Virginia's eyes were very wide, very blue. "Oh, I'm not looking for him. I know where he is. He's inside that building talking to the boat person."

The boatswain suppressed a grin. "Yes, ma'am. We're preparing to leave the dock as soon as he comes aboard."

"Yes, I know. I'm coming with you."

"Ma'am?"

"I said, I'm coming with you."

"Does the captain know about this?" the boatswain asked, puzzled.

"Of course he does. Who do you think asked me?"

Gallagher shrugged, then shook his head in amazement.

When McKay came out of the office, Virginia presented her arm to him and they walked to the *Atlantis* together.

"Welcome aboard, Captain McKay," the boatswain said with a broad smile as Wade and Virginia stepped off the gangplank onto the deck. "The *Atlantis* is ready to get under way, sir."

"Very good, Mr. Gallagher. Have you met Miss Drake?"

"Not formally, sir."

"Miss Drake, this is my boatswain, Mr. John Gallagher."

"Mr. Gallagher, this is indeed an honor," she said, holding out her hand.

The boatswain bent forward, and kissed her fingers. "The honor is all mine, ma'am. It seems the more I see of Wilmington, the more I find to like."

While Virginia blushed at the compliment, McKay cleared his throat. "Mr. Gallagher, would you please prepare us to get under way."

"Yes, sir!" The junior officer went inside the bridge. He pulled down the lever attached to the bulkhead. The brass steam whistle near the forward funnel shrieked for five long seconds, announcing their departure. Walking to the railing, he called to the men standing by the mooring lines on the dock, "Cast off all lines!"

There was a flurry of activity as the dock workers slipped the heavy cables off the bollards, and the crewmen aboard the *Atlantis* hauled them in, hand-over-hand.

"Quartermaster, rudder amidships," McKay said. He went to the speaking tube and opened it. "Mr. Reichman, all ahead slow on the port wheel."

All at once, a shudder ran through the deck as the machinery began to turn, and the port paddle wheel slowly churned the water. The sleek bow of the *Atlantis* edged away from the dock, widening the gap between it and the wharf. Her funnels trailed columns of black smoke which drifted in the breeze, engulfing the shipyard. When she had enough room to maneuver, she headed for deeper water and blended into the boat traffic. Soon the large warehouse of the cotton press came into view, and the *Atlantis* navigated to the western side of the Cape Fear River in preparation to dock at the wharf.

After giving orders to the boatswain on how he wanted the cargo loaded, Captain McKay and Virginia took the ferry back across the river to Wilmington. They strolled east on Market Street and passed the open-air Market House beneath its column supported roof. Dozens of peddlers cried out, trying to sell their merchandise, while the cobblestone streets echoed with iron-shod wheels and the shouts of teamsters.

"My daddy used to say you could find anything you wanted in that place," Virginia told Wade.

"Can you?"

"Heavens no," she said, laughing. "However, little girls believe everything their daddies say. I remember, he'd let me ride on his shoulders as he shopped, and I never went home without a piece of peanut brittle to munch on. How I used to love to come here," Virginia said wistfully.

"Don't you still?"

"Not since daddy died. Mammy comes here about once a week and does the shopping."

McKay held up his hand. "Wait here a minute." He found a peddler selling peanut brittle and bought a bag for a penny.

"Here you are," he said, handing Virginia the candy. "A bag full of memories."

She squealed with delight, then opened the paper bag, offering him some. He smiled and took a piece.

They walked in silence for a few minutes, munching their peanut brittle.

"Have you heard about the area a few blocks north of here, along the river?" Virginia asked, looking at Wade to see his reaction. "It's called Paddys Hollow."

Knowing a lady would never approve of such a notorious place, McKay told her, "No, I haven't. What is it?"

"It's a perfectly scandalous section of town. Anyone searching for wild taverns, gambling houses and brothels can be sure to find whatever he wants there."

"Really? What did your daddy say about that?"

Virginia's lips curved into a smile, and she laughed. "Nothing, if he was smart. Mama would have had his hide if she knew he'd been there."

They waited at the intersection of Second and Market Street while several carriages passed by, then crossed over to Princess Street. As they approached city hall, Virginia noticed Brooke coming down the stairs toward them. She increased the pressure on Wade's arm, and said, "Oh dear! I've got something in my eye. Can you see it?"

When Wade leaned closer to look at her, Virginia raised her mouth to his, kissing him.

Pleased but puzzled, he asked, "What was that for?"

"For being a perfect escort."

McKay gave her a wry smile. "How's your eye?"

Virginia watched Brooke storm away after seeing the two of them kissing. "Much better. I think whatever was in it must be gone."

After leaving Virginia to do her shopping, McKay walked to city hall and waited in front of the building for twenty minutes. When Brooke did not meet him, he went to the second floor and was informed by an elderly lady that Brooke had gone to lunch early and wouldn't return until one o'clock. Perplexed, he sat on a bench in the hall and waited. When it became a quarter to two and Brooke still hadn't returned, Wade grew concerned. Had something happened? He went to her house to see if everything was all right.

Mrs. Snow answered the door and informed him Brooke wasn't home. He didn't mention her daughter's disappearance for fear it might upset her.

As McKay was returning to his ship, he saw Virginia leave a dress shop across the street. She waved excitedly when she noticed him and crossed over to his side.

"How did it go with Brooke?" she asked.

He frowned. "It didn't. She never met me."

Virginia gasped in surprise. "I declare, I don't understand what's gotten into that girl. Leaving a handsome man like you all alone."

"It's all right," he said. "I have plenty to do aboard the ship. We'll be leaving tomorrow evening with the rising tide."

"You will? But I thought you'd wait for a moonless night?"

"Generally we would. There'll be a quarter moon tomorrow, but that doesn't matter because the sky should be overcast."

"Well, if you're leaving so soon," Virginia said, inclining her head and taking his arm, "I consider it my duty for the war effort to show you a good time."

"Thanks, but I don't think I would be very good company this evening."

"I'll bet Paddy's Hollow will cheer you up."

He looked at Virginia in surprise. "I thought decent people stayed away from there."

"They do. But I've always wanted to go." She stopped walking and peered up at him. "Oh, Wade, would you be my escort?"

"I'm sorry but I can't, Virginia. I would never take a lady to such a place."

"Oh please." She gave his arm a little squeeze. "I'd be ever so grateful."

"No. It's out of the question. Think about your reputation."

Virginia paused, frowning. "You're right, of course. What was I thinking? Something like that could jeopardize my standing with the ladies of the Soldier's Aid Society."

"It certainly could."

Virginia folded her arms, pouting. "It seems I never have any fun anymore. I've always done what's expected of me, but my life has been so dull and boring. Until now, that is."

"Until now?"

Virginia batted her eyes. "Yes, silly. Until I met you."

McKay's brow furrowed. "I'm confused. Why should I have any effect on your life?"

Virginia looked at him amazed. "You don't know?"

"No, I don't."

"All right, then. Where shall I begin? You're a brave and handsome blockade-runner captain who has swept the women of Wilmington right off their feet."

McKay smiled. "You're probably just flattering me so I'll change my mind about taking you to Paddy's Hollow."

Virginia lowered her eyes, hurt. "Why, Captain, I would never do such a thing. Besides, I've changed my mind about going."

"You have?"

"Yes. But, I simply can't let you brood all alone. Why don't you come to my house for dinner?"

McKay smiled. "Well, thank you for your kind offer, but I really need to get back to the ship. There's so much I need to do before we leave."

Virginia looked dismayed. "I understand, Captain. Perhaps another time, then."

"Yes. That would be good," McKay agreed, relieved he had an excuse for not going to Virginia's house. He did not want anything to come between him and Brooke.

That evening Judson Bates sat on a cotton bale on the *Atlantis'* deck, explaining to twenty-year-old Howard Dutton what he wanted him to do. Dutton held a tan puppy in his lap he had found that afternoon. Bates didn't want to cut the big, slow-witted man in on the money Reuben was supposed to bring, but he had no choice because Howard was on guard duty that night.

"Look, this nigger an' his family are s'posed to stowaway tonight," Judson explained. "Now I've hollowed out this space for them between the bales of cotton behind the galley. All you gotta do is keep an eye on that big buck, an' leave the rest to me."

Howard nodded, then gave his friend a puzzled look. "How do I do that, Judd? Like this?" He leaned forward, staring hard at Judson.

"No, you fool." Bates picked up the shotgun beside him, thrusting it into Howard's hands. "With this here scatter gun. You're on guard duty, aincha?"

Howard said, "Yeah."

"Well, you just look mean an' hold this gun, an' I'll take care of the rest."

The puppy rolled over, playfully pawing the air while Howard scratched his belly. "All right, Judd. You always know best."

"You're damned right I do. Didn't I get you this job shovelin' coal?"

"Yeah." Howard grinned, then added, "I was surely lucky when I met up with you."

"All right, then. You just let me do the plannin', an' do what I tell you to do."

Howard nodded absently, gazing at his puppy tugging on a shirt button.

"Give me that blasted dog," Judson snapped, motioning for the puppy. "You're s'posed to be on guard duty."

The big man looked up with fear in his eyes. "But I like playin' with Scruffy."

"I know you do, but it don't look right. You're s'posed to be mean."

Howard reluctantly gave the puppy to Judson. "What are you goin' to do with Scruffy? Don't hurt him."

"I won't. I'm just gonna put him in the galley with a bowl of milk. Now you keep watch."

Howard nodded, watching Judson disappear inside the galley. When he turned around, he gasped in surprise. Directly in front of him loomed a huge black man with quick and nervous eyes.

"Glory be! You must be the darkie Judd was talkin' about."

"Yessuh. I brung de silver like I said." Reuben set a lumpy blue cloth on the bale of cotton, untying the corners. "Dis heah's all Callie could git."

Howard's eyes widened in surprise when he saw the gleaming pile of silverware. "That there's a whole heap!"

The black man smiled and laughed. "Yessuh. It sho' is."

Judson stepped outside the galley, hurrying over. "Howard, not so damned loud!"

"Sorry, Judd. Looky here." He grinned, pointing to the silverware. "Looky what the man brung."

Judson gaped in disbelief at the silverware laying on the cotton bale, then stared at Reuben. "Silverware? When you said silver, I thought you meant silver coins."

"No, suh. Dat's all Callie could git from de massa's house," Reuben explained, picking up a large spoon and holding it out for Judson to see. "Dis heah is gooder'n money."

Judson examined the piece. "I guess it'll do. Where's your family?"

"Dey's hidin' among de cotton bales on de wharf."

"Well, go get em."

"Yessuh!" Reuben gave him a wide, grin and bobbed at the waist before disappearing down the gangplank.

An instant later, he came out of the shadows with a woman and three children. The woman stepped onto the ship balancing a toddler on her hip with one hand and leading a young boy with the other. Reuben came up behind her with a girl about five years old.

"Dis heah's my woman, Callie, an' our three young'uns. Dis be Florry, an' dat's Ben an' de one holdin' onto his momma's Elias."

Judson nodded a greeting, then waved for them to follow him to the rear of the cabins. "We gotta get you folks hid. I hollered outta space among these bales of cotton behind the galley."

Reuben looked warily at the small opening.

"I know it's kinda narrow, but it's gotta be that way," Judson explained. "If the captain finds you while we're at sea, he'll throw you over the side. He don't care. You're just another runaway darkie to him."

Judson motioned to Reuben, and said, "Now you scoot back there. Next will go the young'uns, an' then your woman. That way, with the young'uns 'tween you an' her, both of you can hush 'em up."

Reuben folded up his bulk as well as he could, then moved into the narrow opening sideways. After he had gone about three feet, one of the children followed, then another. Callie's slim body stretched the faded material of her dress when she set Ben down.

Suddenly Judson drew a 44-Colt revolver from his waistband, snatching Callie's wrist. "Howard, you keep that scatter gun on Reuben. Me an' Miss Callie are goin' to settle their bill."

Howard shook his head. "But, Judd, I don't think this was part of our plan."

"It is now. This nigger whore will be happy to help her family escape the *massa*. Ain't that right?" Judson asked, eyeing the frightened woman next to him.

"No, Callie!" Reuben shouted, pushing his children ahead of him as he moved between the cotton bales. "Don' you let him touch you!"

Callie looked at Reuben's pleading face, the face that told her not to do it. "I got to, Reuben! I'm sorry, but I got to. I don't want you hurt."

"Howard, you watch him," Judson warned in an excited voice. "Don't let him get out of there."

Howard nervously shifted his weight from foot to foot. "Reuben, I got to do what Judd says. He's smart, an' I gotta listen to him."

The closer the black man got to the opening the more frightened Howard became. "You stop right there, Reuben, or I'm gonna have to hurt you."

"Howard, you mind what I told you!" Judson shouted, struggling with Callie as she tried to go to her husband.

"Reuben, don't you come out!" Howard cried, backing away with the shotgun leveled at the angry man. Howard stumbled on a raised deck plank and both barrels of the shotgun exploded.

Trembling with fright, Howard dropped the shotgun. "I'm sorry, Judd! I didn't mean to do it. I tripped, an' my finger slipped."

No longer able to control the shrieking woman struggling to get free, Judson bashed her across the face with his revolver. Callie's head snapped back, then she slumped to the deck.

Judson rushed to the smoking crevice and saw a tangle of bloody limbs. Reuben lay on top of his children. His chest had absorbed most of the blast and had burst like a ripe watermelon, scattering bloody tissue everywhere. He saw a child's arm, denuded of flesh, dangling from one of the bales, still smoking. Everywhere he looked was blood, punctuated by an eerie silence as if the world stood still in horror.

"Don't make no diff'rence," Judson said with a wave of his hand. "They're just niggers anyway. You get this mess cleaned up before the others get back. I got bizness to tend to."

Howard gawked at the bloody tangle of bodies, then turned to Judson. "What's more important than this?"

74

"I still gotta take care of that bitch. Ain't no way I'm gonna let her live after what she seen."

"Why don't we wake her an' tell her not to say anything?" Howard suggested.

Judson shook his head wearily. "Howard, leave the thinkin' to me. Now I told you what to do."

Howard's shoulders slumped in resignation. "All right, Judd. I'll clean up."

"That's good, Howard. You do that."

Judson dragged Callie into a cabin. While he was unbuttoning his pants, she moaned and began to stir.

"I knew you was just pretendin'. You nigger women always come 'round when you're alone with a man."

Callie's eyes opened, and when she saw what was happening, she began to get up.

"You stay right there," Judson cautioned her, drawing the revolver from his trousers before letting them fall. "You an' me is goin' to have a little fun."

She got back down, watching as he began to rub his flaccid penis. It failed to get hard, and the longer it stayed soft, the angrier he became.

Callie could not get the nightmarish shotgun blast out of her head. She knew Judson intended to kill her also. The strange thing was, she wanted to die. She wished desperately to join her family, because without them, she had nothing to live for. It would be difficult getting Judson to shoot her before he raped her. If she could deny him that pleasure, she would have won a small, but important victory.

"Is dat little bitty thing your cock?" she said, leaning forward to see, then frowned. "Can't be. It's too small."

Judson's face reddened. Once again a woman was making fun of him. "Just you wait. I'll show you how big it is."

Callie pointed at him, laughing hysterically and rocking back and forth.

Judson was afraid Howard would hear her. "Shut up, Goddamn it!"

75

Callie kept right on rocking and laughing. If anything, she laughed louder.

"Look, you nigger whore, I told you to shut up!"

She laughed and laughed, until Judson pointed the gleaming barrel of his revolver at her face, then pulled back the hammer. "I said stop it!"

Callie gave Judson an icy stare, then laughed as loud as she could.

The muzzle blast from the exploding revolver flung her backward, blood spurting from an eye socket. Her body twitched a few times, blood seeping from her shattered cranium, then lay still.

Judson pulled up his trousers, strolling out of the cabin. "Them nigger women sure like their sex," he announced, making a show of buttoning his pants.

Howard had just finished slipping Reuben's body into the river when his friend came outside. "Judd, what was all the laughin' I heard?"

"That wasn't laughin'. That bitch was havin' such a good time, she was cryin' for mercy. Man, them nigger women are hot!"

Howard nodded, thinking how lucky he was to have a friend like Judd. Not many people would go through all the trouble he did to hide the bodies for his partner.

CHAPTER 5

Judson Bates was going to the ship's galley for his morning coffee when he paused to watch four men holding a hose attached to the number two funnel. They were placing it between the bales of cotton to smoke out stowaways. Glad Reuben and his family were gone, and he had nothing to worry about, Judson continued to the galley when he noticed the ferry from Wilmington coming alongside the *Atlantis* with the captain.

"There he goes!" a voice behind Judson yelled. There were shouts and the scuff of feet as people ran across the deck. Finally a sailor wearing a straw hat called, "I got 'em!"

Judson watched with fear as Reuben's son was dragged out from behind a bale of cotton, kicking and screaming.

When someone called for the boatswain, Judson lowered his head so he wouldn't be recognized, then quickly went below.

Captain McKay had just stepped aboard the *Atlantis* when the boatswain came over looking worried.

"Sir, we found a stowaway aboard," John Gallagher said.

"Did you notify the authorities?"

"Yes, sir, I sent Rogers. However, this stowaway is a young black boy who claims his family was murdered by two of our sailors. I think you should hear what he has to say."

"All right, send him to my cabin."

"Yes, sir. Right away, sir."

Minutes later McKay was making an entry in the ship's log, when he heard a knock on the door.

"Come in," he called, setting the pen down on the open page, then leaning back in his chair.

The boatswain ushered the frightened boy in. His shirt was torn and spattered with blood, and his right arm was covered with a thick layer of bandages.

The captain looked at the boatswain, and asked, "What happened to him?"

"He had some buckshot in his arm when we found him, sir."

Puzzled, McKay leaned forward, asking the youngster, "What's your name, son?"

The black boy blinked his big eyes, and answered, "Elias."

"Well, Elias, what happened to you?"

"I bin shot," he said, touching his bandaged arm thoughtfully.

"So I see. How did this happen?"

A tear ran down the boy's right cheek as he remembered the horror of the night before. "When my family hid in de cotton, a man shot us."

McKay nodded understanding so the boy would continue with his story. "That's all you were doing, hiding among the cotton bales? Nothing more?"

"Yessuh."

"Elias, people don't shoot somebody for just trying to stowaway. You had to have been doing something else. Were you stealing?"

"No, suh," the boy answered, frightened.

McKay tried to set the boy at ease. "All right, Elias. I believe you. Where are your parents?"

More tears left glistening trails on his dark skin, which he quickly wiped away. "They's dead. So's my brother an' sister."

"Where are they now?"

"De man threw 'em in de river."

"Do you know who did this?"

Elias nodded, holding up two fingers. "Two white mens did it."

"Do these men belong to this crew?"

The boy nodded again.

"Can you describe them for me?"

"One man was real big. Bigger'n you. An' de other was smaller with a beard an' a black hat."

McKay looked at his boatswain. "Who was on guard duty last night?"

"Howard Dutton, sir."

McKay nodded. "He fits the description. Bates is his friend, isn't he?"

"Yes, sir. And Bates has a beard and wears a black bowler," the boatswain hastened to add.

McKay turned back to Elias. "Can you show me where this happened?"

The boy nodded, pointing to the rear of the ship. "Back there," he said.

McKay rose and took the boy by the hand. "Come on, Elias. Take me to where it happened."

The boy became frightened, trying to pull away. "But I don't wanna' go there!"

"We have to, Elias. If I'm going to accuse anyone of murder, I need to see evidence of a crime."

The three of them went behind the galley, and Elias showed them where his family was murdered. The bales were neatly stacked in two rows and everything appeared in order. McKay looked around a minute and saw nothing usual.

"Elias, are you sure this is the right place?"

The boy nodded. "There was an openin' right heah. But it be gone now."

"Mr. Gallagher, help me move these bales."

Both men grabbed the top bale, lowering it to the deck, then moved the bottom bale out of the way. McKay knelt and examined the deck. The wood was gray and weathered, and it was difficult to tell if it was stained with blood. He looked at the cotton bales on either side of the small passageway, but they appeared normal.

Boatswain Gallagher shook his head. "I'm sorry for bothering you with such an outlandish story, sir."

"That's all right," McKay said, getting up. Suddenly his foot slipped, and he grabbed a cotton bale to keep from falling.

"Are you okay, sir?" the boatswain asked, moving to help him.

McKay waved him back. "Yes. But there's something on this deck." Curious, he leaned over, running his fingers along the wooden planks. McKay picked up several pieces of buckshot, then raised his hand for the boatswain to see. "Look what I found. Let's move a few more of these bales."

The men moved the cotton bales, examining them. One was turned over to hide its bloody burlap cover. As they moved it, a two-inch piece of jaw bone fell to the deck. The shattered bone still had a tooth attached.

McKay's face reddened with anger as he picked up the grisly object. "Mr. Gallagher, is everyone aboard?"

"Yes, sir."

"Good. Have all the men stop what they're doing and assemble on the forward deck."

Several minutes later, all thirty-three crewmen stood in two ranks in front of the bridge. The captain and four armed guards accompanied Elias, while the boy examined the men. Howard's eyes grew big, and he began to tremble as the boy came closer.

"Dat's him! He's de man what done it!" Elias said, pointing at Howard.

Howard glanced at Captain McKay, his eyes shifting nervously. "I didn't mean to hurt nobody! I tripped an' the gun went off."

"I don't want to hear it, Dutton. Save it for the police." McKay nodded to the guards beside him. Two men grabbed Howard and led him away.

The boy continued looking at the men, then pointed to Judson Bates. "Him, too!"

Judson's jaw dropped. "What? You got the wrong man, Capt'n. Howard's already admitted the shooting."

"Yeah, Bates, he did. But you were with him and that makes you guilty as an accessory."

Elias tugged on McKay's sleeve. "Dat man kilt my mama!" he cried, motioning to Judson. "He took her away from us an' kilt her."

McKay had heard enough. "Guards, I want these men put in chains until the police get here."

When the guards stepped forward and seized him by the arms, Judson shook his head in disbelief. "I didn't kill anyone, capt'n! You gotta believe me."

McKay shot Judson a look of contempt. "The boy identified you and Dutton. That's all I need to know."

"You're not goin' to take the word of a nigger stowaway over mine, are you?"

"Bates, I'm not going to argue with you," McKay said, his patience wearing thin. "If you're innocent, then you have nothing to worry about."

"You ain't heard the last of this, Capt'n!" Judson yelled, struggling against the guards as they dragged him away. "I swear I'll get even with you, you nigger lovin' son of a bitch!"

McKay disregarded the man's threats and turned to the boatswain. "Mr. Gallagher, take Elias to the galley and see he gets something to eat. Then take him ashore and have a doctor treat those wounds."

"Yes, Captain. May I add, sir, that you're doing the right thing? Bates has been nothing but trouble since we hired him."

"Thank you for your vote of confidence, Mr. Gallagher. I wasn't sure if I was still popular with the men anymore."

"I believe you are, sir," the junior officer said. "One thing is certain, though."

McKay searched the boatswain's face for an answer. "What's that?"

"You've got their respect, sir. That's a mighty important thing to have when you're commanding a ship in time of war."

McKay nodded in agreement. "Yes, it is. Thank you, Mr. Gallagher."

A few hours later, McKay was checking the barometer in the bridge and entering some calculations in a notebook when the purser entered. "Sir, we have a last-minute passenger."

"Did you show him to his cabin?"

The purser frowned. "No, sir. The passenger is a woman with her Negro maid. I don't know where to put them."

McKay saw Brooke Snow step through the doorway. She was even more beautiful than he remembered. She was dressed in a black velvet jacket with lace around the collar and a red and black plaid skirt. Her auburn hair glistened in the soft light from the window.

When the purser noticed the Captain stare past him and remove his cap, he glanced over his shoulder. "Miss Snow, this is Captain McKay."

"Thank you, but I've already met the Captain," she answered, her eyes locked with Wade's.

"Oh," the purser said in a small voice, then sensed the tension between the two. "With the Captain's permission, I'll return to my duties."

McKay nodded to him and the purser left the bridge.

"Hello, Brooke. Where have you been?"

"I wasn't ready to be found."

"But we were supposed to have lunch yesterday," he reminded her.

A shadow crossed Brooke's face. "I changed my mind. Surely a woman can do that."

"Was it because of something I did?"

She struggled to keep the anger out of her voice. "I'd rather not go into that right now."

"All right, then. Why are you going to Nassau?"

"So I can transfer to a ship going to London," she said, watching his face for a reaction.

McKay was, puzzled. "Why London?"

"Because that's where Burgess & Linden's offices are. You see, I plan to become their new agent in Wilmington."

McKay found her new air of confidence attractive. "That's a great idea except for one thing. All their agents are men."

Brooke nodded. "Yes they are, and that's why I have to go. So I can convince them I can do this job as well as any man." She paused, wondering how she could best explain her situation. "Before my father died, he mortgaged the house and invested heavily in the *Osprey's* cargo. When she was captured, he lost everything. I was faced with the hard reality if someone didn't take up the reins financially, we'd soon lose our home. My mother is still too weak from her attack of yellow fever to cope with such a thing. I fear if we lose the house, I'll lose her, too."

There was an awkward silence while McKay thought of what to say. "If you'd like, I'll write a letter of recommendation," he offered.

"Thank you, Captain. That would be very kind."

McKay frowned, his eyes troubled. "Brooke, I thought we were friends. Why are you being so formal?"

Brooke's gaze hardened. "Because we haven't settled our difficulties."

The boatswain came onto the bridge. He half smiled and touched the brim of his cap when he saw Brooke, then addressed the Captain, "Sir, the police are here for the prisoners."

"Thank you, Mr. Gallagher. Tell them I'll be there in a minute."

"What prisoners are those?" Brooke asked.

McKay remembered what Brooke had said about blockade-runners bringing crime to Wilmington. He was ashamed to admit she had been right. "Last night two crewmen killed a Negro family when they tried to stowaway aboard ship. We found one of their boys, and he told us what happened."

Brooke shuddered at the thought of a whole family being murdered.

McKay changed the subject. "I'll be busy for most of the night until we're clear of the blockade, but I must speak with you. Can we talk tomorrow?"

"If you wish, Captain."

"Thank you. Perhaps after breakfast," McKay said, then replaced his cap. "I can show you to your cabin, if you like."

Brooke nodded. "Yes. I would like to get settled."

McKay showed Brooke and her maid to the second and the third cabins behind the wheelhouse.

The living quarters in Brooke's cabin were Spartan, but then she hadn't expected much in the way of luxurious accommodations aboard a blockade-runner. There were four berths, all empty of course, a small writing table bolted to the wall and the floor, and a tiny chest of drawers with a mirror.

Brooke saw her reflection in the mirror, and a tear trickled down her cheek. She didn't know what she was doing here. If she became a shipping agent for Burgess & Linden, how could she keep the owners happy by showing enormous profits without betraying how she felt? And how could she work with speculators who were the very men she despised? She didn't know the answers to these questions, and the lack of a solution made her feel even more lonely. Although she didn't know what she would do, she was aware of the fact Wade McKay had driven her to this desperate situation, and she hated him for that.

At six that evening the *Atlantis* left the wharf by the cotton press and proceeded to the mouth of the Cape Fear River. She docked at a landing near Battery Buchanan to get the latest intelligence about the blockading fleet's movements. McKay learned the *USS Minnesota*, a large sixty-four gun frigate, bore the Admiral's flag and lay at anchor as a base of operations while the inner squadron patrolled on either side of her at thirty minute intervals. Since the gunboats stopped well short of the *USS Minnesota*, McKay planned to dash through the unprotected gap.

Just after 1 A.M. the *Atlantis* steamed from the wharf. No lights were permitted aboard the ship. The funnels were fitted with special screens to filter out any sparks which might escape, the engine room hatchways were covered with tarpaulins, and even the binnacle was wrapped with canvas so the quartermaster had to peer at the compass through a small aperture. McKay had placed a lookout at the masthead to warn them of approaching enemy ships. Blockade-runners were well versed in the art of remaining undetected. Their low profiles blended in with the sea, while the towering masts of the Federal warships revealed their location.

The *Atlantis* proceeded slowly as she left the safety of the river while the pilot got his bearings. When several miles of ocean lay behind them, the lookout from the forward mast sent a messenger to the captain on the bridge.

A seaman with a black bush of a mustache informed McKay, "Sir, a large ship is anchored two points off our starboard bow."

"Thank you, Mr. Pierce. Keep me informed if anything develops," the Captain said, issuing an order to the helmsman. "Quartermaster, bear five degrees to port."

The lookout in the masthead kept his arm pointing in the direction the Admiral's ship lay, and everyone on the bridge strained their eyes to find her.

"Ship bearing zero-two-five, sir," the boatswain called out.

McKay shifted his telescope to that direction and made out the shadowy form of the three-masted *USS Minnesota*. He turned his gaze to port because he knew the unknown lay somewhere out there. Where would the next ship materialize out of the gloom? He scanned the blackened sea for the danger he knew was lurking just out of sight.

McKay summoned a messenger. "Tell the lookout to keep a sharp eye on the port quarter. We don't want any surprises."

The seaman gave Captain McKay a swift salute, then hurried away.

The sixty-four-gun frigate bobbed in the ocean swell as the darkened blockade-runner steamed closer. Everyone aboard the *Atlantis* grew still. The only movement allowed was when the lookouts turned their heads as they scanned the waters around them for enemy ships.

Suddenly, a ghostly warship emerged from the haze on their port quarter.

"Quartermaster, bear ten degrees to starboard," McKay ordered. Because of the Federal cruiser to port, the blockade-runner would have to pass closer to the Admiral's flagship than intended.

The crew aboard the *Atlantis* held their breath as the gap ahead of them grew smaller. If McKay's calculations were correct, the blockade-runner should slip between the Federal ships with only 500 yards to spare. The temptation to grab the speaking tube and order more speed was enormous, but McKay knew they needed to remain as silent as possible.

Fear heightened the men's senses as the ships drew nearer. The Federal cruiser's bow wave grew louder as it pushed tons of water ahead of it and even the *Atlantis'* paddle wheels seemed to slap the ocean thunderously. The closer the blockade-runner sailed to the big warships, the more threatening they became. Black hulls, bristling with guns and crowned by towering masts, seemed to rise like magic from the sea.

All at once the Federal ship swung toward them, and the ominous sound of drums beating the crew to battle stations drifted across the water.

McKay snatched open the copper speaking tube to the engine room. "Mr. Reichman, all ahead flank!"

A shudder passed through the *Atlantis* as the paddle wheels surged ahead.

The Federal cruiser bore down on her prey, shooting glittering signal rockets from her deck. A blinding flash lit up the horizon as her forward cannon sent a warning shot whistling across the blockade-runner's bow.

Heaving to and letting his ship be captured was the last thing on McKay's mind. "Quartermaster, take evasive action."

The *Atlantis* zigzagged like a frightened rabbit while shells exploded all around her, sending towering geysers of water into the air and sweeping her decks with the spray. Another rocket zoomed across the night sky, pointing out the direction of the chase.

McKay grabbed his telescope and rushed outside the bridge to study the ship behind them. Due to the *Atlantis'* speed, the warship was slipping farther astern and was beginning to disappear into the gloom. McKay turned his head and shouted, so the pilot could hear him above the wail of shot and the crash of spray on the wooden pilot house. "Ninety degrees to starboard!"

The quartermaster spun the spoked wheel, causing the blockade-runner to lean heavily into the turn. Her deck slanted to a thirty-degree angle, and everyone on the bridge had to grab onto something to keep from being thrown across the wheelhouse.

McKay leveled his telescope to see if the Federal cruiser would follow. The warship didn't veer from her course and charged off into the night, her guns thundering at an unseen enemy.

"We've lost them, Captain!"

McKay collapsed the telescope, nodding to the boatswain. "It appears we have, but don't celebrate too soon. We still have the outer squadron to deal with," he reminded him.

Gallagher's expression of joy turned to one of concern. "When do you figure we might encounter them, sir?"

"Well, if they've seen the signal rockets, and I'm sure they have, we could see a few soon. We'll continue on this heading for another hour and that should take us far enough away from the search area."

McKay appeared troubled, clearing his throat with difficulty. "Mr. Gallagher, I would consider it a personal favor if you would check on Miss Snow to see if she's all right. I'd go myself, you understand, but I'm needed on the bridge."

"Of course, sir. I'll do it immediately."

The boatswain walked aft to Miss Snow's cabin and tapped on the door. When he heard the sounds of someone retching, he knocked harder and called, "Miss Snow, are you all right?"

In a few moments, Brooke opened the door, looking pale and tired. "I'm afraid I'm sick. I've never been a good sailor, but I was holding my own until I got tossed out of bed. Then my stomach decided to rebel."

Mr. Gallagher peered past the woman and saw the Negro maid stripping the soiled sheets from Brooke's berth. A chamber pot was on the floor next to it. "I have a guaranteed cure for seasickness," he confided.

"You do?"

"Yes, ma'am. It's an old seaman's remedy. If you're well enough to go to the galley, Cookie can make some of his tea to help you sleep."

Brooke turned green at the thought of food. "I couldn't possibly eat anything now. Can't I stay here?"

"No, ma'am. You need to get out of your cabin and walk around. That's part of the remedy."

The boatswain led her to the galley and sat her down at one of the rectangular tables. The cook and his helper were busy preparing breakfast for the next morning.

"Cookie, Miss Snow needs some of your special tea."

The cook glanced at the boatswain, wiping his hands on his apron. He was a busy little man with a bristling mustache and a sweat-stained shirt. "Yes, sir. I'll brew some right away."

While the cook stoked the fire in the cast iron stove, he described to Brooke the ways to avoid getting seasick. "First, you got men who swear by crackers. Every time they feel the least bit sick, they take a cracker out of their pocket an' nibble on it. Not quickly, mind you. They nibble. All the time they nibble."

The cook filled a pot with water, placing it on the stove while he continued to talk. "Then there's those who lean on the railing an' stare at the horizon when they feel queasy. That works only during the day, however. Never go on deck at night an' look up at the stars. They'll start dancing around, an' before you know it, you're running for the nearest railing."

Cookie opened a square tin and put a heaping spoonful of a mysterious brown herb into a napkin, gave it twist, then sat at the table, waiting for the water to boil. "But I got the best cure of all," he told Brooke. "When you begin to feel sick, look at the horizon, munch on a cracker, and drink some of my special tea. Pretty soon you'll feel drowsy, then find the lowest part of the ship and go to sleep. Works every time," he said with a wink.

Brooke sat at the table holding her head in her hands, half listening to Cookie, watching the room sway this way and that. Suddenly, the smell of the food he was preparing for breakfast caused Brooke's stomach to take a turn for the worse. She ran from the galley and flung her head over the railing.

The night passed without further incident. As the first golden rays of the sun began to light the horizon, the lookout shouted, "Smoke off the starboard bow!"

The captain was inside his cabin taking a nap when the boatswain summoned him to the bridge. McKay expanded his brass telescope, training it on the plume of smoke.

"She appears to be another blockade-runner because of her low profile, sir," the boatswain said with confidence.

"Perhaps she is, Mr. Gallagher, but I doubt it." McKay turned to the helmsman. "Quartermaster, steer one-nine-zero."

When the other ship altered her course to intercept the *Atlantis*, the boatswain shook his head, amazed. "You were right, sir. How did you know?"

"By her smoke trail. If she were another blockade-runner she'd be using anthracite coal for fuel, which is practically smokeless. No blockade-runner would leave a dark smoke trail like that which might give her position away."

The boatswain appeared confused. "But what about her silhouette, sir?"

"Don't be fooled by that. The North converts captured blockade-runners into gunboats and sends them to these waters for that reason."

The captain opened the speaking tube to the engine room. "Mr. Reichman, full speed ahead, and don't spare the bacon."

The boatswain was puzzled. "Bacon, sir?"

"Yes. It's an old trick to get the fires hotter," McKay said.

"Yes, sir. I must remember that."

"You do that, Mr. Gallagher, and we'll make a blockade-runner captain out of you yet."

McKay hesitated, then said, "Thank you for taking care of Miss Snow last night."

"No trouble at all, sir. I was glad to do it."

A silence fell between the two men. Finally the boatswain asked, "Captain, are you and Miss Snow getting along?"

McKay blinked with surprise. "Why would you ask that?"

"Well, I know you have been seeing her, so I wondered why you sent me to check on her yesterday instead of going yourself."

"I told you, Mr. Gallagher," McKay said, irritated. "I was needed on the bridge. Now if I've answered your questions to your satisfaction, is that all?"

The boatswain had never seen Captain McKay so upset, not even while running the blockade. "I'm sorry, sir. I didn't mean to pry."

"Don't be concerned about me. Just tend to your own duties, and we'll get along fine," McKay growled, stalking out of the bridge. He returned a few minutes later, and said in a calm voice, "Mr. Gallagher?"

The boatswain glanced at him. "Yes, sir?"

"Don't forget, one of your duties is to look after Miss Snow and see she is comfortable."

"No, sir. I won't forget," he said, then added, "Would the Captain like me to check on her now?"

"Yes, I would. I will relieve you here."

For the rest of that morning and most of the afternoon, the Federal warship stayed about two-and-a-half miles behind the *Atlantis*. Every so often, she fired a cannon to see if she had gained on the blockade-runner.

At about 4 o'clock a messenger from the engine room came onto the bridge. The man's face was darkened with a mixture of coal dust and sweat.

"Sir, the engineer said the main bearings may burn out soon unless we slow."

McKay motioned for the man to follow him. When they were outside the bridge, he pointed at the Federal gunboat trailing their ship. "Do you want him to catch us so you can spend the rest of the war in a Yankee prison?"

The messenger shook his head. "No, sir."

"Well then, you tell the engineer to find a way to cool those bearings, because there's no way in hell we're slowing."

The seaman nodded and rushed below. A minute later, Brooke came out on deck. McKay was studying the other ship through his telescope and didn't notice her.

"Good morning, Captain."

He lowered his telescope, then turned an admiring gaze to Brooke. Here, amid the harsh realities of war stood the most beautiful woman he had ever known. "Good morning, Brooke. I trust you slept well."

"No, I didn't. I got seasick last night, but Cookie made me something so I could sleep," she explained. "I heard the cannon fire and wondered if I was in for another exciting day."

"I hope not. So far we've managed to stay in front of that gunboat, but the engineer has informed me we may break down soon unless we slow."

"Surely you're not considering that?" Brooke asked, afraid.

McKay smiled. "No. I'm not. But we are far enough ahead I suppose it wouldn't hurt to slow a knot or two."

Brooke pointed to the telescope in McKay's hands, then asked, "May I, Captain? I must have a look at our magnificent pursuer."

"Of course." He handed the glass to her, adding sourly, "But there's nothing magnificent about Federal ships shooting at us."

McKay watched while she put the telescope to her right eye.

"I can't find the other ship," she complained, swinging the long metal tube back and forth.

"Let me help you, Brooke. First, look at the ship, then raise the telescope to your eye," McKay coached as he moved closer to her, steadying the brass cylinder so she could see.

Brooke felt his hands on hers and pushed him away. "How dare you, Captain!"

McKay stepped back, frowning. "I was only trying to help."

His touch had grown cold for her ever since her father's horrible death. "Just like you helped my father?"

McKay shook his head with dismay. "So that's what this is all about."

"Yes, it is. Did you think I would forget so quickly?"

"No, I didn't. That's what I wanted to talk to you about."

Trembling with rage, Brooke rushed to her cabin, slamming the door. At that instant, the Federal gunboat fired her cannon, and somehow the timing of the explosion seemed very appropriate.

As the day wore on, the ship pursuing the *Atlantis* dropped farther astern, and by early evening her smoke trail had disappeared altogether.

The next day was uneventful, until they approached Nassau later that night and saw the lights of a Federal warship ahead of them.

"Another gunboat, sir," the boatswain said.

McKay nodded agreement. "She's going about her normal patrol so she hasn't spotted us. Her presence doesn't make much difference, though. We can't sail into Nassau harbor in the dark because of the coral reefs in the water. We'll anchor in the lee of New Providence Island for tonight, then continue to Nassau at first light."

When they were anchored, McKay went below to the engine room. As he climbed down the ladder, the temperature rose twenty degrees and the smell of machine oil and coal dust assailed his nostrils. Vibrations from the bilge pumps and heavy machinery throbbed through the rungs of the ladder, and the sound of escaping steam hissed from a drain cock.

Mr. Reichman, the Chief Engineer, was in baggy, gray trousers with a grease-stained rag stuffed into his back pocket, and red suspenders, but no shirt. Sweat glistened on his bald head as he peered at a mass of gauges on the front of one of the boilers. He turned when he noticed the captain's reflection in the glass.

"Hey, Chief," McKay said as he stepped off the ladder. "I wanted to thank you for holding this ship together. How did you keep those bearings from burning out?"

The engineer wiped a grimy forearm across his sweat-beaded brow, and said, "Well, sir, I ran out of grease. So I got some olive oil from the galley and mixed it with a little gunpowder from the arms cabinet. It made a thick paste, and I slapped it on those bearings. Kept 'em good and cool."

McKay chuckled. "First bacon--now olive oil. Maybe I should make the galley part of the engine room."

The Chief Engineer scratched his head, making another smudge, and grinned. "You know, sir, that's one hell of an idea."

Next morning, the *Atlantis* lay at anchor two miles off the palm tree-studded beach of New Providence Island. The ship didn't get underway until 9 o'clock because the Bahama Bank pilot had insisted he needed good light to find his way safely through the coral heads. The Negro pilot was a barefoot scarecrow of a man who wore a straw plantation hat and sat on the turtle-back cover near the tip of the bow, pointing in the direction the helmsman was to steer.

When the *Atlantis* tied up to the wharf in Nassau harbor, most of the men gathered on deck to gaze in awe at the spectacle around them. Cotton was piled high on the wharves, and the long lines of dark-skinned stevedores resembled columns of ants carrying their booty down into the holds of merchant vessels. Most of these ships bore the British flag, and after the laborers crammed their cargo spaces to bursting, they stacked the bales on deck. Here and there were to be seen the lead-gray blockade-runners with their short, rakish masts, either discharging their cargo of cotton, or loading vital supplies for the Confederacy.

Brooke stood at the railing, watching the flurry of activity on the wharf. A wide-brimmed blue bonnet shaded her face from the intense tropical sun.

"Hello, Brooke. I have something for you," Wade said, handing her an envelope. "It's the letter of recommendation I promised."

She smiled gratefully. "Thank you, Captain."

McKay nodded, and a silence fell between them. His dark, handsome features did not reveal the disappointment he felt from her brief reply. "When does your steamer sail?" he asked.

"At seven this evening. I'll be traveling to Southampton on the *RMS Triton*."

"I see," McKay said, then paused, searching for the right words, because suddenly the right words seemed very important. "I have

93

to meet the Harbor Master in a few minutes. May I see you before you leave?"

"I'm afraid not, Captain," Brooke said in a calm voice, her face giving away none of the turmoil inside her. "I have so many things to do before then."

Willie Mae, Brooke's maid, came out from her cabin.

Brooke turned to her and smiled. "Good morning, Willie Mae. I was just telling the Captain we have quiet a bit to do when we go ashore. Isn't that right?"

"Oh yes, ma'am." The maid frowned. "Umm-mmm. Lordy, there's a whole heap of things to do."

McKay removed his blue naval cap. His fingers nervously played with the brim. "How long will you be gone, Brooke?"

"I'm not sure. At least a month, maybe longer."

McKay forced a smile. "Well, maybe we'll meet again when you return."

"Perhaps," Brooke said, extending a slender hand to him. "So long, Captain McKay."

"Goodbye, Brooke," he said, giving her a brief smile of farewell. "Have a safe voyage."

"Thank you, Captain. Come along, Willie Mae." Brooke walked down the gangplank to the wharf. The maid followed behind, shaking her head and mumbling in a low voice.

McKay pulled on his peaked cap, staring after Brooke until she was out of sight. Then he marched to the bridge and growled at the deck hands because they weren't moving fast enough.

CHAPTER 6

Two weeks in Nassau seemed an eternity to Captain McKay. The Harbor Master told him because of the backlog of ships being loaded, he would have to be patient and wait his turn. Although the delay was inconvenient, it didn't matter because the Confederate shipping agent had said the *Atlantis'* cargo of 6,000 Austrian rifled muskets and 500 sabers hadn't arrived from Europe yet.

On the other side of the Atlantic Ocean, Brooke Snow stood on the fog-shrouded deck of the *RMS Triton* watching the ship dock in Southampton, England. The deck hands tossed heaving lines from the ship to workers on the wharf, who then hauled them in so they could get to the heavier mooring cables. When the lines were secured and the gangplank was in place, Brooke and her maid went ashore and boarded a train for London.

What Brooke didn't notice was the bearded man in the shadows reading a newspaper. As Brooke and her maid boarded the train, he folded the paper and followed them.

The fog dissipated as the train chugged away from the coast. Brooke sat in the window seat, gazing at the rolling countryside sprinkled with small villages consisting of vine-covered cottages with thatched roofs and little flower gardens. After a while, Brooke became lost in thought. It occurred to her if she became a shipping agent, she would be breaking the law by running war materials through the blockade. She'd become a criminal--the target of every Federal soldier and sailor. Brooke shuddered at the idea someone might be watching her at this moment. Cautiously, and without attracting attention, she scanned the passengers on the train. Could the man across the aisle be a spy? How about the man in back of her, hiding behind a newspaper?

Willie Mae saw Brooke's worried expression, so she reached over and held her hand. "What is it, chile? What's troublin' you?"

Brooke glanced at Willie Mae, then forced a smile. "I know this sounds awful, but I'm questioning my decision to become a shipping agent."

"Why's that?"

"Because I'm afraid Mr. Burgess will think I'm nothing but a silly woman for coming here. I'm also afraid the Federal government will treat me like a criminal. They might even send someone to arrest me."

Willie Mae's brown face crinkled into a warm smile. "Well, ain't nobody gonna arrest you while you're in England, chile. And as far as Mr. Burgess goes, since when have you ever cared what other folks think. You just follow your heart, honey, an' you'll never be sorry. If dat means comin' to England and becomin' de best shippin' agent there is, then dat's what you gotta do. You never saw your papa back down from a challenge, did you?"

An image of her father slipped into Brooke's thoughts. She never considered he had taken his own life--not for a minute. "No. I didn't."

"All right, then. You be de girl he'd be proud of."

Brooke squeezed the maid's plump hand. "Thank you, Willie Mae. You always find a way to put things into the proper perspective."

When Brooke's train arrived in London, she took a hansom cab to the Burlington Hotel on Kings Road where she checked in. The first thing she did was to soak in a hot bath. The blockade-runner she had traveled on didn't have the facilities to bathe. Although Brooke regularly used the shower on the *Triton*, she couldn't settle back and relax as she could in a bathtub.

After Brooke finished her bath and brushed her hair, she and Willie Mae went shopping. Fortunately there were a half-dozen dress shops within walking distance of the hotel. In one of them

Brooke found some gloves for herself and a hat for Willie Mae. The two then ate lunch at a sidewalk cafe before going back to the hotel.

Several tables away, a man looked up from the newspaper he was reading. When Brooke left the cafe, he tossed some coins onto the table, then followed the two women.

Philip Burgess folded his hands on his desk, looking at the woman standing before him. "Miss Snow, why should I hire you as my agent in Wilmington?" The man's thinning straw-colored hair was parted in the middle, and he had a wispy moustache which was waxed and curled at the ends.

"Because I have all of my father's contacts, and I know the business inside and out," Brooke explained.

"These are your only qualifications?" Philip could see just by looking at her that she had more to offer. She was a beautiful woman, and such a woman could be very persuasive around men. Nevertheless, most men felt females had no place in the business world. Could her charm convince them otherwise?

"No, sir." Brooke opened her handbag and removed an envelope, handing it to him. "I have a letter of introduction from Captain McKay."

Burgess put on his gold, wire-rimmed spectacles, then examined the letter. After several minutes, he said, "I see here the Captain thinks quite highly of you."

"Captain McKay is a dear friend," she explained. "However, I doubt our friendship has influenced what he wrote in that letter. I am willing to work hard to make your trade in Wilmington extremely profitable."

Mr. Burgess nodded, setting the letter on his desk. "How do you propose to do that, Miss Snow?"

"All of the businessmen who attend your auctions came to my father's funeral and offered to do whatever they could to help. I'm sure when they find out I'm the new agent for Burgess & Linden, they will be generous in any dealings we have."

Philip smiled, nodding, "You have a point, Miss Snow. I like the way you think."

His response gladdened Brooke. "Thank you, sir."

"I would like to discuss this further, but unfortunately I have another appointment," he said, taking off his spectacles, then carefully folding them. "Perhaps we can talk over dinner this evening."

Brooke hoped the invitation to dinner was business, and nothing more. "Yes, Mr. Burgess. I would like that."

Philip smiled at the thought of spending the evening with such a beautiful woman. "Excellent. I'll come by your hotel at seven."

That evening, Brooke and Philip Burgess went by carriage to The Royal Oak restaurant. The dining area was divided into many small rooms with no more than two tables in each. All of the furnishings were impeccably chosen, from the paintings on the walls to the comfortable chairs and the elegantly patterned silverware. The restaurant was so intimate and cozy, she felt like a guest in someone's house.

A maître d' in a long, black dinner jacket seated them at a small table and announced the specialties for the evening. After ordering for both of them, Mr. Burgess smiled at his guest. "I'm glad you could join me, Brooke. I don't have dinner with a beautiful woman very often."

"Thank you, Mr. Burgess," she said, blushing.

He smiled, then reached for her hand and gave it a light squeeze. "Call me Philip."

Brooke slipped her hand from his. "Very well, Philip. Is there a Mrs. Burgess?"

"Yes, there is. My dear mother, bless her soul."

"She must be very proud of her son," Brooke observed with relief.

Philip raised a water goblet to his lips, taking a drink. "I rather fancy she is. I do try so."

Their waiter returned with a bottle of burgundy. He opened it and poured a small amount in a wine glass, handing it to Mr. Burgess. Philip swirled the red liquid about the sides of the glass and inhaled the wine's bouquet before taking a taste. He nodded to the waiter. The man poured them each a glass, then returned the bottle to the table.

During dinner the conversation turned to the war, and Philip Burgess confided, "Your war has been a blessing to us all, you know."

Puzzled, Brooke lowered her fork. "Oh? How is that?"

"Well, our country was in a mild depression, you see, and the war helped pull us out of it. No one is fighting anymore, except your people, so we were able to buy surplus arms and munitions at a splendid price. Then we trade them for cotton, which you Americans grow so well, and we make a handsome profit."

All evening long Brooke was wondering how she would approach the subject of inflation in the South. She intended to ask Mr. Burgess to lower his profit margin, so it might ease the suffering back home. The time had come, and she could remain silent no longer. "Mr. Burgess, do you realize what a horrible situation you're creating?"

Philip was taken aback, and set down his glass of wine. "I'm afraid I don't understand."

"Between your high prices and the greedy speculators in my country, the average citizen cannot afford to buy the necessities of life."

Philip patted his mouth with a napkin, then tossed it onto the table. "Well, I don't see where that's any of my concern. I'm in business to make money."

"And you still can. I'm just asking you to lower your prices a bit."

Philip shook his head at this ridiculous suggestion. "I can't do that."

Brooke's voice rose in anger. "I thought you might be compassionate enough to want to help, but I can see I was wrong."

Philip looked at the attractive woman across from him and thought what a pity it would be to let her walk out of his life. "Miss Snow, I was prepared to offer you a position as our agent in Wilmington. However, now that I know how you feel, I think it would be a mistake."

Brooke needed this job, and she refused to let it get away from her. "Mr. Burgess, I have given this matter considerable thought, and I think I may have a solution. If we divide your cargo into smaller lots, not only will it be easier to sell, but it will be distributed more evenly. That way, no one can have a monopoly to drive up prices."

Philip considered this a moment. "What's to stop the speculators from buying up all of the small lots?"

"Nothing. But if we divided them small enough, and maybe staggered the times they're sold, I think it would give others a chance to bid."

"That might work," Philip conceded. He liked this woman, not only because she was attractive, but she had brains and could be a valuable asset to the company. "All right, Brooke. You can have the position in Wilmington on a trial basis. However, if I'm not satisfied at the end of three months, you'll be replaced."

Brooke smiled, relieved. "Thank you, Philip! You won't be sorry."

After dinner they went to see Sarah Bernhardt in *The Passerby*. Brooke had always loved the theater, and she became so engrossed in the play she didn't notice Philip staring at her.

When the show was over and they returned to their carriage, Philip turned to her. "Brooke, it's early yet, and my house is nearby. Why don't we go there and talk some more about your ideas?"

Brooke frowned. "Not tonight, Philip. I'm tired from the trip and all."

"Of course you are, my dear," he said, then stared out the carriage window at the fog-shrouded street. A bearded man stood at the curb, hailing a carriage. Philip watched the man, then broke the silence by saying, "I'm afraid I was a little premature offering you a job."

Brooke shot him a troubled glance. *Was it because of her refusal to go to his house?* "Oh?"

"Yes. My business partner has to approve, also."

She nodded understanding. "I see. When can I meet him?"

"Mother will be at the country estate this weekend. She owns fifty-one percent of the firm," Philip said with a wry smile.

Early the next morning Brooke and Philip and Willie Mae left London in a double-brougham coach pulled by four fine looking black stallions. The road led up the gentle hills where goats and sheep grazed in lush pastures and through serene villages with small white churches.

Farthington, Philip Burgess' country estate, was everything Brooke had imagined it would be. It appeared to be an old castle, and indeed it was. The ancient vine-covered building of pale red brick was accented by facings of white stone. A lily-sheathed pond, complete with white swans, lay to the side of an old stone building with stained-glass windows which was once used as a chapel.

"This is gorgeous!" Brooke exclaimed.

"Sir Henry Burgess built it in 1484," Philip said, then gestured to the center of the house. "The original building is in the center and the two wings were added later."

"It's nearly four hundred years old?"

"Yes, but I assure you it has all the latest amenities," Philip said, amused. He tucked Brooke's hand into the crook of his elbow, then led her along a stone walk toward the house. "We have gas lights, and several large cisterns around back keep the house supplied with water year-round."

The arched entryway had two ten-foot doors with quarreled-glass windows. Philip held one of the doors open and they passed through an elegant marble hallway, then entered the parlor to the left. Soft sunlight from an open window bathed the small desk where Cordelia Burgess sat.

Philip's mother relaxed the pen and looked up from the letter she was writing. The distinguished-looking woman had bright, inquisitive eyes and thick greying hair which was twisted up in a knot on the back of her head. "Philip, who's this?"

"Mother, I want you to meet Miss Brooke Snow. She's my newest agent in Wilmington, North Carolina."

Cordelia smiled. "Well, it's about time you realized women can be employed right alongside men." She turned to Brooke, nodding with conviction. "I've been telling him that for years!"

"Well," Philip said, "Brooke convinced me she possesses the skills we are looking for."

"Jolly good for her." Cordelia stood up, taking Brooke's arm. "Come along, dear. You must tell me how you persuaded Philip to give you the job."

Friday morning Brooke and Philip went for a stroll in the countryside and visited a quaint little village with stone cottages and thatched roofs. She found all the people charming, and they spent an hour exploring the town.

As Brooke and Philip left the village, they heard the sounds of children playing and saw a group of people having a picnic on a hillside. A woman beckoned to the couple to come and join them. The two accepted and were led to a large table filled with food. They sat and chatted with their new friends while eating bread, slices of ham, cheese with plenty of wine. Afterwards, when the wine had time to work its magic, they sang and danced the afternoon away.

On the way back to Farthington, Philip put his arm around Brooke and moved closer to steal a kiss. She pushed him away, then suddenly thought maybe she was being too hasty. Here was a man who could obviously help her. "No, Philip! Not like this."

"I--I'm sorry," he stammered. "I couldn't help myself." He was relieved when he saw Brooke did not appear to be angry. "What did you mean when you said, 'Not like this'?"

"I meant this is so sudden, Philip. We barely know each other."

"Oh," he said, nodding. "Then you're saying there is hope for us after we get to know each other better?"

"Yes, I am," she said with a shy smile.

Brooke didn't object to Philip as a suitor. He was above average in looks, but he just wasn't what she had in mind for herself. An image of Wade McKay slipped into Brooke's thoughts. She forced him from her mind, angry with herself for being so weak.

Philip was the perfect companion for the rest of the weekend. He was funny and charming, and he possessed a certain wit Brooke found enjoyable.

Saturday they went ballooning in a field about five miles north of Farthington. Long before the carriage got there, they could see the yellow, red, and blue air-filled bag through the trees. Scattered about the field were crates of iron filings and vats of sulphuric acid used to produce hydrogen. This gas was then pumped through a hose to the balloon. Brooke and Philip were escorted to the gondola by a man clad in a long yellow duster and a checkered cap. He handed each of them goggles, then put on a pair he had slung about his neck.

It was the most thrilling experience of Brooke's life. When the balloon lifted off, she clutched Philip's arm, terrified. He smiled, holding Brooke close. This time she did not push him away. After a while she relaxed, and gazed in awe at the countryside below. The rolling, tree-lined hills were transformed into a patchwork quilt of various shades of green and gold, bordered by winding silver ribbons of water.

An hour later the balloon touched down in a meadow. Holding onto a rope, the assistant leaped out of the gondola and tethered the balloon to a nearby tree. Brooke was sorry to see the flight end, but the trip had taken them ten miles away from their point of departure and it was time for them to go back. In a few minutes, their carriage appeared and whisked them to a marina on the coast where Philip kept his sailboat. The *Siren's* hull and deck were constructed of varnished teak and the brightwork gleamed.

Brooke stared at the boat in disbelief. "I don't want you to take this the wrong way, Philip. You have a beautiful boat, but I just spent three weeks on the ocean. I was ill most of the time, so I hope you can understand why I don't want to go on the water right now."

"Of course, Brooke. I wasn't thinking." Philip paused, considering their options. "Would you like to go to dinner instead? I know an excellent restaurant where they serve the best prime rib in all of England."

Brooke smiled with relief. "Yes. Dinner sounds lovely."

Sunday, their last day in the country, came all too soon. Brooke needed to get back to London that afternoon so she could board her ship, and Philip needed to return to work Monday. While Willie

Mae packed their belongings, Brooke went downstairs to see Mrs. Burgess. She found Cordelia watering her plants in the parlor. The older woman smiled and set down her brass sprinkling can when she saw Brooke enter the room. "Good morning, dear. Did you sleep well?"

"Yes, Mrs. Burgess. I thought now might be a good time to tell you how much I've enjoyed my stay at Farthington."

"Well, we enjoyed having you, my dear. I only wish you could visit longer."

"So do I. Everything here is so beautiful."

"Thank you." Cordelia's smile faded. "Brooke, we need to discuss something which is very important. Have you considered why Philip asked you to come with him this weekend?"

"Yes. He said he needed your approval before he could hire me as a shipping agent."

Cordelia shook her head. "No. He doesn't need my approval for that. He invited you because he likes you."

"I like your son, too, Mrs. Burgess."

"That's what troubles me, my dear. You see, Philip comes from nobility. The Burgess name is respected throughout England. I don't know much about your customs in America, but here nobility marries nobility."

"Mrs. Burgess, are you telling me not to marry your son?" Brooke asked, shocked.

"No, my dear, not at all. I am merely suggesting there are those who would frown upon such a marriage. Things might prove difficult, so you must determine how prudent such a union would be."

"Mrs. Burgess, let me put your mind at ease. I have no designs on your son."

Cordelia smiled. "Philip was right. You are a smart woman."

The conversation during their coach ride back to the city was sparked with fond remembrances of the good times Brooke and Philip had enjoyed. As they neared London, a silence fell between them and each was lost in their own private thoughts.

As the carriage wound through the narrow cobblestone streets, Philip presented Brooke with a letter of introduction to give to the Harbor Master in Wilmington. In it he explained she was their new shipping agent and should be accorded all the respect and privileges an agent was due.

When the coach stopped at the wharf, Brooke leaned over and kissed Philip on the cheek. "You've been a dear, Philip. Thank you for the job and a wonderful weekend. I'll never forget it."

"The weekend doesn't have to end so soon," he said, taking her hand. "We can go anyplace you like. Just name it."

Brooke smiled. "Yes, it does need to end. I've been away from my family and friends for too long. Besides, I have a new job, you know. I need to get busy organizing a wonderful auction so I can impress my employer."

Philip smiled at her attempt at humor. "All right, then. Perhaps I'll come to Wilmington, and we can resume where we left off."

"Yes, Philip. I would like that."

The coachman opened the door and lowered a folding set of stairs. Philip got out and held Brooke's hand as she descended from the carriage. Willie Mae, holding on to her new red-feathered hat, awkwardly climbed down from the driver's seat.

Brooke took Philip's arm as they crossed the planked wharf to the steamship. Willie Mae followed them while two burly stevedores removed five trunks from the carriage, placing them on a handcart.

A moment later the bearded man Brooke had seen earlier slipped aboard the ship, then knocked on cabin door 6A. When the door swung open, the man handed an envelope to someone inside, then quickly left the ship.

After the last crate of Austrian rifled muskets was lowered into the hold, McKay ordered the hatches battened down in preparation for getting underway that evening. After fifteen days in port he was anxious to get back to sea. Since Nassau was a British colony, the Southern ships were safe there, but outside the five-mile limit the sea belonged to no one. Every few hours the smoke trail of a Federal cruiser drifted up from the horizon, reminding McKay of the danger out there.

That evening the moon was a luminescent fingernail in the eastern sky as the *Atlantis* glided out of Nassau harbor while a ten-knot breeze ruffled the surface of the ocean. After she had sailed seven miles, Captain McKay ordered a rocket launched over her stern, toward the island. Hopefully this would fool any patrolling ships into thinking a blockade-runner was being chased to Nassau and thus draw them away from the blockade-runner's trail. Anxious seconds turned into minutes, then the minutes to hours, and the crew began to relax when it became apparent the *Atlantis* had escaped detection.

As the sun's first golden rays streaked across the ocean, McKay stood on the starboard paddle wheel box, scanning the horizon with his telescope as the boatswain came up beside him. A brisk morning breeze swept along the deck of the *Atlantis*, tugging at the captain's blue frock coat. "We're all alone, Mr. Gallagher. The sea belongs to us."

The boatswain nodded, then stared past the captain and pointed out to sea. "No, it doesn't, sir. It belongs to them!"

McKay followed his gaze and saw a pod of bottle-nosed dolphin who were frolicking in the shimmering bow wave. One zoomed out of the water in a breathtaking leap, the sunlight transforming each droplet of water into a radiant diamond. At the height of his leap, he arched his sleek body toward the sea, slipping beneath the waves with hardly a ripple.

"Indeed, it does," said McKay, mesmerized. "Amazing animals, dolphins. They play in the ocean like they haven't a care in the world." He finished the thought silently to himself: *Unlike me.* McKay wondered how things had gone so wrong these last few months. First having to change his base of operations from Charleston when the blockade closed that port, then meeting and losing a woman he was so strongly attracted to she lived in his thoughts constantly.

"They're a sign of good luck, sir!"

McKay nodded. He had heard that said. He closed his eyes, offering a silent prayer this was true.

Others soon joined the two men, shouting encouragement each time a dolphin leaped into the air. It seemed to spur the animals on, for the louder the men cheered, the higher the dolphins leaped.

The dolphins stayed with the *Atlantis* for twenty minutes, then disappeared under the waves as suddenly as they had come.

The following day went smoothly, and the blockade-runner had a good passage. As night fell, they neared the coast somewhere north of Fort Fisher. The ship slowed every half hour to take a sounding. A bit of tallow was placed in the base of the sounding lead and this was used to pick up whatever type of bottom they were passing over.

McKay stood next to the pilot as he examined the lead. "The depth is right, but there's too much shell. We're north of where we want to be," the pilot said.

McKay glanced at the horizon. Since the darkness did not reveal any landmarks to tell him where they were, he had to rely on the pilot's judgement. Quartermaster, steer one-nine-zero."

They proceeded on that course for two hours, stopping every twenty minutes to inspect the sounding lead. After taking several samples close together, the pilot grinned, holding out the lead for McKay to see. "Black sand, Capt'n. We need to turn here."

McKay ordered the quartermaster to steer toward the shore until the water was twenty-five feet deep, then turn south and follow the coast.

The sky began to lighten in the east, revealing a bank of storm clouds. As the weather continued to deteriorate, the wind and waves increased and driving sheets of rain lashed the deck and wheelhouse. Although the visibility was reduced to zero, it helped the blockade-runner remain undetected.

Suddenly a Federal cruiser plunged out of the squall a hundred yards ahead, and the quartermaster spun the wheel to starboard, avoiding a collision. The *Atlantis* didn't respond to the helm fast enough, and the cruiser's bowsprit invaded the foredeck of the blockade-runner, sweeping away the foresail rigging. A moment later the Federal cruiser pulled free of the other ship and disappeared into the rain choked gloom.

Men ran toward the bow to see what damage was done. Several stays holding the mast upright were swept away, prompting the lookout at the masthead to scramble down the shrouds as fast as he could. Two crewmen were busy with axes, cutting the tangled knots of rigging strewn on the foredeck. Fortunately the cruiser's deck was higher than the blockade-runner's, so the damage was minimal and could be fixed.

As the crew worked, the rain tapered off and with it went the *Atlantis'* cover. The Union warship swung around, opening up with her bow chaser. A shot whizzed across the blockade-runner's bow.

With his ship about to be blown out of the water, McKay gave the order he had prayed he would never have to give. "Williams, get the white ensign from the storage locker beside the bridge."

The boatswain turned toward the captain in surprise. "But, sir, we can't surrender without a fight!"

McKay walked to the bridge while he spoke. "I have no intention of surrendering."

Just then a shot raised a geyser of water next to the ship, striking the hull at the waterline, loosening a plate. The Captain grabbed open the speaking tube to the engine room. "Mr. Reichman, stop all engines!"

Minutes later a white ensign fluttered from the halyard, and the cruiser ceased firing. The warship slowed to a stop about fifty yards away and lowered a boat. "How much steam do you have?" McKay asked the engineer.

"Nearly a full head, Captain."

"Good. Wait for my signal, then go to flank speed."

When the Federal launch was far enough from the cruiser, the Captain bellowed into the speaking tube, "Now, Mr. Reichman! Now's your time! Give her everything you've got!"

The engines throbbed to life, setting the paddle wheels in motion.

The men in the launch hollered, firing their sidearms in desperation at the fleeing blockade-runner. A golden-tailed rocket roared off the Federal cruiser's deck while she steamed to pick up the rest of her crew.

"Mr. Gallagher, shoot a few of those signal rockets to port."

Soon the blockade-runner was far ahead of the cruiser and launching her own rockets to confuse any pursuers. The *Atlantis'* chances of making New Inlet ahead of the Federal ship were getting better every moment. A sudden scraping along the bottom of the hull gave an ominous warning. Though the men braced themselves, they were still knocked off balance when the blockade-runner lurched to a stop on the sandbar.

McKay rushed to the speaking tube and shouted, "Full reverse, Mr. Reichman!"

The *Atlantis* shuddered as the engine and paddle wheels strained, but the ship did not move an inch.

"All stop!" McKay looked out to sea. The Federal cruiser had halted a quarter-mile away. *Was the Yankee captain being cautious, trying to figure out what the blockade-runner was up to, or was his ship having troubles of her own because of her deep draft?* McKay turned to the boatswain. "Mr. Gallagher, grab all the crew you can find and meet me at the stern."

Three crewmen went with McKay to a small cabin off the bridge. He took a brass key from his pocket and opened the door. The room contained a gun cabinet with a dozen Enfield rifle-muskets and three wooden boxes of cartridges. He unlocked the padlock on the front of the case and removed the heavy bar which secured the rifles.

"Take two muskets apiece and some ammunition," McKay said.

The men grinned, filling their pockets with percussion caps and cartridges, then grabbing the muskets.

In a few minutes, thirty men were assembled at the stern. On the deck were two coils of line tied to two sixty-pound kedge anchors.

"All right, men. We've been given a little extra time because that Yankee gunboat has probably run aground also. We're going to take advantage of that. I want two boats to take these anchors out three hundred feet and set them thirty degrees apart. I'll wrap the ends of the lines around this capstan, then we'll reverse the engines while the ship is winched backward. Any questions?"

A cannon thundered aboard the Federal cruiser, hurling a ball at the *Atlantis*. The ocean exploded fifty feet to starboard, drenching the men on the blockade-runner.

"Yeah, Capt'n. I have a question," a tall, lanky man said. He had a thick tangle of beard and water was dripping from his wide-brimmed hat. "Do these here muskets mean what I think they do?"

McKay nodded. "Yes. I know blockade-runners don't fire on Federal ships, but this time we're going to defend ourselves. I want two men in each boat to carry a musket. We'll also leave two men here to concentrate on that damned gun crew which keeps shooting at us."

The man grinned, grabbing a musket. "Capt'n, you know I ain't one to brag, but that gun crew is as good as dead."

Ten men went to each dinghy, lifted them over the railing, then set the boats in the water. Boatswain Gallagher got in the first boat and took charge as it shoved off. When it became apparent what was happening, the Federal sailors launched two boats of their own. Setting the kedge anchors now became a race between the two crews. The crewmen from the *Atlantis* only had to row 300 feet, but unfortunately they drew fire from both the gunboat and the sailors in the two launches coming toward them.

Geysers of water erupted around the first dinghy as the Federal guns tried to get the range. A puff of white smoke rose from the gunboat's foredeck. The shell screamed on its deadly mission, splashing into the sea twenty feet before the dinghy. It exploded, blasting a circular seismic wave and tossing a column of white water high into the air. The spray cascaded down, drenching the cowering men.

As bullet and shell splashes kicked up the water around the dinghies, the Confederate marksman on the blockade-runner loaded the British Enfield rifle and adjusted the sights. He knelt by the railing, took careful aim at a gunner on the Federal ship and fired. A moment later the sailor grabbed his chest, slumping over the barrel of the cannon he was loading. Another man pulled him to safety, then took his place.

Boatswain Gallagher stood in the dinghy to show he wasn't afraid, shouting encouragement to his men. "Come on, men! Throw your backs into it! We can't let that other boat beat us! We're nearly there!"

An officer in the first Federal launch raised his pistol, firing at the Confederate dinghy.

The Northern bullets made their odd whistle as they whipped past Gallagher. He thought about sitting down, but he couldn't because the men needed him to lead the way. "Come on, boys! Just a little farther! Show those Yankees what you're made of!"

The Federal cannon jetted a cloud of gray-white smoke, hurling the 8-inch shell like a mighty thunderbolt. It burst in the air like a sudden small gray cloud from which fizzing white smoke trails spiraled earthward. A sudden explosion from the dinghy's bow filled the air with wooden splinters. White-hot shrapnel tore away most of the first bench seat. The Confederate sailor who was sitting there lay in the bottom of the boat, holding the ragged stump of his left leg. Blood mixed with the seawater as it ran down the lower hull planks, tinting it a bright red. The blast threw Gallagher off his feet. He sat up, looking himself over. Other than a few cuts, he was fine. Gallagher crawled to the bow, whipped off his belt, then knotted it about the wounded man's thigh. He grabbed a large wooden splinter and jabbed it through the loop in the belt. Then he twisted the wooden handle of the makeshift tourniquet, stopping the flow of blood.

Bullets were whizzing through the air and thudding into the boat's hull. One man was struck in the arm and the chest by the same bullet. Another man crumpled forward after being shot in the shoulder. Boatswain Gallagher shouted to the man nearest the kedge anchor, "Throw the damned anchor overboard before we all die!"

The man didn't have to be told twice. He grabbed the anchor, stood up to toss it, then pitched forward into the water with three shots to his chest. Only one crewman with a musket was still alive. He loaded his gun, fired and began the process again. Gallagher crawled over to the other rifle, jerking it free from a dead seaman's grasp. He found some bullets in the man's pockets, then sat in the bloody water in the bottom of the boat. Gallagher tore a cartridge open with his teeth and poured powder down the barrel, then pushed in a bullet with his thumb, ramming it down hard. He cocked the hammer and pushed a percussion cap onto the nipple. His first target was the officer shooting at them from the launch. He took aim, squeezing the trigger. A sailor next to the officer dropped his oar, grabbing at his throat with crimson fingers. Gallagher cursed his lousy aim and loaded his musket again. His next shot brought a look of total surprise to the officer. The man rose, threw up his arms and fell backward with a bullet in the chest. The Federal launch lost no time turning around. None of the sailors wanted to continue now their commanding officer was dead. The second boat slowed to a stop while the men decided what to do. The next bullet struck a sailor in the jaw, convincing the others to return to the ship. He leaned forward, spitting up bloody teeth and bone.

Gallagher lowered his musket when he saw the boats turn back. "Cease fire, men. They've had enough."

Now that both kedge anchors were set, the lines were then coiled around the *Atlantis'* rear capstan and eight men took turns turning it. When the anchors bit into the sea bottom, the blockade-runner reversed her paddle wheels, inching backward. A cheer rose from the crew while the dinghies returned to the *Atlantis*.

The *Atlantis'* effort to get off the sandbar was not missed by the other Federal cruisers. Afraid to come too close because of the shallow water, one ship slowed to a stop about a quarter mile off, firing at the blockade-runner.

When the *Atlantis* was in deeper water, McKay said, "Take those lines off the capstan and throw them overboard."

The Captain turned around, looking out to sea. The sky had lightened enough for him to make out another cruiser steaming toward the *Atlantis*.

A seamen near him said, "Well, sir, we know they can't come in this close or they'll go aground, too."

McKay wondered if he could lure them close enough for that.

Another explosion rattled the mast tops and pieces of hot metal rained down onto the bridge. "Quartermaster, steer twenty degrees to port. I need some sea room."

McKay heard the distant muffled roar of cannon fire from the shore. A battery from Fort Fisher was alerted by the sounds of battle and had set up their long-range Whitworth cannon on the beach.

"Thank God for Colonel Lamb!" McKay said. "He's sent a battery to our defense!"

The boatswain raised his telescope in the direction the Captain pointed. "I count two cannon, sir. Aren't they beautiful?"

"They surely are!"

McKay shifted his gaze to the cruiser behind the *Atlantis*. Her bow chasers, thundering. The cannonballs shrieked through the air, plucking the surface of the water around them.

"Come on," McKay encouraged the shore battery. "Hit her a few times so she knows how it feels."

A sudden sheet of smoke and flame erupted from the warship's starboard side as the force of the broadside rocked her in the water. An exploding shell disintegrated the blockade-runner's rear deck into a thousand jagged missiles, flinging McKay against the railing.

The quartermaster helped the Captain to his feet. "Are you all right, sir?"

"Yes, I just got the wind knocked out of me. And you?"

"I'm fine. Just scratched up a bit. So are you," he pointed out.

McKay looked himself over, then ran a hand across his face and found blood on his fingers.

After surveying the damage to his ship, the boatswain remarked, "Well, we're sound structurally and making fifteen knots, so I guess things could be worse."

A cheer arose from the deck hands, and McKay saw them pointing at the nearest Federal warship and howling with delight. Dense smoke engulfed the ship's forward deck, and she was losing speed.

"It looks like the Yankees have had enough," one of the mates cried.

The men jeered the departing vessel. The Captain wanted to join in the celebration but, considering his station, only looked on, smiling.

Twenty minutes later, they saw the huge earthworks of Fort Fisher in the distance. The walls had a bumpy serpentine appearance created by the evenly spaced mounds of sand which rose between the gun emplacements. When the *Atlantis* passed the Northeast Bastion with its bright red and white Confederate garrison flag snapping in the sea breeze, some of the men saluted, and others took off their hats and placed them over their hearts. They knew they were safe once again under the fort's mighty guns.

The sleek, blockade-runner passed the towering mound battery guarding New Inlet and slipped into the Cape Fear River before docking at Craig's landing.

A column of six Confederate soldiers rode up to the wharf as the cargo boom on shore was raising a brass cannon barrel from the ship's hold. Although Colonel Lamb was wearing only his uniform trousers and a white cotton shirt which gave no hint of his rank, Captain McKay recognized him instantly.

"Colonel, I was hoping we'd get a chance to meet again."

The fort's commander dismounted, and the men shook hands. "So was I, Captain. How are you?"

"I'm all right, but my crew isn't. Four of my men were killed and seven wounded."

Colonel Lamb motioned to one of his staff. "Lieutenant, go to the fort and bring back the surgeon and two of his assistants. Tell him there are wounded men aboard the *Atlantis.*"

The lieutenant mounted his horse, then kicked him into a gallop toward the fort."

Colonel Lamb motioned to the cannon being swung ashore. "What guns are these? The Confederate Ordinance Bureau didn't say anything about new guns."

"They're a gift from Burgess & Linden, sir."

"A gift?" asked Colonel Lamb.

McKay nodded. "Yes. You've done such a magnificent job protecting blockade-runners they thought maybe you could put these to good use."

"Of course I can. And a hundred more besides."

"Well, we didn't bring that many," McKay said with a chuckle. "But we've brought you two 12-pounder Napoleons and twenty cases of ammunition."

"Splendid! I know just where to put them."

"I also wanted to thank you for sending that battery to our assistance. We were in a tight spot until their cannon fire struck a Federal cruiser and drove it away."

"I suspected you might need help when we heard the gunfire," Lamb said, then shook his head. "It's been a terrible year. The Union blockade is growing tighter, and it's slowly strangling us. We've lost over thirty ships just off this port alone."

"You almost had another," McKay said, motioning to the damaged stern of the *Atlantis.*

The men walked over to examine the wreckage. A quarter of the wooden rear deck was gone, showing some iron structure members.

Colonel Lamb took McKay aside and said, "I'm afraid things are going to get worse. There's been talk of an invasion."

McKay's face registered a mixture of surprise and concern. "I can't believe the Yankees would try anything so foolish. Certainly they know their plans would be doomed from the start."

"I suspect they'll come prepared for quite a siege. I've made the fortification as strong as I could. But I fear it won't be enough. Apparently the Confederate Ordinance Bureau believes Fort Fisher is low priority, so they send men and supplies grudgingly. There's also a rumor," Colonel Lamb confided, "General Bragg is going to replace General Whiting as commander of the Wilmington Military District."

McKay's eyes widened in surprise. "That can't be! General Bragg's career has been followed by one disaster after another. How could Jefferson Davis put him in charge of the South's last open seaport?"

Colonel Lamb shook his head. "I don't know. I guess we'll have to make the best of it."

McKay tried to remain positive. "Everyone has confidence in you, Colonel. After all. Look what you did with Confederate Point when you only had sand dunes and sea oats to work with."

Colonel Lamb nodded, then looked at the massive fortification guarding the mouth of the Cape Fear River. "Yes, but I'm afraid I haven't done enough."

When the cannon and munitions were unloaded, the *Atlantis* slipped her moorings, then steamed up the Cape Fear River to Wilmington. After she had discharged her cargo, McKay walked along the waterfront until he came to the kerosene-lit streets of Paddy's Hollow.

Tinkling piano music, punctuated by a sea of voices and peels of laughter, filtered out of the Green Parrot tavern and drifted into the street, beckoning the sailors and dock workers. The odor of stale beer and cigar smoke flooded over McKay as he pushed the door open and made his way through the boisterous crowd. It was Friday evening, and the tavern was filled with rough-looking characters from the waterfront who had just been paid.

McKay spotted Amber at the bar and nodded a greeting. She was chatting with two men and smiled at him. The men laughed at a joke she had told them, then she excused herself and sauntered over toward McKay. Her vermilion dress showed off her womanly curves and exposed an ample amount of cleavage.

"Hello, Captain. It's good to see you again."

McKay could tell by the smile in her eyes this wasn't just barroom talk to make him feel good. "Thank you. I'm glad to be here."

Amber pulled up a barstool and sat. "A lot has happened while you were away." She motioned to the bartender to bring them two beers. "Bates and his friend are free."

"What? How can that be?" McKay asked surprised.

Amber shrugged her shoulders. "A fouled-up legal system. What else?"

"I don't understand?"

"Well, the way it was explained to me, when there's white on black crime, the charges are the same. Murder is still murder. But it seems a black man can't testify against a white man in a court of law. Without the boy's testimony there is no case, so the police had no choice but to let the men go."

McKay shook his head in disbelief. "Damn! I can't believe such a stupid law exists."

"It does. And Elias seems to be telling the truth because when the police fished the mother and father out of the river, both of them had gunshot wounds."

"They didn't find his brother and sister?" he asked.

"Unfortunately, no. Each day that passes makes it less likely they will."

"What did the police do with Elias?"

"He was sent back to the Deering Plantation because he's still theirs legally. Charles Deering said he would care for him until the boy turns seventeen. Then he'll give him his papers and make him a freedman."

The bartender brought their beers. After taking a sip from her glass, Amber said, "The police also caught the man who killed Mr. Snow."

"They did? That's wonderful!"

"Yes, it is. A bum pawned an expensive walking stick with a gold tip. The pawn shop owner became suspicious and notified the police. They arrested the bum and asked where he had gotten the cane. He told them he had found it. Well, the police didn't believe that. They showed the walking stick around, and it was identified as belonging to Curtis Snow. Then the man admitted it was stolen in a robbery. Seems he was passing by the shipping agency and saw Mr. Snow through the window. This man had a knife and went inside to rob him. Mr. Snow picked up the gun he had on his desk and they struggled. Unfortunately Mr. Snow was shot. The bum heard someone coming, probably you, and was scared off before he could take Mr. Snow's wallet. He panicked, grabbed the walking stick, and fled out the back."

McKay smiled hopefully. "Maybe Brooke will see me now her father's murderer has been arrested."

"Brooke still hasn't made up with you?"

He stared at his beer. "No. She came aboard ship as a passenger, but she insisted we still have problems."

"Well, at least she's talking to you. That's a start."

McKay nodded, taking a drink from his glass.

"Is there anyone else?" Amber asked, eyeing him.

"No. I haven't had the time or desire to go out with anyone."

"Are you sure? The woman doesn't have to be someone you're seeing. Maybe she's just an acquaintance."

McKay thought a moment. "I met a girl named Virginia. But Brooke couldn't be jealous of her. They're good friends."

"Oh, don't be so sure," Amber said with a laugh. "When there's a man involved, women watch their friends carefully."

McKay paused to think. "Well, Virginia did show me around the town one day."

"Could Brooke have seen you with Virginia?"

"I suppose so. I was meeting her for lunch later, but she never showed up."

Amber smiled. "I think we may have discovered the reason why she stood you up. Go to Brooke and tell her the same thing you told me."

McKay grinned. "You women have it all figured out, don't you?"

Amber laughed. "If we did, none of us would have a care in the world. I just get lots of practice from talking to the men who come in here." She paused, smiling. "You know, you men are lucky."

He glanced at her. "How's that?"

"You have someplace to go to when you're down. A woman doesn't. She can go to her mother, but there are some things women don't want to share with their mothers."

"I never looked at it that way," McKay said.

"You should," Amber pointed out. "Where do you think Brooke goes with her problems?"

He shrugged. "I don't know."

"Wouldn't it be wonderful if she came to you? Maybe you should offer to listen for a change."

McKay mulled over what she said. "That's good advice, Amber, but how do I get Brooke to talk to me?"

Amber thought a moment. "Well, both of you were on a ship for two days. I'm sure that gave you lots of opportunities."

"Yes, it did. But we didn't do much talking."

"Did she come back with you?"

"No. Brooke went on to London. She needed to meet the owners of the shipping company."

"Well, I think I would wait for her in Nassau. Then she'll have no choice but to ride back with you."

"I suppose I could," he said, thinking how he might arrange a stay in Nassau. Finally an idea came to him, and he grinned. "Amber, you've done it again! That's a brilliant plan!"

"Thank you," Amber said, smiling. "But it's merely providing the opportunity. The rest is up to you."

The blockade-runner *Silver Spray* steamed away from the wharf as Judson Bates leaned against the ship's railing and watched the twinkling lights of the waterfront, thinking about the events of the past two weeks. When he and Howard were arrested and thrown into that small eight-foot cell, he thought his luck had run out. Then that fat lawyer Thad Corben came to visit him. After speaking with Judson, Corben advised the Chief of Police about a recent decision in Georgia involving a white man who beat a slave to death. The beating was witnessed by two other slaves, but no one was allowed to testify because they were black. The Chief had done some checking on the law and later released them for lack of evidence.

Judson was fortunate to get a job on another blockade-runner so quickly. He suspected it was partly Howard's doing, along with the fact the *Silver Spray* needed men. He was thrilled to be leaving the city that had caused him so much trouble, but hated to let Captain McKay get away with having him thrown in jail.

The following morning, McKay took the ferry across the river and hired a carriage to take him to the Deering Plantation. The road passed through vast pine forests which provided turpentine, timber and rosin, and made the Cape Fear area prosperous.

After a three-hour ride, the forest began to clear as they neared the lower Cape Fear River, and the trees gave way to lush, green rice paddies. Overhanging limbs of the enormous live oaks on either side of the road intertwined, creating an arched canopy which dripped with Spanish moss and announced they were nearing the plantation house. At the end of the long, tree-lined road stood a stately Greek Revival mansion with six white, fluted Corinthian columns. Over the entrance, which was surrounded by side lights and crowned with an elaborate etched glass fanlight, projected a small balcony with a brass swag lantern. On either side of the main house extended two wings of red brick, topped with terra cotta tile roofs, and decorated with numerous rectangular windows with black shutters. Off to the side were several white trellises overgrown with purple morning glories. Behind the plantation house McKay could see box-like, tiny brick buildings with cedar shake roofs. In front of the slave quarters a half dozen bare-footed Negro children were noisily playing tag, while a shy little girl of about five or six clung to the folds of her mother's dress, fixing them with her expressive eyes.

When the carriage stopped, McKay instructed the driver to wait. He climbed the steps to the porch and pulled the heavy brass door bell. After several moments a Negro house servant opened the door.

"Tell Mr. Deering Captain Wade McKay is here to see him."

The woman ushered him into an enormous, high ceilinged foyer with a winding staircase. The servant left, and several minutes later a white-haired, stooped shouldered gentleman shuffled into the room.

"Mr. Deering, how are you?"

The old man looked up, nodding. "Tolerable, Captain. And you?"

"Fine, sir," McKay said, then added. "Mister Deering, you must be wondering why a sea captain from Wilmington would come all the way out here."

"Yes, I was."

"I'll get right to the point, then. Mr. Deering, I would like to purchase Elias."

Charles Deering looked up at McKay with curiosity. "Why would a sea captain want him?"

"Well, Sir, his family was killed on my ship, so I feel a responsibility toward him."

Mr. Deering brought his fingertips together. "Of course, Captain, I can understand your concern. But I am willing to provide for Elias until his seventeenth year. After that, he'll be a free man and can go wherever he chooses."

"I'm aware of that, sir. I plan to give him a job as a cabin boy on my ship."

Mr. Deering smiled with approval, then asked, "Would this lead to an apprenticeship?"

"Most likely it would."

"My word. I can't offer anything to compare with that."

The old man led the way into the drawing room and carefully let himself down into an armchair behind a desk, motioning the Captain over. When the other man sat opposite him, he said, "You must understand, Captain McKay, I'm not in the business of selling slaves. But since that horrible tragedy claimed Elias's whole family, I feel like the boy deserves another chance. A chance at something better."

"We all feel the same way, sir."

Mr. Deering retrieved a ledger from the left hand drawer. After looking through it, he said, "Well, according to the latest tax assessment, Elias is valued at five hundred dollars."

"And I'm sure he's worth every penny," McKay said. He took a leather pouch from inside his coat. "I presume payment in gold would be acceptable."

"Of course," Mr. Deering said, astounded. He hadn't seen gold since the beginning of the war.

McKay counted out the money while the white-haired gentleman wrote a bill of sale.

The transaction completed, the men went outside to the slave quarters. The children had run off to continue their game somewhere else, and were replaced by an elderly, black woman in a rocking chair. She was mumbling to herself and weaving a basket from palmetto fronds. McKay said hello, but she carried on with her task, speaking to someone who wasn't there. He entered the third cabin behind Mr. Deering, and saw it had a pounded dirt floor and was furnished with several beds, a table with four chairs, and a simple chest of drawers. Elias sat at the table, looking up when the men entered. Captain McKay squatted next to him and said, "Hello, Elias."

Recognition flashed in the boy's eyes.

"I've come to take you home with me. Would you like that?"

Elias glanced at his master. Mr. Deering smiled, nodding it was all right. "Yessuh. I'd like dat fine."

McKay stood. "All right then, Elias. All that remains is for you to gather your belongings."

"Elias," Mr. Deering said, "I'm having a trunk brought from the house you can put your things in. If you want, you can put your family's belongings in there, too."

"Thanky, massa."

The old man smiled, patting him on the shoulder. "No, Elias. I'm not your master anymore. Captain McKay is. He appears to be a fine man. He's offered you a job on his ship."

The boy's eyes grew wide with wonder. "Never sailed on no ship befo'."

"It's a terrific opportunity for you," Mr. Deering said. "There's nothing for you here, Elias. The war has changed everything. I don't even know if this plantation will survive. That's why it's important for you to take this chance and learn as much as you can."

The boy nodded, then hugged Mr. Deering shyly.

When the carriage arrived at the wharf, Elias was reluctant to go aboard the *Atlantis*. Suddenly, all the horrible memories of that night when his family was murdered came flooding back.

McKay placed a hand on the boy's shoulder and asked, "What's the matter, Elias?"

"I's afeared."

"There's nothing to be afraid of, Elias. The men who did those terrible things aren't here anymore."

Elias still refused to go up the gangplank, so McKay tried a different approach. "Do you like to fish?"

"Yessuh."

McKay nodded, smiling. "So do I. When I was a young boy growing up in South Carolina, I used to fish just about every day. Do you know anything about this river?"

"Sho' do," the boy announced proudly. "My Paw an' me fished behin' de plantation plenty."

"You did? Then maybe you could show me the best spots."

Elias shrugged, looking about. "Don' know nuthin' 'bout de river heah, suh."

"You don't?"

"No, suh. Is it deep?"

"Yes," McKay replied. "I have some fishing poles on my ship. Why don't we get them and give it a try?"

Elias hesitated, unsure. "I'd like to stay heah, if dat's all right."

McKay smiled. "Sure it is. But I'll bet the fishing is better from the ship. You'll be able to get your line out farther in the water."

What the Captain said made sense, and the boy's fascination with fishing made him ask, "If we catch us a mess o' catfish can we have 'em fo' supper?"

"Sure we can. I'll have the cook fry them up special."

They went aboard and got two cane fishing poles out of the ship's lazaret, then they went to the galley to get some bait. Cookie was preparing roast beef for supper and gave them some strips of the raw meat. Before long, they had caught seven fish between them. McKay put the fish in the ship's cold storage locker, because he needed to take the *Atlantis* to Cassidy's Shipyard that afternoon for repairs to the rear deck. Elias prowled the bridge, observing with interest the activity of the men around him as they prepared the *Atlantis* to get underway.

CHAPTER 7

Judson Bates and three other men climbed the stacks of cotton bales on the *Silver Spray's* deck, shoving the bales one-by-one into the water to lighten the load. A Federal cruiser had pursued the blockade-runner throughout the night and into the morning. Now the ship could clearly be seen, and Judson paused to watch from this excellent vantage point. She bore the same silhouette as a blockade runner, but at her masthead flew a United States flag. The warship had steadily closed the distance between them, and a series of orange flashes indicated her cannon had begun firing. Judson forgot the remaining bales and scrambled for cover.

"Smoke off the starboard bow!" the lookout called from his position in the foremast, raising his arm in the direction of the new threat.

The smoke trail of a cruiser was visible above the horizon and, like a dirty finger, pointed out another Federal gunboat.

The *Silver Spray* heeled to port in her high-speed turn, and the cruiser behind maneuvered inside to shorten the distance separating them. Shrieking cannonballs ripped the water around the wildly twisting and turning blockade-runner as she steamed through sheets of spray, cascading all about her.

Judson peeked out the doorway of the galley just as a shell wailed through the rigging, sending a shattered spar crashing to the deck. He leaped away from the door, then slammed into the bulkhead where the watch assignments were posted.

Suddenly towering geysers of white water obscured the rakish profile of the *Silver Spray* as an avalanche of shells burst around her. A tremendous explosion rocked the ship and shrapnel and debris rained down in a deadly torrent. Thick smoke filled the galley, and Judson crawled panic-stricken along the sloping deck. He headed for the patch of light that shone from the doorway and soon cool sea air was filling his lungs. The constant noise and vibration of the engines had ceased, leaving the ship strangely quiet and wallowing in the seas. She took a sluggish roll to port, recovering slowly. Judson knew the vessel was sinking and scrambled to the high side. Dazed men crawled from every part of the smoking ship, searching for a safe haven. Judson saw Howard climb out of the engine room hatch, his face darkened with sweat and coal dust.

A launch loaded with Federal sailors came alongside, and the captain, a man with fierce blue eyes and an iron-colored beard, charged aboard, waving a cutlass. A swarm of men wearing black tams, dark blue middy shirts, and bell-bottomed trousers, followed him, armed with pistols. They invaded every part of the ship, searching for any sign of resistance.

"I am Captain Travis of the blockade hunter *USS Black Prince,*" the Federal officer thundered. "According to the Articles of War, I place this vessel and her crew under arrest by authority of the United States Government!"

Crews on blockading duty earned prize money for each blockade-runner they captured. The Union sailors grumbled as they rounded up the Confederate prisoners. They were angry because of the sinking condition of the *Silver Spray* and the probable loss of any prize money. Less than an hour after they transferred everyone to the Federal cruiser, the *Silver Spray* rolled over, and with a dying gasp, sank by the stern.

Five days later, in New York City, twenty-nine-year-old Commander Michael Van Treese returned from lunch to the Navy Department and found a dispatch on his desk. It advised him the blockade-runner *Silver Spray* had been sunk by the *USS Black Prince* and the crew captured. The prisoners were enroute to New

York Harbor on the *USS Empire State* and would arrive that day, the twelfth of August. The commander fumed at the bureaucratic system which allowed these dispatches to be late. How was he expected to interrogate prisoners if no one kept him informed of what was going on? He checked his appointments for the rest of the day and saw every minute was accounted for. The commander knew Admiral Foster wanted all prisoners interrogated upon their arrival in case they might turn up some valuable information. He would have to cancel the rest of his appointments.

The prisoners arrived that afternoon, and Commander Van Treese and a stenographer conducted the first of many interrogations which would last well into the evening.

Two burly guards led Judson Bates into a room and instructed him to sit in a chair in the center. A young commander with sandy hair and a bushy moustache sat at a table beside an ensign who was armed with a pencil and pad of paper, ready to take down the prisoner's every word.

"Mr. Bates, I am Commander Van Treese and this is Ensign Peel. We need to ask you a few questions."

Judson shifted uncomfortably in the chair. "Aw right."

"Are you a citizen of the United States?"

"Yes. I am."

The commander leaned forward, placing his arms on the table. "Mr. Bates, how did you come to be on the *Silver Spray*?"

"I was one of the crew."

"What was your job?"

"I was a deck hand."

Commander Van Treese looked at his notes. "Were you aware if you were caught trying to run the naval blockade, you might spend the rest of the war in prison?"

"Yes. I was."

"Then why did you do it?"

Judson shrugged his bony shoulders, and said, "Well, jobs are hard to find an' the pay's good."

Van Treese's eyes grew cold. "No job is worth your freedom."

Judson flashed a look of indignation, and spat, "Maybe so. But it's better'n starvin'."

The commander didn't miss a beat, continuing with the questions. "What is your captain's name?"

"Captain Augustus Horne."

"How many crew members were on board at the time of your capture?"

Judson thought a moment. "Thirty-three, I 'spect."

Van Treese gave him a small, grave nod. "Did the *Silver Spray* carry any passengers?"

"I don't believe so."

"Did anyone dress differently than the rest of the crew, or receive special treatment from the captain?"

Judson's face clouded up in thought for a minute. "Come to think of it, there was a man who didn't seem to fit in with the others. Didn't see him do nary a lick o' work, neither."

"What was his name?"

Judson stroked his chin. "Bill--Bill Latimer. He's a strange one for sure--always stayed in his cabin."

Van Treese nodded while he jotted something on the paper before him. "What type of cargo did your ship carry?"

"Mostly cotton. We also had some tobacco an' a few dozen barrels of rosin an' turpentine."

"What was your destination?" the commander asked.

"Nassau."

"What sort of cargo were you to pick up?"

Judson looked at him in disbelief. It was insane to believe a lowly deck hand knew what the next cargo might be. "I don't have any idea."

Commander Van Treese leaned forward, asking pointedly, "Was that cargo munitions destined for the Confederacy?"

Judson crossed his arms, glaring at Van Treese. "I done told you. I don't know. They hired me in Wilmington jest before we left."

"What other blockade-runners were docked in Wilmington while you were there?"

"I seen three ships before we left. The *Atlantis*, the *Chicora*, and the *Advance*."

"Can you give us any information about them?"

"Like what?"

"Anything. Their schedules or their cargos. How they're constructed. Things like that."

"Well, the *Atlantis* is a side wheel steamer with two funnels. One before an' another aft of the paddle wheel boxes. They renamed the *Let Her Be* the *Chicora* when she was sold 'bout three months ago. She's a side wheel steamer, too; so's the *Advance*. The *Advance* got two funnels also, but she's easy to spot 'cause they're behind the paddle boxes."

The commander looked Bates over and said, "You look like you're in good condition. Why aren't you in the military?"

"Got no cause. I figure whatever it is you soldier boys is fightin' 'bout ain't no concern of mine."

"I find that hard to believe."

"It's true. I ain't got no slaves. An' Northerners never done me no harm. The only folk who have, has been my own people."

"How's that?" Van Treese asked.

"Oh, you know how uppity folks can git. 'Specially when they figure you ain't their kind."

Commander Van Treese sensed he was hiding something. "Have you ever been arrested?"

Bates grinned and shook his head. "No, sir."

"We can check your record, you know."

"I ain't got nuthin' to hide."

"Mr. Bates, can you tell us anything about how the blockade-runners elude the blockade?"

Judson smiled and laughed. "Shore can, capt'n. I reckon I can help you there. The Confederate Signal Corps done set up range lights to help us navigate the river an' the inlets. When we git to Fort Fisher, the lookouts give us detailed reports 'bout where the Yankee ships are."

Van Treese leaned forward, folding his hands. "Mr. Bates, may I be candid with you?"

"Shore."

"It is my opinion you are fucked."

Judson looked scared. "Why?"

"Most of your crew is English, so we can't hold them for more than a few days. However, since you're a citizen of the United States, we can imprison you at Fort Lafayette until the end of the war."

Judson narrowed his eyes. "But I didn't do nuthin' 'cept try to make a livin'."

"I'm sorry, Mr. Bates. It looks like the rest of the crew left you holding the bag."

Commander Van Treese rose from his chair, motioning to the two soldiers who were standing near the door. "Guards, take this man back to his cell."

The next morning, Commander Van Treese came into Admiral Foster's office carrying two mugs of coffee. The room was deserted. He heard the sound of water splashing in the bathroom so he placed one of the mugs on the desk and sat in an armchair. When the Admiral entered the room, he set down his cup and rose respectfully.

"Good morning, sir."

"Good morning, commander. Ahhh, I see you've brought me some coffee. Bless you." He raised the mug in a mock salute, taking a sip. Years of command at sea had weathered the senior officer's face, and the massive muttonchop whiskers which covered his cheeks swept up to join his white moustache. The Navy had assigned him to its office in New York City the previous year, and he had complained ever since about being put behind a desk. As a result, he spent as little time there as possible.

Van Treese picked up his mug, and said, "I interrogated the prisoners that came in yesterday, sir."

"How did it go?" The admiral spooned some sugar into his coffee, stirring it.

"Well, most of them were English, so we can expect a visit from the British consul demanding their release. I'll try to get as much information as I can before we let them go."

"Excellent. I've been under a lot of pressure from the Secretary of the Navy to put a halt to all this blockade-running. He says Wilmington is a thorn in the President's side, and whatever bothers Mr. Lincoln bothers him. He's demanding it be closed as soon as possible."

Van Treese nodded in understanding. "Admiral, I believe one of these men might help us achieve that."

"How?"

"As a spy, sir. The man I have in mind is an American named Bates. We found a copy of a Wilmington newspaper on board his ship. An article from that paper says Bates and another man were arrested for murdering a slave family about a month ago."

"How did he get free?"

"Through a legal technicality. However, I get the impression he is still bitter about his arrest. If we try to strengthen this belief, we could sway him enough to help us."

"But a murderer," the admiral protested. "I don't know if I want such a man working for us."

"May I remind the Admiral that he wasn't convicted, merely accused. Besides, what choice do we have? You said yourself the Secretary of the Navy wants to stop all the blockade-running. Maybe Bates could help us do that."

Admiral Foster nodded. "I guess you're right. Due to the nature of their work, most spies are nefarious characters anyway."

Van Treese smiled, leaning forward in his chair. "Exactly, sir. I've already planted the idea that because he is an American, we will imprison him while the rest of his crew gets off with just a slap on the wrist."

"Perfect. You keep talking to him, commander, two or three times a day if necessary."

Judson Bates was frightened. First he was put into a cell by himself, now Commander Van Treese was questioning him again. The navy officer's eyes were cold and hard as steel as he demanded, "Why didn't you tell me you were arrested for murder, Bates?"

Bates shifted uncomfortably in his chair. "I haven't been arrested."

Van Treese picked up a Wilmington newspaper, waving it at Judson. "This newspaper was confiscated from your ship. I found an article which says you and another man were arrested for murdering a slave family."

Bates licked his lips. "That ain't me."

"Yes, it is, Bates. Several of your shipmates have confirmed it. Why didn't you say anything about this when I asked you before?"

Judson squirmed in his chair. "I was scared and figured you couldn't check because of the war."

"We have many ways to find out if you're telling us the truth. Don't ever lie to me again." The commander set the newspaper back on the table, and said, "You realize this information changes things dramatically."

"How's that?"

"Before we could just keep you in prison until the end of the war. Now you'll probably be hanged."

"Hanged? But why?" Judson asked, alarmed.

"Mr. Bates, you'll be retried for murder because you're up North now, and we have laws which allow a black man to testify against a white man in a court of law."

Judson shook his head wondering how he became involved in such a horrible mess.

"Your situation is hopeless, unless. . ." Commander Van Treese paused to see what Bates' reaction would be.

Judson perked up. "Unless what?"

"Unless we make a recommendation for leniency on your behalf. If you help us, then we'll help you."

Bates eyed the commander suspiciously. "How would I do that?"

"By providing us with information so we can capture Wilmington and put an end to blockade-running."

"You mean by bein' a spy?"

"Yes, I do."

Judson scowled. "You got the wrong idea about me."

Van Treese leaned forward, placing his elbows on the table. "Why do you say that?"

"'Cause I ain't important enough to help you do any of those things."

"Don't sell yourself short. If we put you in the right place, and you give us the information we need, the war can be shortened by at least a year and thousands of lives could be saved."

"An' if I did this, then you will speak up for me?"

"Yes. Of course I will."

Bates considered this, then asked, "Can you promise I'll go free?"

Van Treese folded his hands. "No. However, I can tell you this. Whenever the Government makes a plea for leniency, it is usually granted."

Bates rubbed his chin, unsure. "If I agree to this, do I git out of my cell right now?"

"Not immediately. We need to work out a few of the details first."

Judson thought about his situation. He didn't want to be executed, and he had no fondness for Wilmington. Then he recalled how Captain McKay had him arrested. Now Judson would have a chance to help arrest him! "Aw right, commander," he said. "I'll do whatever you want."

Van Treese leaned back in his chair, smiling. "You decided wisely, Mr. Bates."

Virginia sauntered along the ornate iron fence which bordered the house Burgess & Linden rented for their crews, shifting her yellow parasol to the other hand before opening the gate. Elias sat on the front steps with a fishing pole across his lap, tying a new hook and sinker to the nearly transparent line.

She smiled. "Hello. Are you going fishing?"

The boy looked up. "Yes'm. De capt'n an' me goin' early tomorrow."

"That sounds like fun. By the way, my name is Virginia. What's yours?"

"Elias," he said, returning to tying his fishing line.

"Nice to meet you, Elias. I'm also a friend of the captain's." When the boy said no more and busied himself with the fishing pole, Virginia asked, "How long do you expect to be gone?"

Elias answered without looking up, "Most of de day, I reckon."

"That's a long time. You're taking a lunch, aren't you?"

He shrugged his shoulders. "Don't know."

Virginia leaned forward toward the boy. "Would you like some nice fried chicken and apple pie to take along?"

Elias looked up, smiling. "Yes'm. I'd like dat fine."

"Well, then I'll just have to fix you some."

"Thanky, Miz Virginia."

"Is Captain McKay around?"

"Yes'm. Does you want me to fetch 'im?"

Virginia's eyes came alive, and she twirled her parasol playfully. "No, Elias. Why don't I surprise him?"

Virginia entered the house and heard voices in the kitchen and went to investigate. McKay was sitting at the table with a cup of coffee while the ship's cook stood at a butcher block table with a knife in one hand and a potato in the other. They were discussing the finer points of chopping vegetables.

Cookie began to slice the vegetable with short, deliberate stokes. "It's a real pleasure working with the potato, especially on a moving ship. First I quarter it, so all the pieces have a firm base to work from. Then I hold it like this and slice . . ."

When Virginia entered the room, Cookie stopped talking and looked up. McKay turned to see what had gotten his attention. "Virginia! What a surprise," he said, rising from his chair.

"Good morning, gentlemen. Can I join this fascinating discussion?"

"Sure, you can," Cookie said. "I was just explaining to the captain how I've chopped vegetables on a ship for twenty years, and I still have all of my fingers. There's a secret to it, you know."

"I imagine there is," she said.

They listened to Cookie for a bit, and when he finished, Virginia said to McKay, "I hear you're going fishing tomorrow."

"Yes. I promised Elias we'd go."

"Can a lady come too, or is it for men only?"

Since McKay had no intention of becoming involved with Virginia, he didn't see any harm in letting her come along. Perhaps he would invite Bosun Gallagher to keep her company. "We'd be glad to have you come with us. Can you fish?"

"No, I'm afraid not. But I'll bring lunch, and I'm told I make some mighty good fried chicken and apple pie."

"Well then," McKay said, smiling. "I don't see how we could afford to leave you behind."

The next morning they rented a carriage and went south along rhe Cape Fear River. An impenetrable tangle of wax myrtle, yaupon holly, and red cedar made the banks inaccessible until a marshy area opened up to let them view the river through the cord grass and centuries-old cypress trees. When the carriage stopped, McKay and Elias grabbed their fishing poles and disappeared down a winding dirt path which led to the water while John Gallagher stayed behind to help Virginia.

"Those two are true fishermen," he said with a chuckle, gazing after them.

"Yes. If I were a little girl, I'd be going with them."

"You would? Were you a tomboy?"

Virginia smiled. "Yes. The biggest."

"Did you wear pigtails?"

She nodded. "Until I turned seven, then my mother took them out of my hair. She said wearing pigtails and britches wasn't ladylike."

John Gallagher imagined her as a young girl. "I'll bet you were cute."

She shrugged her shoulders. "I guess I wanted to be a boy because they got to do all the fun things."

"Oh? Like what?"

She took a blue and white quilt out of the back of the carriage, and said, "You know what I mean. A young girl wasn't allowed to get dirty or catch frogs. They were taught to wear dresses and stay clean, so people would think they were charming."

"It must have worked. You turned into a beautiful woman."

She smiled, handing one end of the quilt to Gallagher, then opening up her end. "Thank you for saying that. Do you really think I am?"

"Oh, yes! I thought that when I first saw you," he said, helping her spread the quilt on a nice shady spot.

"What does Wade think? Does he ever mention me?" Virginia asked, kneeling down to smooth the wrinkles from the blanket.

"Gosh, yes. He talks about you all the time," Gallagher lied. The captain never spoke about her, but he was too much of a gentleman to tell Virginia that. He felt strange telling her about another man when he wanted to be the object of her affections so badly.

"What does he say?" she wanted to know.

Gallagher thought a moment. "He said he was excited about you coming along. So was I."

Virginia walked over to the carriage to get the picnic basket. "What else did he say?"

"Let's see. He . . . ah . . . "

The joy drained out of Virginia's face. "Wade doesn't talk about me at all, does he?"

Gallagher gazed into her eyes. "No. He doesn't."

She frowned. "I don't understand! What am I doing wrong?"

"Absolutely nothing. He's in love with Brooke."

She set the basket on the ground and turned away, her eyes moist.

Gallagher moved behind her, holding her arms. "Virginia, Wade may not love you, but I do. You're all I think about."

She dried her eyes with the corner of a handkerchief, then turned, smiling at him. "You're very gallant, John. Nevertheless, you needn't tell me that so I'll forget Wade."

"Oh, but I'm not!" John protested.

Her gloomy face appeared doubtful.

"I'll prove it's true. Virginia, will you be my girl?"

Virginia was stunned. "This is so sudden, John. I need time to think."

Disappointment showed on Gallagher's face. "All right. But before you answer, let me say this. If you become my girl, I'll do everything in my power to make you the happiest woman in the world."

Virginia had no doubt John meant what he said. Then her thoughts turned to Wade, and she knew she could never find happiness anywhere else but in his arms.

A few days later, a guard led Judson Bates into Commander Van Treese's office. The commander was at his desk and a small man with dark suspicious eyes sat to his left. "Sit down, Bates." Van Treese motioned to the man next to him. "This is Lafayette Baker, head of the Secret Service. He wants to speak with you."

The man's penetrating gaze fell upon Judson. "Mr. Bates, the commander tells me you want to become an agent for the United States. Why is that?"

"Cause I don't want to git executed."

"Executed for what?"

Judson shifted in the chair uneasily. "You know."

"Yes. I do. However, I want you to tell me."

Judson scowled. "Aw right, fer murder. I was accused of killin' some darkies."

"Did you kill them?" Baker asked.

"Blazes no. They done arrested the wrong man."

Baker nodded. "Yes, I know. And all of the jails in this country are full of innocent men."

Judson glared at him.

"Mr. Bates, you're a criminal. If you became an agent, why should we believe anything you tell us?"

Judson thought a moment. "'Cause I got no reason to lie. It'd interfere with my plans. There are folks I aim to get even with."

Baker nodded for him to go on. "Like who?"

Judson smiled for the first time since he'd been captured. "The man who got me arrested. Capt'n Wade McKay."

"Who is Captain McKay?"

"He's capt'n of the blockade-runner *Atlantis*. I had me a job as deck hand on his ship before I went on the *Silver Spray*."

Baker leaned forward, glaring at Bates. "I don't want your revenge to interfere with our mission."

"It won't."

"For your sake, see that it doesn't."

Commander Van Treese and the Secret Service agent spoke quietly for a moment. Then Baker stood up. "Mr. Bates, I'm going to take a chance. We need the port of Wilmington closed. With no supplies coming through the blockade to sustain its army, the Confederacy will have no choice but to surrender. Unfortunately, Wilmington is guarded by Fort Fisher, a strong coastal fortification."

Bates nodded. "I know it well."

"You do?"

"Yeah. Every time we went down the river I seen soldiers and slaves haulin' sand to build up the walls."

"Have you ever been inside?" Baker wanted to know.

"No. I ain't had the pleasure."

"That's what bothers me. I have no reliable intelligence about the inside of the fort," Baker fumed.

Judson saw where the conversation was headed. "I reckon I can git some for you," he volunteered.

Baker leaned forward. "If you could, it would help greatly. If its defenses were to be weakened, it would give us the chink in their armor allowing us to push an invasion force through. You are to provide us with that chink."

Judson scratched his head, unsure. "Me? But how?"

"In nine days there will be a prisoner exchange in Richmond. You and your shipmates, excluding the captain and the pilot, will be among them. You will be contacted there by one of our agents. With his help, you will infiltrate the staff of Confederate General Braxton Bragg. We will supply you with information about the Federal army's movements and strengths. We want you to reveal this information to the general. Tell him when you were a prisoner, they recruited you as a spy for the North, but you want to become a double agent and work for the Confederacy. He will be suspicious of you at first. However, when this information you give him proves correct, he will be inclined to listen to whatever you have to say."

Baker looked at Commander Van Treese before continuing. "According to our intelligence, General Bragg will be assigned to command the Wilmington District in a few weeks. An organization of Union sympathizers known as the Order of Heroes will contact you in Wilmington. For security reasons we cannot divulge the names of any of these people. Therefore, they will get in touch with you."

"Why can't I know who they are?" Bates asked.

"In the event you were to be captured, you can't reveal anything you don't know. Also, we would be foolish to tell you who our agents are in case you defect."

"Deefect?" Judson asked.

"Yes. Go over to the other side and work for them."

Bates waved his hand in dismissal, grinning. "Ain't no need to fret. Those folks was fixin' to hang me down thar. Besides, I ain't done with Capt'n McKay yet. Not by a far sight. Me an' him got a bone to pick."

Over the following eight days Lafayette Baker explained what Judson Bates was to do when he was exchanged.

CHAPTER 8

Whenever the *SS Mercury* rolled in the seven-foot swells, Brooke Snow's stomach followed every sickening motion the ship made. She munched on a stale cracker while watching the bumpy horizon, promising herself she would never venture onto the ocean again. Unfortunately she had six more days before the ship docked in Nassau and another two to Wilmington. She had learned to stay away from the nauseating fumes emanating from the galley's smokestack because they reminded her of the greasy food the cook was preparing for lunch. Sometimes an errant wind would waft the smoke in her direction and make her sick again.

Peter Reynolds was taking his morning stroll on the deck and approached Brooke. She liked the energetic young man who always seemed to have a smile for her.

"Good morning, Miss Snow. I'm glad to see you're enjoying the fresh air," he said. Reynolds was pleased to see her.

Brooke straightened up, forcing a weak smile. "Hello, Mr. Reynolds. I may be on the deck, but I'm not enjoying anything."

Reynolds became concerned. "Oh? What's wrong? Are you seasick?"

"A little," Brooke confessed.

"I've heard it helps to keep some crackers in your stomach," he suggested. "Keeps things from sloshing around down there."

She held up a cracker, and they laughed.

"Well, I guess that blows that theory."

"Yes," she agreed. "I imagine it does."

Wanting to be of some assistance, he said, "Why don't you sit in a deck chair, and we'll talk. Maybe the conversation will take your mind off the sea." He found a chair and brought it over for her. Brooke smiled a thank you and gathered the folds of her skirt before sitting.

He pulled another wooden chair close to hers. "Where are you going when we reach Nassau?"

"Wilmington, North Carolina."

He nodded. "Is that where you're from?"

"Yes. I live there with my mother," Brooke said, fighting the urge to vomit.

Peter said, smiling. "A North Carolina girl! I should have known by your accent."

"How about you?"

"I'm from Atlanta, ma'am."

Brooke became troubled. "Oh, dear! I've read General Sherman and practically the whole Yankee army is laying siege to Atlanta."

His smile disappeared. "Yes. I'm worried about my family."

"Are you married?"

He nodded. "I have a wife and two little girls."

"Oh, dear! What are you going to do?"

Peter shook his head, frowning. "I don't know. I haven't seen my children for nearly two months. First I went to Liverpool on business and now this."

"It must be difficult being away and not knowing if your family is all right."

"It is. I miss my little girls terribly."

Brooke thought it odd he hadn't mentioned missing his wife. "What sort of business are you in?"

"I'm a purchasing agent for the Confederate government."

"Good heavens! Isn't this a coincidence? I'm Burgess and Linden's new agent in Wilmington."

"Really? We'll probably be doing business in the future."

"I hope so," she said, pausing. Brooke's curiosity got the better of her, and she asked, "Before, when you mentioned missing your family, you didn't say anything about your wife. How come?"

Hesitating for a moment, Peter said, "We don't get along anymore."

She waited for him to continue.

He looked out to sea as he spoke. "I'm not sure why that is. Maybe it's because of the war. We lived in Richmond when I was an advisor on President Davis' staff. I'd work some pretty long hours because of all the difficulties a new government experiences. As a result, I didn't get to see my wife much. I guess we just grew apart."

Brooke put a reassuring hand on his shoulder. "I'm sorry to hear that. What brought you to Atlanta?"

"I needed time to be alone to sort things out, so when this job in Atlanta opened up, I took it. Although taking this job meant moving it was all right because we'd be going farther away from the war. I also knew I'd be gone from home a lot and thought that might help."

"Did it?"

His eyes grew sad. "No. I miss my girls more than ever, but the prospect of coming home to their mother hasn't brightened. I may try to get my old job back so I can be with my children."

"That would probably be best. They need their father."

His eyes filled with tears. "They do, but I need them more!"

While Captain McKay inspected the deck load of cotton bales on the _Atlantis_, he explained to Elias how to properly load a ship. The boy was wearing a blue peaked cap and the seamans clothes McKay had bought for him.

When the captain finished, he told Elias to see if the cook needed any help, and walked to his cabin. Just then, the sound of a carriage halting at the dock caught his attention. Inside the cab two lovers were kissing passionately. McKay wondered who the lucky sailor was. He longed to share romantic moments such as this with Brooke. As he turned to go, he was startled to see his boatswain and Virginia stepping from the carriage and walking hand-in-hand to the gangplank. McKay went about his business, pretending not to notice.

A short while later, the boatswain reported to him in his cabin. McKay was seated at his desk, the bill of lading spread before him. He set the pen down on the ledger before him. "Mr. Gallagher, I'm gratified to see you could join us today. I thought for a while we might have to leave without you."

"I'm sorry, sir. I was delayed for personal reasons."

McKay rose and walked to the window, gesturing outside. "Yes. I saw your reason walk to the gangplank with you."

"I'll never be late again, sir."

"See that you aren't. I have enough to tend to before we get underway. I don't need to be assuming your duties, too. Never let your personal life affect the affairs of this ship again. Is that understood?"

The boatswain nodded, embarrassed. "Yes, sir."

McKay dismissed his boatswain and went back to work on the bill of lading. After several minutes, he put down his pen and began wondering what he would say to Brooke when they met in Nassau. He envied Mr. Gallagher, not for his romance with Virginia, but for knowing the bittersweet joys of parting and having a woman anxiously awaiting his return. A man needed to feel that someone cared--it helped him get through all the day-to-day trials of a life at sea.

When it came time for the *Atlantis* to get underway, Captain McKay joined his boatswain and the quartermaster on the bridge. "Mr. Gallagher, is everything in order for getting underway?"

"Yes, sir, it is. A twenty-five-knot wind from the southwest is pushing us against the dock, which may make for a difficult departure because of the tight berths."

McKay recalled the ships along the crowded wharf. "Very well. Cast off all lines except the aft spring line. Double it up and put out some extra fenders," he said.

The boatswain hurried out of the bridge and repeated the Captain's orders to the men standing by the mooring lines on the dock. They slipped the heavy lines over the bollards and dropped them into the water while the deck hands hauled them in hand-over-hand.

McKay pulled a lever on the forward bulkhead causing the brass steam whistle to wail for five full seconds, announcing the ship's departure. He opened the speaking tube to the engine room, and said, "Mr. Reichman, reverse the starboard wheel. Quartermaster, steer forty-five degrees to starboard."

The deck began to tremble as the machinery came to life and the starboard paddle wheel began churning the black water. The ship's bow fought the wind and the current and slowly moved away from the dock while the rear spring line groaned under the strain as it helped the vessel to pivot. When the *Atlantis* had maneuvered far enough into the wind, McKay called down to the engine room, "All stop, Mr. Reichman." Then he said to the boatswain, "Mr. Gallagher, have the men cast off the spring line."

"Aye-aye, sir!"

When the two mooring lines had enough slack, the men on the dock slipped them off the bollard, dropping them into the water.

"All ahead two-thirds, Mr. Reichman. Quartermaster, rudder amidships."

The paddle wheels began to turn and propelled the ship out into the river while her funnels trailed volumes of black smoke, obscuring the dock. The boatswain recalled with pride how everyone on shore had stopped what they were doing to watch the expert handling of the *Atlantis* as she maneuvered away from the crowded dock.

At one in the morning all eyes on board the darkened *Atlantis* focused on the Mound Battery at Fort Fisher. They were waiting for the signal lantern to indicate it was safe to make a dash through the blockade. The lantern was fitted with a green lens and shrouded to reveal only a sliver of light to the waiting ship, concealing it from the Federal fleet.

A green light appeared above the battery, moving back and forth.

The blockade-runner already had raised steam, and the ship responded instantly. Speed was necessary because the situation changed minute by minute as the cordon of Federal ships went about their patrols. The latest intelligence showed the *USS Wabash* lay at anchor about thirty degrees off the inlet and five miles out to sea.

Every available man stood watch on deck for any sign of the Federal warships. All lights were extinguished. The only thing that might alert the enemy was the muffled throb of the machinery and the sound of the bow cutting through the water. The shipyard had fitted the paddle-wheel boxes with skirts to deaden the sound of the paddle-wheels churning the ocean.

Three hours later, Captain McKay dismissed the watch. Everything had gone smoothly and they slipped out of the inlet without alerting a single Federal ship.

During the afternoon of the second day, the lookout sang out from the masthead, "Smoke off the port quarter!"

McKay stepped outside the bridge, and climbed the stairs to the port paddle-wheel box. He trained his telescope on the distant smoke trail. Hearing the boatswain move beside him, McKay handed him the telescope, noting the time on his pocket watch.

"She looks to be a Federal warship, sir," the boatswain announced.

"An astute observation, Mr. Gallagher. It's now 1:20. He should make his intentions clear within the next hour."

At 2:30 McKay noted with annoyance the Federal warship had gained on them, and they would soon be within range of her cannon. Because of her speed and low profile, he suspected the ship was a captured blockade-runner. He also knew with the heavy load of cotton and turpentine the *Atlantis* was carrying, the Federal gunboat would eventually overtake them.

McKay recalled the time his engineer had thrown bacon into the furnaces producing a heavy black smoke which hung over the water. A ship could become lost in such a cloud. Opening the speaking tube to the engine room, he said, "Mr. Reichman, we need more smoke. I want you to burn some bacon in the furnaces."

When McKay saw the smoke trail wasn't thick enough, he ordered some deck hands to carry a cotton bale and a barrel of turpentine down to the engine room, and said in the speaking tube, "Mr. Reichman, I want you to soak some of that cotton with turpentine and burn it. That should make the fire hotter and produce the smoke I need."

The white smoke from the gunboat's bowchasers told McKay she had closed within range. Several seconds later, an explosion thundered across the water, and a cannonball kicked up a foaming geyser of water behind them. The shots moved closer and closer with geometric precision, until they caused the water to boil alongside the blockade-runner.

The *Atlantis* turned into the wind and dense, black smoke from the twin smokestacks began to drift behind them, obscuring the Federal cruiser. When the smoke was thickest, McKay ordered the quartermaster to steer forty-five degrees to starboard.

By the time the men aboard the Federal cruiser realized the blockade-runner had altered her course, they had lost valuable ground and were out of range for her cannon. Despite the fact they were only three hours out of Nassau, and their prize might get away, the warship continued the chase in hopes the blockade-runner may break down.

Several hours later, the *Atlantis* sailed into Nassau harbor while the Federal warship watched from a distance. United States ships had to stop their pursuit because of the five-mile limit.

After securing his ship, McKay went to the steamship lines where Brooke had booked passage for her trip to England. Inside he found an agent behind a long counter, writing in a ledger. "Did a young lady by the name of Brooke Snow buy a ticket to Wilmington, North Carolina, within the past week?"

The agent put down his pen, scratched his head, thinking a moment. "I don't remember the name. Was she good looking?"

McKay smiled. "Yes. As a matter of fact she is."

"Then she hasn't been here. I would have noticed it if she had."

"Would you inform me if she comes in? There's a ten-dollar gold piece for you if you do."

"Certainly, sir. I'll let you know the minute she arrives." The agent got a piece of paper and a pen. "And you are?"

"I'm Captain McKay, the master of the *Atlantis*. If you see her, send a messenger to me immediately. I'll be aboard my ship."

"Yes, sir."

When he got back to the ship, McKay went below to the engine room. As he suspected, he found his engineer prowling among the machinery and wiping it lovingly with an oily rag.

"Mr. Reichman, I noticed our speed fell off a few knots toward the end of the voyage. What happened?"

The engineer stuffed the rag into his back pocket and gestured to the boilers. "Well, sir, I imagine burning all the turpentine and cotton clogged the boiler tubes."

"How long will it take to clean them?"

"Oh, should take a couple of days, I guess."

"I also heard a ticking sound coming from the engine."

The engineer stroked his chin. "Ticking, sir?"

"Yes."

"I didn't notice any strange noises, sir. Maybe it came from the paddle-wheels."

"Perhaps. Nevertheless, it sounds like it could be trouble. Look into it when you get the chance."

That evening boatswain Gallagher had watch. Making his rounds, he climbed down the ladder to the engine room when he saw the engineer and a fireman running a large brush into a boiler tube.

"What are you doing?" he asked the engineer.

"The captain noticed we were losing speed, so I'm cleaning these boilers. These furnaces weren't meant to burn turpentine and cotton. It clogs everything up," he said, shaking his head in disgust. "Oh, and he also mentioned a ticking noise. Did you hear where it was coming from?"

"No, Chief. I didn't hear anything."

The engineer shook his head. "Strange. He said it was quite noticeable. Well, I'll have a look around when I'm through here."

Several days later the engineer went to the captain's cabin to make his report.

"Sir, I've finished cleaning the boilers and the furnaces, but I can't find anything wrong with the machinery that would produce a ticking sound. Could you help me track it down by pointing out where you heard it?"

The men went to the port paddle-wheel box and listened to the engines.

"There it is," the captain said, gesturing to the main bearing journals. "Over here. Listen closely."

The engineer cupped his right ear, turning to the area the captain pointed out.

"There it is again. Do you hear it?"

"No, sir," the engineer said. The man continued to listen, shaking his head with irritation. *Twenty years in the engine room with machinery noises must have made my hearing less sensitive.*

The engineer sat on a wooden plank of the scaffolding, amid panels he had removed from the paddle-wheel box, examining the shaft that led to the engines. Not finding anything wrong, he applied a thick coating of grease to the gears and bearings. This was the third time he had attempted to locate the problem the captain had mentioned. Twice he had dismantled most of the engine and meticulously cleaned and examined each part for excessive wear or stress cracks. He found nothing. He assembled the paddle-wheel box, then went to get the captain. As he had done before, Captain McKay listened to the throb of machinery, frowning. "I can still hear it, Mr. Reichman. I want that fixed before we leave port. We can't afford any breakdowns."

While the engineer was going down the stairs, he saw one of his crew about to leave the ship.

"Davis, I need a hand. I want you to get some engine parts machined and some new ones made."

147

Davis frowned, disappointed. "But, Chief, I got a date."

"Tough. This is more important."

Three days later, when the boatswain was on his way to the engine room to tell Mr. Reichman the new parts had arrived, he saw a young boy walk onto the ship and look around.

"May I help you?"

"Yes, sir. I have an urgent message for Captain McKay," the boy said, clutching an envelope.

"The captain's not here right now, but you can leave that with me. I'm the officer in charge."

The boy handed Gallagher the envelope. "All right. Would you see he gets this right away, sir?"

"Yes. I will."

He gave the boy a tip and went below. The engineer was cleaning some parts in a pan of turpentine and looked up when he heard the boatswain come down the ladder. He wiped his hands on a rag, and said, "Hello, John."

"Hi, Chief. Say, those parts you've ordered have arrived."

"Thanks. Maybe they'll perform the miracle I need."

Boatswain Gallagher fingered the envelope in his hand. "Chief, when I was coming to see you, I ran into a messenger with a note for the captain. It's addressed to him, and it's marked urgent. Do you think I should open it?"

"You're in charge of the ship, aren't you?"

"Of course."

Reichman spotted a piece of machinery which needed his attention, and walked over to it while he spoke. "Then open it. It sounds important."

The boatswain opened the envelope and read the note. It said Miss Snow had arrived and purchased a ticket to go aboard the *Atlantis*, but nothing else. He put the note in his pocket and thought of something to tell the engineer. "It says a new shipment of coal has arrived."

"Oh, that's old news," the chief said with a wave of his hand. "We've already got our coal. The only thing holding us up is this damned engine."

Boatswain Gallagher nodded, smiling. Now all the delays made sense.

CHAPTER 9

Judson Bates jerked and swayed with the motion of the train as he sat on the wooden floor of the stuffy railroad car, shoulder-to-shoulder with two hundred other ragged prisoners of war. At seven o'clock that morning, 1,200 men were loaded onto a train at Fort Lafayette, near New York Harbor. He had learned from Mr. Baker they were headed for a small town outside Richmond, Virginia, for a prisoner exchange with the Confederates.

The train wheezed to a stop amid a cloud of steam and the clangor of the locomotive's bell. The railroad car's doors were flung open, and Federal soldiers armed with bayoneted muskets roused the men to their feet and out of the car. Judson moved along with the crowd, and soon stood squinting in the sunlight alongside the train. Orders and shouts filled the air as the soldiers assembled the prisoners into ranks and marched them to a large fenced-in area a mile away.

Groups of bearded Confederate soldiers milled around dozens of large Sibley tents in the prison compound, speculating about their fate. In a short while, the gates opened, and three horse-drawn wagons cleaved the crowd. An unruly mob of prisoners surged forward when the aroma of food drifted over them. Although they were prisoners themselves, the Confederate officers tried to maintain discipline by forming their men into orderly lines.

After waiting for what seemed like an eternity in line, Judson finally made his way to the wagons. A gruff soldier thrust a mess tin and a cup into Judson's hands, and another man ladled a watery beef stew into his tin from a huge fire-blackened pot. A piece of hardtack and a cup of lukewarm coffee completed his meal. Judson found a small grassy area away from the crowd and sat alone. As he dabbed the hardtack into the stew to soften it, he heard a familiar voice.

"Hey, Judd. I'm shore glad I found you. I was beginnin' to think I'd never see you again."

Judson shaded his eyes and looked up to see Howard towering over him, holding his small cup and mess tin. "Good to see you, buddy. How you been?"

Howard sat with his friend, brooding. "I'm all right, I guess."

Judson could see something was troubling the other man and asked, "What's gnawin' at you?"

The big man stirred the watery beef stew, shaking his head. "Them soldiers said some terrible things."

"What did they say?"

Howard set his stew down and looked at Judson. "They said you'd leave, an' I'd never see you again. They also said they'd hang me for what I done. Those men scared me bad, Judd."

"Well, they were wrong. I'm here, ain't I?"

"You shore are, Judd."

"See. And they didn't hang you, neither."

"Lord, no. I reckon we're mighty lucky for bein' traded so soon, ain't we?"

"We shore are," Judson said, remembering the deal with Lafayette Baker.

"What's the first thing you're gonna do when we get set free?" Howard asked happily.

Judson paused, thinking. "I 'spect I'll find me a pretty woman an' get buck-naked. Then, after I've screwed my brains out, I aim to go to Wilmington. I got business there."

"What sort of business?"

Judson briefly considered telling Howard about his spying mission, but decided against it. "I got me a bone to chew with that nigger-lovin' Captain McKay."

"'Bout what?'"

"I'm itchin' to settle with him for the way he got us arrested an' for takin' that nigger kid's word over ours." The more Judson thought about how they were treated the angrier he became. "He had no call to treat us that'a way. No call at all."

Howard was quiet. Suddenly he smiled and said, "Know what I'm gonna do when we get free?"

"Uh-uh."

"I'm goin' to get me another puppy."

"That's nice, Howard."

"Then I'm goin' to Wilmington with you 'cause we're friends. Ain't we, Judd?"

Judson smiled, patting his friend on the shoulder. "You betcha, Howard."

A Neanderthal-like sergeant awakened Judson before dawn screaming at the top of his lungs for everybody to fall-in outside. The mess wagons had arrived, and the servers were ready to feed the prisoners. He rolled out of his blanket and sat for a minute on the dirt floor of the tent, studying his surroundings as the sleep left his brain. Scores of men lay on the ground in various stages of coming awake. Howard sat up a few feet away, yawning.

After they had eaten, the prisoners were assigned numbers and marched seven miles to the outskirts of Petersburg, Virginia. They marched single-file down the main road, which hadn't seen any traffic in months, carrying a flag of truce. The landscape appeared as a large wound in the earth, pockmarked with gaping, muddy holes, and torn and broken trees. The procession passed thousands of Federal soldiers who were curiously watching from their trenches. These entrenchments were unlike anything these men had ever seen before. They had a sense of permanence about them with their shored-up sides made of logs, and they were dotted here and there with artillery batteries.

Half a mile in the distance, the Confederate earthworks bristled with row upon row of lethal-looking *chevaux-de-frise,* sharpened stakes used as infantry obstacles. A column of men came down the shell-cratered road to meet them. Those in front wore Confederate gray, carrying a similar flag of truce. Behind them came hundreds of ragged Union prisoners. A chorus of cheers arose from behind Judson when the Federal soldiers saw their captured comrades.

The two companies stopped several hundred feet apart, and six officers from each group met halfway between them to negotiate the exchange. When all was in order, a Federal sergeant began calling out numbers, and one-by-one each prisoner came forward and gave him his name when his number was called. The Confederate soldiers repeated the procedure. As the men were exchanged, they were checked off a ledger by both sides.

The gaunt prisoners, many of them missing limbs, staggered forward in pairs to support one another. Occasionally three came forward together, the one in the middle being dragged by the other two, or several would carry a blanket on which lay a friend unable to walk or stand. A doctor and stretcher bearers stood ready to assist the injured men. Tension was evident in the faces of the officers whenever they witnessed the heartrending displays.

When Judson's number was called, he gave the officers his name and waited for the prisoner they were exchanging him for to step forward. Soon a ragged man being helped by another came limping over to the group. His haunting, sunken eyes stared out from an old man's bearded face, his body so emaciated he probably weighed less than a hundred pounds. Judson wanted to look away, but his eyes were drawn to the skeleton of a man before him. He lingered a moment more, then hurried past the ghostly image of this old/young man who had seen too much of the horrors of war.

As Judson neared the Confederate lines, men rushed forward, gathering around him as if he were a hero. To assume the role, he managed a limp and was helped behind the lines.

Being freed wasn't at all what Judson had expected. It was almost like being in prison again because the Confederate Army detained the men while it debriefed them to find out if anyone was planted as a spy. It was a difficult enough task to check military records for most of the men, but Judson presented a unique problem.

Since he was captured on a blockade-runner, it was necessary to request a report of the incident from the Navy, and a crew list from the company who owned the vessel.

A week later the army released Judson and Howard, and they traveled to Richmond by train. True to his word, Judson went in search of a bawdy-house while his friend looked for another puppy.

As Judson roamed the streets, the sound of honky-tonk piano music lured him into a tavern. Inside, female heads turned, gazing at the new customer and smiling, hoping to get him to join them. Most of the women wore revealing frilly undergarments. Judson nodded to a pretty redhead in a short, black chemise, and the woman sauntered over.

"Hello, stranger. My name is Sybil," she said with a provocative smile.

"Mine's Judd, ma'am," he said, tipping his bowler hat.

"What's your pleasure, Judd?"

"First I'd like to have me a drink, then how 'bout you an' me go upstairs for a ride?"

"Sure. I'd love to," she said, motioning to the bartender. "What'll you have?"

Judson slapped the bar. "Give me some of the best whiskey you got. I want to celebrate."

She sat on a barstool, crossing her legs and lighting a cigarette. "Oh? What are you celebrating?"

"Freedom, ma'am. I just got paroled from a Yankee prison."

"You were a prisoner of war?" she asked astounded.

The bartender brought over a bottle and poured a glass of whiskey. Nodding his thanks, Judson said, "Yes, ma'am. I sure was."

"Well, this is an honor. I'll have to show you a real good time."

"Thank you, ma'am. Been a while since I had me a good time."

When Judson finished his drink, Sybil took him by the arm and led him upstairs to a vacant room. He turned away from her as he undressed.

"Don't be modest, honey. Let me help you," she said coming around and unbuttoning his pants.

Her sharp intake of breath, when she saw how small he was, made Judson snap sharply, "What's the matter? Ain't I man enough for you?"

"No, it isn't that, honey. You surprised me is all."

"I was injured," he lied. "I took a Yankee ball in the groin at Cold Harbor. It messed things up real bad down there."

"Oh, you poor thing! Let mama take care of it for you," she cooed, pushing him toward the bed.

When he was unable to perform, Sybil lay on the bed, stroking his chest. "Don't worry, honey. It happens to the best of them. I've been with a lot of men, so believe me, I know."

A humiliated Judson frowned, complaining bitterly, "Fuckin' war! The mechanics of nature don't work worth a damn anymore."

She smiled sweetly, touching his arm and said, "We can try again if you'd like. Why don't you just lie back, and let Sybil do all the work?"

Someone knocked on the door, and Sybil put on a robe to answer it. It was a friend, and she went into the hall so they could talk in private.

Judson heard another woman's voice, then soft laughter. An immense hatred raged inside him. He knew they were talking about him.

When Sybil returned, he said, "I know what'll get me excited."

Loosening her robe, she asked, "What's that?"

"Tying you to the bed."

"Whatever you want, honey. Only don't tie me too tight."

"I won't," he promised.

"What are you going to use for ropes?" she asked.

Judson looked around. "The belt from your robe looks long enough."

She untied her belt and gave it to him.

"Now take off the rest of your clothes, an' lay on the bed."

Sybil shed her garment and did as he instructed. He raised her arms, tying both of her wrists to the headboard.

"Hey! Not so tight!" she complained.

155

"You want to please me, don't you?"

"Well, yeah. But take it easy."

Judson tore the top sheet off the bed, ripping it into strips.

"You'll have to pay for that," she snapped.

"Uh-uh. I don't have to pay for a damned thing," he said, as he spread her legs wide, tying them to the posts at the foot of the bed. "But you're goin' to pay right now for laughin' at me." He used the remaining strips of torn bed sheet to reinforce the restraints to her wrists, leaving just enough play to enable her to squirm for his delight.

As Sybil lay sprawled in her nudity across the bed, Judson decided it was time to show Sybil who really was in control. He clenched his large hand into a fist, smashing it into her face. As Sybil lay moaning and dazed, he pulled his handkerchief from his back pocket and crammed it into her mouth, securing it with a piece of his sweaty undershirt which he tied around her head. Sybil struggled frantically to reach the alarm cord which hung near the head of the bed--a device which was used to signal the bouncers downstairs in case of trouble. She began crying in muffled agony as the restraints cut into her wrists.

Amused, Judson picked up the end of the alarm cord, dangling it just beyond her grasp. "Is this what you're after?" he asked, teasing her.

Sybil's eyes grew wide with fright as she fought harder to grab the cord. Judson continued to tease her. "What's the matter? Did I tie your ropes too tightly?"

Sybil fought desperately as she tried to pull her hands free. All the while Judson tormented her by tickling her fingertips with the end of the cord. "Here it is! Be quick now."

Sybil lunged in a final futile effort to seize the cord, then squeezed her eyes tightly shut, sobbing uncontrollably.

Judson, grinning broadly, showing missing and decayed teeth, said in a sinister tone, "Say bye-bye to the cord; you won't be needing it anymore." He tied the alarm cord to the handle on the window sash, far from Sybil's reach.

Judson stood next to the bed, gazing down at her. "You look real fine, Sybil. But somethin's missin'."

He hopped off the bed and inspected the items on her dressing table: a looking-glass, hair brush, the usual assortment of creams and perfumes. Nothing caught his attention. The chair beside the table had heavy wooden legs with ball and claw feet. He smashed it against the brass bed frame until it lay in pieces on the floor. One of the legs had a splintered end, and he picked it up excitedly. Here was the instrument he was searching for.

Judson was so drained by his sexual release he fell into a blissful sleep. Jerking awake, Judson surveyed the room. Sybil's lifeless body lay on the blood-soaked mattress like a butchered animal on a sacrificial altar. The sight repulsed him, yet he could feel himself becoming aroused. The events of that evening came to mind, her helplessness, and his incredible pleasure exacting revenge for what women had done to him in the past.

There was a pan of water on the dresser and Judson cleaned himself up. He pulled on his trousers, examining the remnants of his shredded undershirt. Irritated it was reduced to rags, he donned his shirt.

Quietly he opened the door a crack to see if anyone was in the hallway. It was deserted, so he slipped out of the room, creeping down the stairway. By now the bawdy-hall was filled to capacity with boisterous patrons, each hoping for an evening of pleasure with one of the scantily dressed ladies of the evening. Judson was confident his footsteps on the staircase were muffled by the carefree sounds of piano music which filled the room and spilled into the street. The room stank with a mixture of stale beer and sweat and was permeated with heavy smoke which provided the perfect cover for Judson as he made a quick exit out a side door. Once outside, Judson went down the alley and around to the front of the brothel. He found Howard sitting on the planked walk playing with a small puppy.

"Hey, Howard," Judson called.

Howard swung around with a smile on his face. The puppy cocked his head quizzically to see what all the excitement was about.

"Hey Judd, I've been waitin' for you."

Judson held his arms wide, grinning. "Well, here I am."

Howard picked up the puppy, cradling it like a baby. "This here's Rascal. I saw this litter of six puppies, an' the owner said I could have one."

Judson's smile vanished. "We ain't takin' no dog to Wilmington, Howard."

"Why not?" Howard asked with a sinking heart.

"'Cause he'll be fussin' the whole time."

Howard rose, still holding the puppy. "But, Judd, he won't make a sound. You won't even know he's around."

"Look, Howard, either he stays, or you ain't goin'."

The big man smiled sweetly at the puppy in his arms. "Judd says I can't take you with me, Rascal. You go home to your mama now, you hear." He set the puppy down and walked away without looking back.

Rascal stared after him confused, wondering if this was another game.

Judson patted his friend on the back. "Now you're talkin' sense, Howard. Let's you an' me check the train schedule."

They hadn't walked more than ten steps when the puppy began jumping on Howard, crying to be picked up. Judson scowled and kicked the dog, and the puppy yelped and fell in the dirt.

Howard exploded. He snatched a startled Judson off the ground, shaking him violently in the air. "Don't you ever hurt Rascal again, or I'll hurt you!"

For the first time Judson became frightened of Howard. He grinned nervously at the big man. "Settle down. I was only funnin'. We can take the dog with us."

Howard eased Judson to the ground, asking wide eyed, "You mean that?"

Judson's confidence was returning. He felt in control again. "Of course I do. But the minute he puts up a fuss, he goes."

158

Howard was so happy he couldn't sit still. He hopped from one foot to the other, clapping his hands. "He won't make a fuss, Judd. I promise he won't."

"All right then. Fetch the damn dog."

CHAPTER 10

A carriage stopped at the wharf alongside the *Atlantis*, and Captain McKay and Elias emerged from the cab loaded down with packages from their shopping excursion ashore. As they boarded the ship, the boatswain emerged from the engine room hatch.

"I have a message for you, sir. It's marked urgent."

McKay put the envelope in his pocket. "Thank you, Mr. Gallagher. I'll be in my cabin if anyone needs me." He gave several packages to Elias, and said, "Take these to Cookie, and see if he has any chores for you."

When McKay was seated at his desk, he opened the note and saw Brooke had purchased a ticket that morning to travel on his ship. During the voyage from Wilmington he had practiced what to say to her when they met, but now the words he had prepared so carefully eluded him. As he tried to recall them, there was a knock at the door. "Come in."

The chief engineer, his face puffy and glistening with sweat, entered wearing his characteristic red suspenders and baggy, grease-stained pants. "I think I've got that problem licked, sir. I've replaced some parts, and the engine's running like new."

"That's wonderful news, Chief." McKay noticed the engineer's disheveled appearance and was afraid he might have been too demanding. "I hope I haven't worked you too hard. You do understand your task was vital to the safety of this ship?"

The engineer smiled. "Yes, sir. Don't give it another thought. I love messing with engines, and having a problem to solve makes it all the more interesting."

"Good. Let's check those engines," McKay said, standing up.

The men made their way to the paddle-wheel box and listened while the engines were running.

"You're amazing, Chief. I don't hear the ticking anymore," McKay said astounded. "Get the ship ready to sail on the evening tide."

Later that afternoon Captain McKay greeted Brooke Snow and Peter Reynolds as they came aboard the *Atlantis*. "Brooke, you look wonderful! England must agree with you."

"The country is beautiful," she said, "but if I'm aglow it's because I have wonderful news. I'm Burgess and Linden's new Wilmington agent."

McKay beamed. "That is wonderful news. Congratulations."

"Thank you. Oh, Wade, I want you to meet a friend," she said, turning to Peter and placing a hand on his arm. "This is Peter Reynolds. He'll be sailing to Wilmington with us."

McKay noticed her gesture and wondered if it had any special meaning. "Delighted to meet you, Mr. Reynolds," he said, extending his hand.

Peter shook it, and said, "Thank you, Captain. The pleasure is all mine."

"Are you going to Wilmington on business?"

"No. Actually I live in Atlanta, but General Sherman has made it impossible for me to go home."

"I'm afraid I have bad news then," McKay said. "Atlanta surrendered to Union forces on September third."

"That can't be!" Peter Reynolds moaned. "My family's there."

Brooke turned to comfort the distraught man. "I'm sure they're all right, Peter. The army won't harm civilians."

"I wish I could believe that."

"It's true," McKay said. "If anything, it'll probably ease their situation. Contrary to what you might have heard, the Federal Army

161

is not made up of barbarians. I'm sure they'll give the people of Atlanta whatever food and medicine they need."

Peter shook his head, moaning, "It's all my fault. I shouldn't have left them alone!"

"Don't blame yourself," Brooke said. "You had no way of knowing."

"Yes, I did. In wartime anything can happen. Now my family is being held prisoner."

McKay placed a hand on Peter's shoulder. "Mr. Reynolds, please try and calm yourself. Why don't you go to the galley and have some coffee while we prepare your room?"

Peter nodded, and Brooke led him to the galley while the captain went to get the ship's doctor.

The *Atlantis* got underway that evening beneath an overcast sky while a fifteen-five-knot wind blew out of the north.

Throughout dinner, McKay kept a close eye on Brooke and Peter. He wasn't comfortable sharing her attentions with another man.

"So, Mr. Reynolds, what do you do?" asked McKay, being careful to keep the conversation away from the surrender of Atlanta.

Peter was sipping a glass of red wine, then set it down. "I'm with the Confederate Ordinance Bureau, Captain. My job demands I travel to Europe to purchase supplies for our military. I wouldn't doubt that some of the cargo on this ship is aboard due to my efforts."

McKay nodded. "That's probably true. Perhaps you can help a friend of mine and do the South a great service."

Peter was cutting a piece of beef and looked up. "Oh?"

"The last time I put in at Fort Fisher I spoke with Colonel Lamb, and he mentioned the Ordinance Bureau is slow to send him the materials he needs. I thought you might look into it."

"Certainly, Captain. I'll do what I can."

McKay turned, and said, "So, Brooke, you haven't told me anything about your job."

She smiled, lowering her fork. A black silk hair net held her auburn hair in place, and she was wearing a sapphire-blue, velvet bolero jacket edged with ribbon and decorated with silver beads. "When I spoke to Mr. Burgess, he politely told me he wouldn't hire a woman. He said they were frowned upon in the business world."

"They are," McKay agreed. "How did you convince him otherwise?"

"I gave him some of my ideas."

McKay reached for his water, taking a sip. "Which are?"

"I told him I have the support of father's business associates. I also told him about an idea I have to ease speculation."

"Really?" McKay asked, intrigued. "How do you intend doing that?"

"By dividing the cargo at auction into smaller lots," she explained. "It would give more people a chance to bid. The way it is now, two or three speculators buy the entire cargo."

"I see, but what's to prevent these same men from buying all the small lots?"

"Not a thing," Brooke admitted, "but it might give others a chance where they had none before."

"It sounds good in theory, but will it work as intended?" McKay asked.

"I think it will with a little fine tuning," she said.

Cookie placed a platter of his specially prepared tuna steaks on the table, and McKay helped himself.

After an eating silence, Brooke asked, "What do you think of my idea, Peter?"

"What?" He looked surprised, then embarrassed. "I'm sorry. My mind was elsewhere. When you mentioned fine tuning, I thought of our piano at home. My wife would play the most marvelous songs. Once a week we would gather in the parlor, around the piano, and sing. I'd hold my little girls on my lap, and they'd join in, too." His eyes took on a tortured look. "Now, I may never know that joy again." He glanced around tearfully. "Excuse me for going on so. I think I need some fresh air."

Peter folded his napkin, and the others watched him leave in silence.

* * * *

A soft rain pelted the bridge during McKay's watch that night. While gazing through the water droplets on the window, he puzzled over what he might say to Brooke when they were alone. McKay had intended to tell her of his love when she came aboard, but with Peter Reynolds always by her side, finding the proper time was difficult.

When the boatswain came to relieve him, McKay looked at his pocket watch and saw it was a little before midnight. Thinking Brooke might still be up and they might have a chance to talk, he pulled on his cap and went to her cabin. Before he got there, he saw Peter Reynolds at Brooke's door talking with her. To McKay's amazement, Peter went inside and closed the door.

Brooke Snow was sitting at her desk writing a thank you letter to Jason Burgess for selecting her as his new agent when a knock on the door broke her train of thought.

"Who is it?"

"It's Peter Reynolds. I need to speak with you."

"Let me get my shawl, then we can go for a walk."

"It's raining outside. Can I come in?"

"All right. Just a minute," she said, glancing in the mirror to make sure she was presentable, then opening the door.

Peter stood in the rain clutching a doll in each hand, obviously upset. "These were for my two little girls," he said, holding the dolls out for her to see. "I can't give them to my daughters now. I don't even know if they're alive. What am I going to do, Brooke?"

"Come inside, Peter, before you get soaked."

Peter tramped in, clutching the dolls and pacing back and forth.

Brooke was nervous. She was alone and could smell alcohol on the man's breath. She had never let a man in her bedroom before, let alone someone she had just met only a short time ago. "Peter, you mustn't let yourself become so upset."

"I can't help it. I can't sleep. Whenever I think about my little girls, I see them crying in the street, and no one is there to comfort them."

"Why don't you see Cookie, and he'll fix something to help you sleep," Brooke said, remembering the strong tea the cook had given her when she was seasick. The potent concoction had knocked her out for nearly a day.

"I just need someone to talk to. Someone who cares."

Brooke's eyes softened. "I care, and I'll listen, if that's what you want."

He sat on the bed, collecting his thoughts. "I guess the reason why I feel so terrible is I'm supposed to be responsible for their safety. I should never have left them in the first place. It's inexcusable for a father to do that."

"Why don't you go home when we reach Wilmington? Even if you're captured, you could probably find out if your family's safe."

"I've thought of that, but I can't bring myself to do it! I guess I'm just a coward."

"I don't think you're a coward. It took great courage to say what you just did."

Shaking his head, Peter said, "No, it didn't! I'm just a weakling cowering in a woman's room, afraid to show my face." He sat on her bed, hanging his head in despair. "I hate this terrible war so much I'd do anything to end it."

Brooke had no idea his depression had become so serious. "I'm going to get the doctor."

Peter reached out for her. "No! Please don't leave me!"

"Maybe a sedative would help calm you," she suggested.

"Just hold me," he begged, staring into her eyes. His pleading face was streaked with tears. "I need to have the security of someone's arms around me."

She sat beside him and held him, soothing his fears and rocking him like a baby.

After a while, Peter fell asleep.

*   *   *   *

"Evenin', ma'am."

Amber, who was socializing with the customers at the bar in the Green Parrot, turned her head to see who it was. The short man had brown hair slicked down with perfumed Macassar oil and sideburns which extended down into a beard. He held a black bowler hat in his hands.

"Hello. My name is Amber," she said, extending her hand.

"Mine's Judson, ma'am." He shook her hand, then pointed behind him. "This here's my friend Howard."

Amber glanced past him, smiling. "Hello, Howard."

He tipped his hat, and Rascal peeked out from under his coat. "Evenin', ma'am."

She leaned back against the bar. "You boys must be new here."

"Not exactly. I left here on a blockade-runner last July, but it was captured. We were just paroled from a Yankee prison."

"A war hero, huh?"

"If that's what a hero is. Yes, ma'am," Judson said, smiling.

"What brings you to town?"

Lafayette Baker had told Judson to meet a man at this tavern. He would not tell him who he was, but the Secret Service man had given him a small patriotic pin to wear. "I got business with General Bragg," Judson said.

"I read in the paper he'd been assigned to command the Wilmington Military District. I don't believe he's in town yet, though."

Looking around, Howard asked, "Ma'am, where do they keep the parrot?"

"The what?"

"The green parrot they advertised out front."

Amber stifled a laugh. "We don't have any bird, honey. That's just the name of this tavern."

"Oh," Howard said, looking perplexed and petting the puppy in his coat.

"So why don't we go upstairs for a while?" Judson asked.

"Sure, honey. Anything you want," Amber said getting off the bar stool.

At that moment, a huge man with a wiry black beard grabbed her from behind and spun her around. "Hey, Amber. How's my favorite girl?"

She broke into a grin when she saw who it was. "Hello, Shawn! Where have you been?"

"Down at Smithville. They're buildin' a small fort there to protect the river."

"Oh, Shawn, this here is Judson and Howard," she said, indicating the two men. "They're new to Wilmington."

Shawn extended his big hand, grinning. "Pleased to meet you. Where you boys from?"

Judson shook hands with the man. "Hampton Roads, Virginia."

Shawn nodded. "Good people there. You a fisherman?"

"Nah, I never had enough money to buy a boat, so I worked in a fish market. When the war began, I came to Wilmington lookin' to hire on a blockade-runner. I heard that's where the money was."

"You heard right. But I guess I don't need to tell you it's not what it used to be. The blockade has gotten so strong a man takes his life in his hands every time he goes beyond the river."

"The Yankees captured Judson, but he was just released from prison," Amber said.

Shawn scratched his beard and said, "That a fact?"

"Yes, sir. They paroled me about two weeks ago."

"I'll bet you got a right good tale to tell. Well, you got to tell me all about it sometime." Shawn glanced at Amber and gave her a playful squeeze. "Right now, this little lady an' me got business to take care of. Ain't that right, darlin'?"

Amber grinned playfully, then frowned. "I'd love to, but Judson asked me first."

Judson smiled good-naturedly and said with a wave of his hand, "You go ahead. I'm s'posed to meet a friend pretty soon."

"You sure?" Amber asked, her arms intertwined with Shawn's.

Judson nodded. "Yeah, you two have a good time. I'll get me a drink and wait for my friend."

Judson watched them leave, admiring how Amber jiggled in all the right places every time she moved. Her lush body created a desire in him which needed to be satiated. He looked at the other girls and didn't find any that were as appealing, so he went to the tavern across the street. Howard said he had to feed Rascal and went in search of a restaurant.

Loud piano music beckoned Judson to enter the smoke-filled establishment. In front were tables filled with people playing cards or talking. To the left a half dozen girls were dancing on stage, throwing their dresses into the air, being ogled by some boisterous men in the first several rows of tables. Judson weaved through the throngs of people coming and going, finally making it to the crowded bar. A blonde girl in a blue dress caught his eye as she walked by, and he followed her to the end of the bar.

"Evenin', ma'am," Judson said, taking off his hat. "My name's Judson. I just had to tell you that I watched you sashay by, and you're the prettiest gal I've seen in a long time."

She gave him a warm smile. "Thank you, Judson. I'm Iris."

"If you don't mind my company, ma'am, I'd like to skip the preliminaries an' go right upstairs."

"I couldn't think of anything I'd like better," she said, taking him by the hand.

When they were in the room, she turned to Judson and asked, "What would you like?"

He took some rope from his pocket, dangling it in front of her. "If you don't mind, there's a game I'd like to play."

"Oh, I like games!" she said.

Judson's lips curved into a smile. "Good. Because you'll love this."

Judson rolled off the dead girl and felt the cooling mixture of blood and semen against his genitals. Iris lay beside him, her hands and feet tied to the bedposts. He retrieved the ivory handled knife from between her legs and tasted their combined juices on the blade. The salty taste thrilled him like nothing ever had before.

* * * *

The next morning at breakfast, McKay saw Brooke and Peter Reynolds come into the small dining room together.

"Good morning. I trust everyone slept well," McKay said.

"Yes, I did, Captain," Peter Reynolds replied, glancing at Brooke. "It took a while, but I eventually managed to get some sleep."

McKay wanted to make a snide remark, but thought better of it. "Good for you. How about you, Brooke?"

Cookie poured her some coffee, and she took the mug gratefully. "Very well, Captain. I think the ocean air helps."

McKay hoped Brooke would mention the night before. He needed an explanation as to why Peter was in her cabin at such a late hour.

"Yes. It does," he admitted. "I also find the motion of the sea and the sound of the waves very restful."

"So tell me, Captain McKay. How did you sleep?" Brooke asked, adding some cream and sugar to her coffee.

"Not well. Something was troubling me."

"Does it concern our voyage?" Peter asked with concern. He was buttering a biscuit and looked up.

McKay considered telling him what he had seen when it occurred to him that might not be wise. Brooke had never told him she cared. She probably still blamed him for her father's death. He chose something else to discuss. "It might. I'm troubled by the naval blockade. It's growing stronger every month."

"Brooke assured me if anyone could get us to Wilmington safely, it was you," Peter said, glancing at her.

McKay saw Brooke smile at him self-consciously.

"I have every confidence in your abilities, Captain," Brooke said.

"Thank you for your trust, Miss Snow. I hope I can live up to your expectations."

"I know you will. You haven't disappointed me yet."

McKay smiled mechanically, thinking to himself, *If only I could say the same about you.* "By the way, Miss Snow. The police have arrested the man who murdered your father."

Brooke stopped cutting her ham and looked up. "They have? That's wonderful news!"

"Yes, it is. Seems this man tried to rob your father's office, but was scared off before he could take any money. All he got was a walking stick. A bit of bad luck for him because it linked him to the crime."

Brooke felt foolish for blaming Wade for her father's death. She made a mental note to apologize when they could be alone.

McKay tapped the glass on the bridge's barometer and saw it had fallen to nine hundred and ninety-seven millibars. He entered the new reading into the ship's log, then went outside to check the wind. Driving rain lashed at him when he opened the door, and he could hear the wind howling in the rigging. The enraged waves of the slate-gray sea leaped twelve feet into the air to form whitecaps and mix their blowing spray with the sheets of rain.

After determining the direction and velocity of the wind from the anemometer, he noted with apprehension it had increased to forty-three knots and blew from the south-southeast. Some of the worst storms and hurricanes had occurred in September and had come from the same direction. He was uneasy being this far from land if they were in for a serious blow. As he turned to put the anemometer away, he saw Brooke stagger across the pitching deck toward him. He put the instrument in its box and went to her aid.

"Brooke, it's too rough on deck. Please stay inside."

"I had to see you," she shouted so she could be heard above the wind.

McKay also wanted to talk to her. They needed to seek shelter, but he did not feel comfortable with so many people in the bridge. "Let's go to my cabin," he said, placing a protective arm around her.

They clung to each other for support, until they were inside his cabin behind the pilothouse.

"What was it you wanted to talk about?" he asked, unfastening the gold buttons on his damp, blue coat.

"I want to apologize for blaming you for my father's death," she said, taking off the dripping wet shawl and shaking it out.

"I can understand why you'd believe I was guilty. But it still hurt to think you could even suspect me."

Grasping his hand, Brooke said, "I know, Wade, and I'm sorry. Can you ever forgive me?"

He frowned, wondering why Peter went to her room last night.

Brooke was saddened because he still seemed angry with her. "What's the matter, Wade? When we sailed to Nassau, you wanted to mend things between us. Now you act like that's the farthest thing from your mind."

He became surprised. "I'm acting different? How about you?"

"What do you mean?"

"You know very well. First you've been overly friendly with Peter, then you let him into your room last night."

Brooke's jaw dropped. "You were spying on me?"

"No, I wasn't. I just happened to see him at your door when I left the bridge, and don't change the subject."

"I suppose when you leave the bridge it takes you by my cabin?" she said, crossing her arms.

McKay became flustered. "No, it doesn't. I went there because I needed to speak with you."

Her gaze softened. "You did? About what?"

He shook his head in irritation. "There you go changing the subject again."

"No, I'm not. I'm just curious."

McKay hesitated, unsure how to proceed. "Very well. I wanted to tell you about your father and discuss our relationship."

"Ah-ha!" Brooke said. "I knew something else was troubling you. I didn't believe that story about the naval blockade for a minute."

"You're very observant."

She moved closer, taking his hands in hers. "I'm observant because I care about you."

Suddenly words didn't seem powerful enough to convey the overwhelming feeling McKay had for Brooke. He gathered her into his arms, kissing her like he had dreamed of doing for so long.

Just then the deck heaved, and it took McKay a moment to realize this erratic movement was due to the storm-tossed ocean. His years of training as a sea captain took over. Reluctantly releasing Brooke, he said, "I'm sorry to leave you, dear, but I have to see to the ship."

Brooke gazed into his eyes, whispering, "I know you must. Hurry back to me, my darling."

The intoxicating nearness of her inspired him to kiss her again. The touch of her lingered on his lips as he rushed out the door.

As McKay fought to the wheel house against the wind-driven spray, it occurred to him he never found out what Peter was doing in Brooke's cabin the night before. When he got to the bridge, he found the boatswain directing the quartermaster as monstrous waves crashed into the bow, sweeping the windows with foaming water. "What is our situation, Mr. Gallagher?"

"I'm trying to keep the ship headed into the seas, sir, but the waves keep turning us broadside."

McKay nodded, analyzing their plight. He noticed the bow was pounding into the waves and called down to the engine room to reduce speed. The strain on the hull could also be eased by keeping the ship at an angle to the seas, thus providing more support. "Quartermaster, I want you to steer forty-five degrees to the waves so our bow cuts into them on an angle."

Before the man could turn the spoked wheel, a mighty wall of water picked up the stern like a giant hand, shoving the ship forward. The bow rose on the crest of the wave for a long moment, then plunged into the gaping trough before it. The prow buried itself into the sea, and the ship appeared certain to descend to the depths, when it rose again, flinging spray its entire length.

McKay crashed against the binnacle with a force that left him breathless. He swung around and saw the quartermaster paralyzed with fear, clutching the wheel. To prevent the ship from capsizing when the next towering wave crashed on top of them, McKay pushed the terrified man aside, spinning the wheel to port.

The maneuver wasn't quick enough, and the ship was flung like a toy by the next gigantic wave. Tons of foaming water smashed the windows, and the bridge creaked as if it were going to be ripped from the deck. Everything loose in the pilothouse was thrown to starboard, and McKay clung to the wheel to keep from being swept into the bulkhead or out the door. He looked to his right and saw nothing but the infuriated sea as the ship continued its sickening roll. At this point the wheel was useless as a navigational aid, but McKay maintained his grip on it, hoping the ship would recover.

For the longest time the *Atlantis* lay on her side, then ever-so-slowly she began to right herself. When she was nearly straight and level, another wave crashed down on them, burying her starboard rail into the sea. Water gushed through every opening on the starboard side of the bridge. Each time the ship was thrown on her beam-ends she recovered more slowly, as if taking half of the ocean with her. When she finally did right herself, the water flowed out of the doorway. The boatswain released his grip on the binnacle, looking through the window. He saw the wave had tossed the *Atlantis* exactly where Captain McKay had wanted it.

Grasping the speaking tube with both hands, McKay hollered down to the engine room. "Mr. Reichman, is everything all right down there?"

There was no answer. McKay fought to control his emotions as he felt his ship slipping away from him. "Mr. Reichman?"

A small voice answered. "I'm here, sir. I been tossed around the engine room like a child's ball."

"How are things?"

"Well, sir, I haven't had time to check, but from what I can see some coal has spilled from the bunkers. I'm worried some of it may get in the bilge pumps and clog them. A few of my men got bounced around pretty good. However, it doesn't look like their injuries are anything serious."

"That's good. How are the engines?"

"They appear to be all right, sir. I'll know more in a few minutes, though."

"All right. Keep me informed."

"I will, sir."

McKay felt they had a fighting chance since the ship still had power. If he could maintain their position to the seas, they might escape without further damage. "Mr. Gallagher, keep an eye on the waves behind us. Let me know if they start to gain on us."

The boatswain rushed to the doorway, looking out. No more than a minute later he said, "A monstrous wave is coming behind us, sir."

"Quartermaster, take the wheel." McKay grabbed the speaking tube to the engine room. "All ahead flank, Mr. Reichman!"

A shudder passed through the deck as the engines increased their tempo and the paddle wheels surged ahead. McKay hurried to peer over the boatswain's shoulder and saw a wall of green water bearing down on them. All he could manage to say was, "God, help us!"

Precious minutes later the wave began to recede as their speed checked its advance.

McKay slapped the boatswain on the back, grinning. "Good job, Mr. Gallagher."

"Thank you, sir."

For the next few hours McKay monitored the ship's progress, adjusting the speed when necessary. When the barometer began to rise, and it appeared they were leaving the hurricane behind them, McKay turned over command of the bridge to his boatswain and went to check on Brooke. He found her in her berth, very pale and seasick. Although he wanted to find out what Peter Reynolds was doing in her cabin the night before, he put his own concerns aside. Getting a cup of tea from the galley, he went to her cabin and sat at her bedside while she drank it.

"Wade, I don't want you to see me like this. I must look awful," Brooke said, struggling to get up.

McKay pushed her back. "Nonsense. You're beautiful. Besides, you need someone to take care of you. Drink your tea now."

Brooke smiled, sipping from the cup he handed her. It was wonderful to have someone watch over her. Just like her daddy did when she was a little girl. She fell asleep a short while later, and McKay quietly let himself out.

The hurricane had performed a miracle. The Federal fleet had sailed up to Beaufort to ride out the storm in the safety of the harbor, leaving the ocean off Fort Fisher free of any blockading vessels.

For the first time the *Atlantis* was allowed to sail into the Cape Fear River without any interference.

An anxious crowd had gathered on the wharf to watch the *Atlantis* dock. The strange mixture of humanity represented every level of the social structure in Wilmington. There were shabbily dressed workmen, and men in high-crowned hats and frocked coats with ladies in colorful crinolines, holding parasols.

When the gangplank was in place, Virginia Drake rushed aboard. She found Captain McKay, throwing her arms around him. "Oh, Wade, I'm so glad you're safe!"

McKay was taken aback. "Thank you, Virginia. Ah, John Gallagher is in the pilothouse, and I'm sure he'll be eager to see you."

Virginia gazed up at him, tears of joy in her eyes. "Don't you know it's you I love? When I heard about the storm, all I could think of was you."

McKay pushed away from her, stepping out of the way as a stream of people came aboard the ship. Now the *Atlantis* was in port, the deck became a flurry of activity. Workmen were removing the battens from the forward hatch so they could begin unloading the cargo.

"I'm flattered, Virginia. But I . . .I don't love you. John does, and he's a fine man."

She moved closer, grabbing his arm. "Not as fine as you."

Pushing her hand away, McKay said, "Look, Virginia, you need to understand there has never been anything between us, and there never will be."

Virginia's eyes grew moist. "A girl can hope, can't she?"

Brooke, emerging from her cabin just in time to see the two of them together and called to the other woman. "Oh, Virginia!"

"Yes?"

"Could you come here for a minute? I need to speak with you."

Virginia sauntered over to where Brooke was standing.

Placing her hands on her hips, Brooke said, "Look, Virginia, I know what you're doing. Either you stay away from Wade, or I'll tell the ladies at the Society what you've been up to."

"Why, Brooke, whatever do you mean?"

"You know very well. No decent woman would go to Paddy's Hollow and do the things you do."

"And you mean to tell them?" Virginia's eyes widened as she thought of the effects that would have. She hated the idea of Brooke having something over her.

"They won't hear it from me if you do what I say."

"Is that a threat?"

Brooke's gaze turned cold. "No. It's a promise."

Virginia tilted her head and said, "I'll think about it, Brooke. By the way, have you seen John Gallagher?"

"He's probably on the bridge. You'd do well to spend more time with him. Maybe some of his principles will wear off on you."

"Thank you, but I don't need your advice," Virginia said in a huff, stalking off.

McKay came over to Brooke with a grin. "You look well after your encounter with Virginia. What did she want?"

Brooke's lips curved into a smile. "We needed to straighten out a few things--woman-to-woman."

"Oh? Am I allowed to ask what they were about?"

Brooke's smile turned mysterious. "I'd rather you didn't." Her eyes softened, and she took Wade's hand. "Thank you for taking care of me yesterday."

"You're welcome. Oh, by the way," he said, handing her some papers. "This is your first official duty as Burgess and Linden's agent."

"What are these?"

"They are two copies of the cargo manifest. Keep one for yourself and take the other to the auctioneer you hire. I suggest Mr. Wilkes Morris, he's the best in the business. Tell him about your idea to divide the cargo into smaller lots. He works for you, so he'll listen."

"Thank you. Lord knows I need as much help as I can get," Brooke said with a laugh.

Peter Reynolds strolled over, looking confident and in control for someone who had just been through such a harrowing ordeal.

"Hello, Peter," McKay said. "As a member of the Ordinance Bureau, I have a copy of the cargo manifest for you."

"Thank you, Captain," he said, looking it over. "I trust the military supplies will be unloaded first."

"Of course. I'll give instructions they should be taken to the railroad depot, if that's all right with you."

"Yes, it is, Captain. Where can I go to wire the Bureau of my arrival?"

McKay gestured to the Northeast. "You'll need to go to the telegraph office at Front and Market."

Brooke said, "Oh, Peter, before you go, would you come to dinner at my house this evening? Captain McKay will be there too."

"I'd be delighted. What time?"

"Around seven. Is that all right?"

He smiled, nodding. "Sure. Can I bring anything? Some wine perhaps?"

Brooke shook her head. "No. Just yourself."

When Brooke had finished giving him the directions to her house, McKay said, "I wasn't aware I was invited to dinner."

"Of course you are. I want to see you, but since I've been away for over a month, I need to spend this evening with my mother. This way I can be with both of you at the same time."

"But why did you invite Peter?"

Brooke grew serious. "He's new in town, and I feel sorry for him because of what happened to his family."

McKay hesitated, unsure of how he should proceed. "Speaking of Peter, what was he doing in your room the night before last?"

Brooke had wondered when Wade would ask her about this. She chose her words carefully. "He was upset about his family and wanted to talk. I let him in because it was raining."

"All you did was talk?"

"Yes," Brooke frowned, folding her arms. "You're making me uncomfortable with all these questions."

"I'm sorry. I guess I mistook your being kind to him for affection."

She took his hands in hers, batting her eyes to let him know what she was about to say was meant in fun. "Why, Captain McKay, there's only one man for me, and that man is the captain of the *Atlantis*."

The bar at the Green Parrot tavern was abuzz with details of the prostitute's grisly murder across the street. Judson Bates sat with a glass of Irish whiskey, listening, when a voice asked, "Is that a patriotic pin you're wearing?"

Judson turned, looking at the young man. "Yes, it is."

"I thought so. I've seen some of my friends back home wearing pins just like it. My name is Peter Reynolds. May I join you?"

"Shore. Pull up a chair."

Peter sat and said, "Uncle Lafayette says the war will drag on for another two years. I hope he's wrong."

This was the phrase Secret Service Agent Lafayette Baker said would identify his contact. Judson gave the countersign. "Yes, but if General Lee can hold onto Richmond and mount another invasion in the spring, it may force the North to consider peace."

Peter Reynolds said, "I agree. But enough talk of the war. I'm famished. Have you eaten lunch?"

"No. I haven't," Judson admitted.

"Good. I know a restaurant which serves the best black-market steak along with a superb twenty-year-old burgundy."

The men left the tavern and walked to the Golden Age Restaurant where they were seated at a corner table.

"What am I supposed to do now I'm in Wilmington?" Judson asked.

"Don't ask me anything here," Peter cautioned in a low voice. "I rented a room. We'll go there later and talk."

After the men had eaten, they walked to a shabby boarding house two blocks away. Peter Reynold's room consisted of little more than a single bed and a battered writing table with a kerosene lamp.

"I have been assigned to General Bragg's staff as an advisor," Peter said. "I will appoint you as one of my scouts. On or about December 13th, the North will send sixty ships with about seven thousand men, to try and take Fort Fisher. You are to tell the general you overheard one of the officers talk about the invasion when you were a prisoner."

Judson was confused. "Why would he believe me?"

"He won't. However, when the invasion fleet appears, like you said it would, he'll be inclined to listen to whatever else you have to say. This invasion will be a ruse. After a heavy bombardment and landing troops for an assault, they will turn back saying the fort is too strong to take. This whole plan is merely to feel out the Confederate defenses and to give you credibility with General Bragg."

Judson nodded. "I understand. What happens then?"

"The Federal retreat will further convince General Bragg Fort Fisher is invincible. So when the real attack comes in January, he'll be so flushed with his recent victory he'll be overconfident. You are to help make him believe the fort can't be taken. Then, when the Federal Army makes a landing north of the fort, advise him to keep his troops in reserve so they can protect Wilmington."

Judson could feel a surge of power as they discussed the plans. Pretty soon Fort Fisher would fall, and so would Captain McKay.

When McKay arrived at the Snow residence, he found Peter Reynolds already there. In a sad voice Brooke's friend recalled what life was like in Richmond and Atlanta during the war. McKay took a seat in the parlor, listening quietly. As much as he tried to like the man, something disturbed him about Peter. It wasn't that he saw him as a rival for Brooke's affections. It was something else, something not readily apparent. Perhaps, McKay thought, Peter's odd behavior was due to all the stress the man was under.

A light-skinned Negro servant girl entered the parlor and nodded to Mrs. Snow everything was prepared.

Mrs. Snow led the others to the dining room, where the rich mahogany grain of the table peeked out from under a white lace tablecloth, and five types of colorful fruit filled a Waterford crystal bowl in the center. A score of plates held warm corn muffins, green beans, mashed potatoes, and roasted meat, while red wine and elegant, silverware glinted in the candlelight from two candelabrums. A gray-haired Negro butler stood silently in the shadows, ready to serve the guests anything they desired.

"How did you ever manage this wonderful meal?" Peter asked Mrs. Snow.

She smiled at the compliment, explaining, "Captain McKay was thoughtful enough to bring the beef and wine, while we supplied the fruit and vegetables."

"I was glad to contribute to this wonderful meal," McKay said pleased. "Being a sea captain has its rewards. The most obvious is the excellent pay, but another is the opportunity to purchase items which are difficult to obtain in the states due to the war."

As the meal was being served, Peter announced, "The Bureau told me they didn't have any news of my family."

Voicing her concern, Brooke said, "I'm sorry, Peter. I'm sure they're all right."

"Thank you for saying that. I've tried to convince myself no harm will come to them, but it's difficult."

"When was the last time you heard from them?" Mrs. Snow asked, adjusting the napkin in her lap.

"When I left Atlanta in August."

An uncomfortable silence settled over the table while everyone considered what to say.

"Oh, I nearly forgot," Peter said. "They also informed me I've been reassigned to General Bragg's staff."

"What do you think your duties will be?" Captain McKay asked, picking up his wine glass.

"I'm not sure. I was an advisor to President Jefferson Davis when I was in Richmond. I assume that may be what they have in mind for me here."

McKay changed the subject, addressing everyone at the table, "Has anyone heard about the gruesome murder in Paddy's Hollow?"

Her eyes widening, Brooke set her fork down. "Mother mentioned something about a murder. Didn't you, mother?"

"Yes, but I just heard bits and pieces. I'm sure Captain McKay knows more about it than I do."

Everyone looked expectantly to McKay, and he said, "Well, the other night someone butchered a whore so badly she bled to death."

"Isn't that dreadful? I don't know how those women can expose themselves to such peril," Mrs. Snow said with concern.

"That's the type of life she chose for herself, Mrs. Snow," Peter said in a condescending tone. "I'm sure she was aware of the risks."

McKay resented Peter's remark because his statement made it seem as the victim had a choice. From what he had seen, most women who had become prostitutes didn't have the luxury of choosing. They were forced into that way of life by economics. McKay thought of Amber and wanted to say he knew of a few decent women who were whores, but decorum dictated he remain silent.

"Do the police have any suspects?" Brooke asked.

"No, not yet, but they believe it may have been one of her customers. Whoever it was must have just come in off the street and selected her so quickly nobody remembers him."

"Then it was planned," Brooke surmised.

"Yes. It appears so. That's why you and your mother need to be careful," McKay reminded her. "Two women living in this big house with no man around can be an inviting target for such a fiend."

"I'm sure we'll be safe. Neither of us goes to Paddy's Hollow," she pointed out.

McKay frowned. "I know you don't, but you do go to the riverfront quite often, and there's always a lot of rough characters around."

Brooke's voice took on a defensive tone. "I have no choice. My business takes me there."

"Why don't you go with a friend?" McKay asked her.

"Maybe you can go with Mrs. Grady from next door," her mother suggested.

Brooke knew she was outnumbered, so she relented. "I guess I could."

They ate quietly, then Mrs. Snow asked, "Isn't it a shame about poor Mrs. Greenhow?"

Lowering his water glass, McKay asked, "What happened?"

"You haven't heard?" she asked.

"No. I've been out at sea for nearly a month."

"Well," Mrs. Snow began, "she was collecting money in England for the relief fund. Then she booked passage on the blockade-runner *Condor*, but it ran aground off Fort Fisher. Mrs. Greenhow did not want to get arrested, so she convinced the captain to lower a boat and put her ashore. She put all the gold she had collected in her dress. Well, the boat capsized, and Mrs. Greenhow drowned weighted down by all the gold she was carrying."

"Oh, no! That's terrible," Brooke said shocked.

"How much gold was there?" McKay wanted to know.

"I heard she had $2,000 in gold sovereigns."

"Have they found her body yet?" he asked.

Mrs. Snow nodded. "Yes. They say a soldier from the fort found her when she washed ashore, but the gold was missing."

Everyone shook their heads with disgust and agreed it was a cruel, heartless act for anyone to steal from the dead.

While listening to the table-talk, Peter was recalling the time he and his family had lived in Richmond before they fled to Atlanta. The Union Army had laid siege to the city, and months of incessant gunfire had filled the streets with dying and wounded men. The ravages of war seemed to be everywhere. Ugly trenches ringed the city, and the beautiful countryside was pockmarked with shell craters and stripped of every living thing. Peter grew to hate war so much he vowed to do all he could to end it. It was then he had become a spy for the Union. He would rather see his beloved South fall in defeat now, while there was still something to save, then have her reduced to ashes later.

CHAPTER 11

General Braxton Bragg strolled among the reinforced gun emplacements at Fort Fisher, wondering how the Federal fleet could ever hope to take such a powerful fortification. He suspected Colonel Lamb, the fort's commander, was an alarmist who saw an imaginary enemy advancing on his position like the relentless waves of the empty sea.

The general's steel-grey eyes stared out from under bushy, hooded eyebrows, and the peculiar way he had of showing his lower teeth like a bulldog gave him a ferocious appearance. His sour disposition was brought about by imaginary illnesses and bouts of depression linked to his declining career. After his defeats at Chattanooga and Missionary Ridge the previous year, he had suffered a nervous breakdown and resigned his command. President Davis refused to accept his resignation and had ordered him to Richmond as his chief of staff. Ten months later General Bragg was sent to Wilmington, North Carolina, to oversee its defense.

He was standing atop the Northeast Bastion which, because of its towering position, commanded an exceptional view of the ocean and the surrounding fort. The crescent-shaped Pulpit Battery behind it was the colonel's command post. Walking alongside the general, Governor Zebulon Vance pointed to the black dots on the horizon, asking, "Colonel Lamb, are those Federal ships out there?"

"Yes they are, Governor. There's been increased activity lately which leads me to believe an invasion could come at anytime."

"From what I've seen, Colonel, you have nothing to fear," assured General Bragg. "This fortification is magnificent. The only weakness I have detected is the lack of soldiers manning the walls."

"I agree, sir. I have five hundred and eighty-three men at last count, and most of them are inexperienced. To properly defend this position, I would need at least six times that number. We also need a sizable body of troops stationed north of the fort so they could attack the enemy rear if he attempts a landing."

"I'll advise President Davis of that," General Bragg said. "In the meantime, I'll issue an order prohibiting white men of military age from leaving the city. Perhaps we can raise some volunteers to help defend the fort. Is there anything else you lack?"

Colonel Lamb nodded. "Yes, sir. I need ammunition and gunpowder. Right now we have only seventy rounds per cannon."

"I'll see what I can do. I need to review the entire situation. Perhaps we can shift some supplies from elsewhere."

"Thank you, sir."

"What sort of precautions have you made for a land attack?" General Bragg asked.

Pointing to the area in front of the fort, Lamb said, "As you can see, sir, the land north of the fort has been cleared of trees for half a mile, and we've built a palisade fence."

General Bragg shaded his eyes, glancing at the land Lamb indicated.

"The fence was built with sharpened nine-foot-high stakes, sir."

General Bragg nodded, crossing his arms. "I think that should be adequate. What other defenses do you have?"

Motioning toward the center of the land face, Colonel Lamb said, "About halfway down the land face is a sally port which will allow troops to rush out and man that fence in case of attack. Two artillery pieces, stationed at the entrance loaded with grape and canister, will keep the enemy from entering the fort through the tunnel. Two hundred yards in front of the land face, I've buried twenty-four torpedoes. Each of them contains one hundred pounds of gun powder."

General Bragg nodded. "Most formidable, Colonel. But I believe it can be improved."

"I would love to hear any suggestions you have, sir."

Bragg gestured to the clearing. "I would like to see a moat across the entire peninsula. Something like to the one Fort Wagner had on Morris Island. Put some men to work on it right away."

"Yes, sir," Colonel Lamb said, and thought, *I suppose he'll want it stocked with alligators, too.*

The colonel disliked the grim general with the bright, piercing eyes who had replaced his friend and mentor General William Whiting. Together he and General Whiting had built Fort Fisher into the mammoth fortification that it was. He also inspired a rare loyalty in his troops. What better man to defend his own creation than General Whiting himself.

That afternoon a steamer took General Bragg up the Cape Fear River to his headquarters in Wilmington. As he sat at his desk writing an order to prohibit men from leaving Wilmington, his aide came into the office.

"General, Peter Reynolds is here to see you. He says he's been assigned to you as an advisor."

General Bragg slammed down his pen angrily, thinking, *Every time the government appoints me to a new duty station they send me another know-it-all advisor.*

"Show him in, Major," he said in an exasperated tone.

Peter Reynolds came into the general's office, and Bragg motioned to a chair in front of his desk. "Sit down, Mr. Reynolds. I understand you're to be my new advisor."

"Yes, sir. I have a letter of introduction from Lieutenant General Thomas."

General Bragg opened the envelope, then looked the letter over. "It says here you were assigned to President Davis's staff and then transferred to the Ordinance Bureau. What could you possibly do for me?"

"Sir, my job in the Ordinance Bureau required me to purchase military supplies from Europe and ship them here. That job also required I have an intimate knowledge of blockade-running in this area. General Thomas thought it would be prudent to have me expedite the transfer of these supplies for you."

"I see. Well, if you're an expert in these matters, I would like you to prepare a written report on the situation and how it could be improved."

"Yes, sir, I'll get to work on that right away. By the way, I have a scout named Judson Bates who claims he has information concerning an invasion of Fort Fisher."

General Bragg leaned forward, eyeing the man curiously. "Where did he come by this information?"

"In a Yankee prison, sir. He was captured trying to run the blockade out of Wilmington. He said while he was being interrogated, he overheard some Union officers discussing an invasion."

"We need to be careful, Mr. Reynolds," General Bragg said. "He may be working for the other side and trying to plant false information. Send this man to me for questioning."

Twenty minutes later, Judson Bates sat across from General Bragg.

"I've been told you have information about an invasion, Mr. Bates."

"Yes, sir," Judson said. He related the plan as Peter Reynolds had told it to him. General Bragg listened, saying nothing.

Finally he asked, "Why should I believe you?"

Judson shrugged his bony shoulders. "Why not, Gen'ral?"

"The South has limited resources. I would need to shift men and material away from a critical area to help defend Fort Fisher. If the North were planning an attack, they might make a feint in this direction when their real objective is elsewhere."

"An' you think they gave me false information knowin' I would go to you," Judson said.

"Exactly."

Judson grinned, shaking his head. "Well, Gen'ral, I'm jest tellin' you what I heard. If this here is true, you might be able to use that information somehow."

After Bates had left, General Bragg deliberated over what he should do. If the Federal army did invade and Fort Fisher fell, he'd be hounded by the press because he'd failed again. His enemies would demand his resignation, and this time they would probably get it. General Bragg did not think he could suffer through another humiliating defeat.

Bragg took an amber bottle of laudanum from the top left drawer of his desk, and opened it. He deliberated over the bottle of cocain-based medicine for several seconds. His doctor had prescribed large doses to arouse his lethargic liver, a side effect from the time he had caught malaria in Florida. In one quick motion, he took a swallow, grimacing.

Then Bragg picked up his pen with renewed strength, writing a request for six thousand troops to be transferred from Richmond.

McKay chided himself as he walked down Water Street on his way to the Green Parrot Tavern. Since his arrival yesterday he hadn't found time to see Amber yet. He enjoyed the woman's company because she was easy to talk to and listened to his problems. Quite often she had offered good advice. The box he carried contained a silk dress he had bought in Nassau for his friend.

When he entered the tavern Amber was facing away from him, talking to the bartender who was wiping a glass with a rag. McKay moved beside her, setting the package on the bar in front of him.

"Does anybody know where I can find Amber?" he said, pretending not to notice her.

The woman swung around, giving him a big hug. "Wade, I can't believe it's really you! I was so worried when I heard about the hurricane."

"It had me a little worried, too, but here I am, safe and sound."

"What's in the box?" asked the bartender.

"Something I picked up for Amber in Nassau."

"For me?" she asked, her eyes widening in surprise.

McKay nodded, handing it to her. "It's a gift. Brooke and I are together again, thanks to you."

She set it on the bar, slipping off the string and wrapping paper. Inside the box was a ruffled, red silk dress.

She squealed with delight, holding it up in front of her. "Oh, Wade, it's beautiful!"

"The shop owner said it was imported from Paris. I hope you like the color. I can't imagine you in anything but red."

"I love the color. Thank you, Wade. You're so sweet," she said, kissing him on the cheek.

Judson Bates came through the door at that moment. When he saw Captain McKay with Amber, he backed into the shadows so he wouldn't be seen. Amber suddenly became irresistible to him.

The next morning Mrs. DeRosset and two women from the Ladies' Soldiers Aid Society came to visit Brooke.

"We heard of your arrival yesterday. Thank God you made it through that dreadful storm safely."

"Thank you for your concern. It's an experience my stomach and I won't soon forget," Brooke said, rolling her eyes and remembering the sickening motions of the ship.

Mrs. DeRosset then explained the reason for her visit. "The ladies and I came by to see if you'll be doing any more volunteer work for us."

"I would like to, but I can only donate one day a week because of my job."

"I understand, dear, and that brings me to another question. How do you justify being a shipping agent and then doing charity work?"

"I'm not sure I understand." Brooke knew what she meant. The same thing had bothered her until she had thought of a solution.

Mrs. DeRosset smiled. "What I'm trying to say is this. Since agents help to fuel inflation by holding these auctions, how can you possibly do volunteer work for us knowing what you do contributes to people's suffering?"

Brooke became irritated and said, "Without people like me there would be no goods at all." Then her tone softened a bit. "I know there are problems with the system we have, but I'm working to solve them."

"You are? What can you do?"

Smiling, Brooke said, "If you'll come by the auction house tomorrow morning, you'll see what I have in mind."

For dinner that evening, Brooke invited all of her father's business acquaintances to her house. She was able to take each man aside and explain the problems speculation caused and remind them how they had promised to help her. Everyone agreed they would do anything they could to help, except one man from Columbia, South Carolina. He was a nervous little man who wagged his finger to demonstrate his point when he got excited.

"Why should I help you?" he argued. "I'm only trying to keep up with inflation like everyone else."

Brooke realized unless everyone went along with her plan it would fail. The other men gathered around, trying to reason with the man.

A distinguished looking gentleman with a white Vandyke beard spoke up. "Pretty soon the war will be over, and we must think about moderating our prices. If we don't, people will remember and make things unpleasant for us."

"That's true," another man offered. "We need to plan ahead if we are to fit back into the peacetime economy."

Brooke was too nervous to sleep the morning of the auction, so she walked down to the warehouse to see if everything was in order. Row after row of numbered crates littered the floor. On top of every crate was a sample of the merchandise the box contained. Every size and description of medicine bottle was displayed along with bolts of different types of gaily colored cloth, brass and bone buttons, lead pencils, boots, shoes, bags of sugar and coffee and various other items. Mr. Morris was very helpful in setting things up and even made some suggestions on how they could run the auction to help achieve a wider distribution. When Brooke told him of her dinner the night before, and how one man might ruin what she was trying to do, Mr. Morris told her not to worry.

"Some cargo had water damage from the storm," he said. "If this man causes trouble, I'll stop the auction and say I can't sell anything more until I assess the damage. We'll hold another auction after he's gone."

"Did some cargo get damaged?" she asked.

"Not much. Fortunately when the cargo was loaded they put the bottled goods on the bottom in case some water got into the hold. A freshwater bath and a quick wipe fixed anything that did get wet."

Shortly before the auction began, McKay came into the warehouse.

"Your father always insisted on having the captain here to boost sales, so I thought I'd give you the same consideration," McKay said, grinning. "Besides, you're much prettier than he was."

"That's very thoughtful, Wade. I'll need all the help I can get."

"You'll do fine," he said, patting her hand.

Five ladies, headed by Mrs. DeRosset, the president of the Ladies' Soldiers Aid Society, walked over to Brooke.

"How pleasant to see you again, Brooke. Hello, Captain," Mrs. DeRosset said, acknowledging his presence. "I heard you had a difficult time during the storm."

"Yes, ma'am. My ship was tossed around so badly several hull plates came loose and some structural members were weakened. The man at the shipyard said the repairs will take a few weeks."

"Oh dear! Well, I'm glad your ship weathered the storm and returned you to us safely."

"Thank you, ma'am."

"Oh, Brooke, what were we supposed to see?" Mrs. DeRosset asked.

"I have an idea I hope will provide a wider distribution for the goods at a lower price. I've divided the cargo into smaller lots so more people will get a chance to bid. When the auction begins, you should notice the speculators aren't buying up everything like they used to. They've promised me they'd take a lower profit to help us through these difficult times."

"That sounds too good to be true. What makes you think they'll keep their word?"

"I appealed to their patriotism and reminded them of a promise they made at my father's funeral."

"Oh? What was that?" Mrs. DeRosset asked.

"Everyone said they would do all they could to help my mother and me. The other night at dinner, I made it known I was greatly concerned about the high prices caused by speculation."

Mrs. DeRosset eyes widened. "And you feel this will work?"

"Yes, I do."

The president of the Ladies' Soldiers Aid Society smiled, and said, "Well, Brooke, I hope things work out for you."

The air was crackling with excitement when the time for the auction arrived. Well-dressed men smoking big cigars walked around the mounds of goods, examining them.

Everything at the auction went according to plan. Even the man who said he wouldn't help was shamed into complying. The ladies from the Soldiers Aid Society smiled, offering their congratulations to Brooke before leaving.

That night Brooke and Wade had the romantic evening alone they had dreamed about since returning to Wilmington. They went to dinner at the Old Dominion restaurant where they discussed the results of the auction over roast duck with wild rice and a bottle of white wine.

Later they took a carriage to Thalian Hall and saw Eloise Bridges' new drama, "Lady Audley's Secret", and then strolled along the riverfront.

"I read in the Wilmington Journal the editors doubt the Yankees will attack here this year," Brooke said. "Of course, there's barely a week left to prove them wrong."

McKay chuckled over the newspaper making such a bold statement. "I guess they must feel pretty safe about printing that editorial."

Brooke's laugh was weak, softened by worry. "Wade, what would you do if you were the Yankee commander?"

McKay thought a moment. "Well, I imagine I'd do the unexpected. Colonel Lamb and General Whiting have had at least three years to strengthen Fort Fisher and the batteries on Confederate Point. They've also done a magnificent job with Fort Caswell and Fort Holmes across the river. Since the North's goal is to close the port of Wilmington, I would bypass the Confederate strength and go there."

She stopped walking. "Oh dear. Are we in danger of being invaded?"

McKay considered his answer carefully. He did not want to frighten Brooke, but she needed to be aware of their situation. "I don't want to sound like an alarmist, but it's possible the North has already launched an invasion."

"What makes you think so?"

"Savannah has fallen within the past week, and no one seems certain where Sherman's army is headed next."

"And you think he may come here?"

McKay nodded. "It's a strong possibility. The North has wanted this port closed for a long time. Now they have a sizable army almost within striking distance."

In her mind's eye Brooke could see her home in flames, just like Atlanta. "Oh dear, that would be the worst thing that could ever happen."

"Wilmington isn't doomed yet. General Lee would send troops from Richmond to try and turn Sherman away. If I were the Yankee commander, I would land an invasion force east of the city. Then the Confederate army would be caught between two Northern armies. With Sherman being the hammer, and the invasion force acting as an anvil, they could destroy anyone who might stand in their way."

"Then the city will be destroyed, too," she said.

McKay saw the anxiety on Brooke's face and felt compelled to ease her worry. "This is all a guess, you understand. No really one knows what will happen."

She turned her face up to his. "The thought of war coming to Wilmington makes me realize I may lose everything which is dear to me. My home, this beautiful city, you. Wade, what will become of us?"

Gathering her into his arms, McKay said, "If the Yankees come, I'll take you on my ship and sail so far away no one will ever find us."

As soon as Virginia heard the auction was a success she went over to Brooke's house to congratulate her. "I'm so happy things went well at the auction."

"Thank you, Virginia." Brooke no longer considered Virginia her friend and was wondering what the woman wanted. "I've worked hard to put this together."

Virginia's smile slipped. "Oh, by the way, it's a shame about Wade and that prostitute he's been seeing."

"What?" Brooke was astounded by this woman's brazen attempt to create difficulty between her and Wade.

"You haven't heard?"

Brooke's gaze turned cold. "No, I haven't. Look, Virginia, I've had enough of your lies. I've warned you what would happen if you caused any more trouble."

"Brooke, you must believe me. This is the truth. I have a friend who's a bartender at the Green Parrot, and he said Wade gave a prostitute who works there an expensive dress. And that's not all. She also kissed him."

"I don't believe you for a minute, Virginia. You're nothing but a lying bitch."

Virginia's jaw dropped in surprise. "Why, Brooke, how dare you say that to me!"

Brooke leaned forward, narrowing her eyes. "It's true! Now get out of my house."

Virginia was shocked. She had never seen Brooke so angry. "I will, but I'm telling you this as a friend. If you don't believe me, check around. Her name is Amber."

Brooke sat down after Virginia left, thinking about what the woman had said. It was obviously a lie, and she had no intention of checking into it.

* * * *

Like Peter Reynolds had said it would, an invasion force of fifty-six warships plus numerous troop transports and supply vessels sailed from Hampton Roads, Virginia, on the morning of December 13, 1864. The Federal ships steamed out of the James River into the Chesapeake Bay, then turned northward and went up the Potomac River, trying to mask the force's intentions. The fleet lay at anchor that night. Then at dawn they turned around and steamed out into the Atlantic and headed southward.

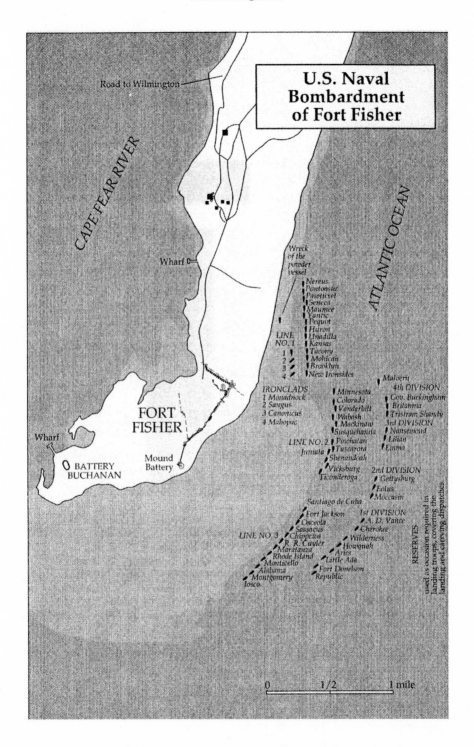

Road to Wilmington

U.S. Naval Bombardment of Fort Fisher

CAPE FEAR RIVER

ATLANTIC OCEAN

Wharf

Wreck
of the
powder
vessel

Nereus
Pontoosuc
Pawtuxet
Seneca
Maumee
Yantic
Pequot
Huron
LINE
NO. 1
Unadilla
Kansas
1
2
3
4
Tacony
Mohican
Brooklyn
New Ironsides

IRONCLADS
1 Monadnock
2 Saugus
3 Canonicus
4 Mahopac

Minnesota
Colorado
Vanderbilt
Wabash
Mackinaw
Susquehanna
Powhatan
Tuscarora
Shenandoah
Vicksburg
Ticonderoga

LINE NO. 2
Juniata

Malvern
4th DIVISION
Gov. Buckingham
Britannia
Tristram Shandy
3rd DIVISION
Nansemond
Lilian
Emma

2nd DIVISION
Gettysburg
Eolus
Moccasin

FORT
FISHER

Wharf

BATTERY
BUCHANAN

Mound
Battery

Santiago de Cuba
Fort Jackson
Osceola
Sassacus
LINE NO. 3
Chippewa
R. R. Cuyler
Maratanza
Rhode Island
Monticello
Alabama
Montgomery
Iosco

1st DIVISION
A. D. Vance
Cherokee
Wilderness
Howquah
Aries
Little Ada
Fort Donelson
Republic

RESERVES
used as occasion required in
landing troops, covering the
landing and carrying dispatches.

0   1/2   1 mile

195

CHAPTER 12

The shimmering sun rose above the darkened sea, and like nature's own artist it painted the sky and the wave tops in the richest hues of apricot and crimson, creating a masterpiece. Captain John Thomas opened the cabin door of the *USS Weybossett's* cramped living space he shared with eleven other officers from the First Brigade of the 117th New York, and saw everything about him was touched with gold.

The twenty-nine-year-old captain tamped tobacco into his clay pipe and pondered how he had come to be on this ship, going off to fight an enemy he held no animosity for. Three years ago he would have thought this was impossible. Could it have been only three years? So much had happened that it seemed like a lifetime.

John Thomas was a journalist for a small newspaper in upstate New York when the War Between the States erupted. Then the war had seemed a million miles away. He didn't give it much thought until Congress passed a conscription act making all men aged twenty to forty-five eligible for military service. It exempted those who paid $300 or provided a substitute. John did not have that much money, and he did not like the idea of someone doing his duty for him. His forefathers had not shirked their duty during the Revolutionary War, and they had paid for his freedom in blood. Now the time had come for him to do his share. On a warm August day in May 1862, he bid his wife goodbye and volunteered for the Union Army.

Because many officers were killed during Virginia's bloody peninsula campaign, John rose rapidly to lieutenant and finally captain. During that time he had grown from the clean-shaven man he used to be, into the muttonchopped veteran standing on the deck of the *USS Weybossett*.

John struck a match and cupped his hands around the bowl of his pipe while drawing steadily on the stem. He had a good feeling about the expedition in spite of being saddled with a controversial commanding officer like Major General Benjamin Butler. Most of the men knew the balding, puffy-eyed general with the drooping moustache as "Old Cockeye" because of a lazy left eye which had a tendency to stray.

General Butler was also recognized for his creative ideas concerning warfare. He once had proposed using jets of water from fire engines to blast down Confederate earthworks and later, when the army's siege of Richmond had stalled, he suggested tunneling under the city and launching a surprise attack from underneath it. His latest idea was filling a ship with gunpowder and towing it near Fort Fisher, then igniting it. He theorized the resulting blast would level the fort and kill the garrison inside. Any soldiers who weren't killed outright would probably suffocate from poisonous gases, he predicted, and the army could merely walk in and claim the fort for the Union. Most military leaders thought the idea of a huge, floating bomb was insane.

Captain Thomas finished smoking, and tapped his pipe against the railing to clean out the ashes before putting it into his pocket. He felt lonely and went into the cabin to write a letter to his wife. He would see action soon, and he wanted to write a few lines to cheer her. The men inside the salon had gathered around a corporal who was playing a mouth organ, and Sergeant Kittredge's strong baritone voice rose to the melancholy strains of Lorena. John Thomas stopped for a moment, listening to the music and thought of home.

Because the Wilmington operation was so complex, the Naval warships did not meet up with the Army's transports until December 18. The ships assembled twenty-five miles off Fort Fisher so the

Confederates would not detect the fleet. The weather was pleasant since the beginning of the operation, but now it began to deteriorate. A terrible gale whipped the sea into a frenzy and forced the Federal fleet to seek shelter at Beaufort, causing another delay.

In the early morning hours of December 24, General Butler's powder boat was towed into the shallow water near Fort Fisher. Admiral David Porter ordered the Federal fleet to steam forty-miles offshore, then drain the pressure in their boilers so they would not rupture from the explosion. At 1:46 A.M. the shockwaves from the thunderous blast raced across the water, rattling the ship's rigging and yardarms.

When the naval fleet steamed into position for the assault later that morning, they discovered Fort Fisher was unscathed. Its garrison flag fluttered in the breeze above walls and gun chambers which were strong as ever. Even the palisade fence suffered no damage and stood gleaming in the sun. Now it was up to the Federal fleet to destroy the fort. When the green and white signal flag was hoisted aloft from Admiral Porter's flagship, the ironclad *USS New Ironsides* opened the bombardment with a savage broadside, sending ten eleven-inch cannonballs shrieking toward the fort. Within moments the entire fleet joined the barrage.

General Braxton Bragg sat in his Wilmington headquarters holding a telegram from Colonel Lamb. It announced the assault at Fort Fisher had begun and contained a request for food, ammunition and, most of all, reinforcements.

Twenty minutes later, Captain Fitzpatrick rang the bell at the slave market, until a crowd of people had gathered. General Bragg stood on a crate of peanuts, addressing the throng. "Citizens of Wilmington. The battle at Fort Fisher has begun! The Confederacy needs everyone to do his duty. Any man who can carry a gun is expected to go to my headquarters and volunteer."

McKay stepped out of the crowd. "As captain of the *Atlantis*, I volunteer my services and the use of my ship."

"Excellent, Captain. That will fit in nicely with what I have in mind. I've just received word General Hoke's division is about to arrive from Richmond by train. We'll need your ship for transportation."

McKay hurried to the boarding house to rouse his crew, then went to Cassidy's Shipyard to get the *Atlantis*. After inspecting the ship to see if she was seaworthy, McKay steamed to the fueling dock and had her bunkers loaded with coal, before continuing downtown.

A large, angry crowd had gathered around General Bragg in the Market Square when McKay came ashore. He waited until a man in a blue frock coat and top hat finished making a patriotic speech, then said to the General, "The ship is at your disposal, sir."

"Excellent, Captain. I've called out the Wilmington Home Guard along with the Junior and Senior Reserves," General Bragg said. "General Hoke's men will be along at any moment. How many men can your ship hold?"

McKay thought for a moment. "Around five hundred, I imagine. How many do you expect?"

"General Hoke has six thousand men, and with the volunteers and local Militia I guess there could be over eight thousand."

Amber stepped down from a wagon, and rushed over to McKay. "Wade, I brought some whiskey and brandy from the tavern. The men at the fort will need it as an anesthetic for the wounded."

Smiling at her, McKay said, "Thank you, Amber. I know it'll be appreciated."

Brooke was on her way to volunteer when she saw Wade talking to a woman with curly red hair. Judging from the way she was dressed Brooke imagined this was the prostitute Virginia spoke of. Her hunch was confirmed when she heard him call her Amber. Brooke decided now was as good a time as any to confront them. "Hello, Wade. Who is your friend?"

Surprised to see Brooke, McKay said, "Oh, Brooke, this is Amber. Amber, Brooke."

There was an awkward silence while the two women sized each other up.

"Amber brought a wagon load of whiskey for Fort Fisher," McKay offered, trying to keep the conversation going.

Brooke raised her eyebrows.

"Yes, but please don't get the wrong idea," Amber explained. "The whiskey is for medical use only. I want to help those poor men as much as I can."

"I do too," Brooke said. "That's why I came to volunteer."

"That's terrific," McKay exclaimed. "I believe the ladies are rolling bandages down at City Hall."

Brooke appeared hurt. "But I want to go to the fort to help tend the wounded."

"Brooke, Fort Fisher is no place for a woman. It's too dangerous."

This was the wrong thing for Wade to say to her. "It is? I guess this is your way of saying, 'Go away little girl. This is men's work'."

McKay frowned. "I didn't mean that at all. I just feel you can do more good here."

"You left out safely, didn't you?"

McKay could see he was getting into deep trouble, but he saw no way out. "Yes. That too."

"Why is it men think women can only do certain things?" Brooke demanded.

He shrugged. "I don't know. Women are just better at them, I suppose."

"Like rolling bandages," Brooke suggested.

"Yes. That's one of them."

Brooke thought a moment, smiling. "I believe you left out scrubbing floors and washing clothes."

McKay was seeing a rebellious side of Brooke which he never knew existed. "Brooke, I haven't time to argue the differences between men and women. You're not going to Fort Fisher and that's final."

Brooke glared at him, crossing her arms on her chest. "Oh? And who made you my lord and master?"

Amber felt uncomfortable and excused herself. "I have to help unload the wagon. Nice meeting you, Brooke."

"Yes," she snapped at the other woman. "It's good to finally meet you."

Amber glanced at Wade with a "What does she mean?" look before she walked away.

When Amber had gone, he asked Brooke, "What was that about?"

"All right, if you insist. Virginia came by my house the other day and said you were seeing a prostitute named Amber. She also said you gave her an expensive dress."

McKay knew he would have a difficult time explaining his way out of this. "Yes, I did. She gave me some good advice, so I brought her a gift. But she's only a friend."

"Is that all she is to you?"

"Yes," Wade answered. "I told you we're just friends. Why must you make such a big thing out of this?"

Brooke stared at him in amazement. "The woman is a prostitute, Wade! Doesn't your reputation mean anything to you?"

"Yes, it does," he said exasperated. "Look, I have a lot to do, so I don't have time to argue right now."

"Oh? Excuse me for taking up your valuable time. I think I'll go roll some bandages," Brooke said, storming away.

Judson Bates wanted to keep a low profile around Captain McKay, so when he saw him get off the *Atlantis,* he motioned to Howard. "Come on. Let's get outta here."

"Just a minute, Judd. Rascal nearly has it." Howard liked to hide a cracker in his shirt pocket and let the puppy find it. The little dog whimpered, nuzzling Howard's pocket for his treat.

Judson noticed Peter Reynolds approaching them, and said, "All right. You stay here. I've got to see what Reynolds wants."

Howard saw his friend walk over to General Bragg's advisor and thought, *Judson shore is lucky findin' himself a good job like that. I wish there was somethin' I could do.* Then it occurred to him. *The Army's lookin' for people to go to Fort Fisher. Maybe I should volunteer.*

Peter nodded a greeting. "Morning, Judson, walk with me. There's something we need to discuss," Peter said, indicating they should cross the street.

When they had gone far enough away from the crowded riverfront, Peter said, "I want you to persuade General Bragg Fort Fisher can defend itself. Tell him it's his duty to keep the port of Wilmington open. To do this, he must place General Hoke's division between the Yankees and the city."

Judson scratched his chin, unsure. "I understand, but I can't tell the Gen'ral what to do."

"I know that. Just give him your opinion."

"What if he doesn't listen to me?" Judson asked.

"Then the Union Army will make a feint toward the city. Bragg will have no choice but to try and check their advance. The commanding Union officer will allow him to bring his division up so he can halt their march. When he does, the Yankees will retreat. Bragg will feel certain he did the right thing, and he'll see your information was correct."

"After that Gen'ral Bragg will listen to whatever I have to say," Judson said with a grin.

"Exactly. Remember, this whole operation is merely to feel out the Confederate defenses and to give you credibility with the General."

Judson nodded. "You've thought of everything."

"I hope I have," Peter said. "If this plan succeeds, it could shorten the war by a year or more."

The appearance of the Junior and Senior Reserves saddened McKay as they tramped aboard the *Atlantis. They're just young boys and old men,* he thought. *Were these the men who were supposed to defend Fort Fisher?* He felt terrible about taking them to what could prove to be their deaths.

General Bragg hurried aboard the *Atlantis,* handing McKay an envelope. "Captain, would you take this dispatch to Colonel Lamb? It's urgent."

"Of course, General."

"Are you loaded?"

McKay looked about, nodding. "Yes, sir. I think I'll need to make two trips with the reserves."

"Fine. I'm gathering some food and ammunition for your next load. They'll probably be at the dock when you return."

"Any word yet about General Hoke's division, sir?"

"They're still arriving by train. Hopefully they'll be waiting for you when you get back."

McKay fingered the envelope in his hands, trying to think of the right way to say this. "I'm concerned about the reserves, sir."

The General nodded. "Because of their age, you mean."

"Yes, sir. I'd like to leave them here. They don't belong in battle."

"I don't want to use them either, Captain, but we need to use what little resources we have."

General Bragg thought a moment. "I'll tell you what. Tell Colonel Lamb I wish to keep the reserves north of the fort. They shouldn't see any action there."

"Thank you, sir."

Brooke hurried away from the riverfront in tears. As she left the wharf, she heard a voice ask, "What's wrong, Miss? Did you stub your toe or somethin'?"

Brooke wiped away a tear and saw a large man holding a puppy. She was apprehensive about talking to strangers after the recent murder, but the crowded wharf put her fears to rest. Brooke answered him because it was the polite thing to do. "No. I just got something in my eye."

"Oh," Howard said. "I stubbed my toe once, an' it hurt like the blazes. I thought maybe that's what you did."

"No. I'm fine. Really," Brooke assured him.

He nodded, scratching the puppy's ears. "My name's Howard. This here's Rascal."

"Hello, Howard. I'm Brooke Snow. Your puppy is adorable."

Howard beamed, and Rascal cocked his head, looking at her quizzically. "Yes, ma'am."

"What kind of dog is he?"

Howard smiled, shrugging his big shoulders. "I don't know, but he's the best darned dog in the whole world."

"I'm sure he is," she said with a grin. "May I pet him?"

"Shore. Rascal's partial to havin' his ears scratched," he confided.

She petted the puppy, and the dog closed his eyes with pleasure.

"He likes you," Howard pointed out.

"Yes. It seems he does."

Brooke's heart had always been captured by baby animals with big expressive eyes, and this puppy was no different. He tugged at her emotions, erasing every bit of her tears.

"You're a good woman. You know how I can tell?"

"Uh-uh."

"Animals are smart," Howard said, stroking Rascal while the puppy nuzzled his hand. "When they take to somebody right off, it's because they're a good person."

"Am I a good person, Howard?"

Grinning, Howard said, "Golly, yes. Look how he's tryin' to get at you."

She smiled, scratching the puppy's ears. "He is, isn't he?" Brooke was curious about the good-natured man. "Do you work around here, Howard?"

"No, ma'am. I used to, but not anymore. Judson Bates an' I-- that's him over there, the short one with the bowler hat--we worked on a blockade-runner 'til the Yankees captured it."

Brooke looked to where he was pointing and saw the other man was with Peter Reynolds. She supposed Judson was asking him for a job on another blockade-runner.

"Being a prisoner must have been terrible," she said.

"Yes, ma'am. But they released us in a prisoner exchange near Richmond 'bout two weeks ago."

"Thank heavens. I'll bet you're glad to be free."

"Yeah," he said glumly. "But I'm thinkin' about goin' to Fort Fisher to fight the Yankees."

"You are?"

"Yes, ma'am. 'Cept I don't know what to do with Rascal. I wouldn't feel right takin' him to the fort with me."

Howard brightened with an idea. "Hey, Brooke, would you watch Rascal for me?"

"I don't know, Howard. I . . ."

The big man interrupted her. "He really likes you. Please!"

Brooke found it difficult to refuse such a poignant request. "Of course I'll watch him for you, and when you want Rascal back just come to city hall. I work with the Ladies Soldiers Aid Society on the second floor. If I'm not there, tell the women what you want, and they will know where to find me."

Howard's whole face crinkled into a warm smile. "Thank you, Brooke. It'd mean an awful lot to me."

The man reached into his pocket, bringing out a cracker.

"Rascal loves crackers. There's this game we play. I hide 'em, an' he finds 'em. We're a team."

"I can see that," she said with a smile.

"Why don't you hide this, an' let him find it?"

"All right," she said, then hid the cracker inside her purse and set it on the ground.

Howard put him down, and the puppy scrambled over to her handbag, barking at it.

"He knows this game well," she observed. Brooke stooped and opened the purse to help Rascal find the cracker. He happily chewed the treat while she petted him. The puppy squeezed his eyes shut, showing her where to pet him by turning his body.

They continued playing with the puppy until the time came for Howard to leave. With his eyes moist, he pulled a handful of crackers from his pocket and said to Brooke, "I have to go now. Would you give these to Rascal so he won't see me leave?"

She nodded. "All right, Howard. I'll take good care of him. You be careful now. You hear?"

"I will," he promised, then hurried away, wiping his eyes.

As the *Atlantis* steamed down the Cape Fear River, McKay stood on top of the port paddle wheel box, thinking of his argument with Brooke. She was headstrong, but maybe that was why he found her so fascinating. She wasn't weak like a lot of other women he had known. Brooke had her own opinions and stood by them, no matter who opposed her. He also had to admit she was gorgeous when she became angry. Her fiery temper made the color rise in her cheeks, and her blue eyes burned with fierce determination.

A low rumble interrupted McKay's thoughts. The sound of the bombardment at Fort Fisher seemed to rise and fall like some far-off thunderstorm. Periods of furious intensity marked the continuous roar, and it became louder as the *Atlantis* steamed downriver. A pall of grayish-white smoke darkened the sky to the south and gave him a sense of foreboding.

The boatswain was also watching the sky, then turned and saw the look of concern on the Captain's face. "It sounds like the boys at Fort Fisher have their hands full, sir."

"Yes, it does. I only hope they can hold on until reinforcements arrive."

After a moment, Captain McKay added, "Mr. Gallagher, post some lookouts around the ship and reduce our speed when we're three miles north of the fort. I don't want to sail into the middle of a land assault and get captured."

Soon the bumpy outline of Fort Fisher appeared with shells bursting all around it, lighting up the smoke-filled sky and kicking up giant geysers of sand. Through the smoke of battle McKay could see the fort's red, white and blue Confederate garrison flag snapping in the breeze above the Northeast Bastion.

When the last mooring line on the *Atlantis* was made fast at Craig's Landing, the Junior and Senior Reserves disembarked. They were then formed into units by their respective officers and marched to the beach where Batteries Gatlin and Anderson were positioned among the dunes. These two small batteries, located five miles north of Fort Fisher and about a mile apart, were expected to stop a Federal landing with their two thirty-two pounder cannons which were supported by four field pieces.

After borrowing a horse from a nearby stable, McKay rode toward Fort Fisher with General Bragg's dispatch.

Galloping along the river, McKay could hear shells scream into the fort, then explode with a thundering crash. Some cannonballs missed their target and either splashed into the river beyond or exploded in front of the fort, spraying sand in all directions. At one point the concussion from a fifteen inch cannonball made the ground heave up and tremble for hundreds of yards around. McKay's horse reared up out of fright and would have galloped out of control if it hadn't been for his expert handling.

When McKay reached the entrance, he found the palisade gate locked and no one there. Shouting for someone to open the gate, he tried to control his terrified horse. Two soldiers ran from the bomb shelter at the base of Shepard's Battery, and removed the huge wooden bar that held the gate shut.

"I have a dispatch for Colonel Lamb. Where can I find him?" McKay asked.

"He's at combat headquarters in the Pulpit Battery, sir. It's right beside the Northeast Bastion," the soldier shouted, pointing toward the garrison flag.

The air came alive with whirring shell fragments and stinging sand as McKay spurred his horse along the half mile-long land-face. Through the drifting smoke of the burning barracks to his right, he could see the pockmarked sand littered with shell fragments. Beyond that the fort's stable lay shattered, the horses either dead or wildly running about.

McKay hopped off his horse when he reached the crescent-shaped mound of the Pulpit Battery, then rushed up the stairs. Colonel Lamb was gazing through a telescope at the Federal fleet, General Whiting beside him.

"Colonel, I have a dispatch from General Bragg."

Lowering his telescope, Colonel Lamb said, "Give it to General Whiting, Captain. He's in charge of the fort now."

The General shook his head. "No, Colonel. You are still in command. I am here simply as an advisor."

McKay handed the dispatch to the Colonel, and said, "I've brought five hundred of the Junior and Senior Reserves with me, sir.

General Bragg said to keep them north of the fort, so I let them off at Craig's Landing."

Lamb nodded. "General Bragg promised me additional reinforcements. Do you know when they might arrive?"

"I'm to bring General Hoke's division to the fort when they arrive from Richmond, sir. They should be coming into Wilmington by train now."

"It will probably take two days to ferry them down here," Colonel Lamb said.

"Yes, sir, at least that long. It's a six-hour trip when you figure all the loading and unloading of the men."

"If the division comes overland, it'll still take two days because of the deep sand on Confederate Point," General Whiting reminded them.

"Either way it'll take a long time, unless we can get another ship," McKay pointed out.

"I may have to commandeer one," General Whiting said, adding, "although that would be exceeding my authority. General Bragg is in charge of the Wilmington District. I can merely suggest things to him."

"Didn't anyone else volunteer their ship?" McKay asked.

Lamb grimaced. "No, I'm sorry to say. There's only one other blockade-runner in port, and she's busy loading cotton. The rest of the ships are too small for what we have in mind."

"So as it stands, we have only one ship," Colonel Lamb said. "How are we going to move that many men in so short a time?"

McKay thought a minute, then said, "I'm not sure I can answer that, Colonel. However, if the troops come by boat instead of marching from Wilmington, they'll be rested and ready to fight when they do arrive."

"Yes, they will, Captain. I want you to start ferrying the troops as soon as you can, but let the cavalry ride from Wilmington. This way we'll have at least some troops at the fort if we need them."

"Yes, sir," McKay said, then pointed out to sea. "Do you mind if I have a look at the Federal fleet?"

"Not at all, Captain. Why don't you use my telescope?"

McKay could see the Federal fleet anchored in three long lines, starting about three quarters of a mile off the beach. The first line contained five ironclads; the second and third contained at least a dozen huge warships each, and beyond them scores of others were held in reserve. McKay recalled the time before the war when he had steamed up Chesapeake Bay and saw the *USS Colorado* with its 52-guns, the 48-gun *USS Minnesota* and the 46-gun *USS Wabash*. He was sure he saw the same ships in the second line, firing fierce broadsides at the fort. A ship was steaming down the second row displaying various flags.

"What ship is that, Colonel? The one with all the flags," McKay said.

"That would be Admiral Porter's flagship, the *Malvern*. He's communicating with the other ships by using signal flags."

"He would make a pretty nice target," McKay observed.

"Yes, he would," the Colonel said. "However, we have less than seventy rounds per cannon, so I issued orders to fire every thirty minutes."

"Don't you think we could fire a couple of cannonballs at that pompous bastard with all the flags, sir?" asked a young Major, who must have been General Whiting's aide. "I'd love to see the Admiral get his coattails wet."

Grinning, Colonel Lamb said to the officer in charge of the battery, "Mr. Carter, train your gun on the Admiral's flagship. I want you to fire two rounds at it. Nothing more."

The gunner smiled. "Yes, sir!"

The gun crew already had the ten-inch Columbiad loaded and prepared to fire. They swung the gun carriage around on its track until it was in position, then corrected the elevation with a handspike. When his crew stepped to the rear of the gun chamber, the gunner yelled *"Fire!"*, then yanked the lanyard.

The cannon's thunderous discharge shook the battery so McKay wondered if it hadn't exploded. When the smoke began to clear, he looked around and saw Colonel Lamb and General Whiting peering over the wall at the ocean. McKay rushed to where they were standing and saw the melon-sized shot arc through the air and splash into the sea twenty yards short of the flagship.

The crew sprang into action as soon as the gun fired. They sponged, swabbed and reloaded the cannon, while another man was raising the elevation a notch. Soon the Columbiad thundered again. This time the shot fell into the ocean right next to the Federal ship, spraying it with water.

"One more shot, sir," the gunner pleaded. "I know we can hit him with one more shot."

Colonel Lamb watched as the Admiral's ship altered course to retreat to safer waters, and said, "No, Lieutenant. We've accomplished what we wanted to do."

The actions of the Pulpit Battery did not go unnoticed by the fleet. Within minutes, shells were whizzing in the air above the battery and exploding on the walls. The men took cover in the headquarters' bomb shelter, waiting for the storm of cannonballs to subside.

General Bragg was walking back to Confederate headquarters at third and Market when he heard someone call his name.

"Sir! Gen'ral Bragg, sir!"

The General turned and saw Judson Bates hurrying to catch him.

"The Yankees came jest like I said they would," Bates said, removing his hat.

Bragg nodded. "Yes, they did. But it was probably a lucky guess on your part."

"No, sir. It weren't no lucky guess. Know what else I heard?"

General Bragg knew he should not listen to this disgusting little man, but Bates had been right about the invasion. "No. What did you hear?"

"I heard them Yankee boys sayin' the fleet's goin' to land an invasion force 'bout five miles north of the fort."

More guess work, General Bragg thought. "I could have predicted that. You aren't giving me anything I don't already know."

Bates looked about to see if they were alone. "Yeah, but I know somethin' else. Somethin' nobody else knows but the Yankee commander."

"What's that?" Bragg wanted to know.

"I know the whole dang Yankee army is goin' to bypass Fort Fisher and march on Wilmington."

Bragg was stunned. "You actually heard this?"

"Yes, sir, Gen'ral."

Bragg shook an intimidating finger at Bates. "If you're lying, I'll have you arrested for giving the army false information during a time of crisis."

Grinning, Bates said, "I ain't afeared. 'Cause I know what I'm tellin' you is the truth."

"What else did they say?"

"Nothin' much 'cept them Yankee boys were laughin' at us. Sayin' we'd be hidin' inside Fort Fisher like a pack of cowards while they march to Wilmington an' capture it with nary a lick o' trouble," Judson said, then added. "Too bad we ain't got any troops to put between the invasion force an' the city."

"I have General Hoke's division, but I've promised Colonel Lamb some reinforcements for the fort." General Bragg stroked his beard, deep in thought. "I know. I'll have his division march down to Confederate Point from Wilmington. That way, they'll be between the city and the Federal Army."

Bates grinned, showing missing and decayed teeth. "That oughta do it, Gen'ral!"

"Yes, it should. If this isn't a trick."

Bates looked shocked. "Gen'ral, I'm a good ol' southern boy jus' like y'self. An' there ain't no way in hell I'd lie to you. Them Yankees are comin'. Shore as I'm standin' here."

Narrowing his eyes, General Bragg warned, "They'd better be. Or you'll be standing on the gallows."

The bells of St. James Episcopal Church rang, summoning the people of Wilmington to attend Christmas services and pray for the deliverance of the soldiers at Fort Fisher.

Sitting next to her mother in church, Brooke Snow noticed Virginia Drake come in with her mother and a young man in uniform. She recognized the soldier as George, Virginia's older brother.

Referring to the Federal assault on Fort Fisher, Reverend Burnell spoke of the barbarians from up north who showed such callous disregard for the Lord's birthday by making war on their fellow men. He also predicted the invaders would be defeated because of their evil ways.

At the conclusion of Reverend Burnell's sermon, the parishioners bowed their heads in prayer while the church's windows rattled in their frames from the bombardment at Fort Fisher.

As the people filed out of church, Brooke's mother greeted Mrs. Drake and her family. "Merry Christmas, Abigail! It's been so long since I've seen you or your daughter. And, George, it's so pleasing to see you home for the holidays. How long are you staying?"

The lanky man said, "Thank you, ma'am. I'm on a two-week convalescent leave."

"Oh dear, I didn't know you had been wounded?" Mrs. Snow asked.

"No, ma'am. Nothing that spectacular. I caught pneumonia standing guard in the trenches near Richmond. Seems they're always cold and wet this time of year."

While their mothers were chatting, Brooke took Virginia aside and said, "Wade explained everything to me. That woman at the Green Parrot was an old friend of his."

"I'll bet she was," Virginia responded. "Doesn't it seem suspicious Wade has only been in Wilmington for five months and already he has an old friend who's a prostitute?"

"Well, he didn't use those words exactly. He said she had given him some good advice, and he was so grateful he bought her a gift."

Virginia's voice took on a superior tone. "An expensive gift from what I heard. But I imagine he's given you ones more valuable than that."

The look of hurt on Brooke's face told Virginia he hadn't. "Oh dear, he hasn't, has he?"

212

"Of course he has!" Brooke lied. "Wade loves me. He also brought my mother a wonderful beef roast and some wine when he returned from Nassau."

When Brooke rode home with her mother later, she wondered about her relationship with Wade. If he truly loved her, why hadn't he given her gifts like he had this other woman?

While Brooke and her mother were attending Christmas services, Union Captain John Thomas climbed into a longboat alongside the troop transport and got ready to storm the beach. Two hours earlier, seventeen warships from the reserve fleet had steamed five miles north of Fort Fisher and began a thunderous bombardment in preparation for the Federal Army's landing.

The Confederate batteries dueled with the Union fleet using their two 32-pounder cannons and four field pieces, but any resistance they offered was soon smashed beneath a tremendous hail of iron.

The closer Captain Thomas' longboat came to the beach, the louder and more terrifying the explosions became. Cannonballs whistled overhead, and the whole beach seemed to erupt in smoke and flames as if in the midst of a great volcano.

As the boats began to run aground in the shallow water, the Naval bombardment ceased and was replaced by the staccato crackle of musketry. Minnie balls buzzed through the air like angry bees, and John jumped into the waist-deep surf to escape them. He drew his sword, holding it high for the men to follow him.

Soon Captain Thomas was joined by thousands of screaming Union soldiers, rushing onto the beach. In a matter of minutes all Confederate resistance crumbled. What was left of the Junior and Senior Reserves dropped their weapons and held up their hands in surrender. As the prisoners were gathered up, Captain Thomas was surprised and saddened to find they had been fighting old men and boys and wondered, *Is this what things have come to? Has the situation here become so desperate these men are all the South have left to defend Fort Fisher?*

The Federal Army could hear the pounding of the Naval bombardment through the trees. Skirmishers were sent out ahead as the First Brigade prepared to make a reconnaissance in force. As the Federal force left the beach and moved southwest, they encountered Confederate pickets from Kirkland's Brigade, the vanguard of General Hoke's division. The Confederate skirmishers traded volleys with the Federal troops, until they realized they were facing three full brigades of about 6,500 men. Afraid of being flanked, General Kirkland ordered his skirmishers to fall back to their main line of defense, a trench stretching across the peninsula from Sugar Loaf Bluff near the river to Battery Gatlin on the beach.

With nothing to stand in their way, the Federal Army advanced on Fort Fisher through the pine trees and the deep sand of Confederate Point. Near Wilmington Road they found telegraph wires from the fort, and one of the troopers climbed the pole and cut the lines. About 2,200 yards from the fort's walls, the soldiers halted and began digging trenches.

Inside of the fort, General Whiting tried sending an urgent request for reinforcements to General Bragg. When he discovered the wires were down, he sent a rider through the fort's gates with a dispatch. Union skirmishers were alerted by the sound of a horse galloping over the wooden bridge from the fort. Within minutes the rider tumbled from his saddle with several minnie balls through the chest.

While his men were busy digging, Captain Thomas went to the commanding officer to see what else needed to be done. As he neared the center of the line, he saw General Weitzel and Colonel Curtis viewing the fort through binoculars.

General Weitzel lowered the field glasses as the captain approached, handing them to him. "Hello, John. Take a look and tell me what you see."

The fort's bumpy outline appeared through a haze of smoke and bursting shells. He counted seventeen cannons between the sodded mounds of sand, but no soldiers manned the walls. "Lots of cannon, but the walls appear deserted, sir. Maybe the Naval bombardment did some good."

"I'm not so sure. The soldiers probably sought shelter in bombproofs. When the bombardment stops, they'll rush to the walls and defend the fort."

Captain Thomas nodded.

General Weitzel looked worried. "Also, those cannons look serviceable. With a Confederate division to our rear, I think it would be suicide to mount an assault. Those aren't old men and boys back there. That's a veteran Confederate division."

"What are you going to do, sir?"

"What any intelligent officer would do. I'm going to inform Major General Butler of the situation and let him decide."

When the Naval bombardment ceased for the day, it was discovered what General Weitzel had said was correct. Hundreds of Confederate soldiers rushed to the walls to defend the fort. Puffs of white smoke erupted from the sides of the parapets as bullets whistled down at the enemy.

Five hours later, a courier arrived with a message from Major General Benjamin Butler calling off the invasion.

CHAPTER 13

Captain Fitzpatrick rushed into General Bragg's office, waving a telegram. "The Yankees have retreated, sir!"

General Bragg lowered the bottle of laudanum from his lips and displayed a rare grin. "By God, we licked 'em!" Then he recovered from his momentary lapse of composure, asking, "Captain, did you read my telegram?"

"No, sir. I heard the news from the boy who delivered it."

"That's the trouble with young folk today," Bragg grumbled. "They rarely listen to anyone, and when they do, they can't keep their mouths shut."

"Yes, sir. Here's your telegram."

The general sat back in his chair, opening the envelope and reading the message with satisfaction. He was worried when the Union troops landed north of Fort Fisher, but fortunately he had General Hoke's division march down from Wilmington. The Yankees had expected to meet light resistance when they advanced toward the city. Instead of just a few poorly trained militia, they encountered a Confederate division and retreated. Bragg sat back, considering what had happened. *Judson Bates had been right again.*

The *Atlantis* docked at the landing near Battery Buchanan amid wild cheering. The news of the Union fleet's withdrawal generated such excitement among the soldiers it spread to the sailors on the ship with incredible speed.

Crowds of jubilant men gathered around Colonel Lamb to congratulate him as he made his way to the blockade-runner. After stopping and talking to more than a dozen men, he finally strolled up the ship's gangplank and went aboard. "Have you heard the glorious news, Captain?"

"Yes, sir. Congratulations on your victory," McKay said.

"Thank you," Colonel Lamb said, allowing himself to smile briefly. "The Yankees will return, of course, but at least we have time to prepare for them."

McKay remembered the damage he had seen when he rode to the pulpit battery. "How did the fort fare, Colonel?"

"Not too badly. Why don't you come with me and see for yourself? I'm checking the damage to see how we might prepare for the next attack."

"Thank you, sir. I'd like that."

McKay borrowed a horse from one of the soldiers and joined the Colonel and two of his aides for a ride along the fort's sea face.

The massive walls were sodded with grass to hold the sand in place, but now they were cratered and void of anything green. Still, the walls had withstood the war's most fierce bombardment and showed no signs of significant damage. The hardened structures, such as the fort's headquarters, barracks, and stables, fared the worst. Wispy tendrils of smoke rose above the burned-out wreckage of the buildings. Most of the stairs leading to the gun emplacements were destroyed, and huge cannon barrels weighing several tons apiece were toppled from their carriages and cast aside as if by some rampaging giant.

"The attack destroyed four of our guns, and we suffered sixty-one casualties," Colonel Lamb explained as they dismounted to examine the muzzle of a cannon which had suffered a direct hit. The shattered artillery piece had tumbled down the sloping wall and come to rest at the base.

McKay knelt and ran a hand over the jagged metal, trying to imagine the awesome power required to do such damage.

"The Yankees will learn from their mistakes," the Colonel continued, "so I'm afraid the next assault will be worse. I've received reports of a large fleet being assembled at Hampton Roads. That's why I need you to take General Whiting to Wilmington, so he can meet with General Bragg and then commandeer a boatload of cotton. I would like you to trade that cotton for supplies in Nassau. I'll have a list prepared of what we need."

Shaking his head, Captain McKay said, "I'm not sure Burgess & Linden would let me do that, sir."

"I've anticipated that. General Whiting will write a letter to the owners explaining he has commandeered your ship and exonerating you of any blame in this affair."

"Thank you, sir. I feel better knowing I have your full support," McKay said.

"You do."

"Then with your permission, I'll leave immediately."

"Permission granted. And, Captain," Colonel Lamb said, extending his hand, "I appreciate everything you've done. Without your help ferrying troops and supplies we wouldn't be celebrating this victory today."

McKay shook his hand and smiled self-consciously at being thanked for doing something he felt was his duty. "No thanks are necessary, sir. I was glad to help."

McKay returned to the *Atlantis* with General Whiting and prepared the ship to get underway. The blockade-runner steamed up the Cape Fear River, docking at the cotton press on the west bank, across from Wilmington. While his ship was being loaded, McKay took a ferry to the city and went to see Brooke. He took off his cap when she answered the door. "Hello, Brooke."

Brooke's face lit up when she saw who it was. "Wade, what a surprise. Why don't you come in?"

"No. I can only stay a minute, then I have to get back to the ship. I came by to tell you General Whiting has commandeered the *Atlantis*. He also wants me to exchange a load of cotton for military supplies in Nassau."

"Oh, dear! That might take weeks."

"It could. However, if Nassau has everything I need, I may be back in as little as eight or nine days."

Brooke's faced clouded with concern. "But, Wade, no one has ever made that trip in less than two weeks before,"

"That's because no one has ever had a faster ship, or a greater cause for speed." He grew solemn. "Brooke, I took a ride inside the fort today and saw the terrible damage. The soldiers need those supplies desperately to fend off another Union assault. Colonel Lamb seems to feel another attack may come soon. That's why he wants me to go to Nassau now, before the Yankees return. He said General Whiting would write a letter to Burgess and Linden explaining everything."

"That's good. I'm sure they'll be wondering why the *Atlantis* hasn't made another run through the blockade."

McKay glanced at her, changing the subject. "About the other day, when I wouldn't take you to the fort. I want to thank you for honoring my wishes by not going."

"I had no choice," she said, then added, "Wade, when are you going to treat me as a real person?"

"What do you mean?"

"I have thoughts and desires like anyone else. I wanted to help those men at the fort, but you couldn't see past my being a woman long enough to let me do that."

McKay was exhausted and didn't feel like arguing. "I'd rather not go into those reasons right now."

"Why? Is it because you know you're wrong?"

"No. It's not that at all. I have a lot on my mind right now, and I don't want to worry about you too."

Brooke was flattered Wade thought enough of her to care about her safety. "I can appreciate that," she said, "but you need to try and understand me too."

"I am, but it's not easy. I've never met anyone like you before."

"That's because there *is* no one like me," she said, her chest swelling with pride. "I'm an original. I'm Brooke Snow. I have my own ideas and I refuse to compromise them because some man tells me differently."

McKay could not believe this was the same woman he had met last July. "I'm not asking you to change. You can do anything you want. Only don't expect me to help you do something foolish."

"Fine. I won't," she returned with a flash of anger.

McKay's eyes softened, and he said, "Listen, Brooke, I don't want to argue. I just stopped by to tell you I'll be leaving right after the ship's loaded. Probably tomorrow night."

Brooke's face became cold. "Fine. You've done your duty. Now if you will excuse me, I have business to tend to."

"Certainly, I need to get back my ship anyway," he said gloomily, putting his cap back on. "I guess I'll see you when I return."

"Yes, I imagine so. Goodbye, Wade. Have a safe voyage," she said in a firm voice.

Brooke waited several seconds to see if Wade would tell her he was sorry, he was wrong about the things he had said. To her disappointment, he turned and went down the steps without a word. Brooke went inside and watched him through a parlor window, her eyes welling up with tears. *If it felt so good to be strong and independent, she wondered, then why was she crying?*

When Judson Bates learned McKay would attempt to run the blockade to get supplies for Fort Fisher, he put his plan into action. Although Peter Reynolds was going to alert the blockading squadron that evening so the Yankees could set a trap for the *Atlantis*, Judson wasn't convinced that was good enough. He needed to be sure the *Atlantis* and her captain would be out of the war forever. It was important to Judson he was the one to strike the blow which brought about McKay's destruction.

Early that morning, Judson rode to the small fort overlooking the Cape Fear River near Wilmington. The battery at Fort Stokes consisted of two cannons and he secretly made a deal with one of the soldiers to sell him a 12-pound explosive shell. Next, Judson went to the docks and purchased some tools, a small sack of coal and a block of tar.

Judson returned to his room and scattered the chunks of coal onto the floor so all he had left in the sack was coal dust. The tar was sold in solid blocks, so he broke off a piece and heated it over a potbellied stove. Judson sat on the floor, examining each piece of coal. The chunk needed to be large enough to disguise a 4 ½ inch shell and able to be split apart easily. When he found the right piece, he cracked it open and hollowed out the middle with a chisel. By the time he had finished, the tar had become soft and gooey, and Judson coated the inside. Next he embedded the explosive shell within the lump of coal and sealed the two halves. Finally, while the tar was still pliable, he put the piece in the sack and coated it with black dust to disguise the seam.

Later that afternoon, Judson walked to the wharf and saw McKay supervising the loading of cotton bales as they came aboard the *Atlantis*. Judson hadn't planned on McKay being out on deck and hesitated. He needed to plant the bomb in the ship's coal bunkers, but he couldn't let anyone see him. A dock worker, unloading cargo from a blockade-runner which put into port that morning, provided the cover he wanted. Judson struck up a conversation with the man and helped him load some crates onto a wagon. All the while, he watched the *Atlantis*.

When McKay left the ship to visit Brooke, Judson Bates scurried aboard, carrying a sailor's ditty bag over his shoulder. He went to the forward hatch and descended the companion ladder. The chief engineer was in the engine room, checking the machinery for the coming voyage. Thinking quickly, Judson stepped through the doorway. "Mr. Riechman, I had hoped I'd find you here. You're the man I came to see."

The balding engineer turned to see who it was, wiping his hands on an oily rag and stuffing it into his back pocket. "Hello, Bates, I heard you got out of jail. How did you manage that?"

"It was simple. The police realized they had arrested the wrong man."

The engineer faced him, folding his big arms. "Is that a fact? How come I heard otherwise?"

"A lot of folks are spreadin' rumors about me. But none of 'em are true. That's why I came to see you. Nobody'll hire me because they think I'm a murderer," Judson said, shrugging his narrow shoulders. His eyes softened, and he hung his head. "Chief, would it be too much to ask if you would speak to the captain for me?"

Although the engineer disliked the man, he found it difficult to refuse anyone who needed help. "All right. Come with me and we'll go see the captain. Maybe he can find a spot for you down here."

"I know this sounds awful, Chief, but I'm afraid to go with you. Captain McKay doesn't like me much, an' I'm afraid of what he might say if I were to ask him. Would you talk to him first?"

"Okay. You wait here until I come and get you."

"Yes, chief. You're the best."

The engineer nodded, then mounted the companionway ladder, climbing out of sight.

Judson found the coal bunkers easily because of the way the blockade-runner was laid out. The ship's designers had placed the bunkers around the boilers to provide protection against enemy shot. Opening his bag, Judson removed the fake chunk of coal. He didn't want the bomb to explode in the river because McKay could merely run the ship aground to keep from sinking. He figured the best chance of killing the man was if it exploded while the *Atlantis* was trying to run the blockade. Surely if his bomb didn't destroy the ship, it would cripple it enough so the Yankees would finish the job. The trouble was, he had no way of knowing when the stokers would shovel the bomb into the furnace. Judson estimated how much coal the ship would burn going down the river, then buried the explosive under that layer.

"Come on up, Bates," the engineer called. "The skipper ain't here, but the boatswain is."

Judson closed his bag and hurried up the ladder to the foredeck.

The boatswain glared at him, his mouth a firm bitter line. "You're not welcome here, Bates. Leave this ship immediately, or I'll have you escorted off."

"Yes, sir," Judson said, picking up his bag. He smiled to himself as he walked to the gangplank. Now McKay and his whole crew would be sorry they ever messed with Judson Bates.

Ever since the Union Army had defeated him so badly at Missionary Ridge, General Bragg's flagging military career had troubled him. What he needed to do was to advertise his recent success on a grand scale. That would mean having an elaborate victory parade in Wilmington and inviting the President and the Governor. The trouble was all the troops at Fort Fisher were jealously guarded by General Whiting and Colonel Lamb. As usual they saw defeat in everything and asked the troops be left to defend the fort. They cautioned the Yankees would return soon and this battle was just a prelude of what was to come. *Who were they to tell him about the strategy of war?* General Bragg fumed indignantly. *He was their superior, by God! And he knew more about military tactics than either of them.*

The General thought of himself as a professional soldier among a horde of civilians who were only playing war. Before hostilities began the Federal army numbered about 15,000 men. Now, with the Northern and Southern armies combined, it had swelled to over a million. He knew how the Northern army conducted warfare because he had been an artillery captain for the Union during the war with Mexico. He also was aware capturing Fort Fisher required an invasion by sea, but the Atlantic ocean could become his ally this time of year. Such a large scale operation would require sixty or seventy ships, and the turbulent waters around Cape Fear were notorious for their winter gales. *No*, Braxton Bragg thought convinced, *The North won't move unless the odds are heavily in their favor. Which means they'll put off another assault until the spring, when the weather will be more agreeable.*

General Bragg had weighed the situation carefully, and it was clear to him he needed a victory parade more than Colonel Lamb needed the troops to guard Fort Fisher. Besides, the soldiers would be gone for only two weeks. What could possibly happen in so short a time?

Ten miles north of Fort Fisher, Peter Reynolds lay on his stomach among the sea oats lining the beach and gazed through his binoculars.

The moonlit surf crashed upon the shore with synchronized regularity, and shadowy ghost crabs emerged from their burrows to scurry over the sand. For the last five nights Peter had lain amid the coarse beach grass searching for the Confederate patrol that usually made their rounds just after midnight. A faint murmur of voices drifted to him on the cool sea breeze, and moments later some riders emerged from the darkness. Two Confederate soldiers were riding along the line of sea oats, searching for anything suspicious. He drew his revolver when one cavalry man dismounted a few feet from where he was hiding. If the sea oats around him moved one bit, he was prepared to fire.

"What's up, Heath?" a voice called. "You fixin' to water that there beach grass?"

Heath shook his head in irritation. "No, I ain't, you blockhead. I'm lookin' fer those bottles of wine we stole from the blockade runner that run aground last month. This here dune looks like it might be where they're hid."

Jim Bob turned his head to the side, leaned over in his saddle and spat a stream of tobacco juice to the sand. Some spittle clung to his whiskers and he wiped his mouth on his sleeve. "Reckon this whole area looks the same at night. But that jest goes to show what I been sayin' all along."

"What's that?"

"That you're crazier'n a loon. You know we done searched every square inch of this beach during the day, so yore a mite tetched if you think you're gonna find a dadburned thing now."

"Never you mind, Jim Bob. It's hid here somewheres, an' I aim to keep searchin' till I find it."

A saddle creaked as Jim Bob swung to the sand, then walked over to the brush. Suddenly the grass rustled to Peter's right as the other man rummaged about for the wine he had stashed.

A cloud scudded across the moon, darkening it, and the soldier cursed, "Damn! Can't see nuthin' in this tall grass."

Jim Bob noticed a rider approach, and said, "You best hurry up, Heath. The Lieutenant's headed this-a-way."

Heath spat another stream of tobacco juice with contempt and glared down the beach. "Shit! Let's get outta here before he comes."

The men swung up into their saddles, then kicked their horses into a gallop down the beach.

When the patrol was out of sight, Peter lit the hooded signal lantern, then opened and closed the shutter in a certain sequence.

Thirty minutes later, a naval launch full of blue uniformed men glided through the roaring surf. Ten Federal sharpshooters hopped out and splashed through knee deep water, rifles at the ready. They took up defensive positions on shore, while the rest of the crew hid the boat where the beach dropped off sharply to meet the ocean.

Peter got to his feet, emerging from the sea oats with his hands raised. "Don't shoot! I was the one who signaled. My name is Peter Reynolds, and I have an urgent message for Admiral Porter."

A tall Federal officer with muttonchop whiskers and wearing a blue forage cap stepped forward, extending his hand. "Hello, Mr. Reynolds, I'm Captain Weir. I also have an important dispatch for you."

The men shook hands, then exchanged envelopes.

"When we hadn't heard from you for so long, we thought you might have been captured," the captain remarked.

"I'm sorry if my absence gave you cause for concern, but I needed to become familiar with the Confederates patrolling the beach before I could signal you."

"I understand your need for caution," Captain Weir replied. "My orders are clear on one point, Mr. Reynolds. I'm not to remain on enemy soil too long or else I might be discovered. So, if you have nothing further to report, I'll return to my ship."

"Everything's in my dispatch, sir."

"Very good. If you need to contact me again, my ship will stay on station until the invasion begins. Good luck to you, sir."

"Thank you, Captain."

When Peter returned to his room, he lit a coal oil lamp, and drew the shade. With nervous fingers he broke open the seal on the envelope from Captain Weir and removed the coded message inside. The dispatch consisted of a meaningless jumble of letters. He took off his left boot and removed a folded piece of paper containing the key and sat to decipher the communication. The first word, or keyword, told him what sequence of the alphabet he needed to use to restore the message.

When the message was decoded, Peter read the dispatch. The Federals had moved the invasion ahead three days, which meant he had less than forty-eight hours to inform Judson Bates of the change in plans.

At four the following afternoon Judson Bates was supposed to meet Peter at his room so they could review their plans, but he never showed. Peter waited thirty minutes longer, then went to Paddy's Hollow to look for Judson. He began his search at the Green Parrot because he knew the man could usually be found there. As Peter expected, Judson was sitting at a table, watching the girls entertain the customers. "Why didn't you come to my place like we had agreed?" Peter muttered under his breath.

Judson gazed at Peter, then nodded to an extraordinary young woman wearing a burgundy dress which exposed a silken thigh whenever she moved. "I plumb forgot. But can you blame me? The way that whore gussies herself up, she'd tempt a preacher."

Peter glanced around. "Yes, she would. However, we have important business. I need to see you privately."

Judson nodded, then angled his head to watch Amber saunter past the table with a young man on her arm. They went upstairs, laughing.

"I know where we can go," Judson volunteered. "There's an empty room upstairs at the end of the hall. The tavern keeps it open for their special customers, so they can have some privacy."

Looking around, Reynolds said, "I guess it will have to do."

"Good. I'll get us some whiskey."

Judson got a bottle from the bar, and the two men went upstairs. The dimly lit hallway gave way to a dozen closed doors and ornate kerosene wall lamps with fire-blackened chimneys. Muffled voices emerged from behind several doors, giving a hint of the sexual activity behind them.

At the end of the hallway Judson tapped on a door and waited. When no one answered, he turned the knob and went inside. The light, airy room was a welcome sight after the darkness of the stuffy corridor. A soft breeze stirred the curtains in the open windows. Judson walked past a round table with five straight-backed chairs to a small bar and filled two glasses with whiskey. He handed one to Peter.

"Last night I received a dispatch from General Terry," Peter said, retrieving the message from his pocket and giving it to Judson. "It says the invasion's been moved ahead three days. That means we must disarm the mine field outside of Fort Fisher tomorrow evening."

Judson looked over the message, nodding. "When do you want to go?"

"We have a lot to do so I want to get an early start. Meet me south of town on River Road at nine P.M. It's about a three-hour ride to the fort, so we should arrive around midnight."

Judson nodded. "How long do you reckon it'll take us?"

Peter shrugged. "About an hour. Maybe more. All we have to do is find the wires and cut them."

"The mines are electric?"

"Yes. They're the latest thing," Peter explained. "You see, contact mines only explode when somebody steps on them. The trouble is, there's no way to be sure someone will do that. With electrically detonated mines, the men inside the fort can wait until the Yankees are in position before firing them. A few well-placed charges could take out an entire brigade and blunt the Union assault."

Judson scratched his head, unsure. "I ain't never fooled with no electricity before."

"There's nothing to it. All we have to do is find the wires and cut them. When we're through, I'll return to Wilmington so I can convince General Bragg to leave his troops where they are so they can defend the city. However, I want you to wait there until morning so you can enter the fort."

Judson grew angry. "What for? So a damned Yankee cannonball can blow up my ass?"

"You'll be all right if you stay in the bombproofs during the bombardment. However, once the land assault begins, I want you to spread panic and confusion wherever possible. In tense situations, badly outnumbered troops will believe anything they have been told. I hope rumors of defeat will keep the fort's soldiers from organizing an effective defense."

Judson chuckled, pouring them both another drink. "Oh, you got the right man for that. Defeat is my middle name."

Peter didn't like to see alcohol being consumed so freely when they had an important job to do. He frowned, saying, "Don't you think you should slow down? We've got a lot of work to do tomorrow night."

Judson's grin disappeared. "I ain't forgot. I'm jest celebratin'."

"Celebrating what?"

"My victory. Folks 'round here never paid me no mind. Thought I was a no account, till I killed me a few niggers," Judson said, grinning. "Then you should-a heard all them righteous sons of bitches holler for my hide. They wanted to string me up. McKay was the worst of the lot, though. He had some piccaninny single me out in front of everybody, then had the police drag me off to jail." Judson leaned back in his chair with a satisfied smile. "Yep, pretty soon all those folks will get paid back for what they done. My only regret is McKay won't be there to share in their misfortune. He needs to pay real bad. But he's sailing to Nassau tonight."

"Oh, that reminds me. I alerted the blockading squadron last night, so they could set a trap for the *Atlantis*."

"Them Yankee boys can try to capture her, but Captain McKay's slicker than goose grease. I got me an ace in the hole though," Judson confided, grinning.

"You do?"

"Yep! I planted a bomb in his coal bunkers. Next time he tries to run the blockade, he'll be blown to kingdom come."

Peter looked at him, amazed. "I'm afraid I misjudged you, Bates. I didn't think you were capable of doing something so sinister."

"There's a lot you don't know about me," Judson said with a wink. He poured them both another glass of whiskey. "Drink up. It ain't every day you get to make history."

The thought of what they were about to do upset Peter. The more he thought, the more he needed a drink to calm his nerves. Peter tossed down the amber liquid, staring hard at the man seated across the table. He felt the need to explain his motives and tell Judson he was no traitor. "I want to make it clear why I'm doing this. I became a Union spy because I could see the war was destroying the South. Not just the people and the buildings, but a whole way of life. At this very minute General Sherman's army is moving across the country like a plague, destroying everything in his path."

Peter took a savage pull from his drink, and continued. "It became personal after Atlanta fell because my wife and children are there. I figure the sooner this damned war is over, the sooner I'll get to see them again. This isn't about winning or losing anymore. It's about protecting my family."

Peter poured them both another glass of whiskey. "Now it's your turn, Bates. Tell me why you're doing this? Is there a reason besides the one you told me about?"

Judson scowled. "You're damned right there is. I'm a man. An' I deserve some respect. I'm tired of all these rich bastards lookin' down their noses at me like I was just some piece of trash."

Judson took another gulp, brooding some more. "I want everybody to know who I am. When I walk down the street, I want them to say, 'Good mornin', Mr. Bates. How are you today?' An' I want the women in this town to sit up an' take notice when I pass by."

"Ah, women," Peter said with a smile, "they're so important. They can make a man feel like a king, or the scum of the earth."

"You got that right," Bates agreed with a grin. "Hey, let's drink to the ladies!"

"By all means," Peter said, raising his glass in a toast. "To the ladies. God bless their little hearts."

When the whiskey was gone, the meeting concluded. Since Peter was drunk, Judson took his friend by the arm to steady him.

As he led the man from the room, Judson saw a door open down the hall. He recognized the man who came out as the fellow who had gone upstairs with Amber. "You go ahead, Peter. I aim to get me a woman."

Peter nodded groggily, staggering down the hallway.

After Peter had left, Judson went over to Amber's door and tapped on it.

"Who is it?" a women's voice called.

"A customer."

"Just a minute, hon."

In a short while Amber opened the door, dressed in a loose fitting robe which revealed a great expanse of her white bosom. "Come on in, honey. I'm sorry you had to wait, but I needed to take care of some personal things."

Judson stepped inside, closing the door. "That's all right. I saw a customer leave, an' I figured I'd save you the trip downstairs."

"Well that was thoughtful. What can I do for you? The usual?"

"No, I have a special request," Judson said, reaching into his coat pocket and bringing out a set of ropes. "I like my women to wear these."

Peter Reynolds was feeling a bit dizzy when he reached the end of the hall, so he sat at the top of the stairs to rest for a few moments. When he felt well enough to continue, he stood, then missed the first step and tumbled to the bottom.

When Peter awoke, he was flat on his back in a strange room, and a beautiful woman with blonde hair was pressing something cool to his forehead. "Where am I?"

"You're at General Hospital number four," Virginia Drake replied. She put a hand on his shoulder when he tried to sit up. "Lie still. You have a nasty gash on your forehead."

"What happened?"

"The man who brought you here said you had too much to drink and fell down some stairs. He also mentioned someone was killed at a tavern."

Peter's memory of the meeting with Judson Bates at the Green Parrot came flooding back. "I remember being at the tavern, but I don't recall anyone being killed. Did he say who it was?" Peter asked, hoping Judson was all right.

"No. He rushed out right away, but he mentioned something about a prostitute."

Peter looked at the woman. "You're pretty. You remind me of my wife."

Virginia smiled. "I'm flattered. Why isn't she taking care of a handsome man like you?"

Dropping his gaze, Peter said, "I don't know where she is. My family was in Atlanta when the Yankees captured it."

Virginia stopped dabbing at the cut. "Oh dear! How awful that must be for you."

"It's been a nightmare, but they won't be prisoners much longer."

She rinsed the rag in a bowl of water. "Oh? How come?"

"The war's going to be over soon," Peter said.

"Well, I don't know," she said, shaking her head. "It's been dragging on for four years now."

"Yes, but the end is near. Trust me."

Virginia figured this was the whiskey talking and didn't give what he said much thought. She was just making conversation to be polite and put him at ease. "How can you be so sure?" she asked.

Peter's eyes clouded over, and his tone became guarded. "Never mind. Just take my word for it."

Virginia finished cleaning the wound, then wrapped a dressing around his head before knotting it.

"So how did a pretty lady like you come to work in a hospital?"

"I do volunteer work for the Ladies Soldiers Aid Society, and this happens to be one of my duties. I work here three evenings a week."

"Today must be my lucky day then."

She looked at him and laughed. "I don't think so. You're a mess."

"I meant because you're here today."

"Oh! That's sweet."

Peter felt the bandage and asked, "You mentioned having other duties. What are they?"

"Oh, I do a lot of things. The day after tomorrow the ladies and I are going to Fort Fisher to give the soldiers a warm meal."

Peter grabbed her arm in a vicelike grip, his eyes wild. "Don't go!"

Virginia was frightened to have this stranger treat her so roughly. The brutal murder of the woman in Paddy's Hollow was always in the back of her mind. "Why not?" she asked.

"Because the Yankees are returning."

She was positive he was disorientated now. "They were just here. They won't come back so soon."

Peter felt woozy and lay down. "Yes they will. Please don't go to the fort. Promise me you won't."

Virginia figured being agreeable might help to relax him. "All right," she said. "I'll stay here."

"Good. I wouldn't want you to get hurt. This war has hurt too many people already," Peter's voice trailed off as he became sleepy.

As Peter drifted off to sleep, Virginia went through his pockets for identification so she could make out the hospital records. She found several papers in his wallet. One stated he was an advisor to General Bragg's staff, but another was a message from General Terry giving the date of the Union invasion. *How did this man come by this information?* she wondered.

Virginia started to go to the front desk to report what she had found when suddenly she smiled and hid the dispatch in her apron pocket.

CHAPTER 14

When the *Atlantis* left the wharf near the cotton press the following evening, McKay felt an incredible sense of freedom. He had made the same journey a dozen times in the last two days, ferrying troops and supplies, but this time it was different. This time the voyage was exciting because it held the promise of his return to the sea. McKay longed to smell the ocean breeze and feel the gentle movement of the deck under his feet as his ship rolled in the swells. Although he was excited at the prospect of going to sea, his relationship with Brooke disturbed him. She was constantly on his mind. He was so close to happiness, and yet it eluded him. Would he ever know a woman's love?

A thunderous explosion rocked the ship, throwing McKay against the starboard bulkhead. The quartermaster fell to his knees, bracing himself by holding onto the spokes of the wheel, while the boatswain was hurled to the deck. As McKay struggled to the copper speaking tube, a sharp pain shot through his right arm and shoulder. "Mr. Reichman!"

No one answered, but McKay heard terrified shouts and screams mixed in with the background of engine noise. "Mr. Reichman, please!"

Again no answer, just more agonizing screams.

Seeing black smoke billowing from the engine room hatch, McKay dropped the speaking tube and shouted, "Mr. Gallagher, get some men and the fire hose, then join me in the engine room."

McKay dashed to the rear hatch, and gazed into the black, smoky hole. He didn't know what awaited him at the bottom, but he had to help those men. Without a thought for his own safety, McKay hurried down the companionway ladder.

The engine room resembled a scene from hell. Thick smoke, illuminated by the flickering orange glow from fires, was everywhere, and scores of men were crying for help. In the dim light McKay could see the balding engineer, spattered with blood and soot, trying to pull a badly burned man to safety. The man's skin was black and hung in tatters. The captain rushed to help, but fell. Struggling to regain his footing, McKay fell back again in horror when he saw what had tripped him. A warm chunk of flesh, with a leg bone protruding, lay across his calf. Through the smoky haze McKay could see bits of the man scattered everywhere. His chest, with no arms and sprouting a head burned beyond recognition, comprised the largest piece. McKay choked back the bile which rose in his throat, and struggled to his feet.

By this time other men had come to the engine room and assisted in removing the injured. Within minutes, the boatswain and two men came running over with the fire hose.

"Fires are scattered everywhere, Mr. Gallagher. Be careful not to get the furnaces wet or you may cause another explosion."

The boatswain nodded, climbing down the ladder.

McKay turned to the engineer, asking, "What happened, Chief?"

"A God damned furnace blew. That's what!" the engineer snapped, shaking his head with disgust. "Don't mind me. I don't handle explosions in my engine room well."

"That's understandable. So tell me what happened?"

"Well, everything seemed to be going along like normal. Then the damned thing exploded. Unfortunately a stoker was shoveling some coal into it when the thing blew. Poor soul was killed instantly, Gunner Larson, I think it was. I believe four or five others were injured. Maybe more."

"Chief, it's important we make Nassau to get those supplies for Fort Fisher. Do you think the furnace will be all right?"

"I don't know. We'll have to shut it down so I can look it over."

"That won't be a problem. I can drop anchor here and still leave enough room for other ships to navigate around me. How long do you think it will take?"

The chief engineer shrugged. "Two, maybe three hours."

"All right, but hurry. We need to sail on the evening tide."

Three hours later, the chief engineer reported to McKay. "I inspected the furnace, sir, and everything's fine. It appears the only thing that kept it from blowing up was having the door open, allowing the pressure to escape. Too bad Gunner was standing in front of it, though."

"It's ironic, isn't it?"

"How's that, Captain?"

"Well, unfortunately Gunner died because he had the door open, but because it was, the rest of the ship lived."

"Yeah," the engineer said, smiling. "I never thought of it that way. Sort of makes him a hero."

"Yes, it does. That's what I intend on telling his family. That none of us would be here if it wasn't for him."

"Got any idea why this happened, Chief?"

"Yes, sir, I do. That furnace wouldn't have exploded without a little help. I think someone planted a bomb in our coal supply."

"A bomb? Who would do such a thing?" McKay asked.

"I have an idea. I don't know if the boatswain mentioned this, Captain. But Judson Bates came on board when you were gone the other day. Said he was looking for work."

"He did? Mr. Gallagher hadn't said anything about it to me."

"Well, sir, I did an awfully dumb thing. I left him alone in the engine room while I went to look for you. I remember he had a canvas bag with him, but I figured it was just his gear."

"And you think he planted the bomb?"

"Yes, sir. By my way of thinking, he certainly had reason, and Lord knows he had the opportunity."

McKay nodded. "I'll tell the police about your suspicions when we return."

The chief engineer slammed a huge fist into his open palm. "How could I be so stupid! I never should have left him alone!"

"Don't blame yourself, Chief. What's done is done. Now I want you to get ready to get underway."

"Right away, sir."

When the *Atlantis* drew abreast of Battery Buchanan, she glided to a stop and dropped anchor. Lookouts were posted around the ship, and the long wait for the signal lantern from the fort began.

A few minutes after midnight a green lantern swayed above the battery indicating it was safe to continue. The men on board the *Atlantis* hoisted the anchor as muffled orders were given and obeyed. Smoke and sparks cycloned into the night sky as the firemen stoked the furnaces with more coal, setting the paddle wheels into motion and propelling the blockade-runner through the black water.

McKay saw the storm of burning embers emanating from the smokestacks and called down to the engine room. "Mr. Reichman, why are there sparks coming from the funnels?"

"I'm sorry about that, sir. The explosion from the furnace blew out the screens in the flues."

"All right then. Cut down on the coal for the next two hours. It's important we maintain an absolute blackout."

As McKay moved away from the speaking tube, he cursed whoever was responsible for the inferior coal they had been getting lately because it produced so much smoke.

Whether the *Atlantis'* discovery was due to the Federal fleet's increased vigilance, born out of frustration for their failed invasion, or just plain bad luck, McKay had no way of knowing. Federal cruisers appeared out of the gloom to his right and left, then a third charged at them from dead ahead, rockets streaking off her deck. The star shells burst in the sky, pointing out the direction of the chase and turning night into day.

McKay appraised their situation and noted the largest warship was off the starboard beam. "Quartermaster, I want you to steer on a collision course with the cruiser to starboard. Mr. Gallagher, tell the engine room to give us all the power they can."

When the boatswain had finished speaking with the engine room, he admitted, "I'm confused, sir. We're sailing right to one of their ships instead of trying to get away."

"On the contrary, Mr. Gallagher, it may be our best chance to escape."

"How, sir?"

"The cruiser to starboard is the closest. By steering directly at her, she'll only be able to fire once with her bow chasers at a small target before we steam past her."

The boatswain was skeptical. "Since the only advantage we have is our speed, wouldn't it be better to steer away from the Yankees and try to outrun them?"

"I believe that may be more risky. We'd have three ships firing at us instead of one or two. By staying close to that ship she'd shield us from the others. The two remaining cruisers would be reluctant to fire since one of their own ships is so near to us."

"So steering at them would be the safest thing to do?" the boatswain asked doubtfully.

"Exactly, Mr. Gallagher."

"Yes, sir. But what if that ship doesn't steer away from us?"

"Put yourself in the place of the captain in the gunboat. Would you continue on a collision course with a madman who has nothing to lose?"

"No, sir. I don't believe I would."

McKay clapped the other man on the back. "Of course you wouldn't. That's what I'm counting on."

Yellow flame blossomed from the gunboat dead ahead as her forward cannon sent a ball whistling through the *Atlantis'* rigging.

"That was awfully close," the boatswain said with concern.

"She won't have time to reload, so I suspect that's the only shot she'll have at us."

When the Federal cruiser veered to starboard, McKay ordered, "Quartermaster, steer more to port. I want you to aim for the center of her bow."

The closer the two ships came to each other, the more anxious the crew became. Men scrambled for cover wherever they could find it. Every time the Federal warship tried to avoid a collision by turning away, the *Atlantis* would turn with her. The blockade-runner was so near to the other ship McKay could see the nervous gun crew rushing to load their cannon for another shot.

When fifty yards separated them, the Captain yelled, "Quartermaster, thirty degrees to starboard! Then I want you to steer so close to the other ship we pass no more than ten yards apart!"

For a moment, McKay thought he had waited too long to change course. The Union warship's bowsprit, like a great lance hurtling through the air, was about to sweep over the blockade-runner's forward railing when the *Atlantis* heeled heavily to starboard in her high speed turn. The Confederate ship passed so near to the cruiser, McKay could see the startled expression on the Yankee captain's face. He could also read the lips of the gunnery officer as he yelled *Fire!*

A sheet of smoke and flame exploded from the warship's side, and the thunderous roar from her cannons blotted out every other sound. Because the blockade-runner was built so low to the water, and the Federal ship so high, the warship was unable to drop her guns low enough to fire effectively. Still, the explosion shattered the windows on the blockade-runner's bridge, throwing everyone to the deck.

Groggy from the explosion and suffering a badly cut left cheek, McKay grabbed the binnacle and pulled himself up, thinking he was terribly wrong about taking this gamble, and as a result the *Atlantis* had suffered a devastating blow. As the veil of smoke cleared, he saw burning embers from the cannon's wadding had started a dozen small fires on the cotton bales, but his ship was still intact. The cannons had fired over their heads as he had expected they would, but McKay hadn't figured on the blast of fiery air which accompanied the cannonballs. He helped the boatswain to his feet, noticing the young man's face was spattered with blood.

"Mr. Gallagher, are you all right?"

"I can't see, sir!" his panicked voice answered.

"A lot of blood has seeped into your eyes from a gash on your forehead. Try to clear them."

The boatswain wiped his eyes, blinking nervously. "It's no use, sir. I still can't see. And it hurts like hell just to keep them open."

"All right, just be still," he advised.

A deck hand was rushing past the bridge with a fire hose, and McKay shouted to him, "You there! Mr. Solari! Drop what you're doing and take Mr. Gallagher below. He can't see. Have Davis look at him. He went to veterinary school, so he's the nearest thing we have to a doctor."

The man laid the hose down, leading the boatswain from the bridge by the arm.

McKay climbed the stairs to the port paddle wheel box, looking behind them to see where the Federal cruisers were. In the golden light of the rockets he could see the ship they had just passed, coming about. Beyond her, two more warships were sailing in pursuit. McKay knew they would have a difficult time catching the *Atlantis* because of her speed. Deciding his ship was safe for the moment, McKay picked up the fire hose and went forward.

Several men were shoving flaming cotton bales overboard, and another was trying to smother a blaze on the foredeck with a piece of burlap he'd stripped from a bale and wet down.

McKay turned the hose's nozzle, aiming the jet of water at the base of the nearest fire. Fortunately the cotton was compressed to remove any air before baling, and this lack of oxygen slowed the fire considerably. Still, putting the blaze out was tricky because of cotton's tendency to smolder and then start burning again.

Suddenly the sea ahead of the *Atlantis* was lit up by rockets and exposed another Federal cruiser bearing down on them, her bow chasers grumbling angrily at the stubborn blockade-runner.

With the blaze under control, McKay gave the fire hose to a seaman next to him and started back to the bridge. As he headed for the wheelhouse, McKay wondered why he hadn't heard any cannonballs whizz through the air or seen splashes near the blockade-runner. Was the Federal gunnery that bad, or was he just plain lucky?

"Look over there, Captain!" a sweating bare-chested seaman shouted, pointing to port and grinning. "They're firing at someone else, sir!"

In the dim light from the rockets, McKay could make out the low-lying hull of a blockade-runner. Her rakish twin stacks, fore-and-aft masts and paddle wheel boxes meant she was the *Agnes E. Fry*. Apparently she was heading for New Inlet and had the misfortune of blundering into the chase intended for the *Atlantis*. McKay saw this as an opportunity to elude his pursuers. "Quartermaster, three points to starboard."

In the next thirty minutes McKay's emotions ran the gamut from exhilaration to sorrow. There was great joy in being able to outrun the Yankee blockade, but the rumble of cannon fire directed at a fellow blockade-runner dampened McKay's enthusiasm. A close fraternity arose around the business of blockade-running and most of the captains knew each other. Captain Fry was a good friend with a fine family, and McKay could not shake the feeling somehow he would be responsible if anything bad had happened to the man.

* * * *

Amber looked at the ropes in Judson's hand with concern. The most important rule in her profession was to always remain in control of the situation. She could not be in control if she was tied up. "Sure, honey, I'll put them on if you want. But only if they're loose enough for me to get out of."

"Yes, ma'am. Anything you say," Judson said grinning.

"What would you like me to do?"

"Why don't you start by taking your robe off an' layin' on the bed?"

Amber discarded her gown, tossing it onto a chair. Her luscious body with its ample breasts and gentle curves was even more breathtaking than Judson had imagined.

"Would you like me to lie on my back?"

"Yes," Judson whispered, his voice barely audible as he moved to the bed, "an' spread your legs."

She did and a small moan of pleasure escaped his lips. He caressed the silken mounds of her breasts, then smashed her in the jaw with a savage uppercut.

The blow stunned Amber, but she quickly regained her senses. She realized she was in deep trouble unless she did something to put him off balance. "Oh, that was wonderful!" she breathed, her eyes burning with desire.

Her unexpected reaction took Judson aback. "You liked that, bitch?"

A small trickle of blood ran down from the corner of her mouth, and she nodded. "Mmmm! It's exciting when a masterful man like you dominates me. Hit me again. But not so hard, I want to be awake so I won't miss a thing."

"I aim to, but I'm going to tie you up first."

"You don't need any ropes to keep me here, honey. Besides, how can I give you pleasure if I have my hands tied?" she asked, reaching out to stroke his thigh.

Judson contemplated the sensual creature before him. "All right. Then you won't mind if I cut this." He drew an ivory handled hunting knife from a sheath on his belt, and she gasped in fear. Chuckling at her reaction, Judson said, "There ain't nuthin' to be afraid of yet. I'm jest fixin' to cut your emergency cord next to the bed."

Amber had figured her best chance to stay alive was if she played along with Judson. Then, when he was sufficiently distracted, she'd try to ring downstairs for help. Now that hope vanished as she watched the cord fall to the floor.

Judson stepped out of his clothes, carrying the knife to the bed.

"What's that for?"

"This is somethin' you might enjoy. Here, let me show you how it works."

Amber lay still as Judson climbed onto the bed and straddled her about the waist, then brought the knife to her lips.

"Kiss it!" he commanded.

She did as he asked with trembling lips.

"That's fine. Now snake your tongue out an' lick it, bitch."

Amber was convinced Judson intended to kill her, but she had to gain his trust if she hoped to escape. If she could keep him busy long enough, perhaps one of the bartenders might notice her absence and investigate. She moistened her lips erotically, then played her tongue over the blade's glistening surface.

Judson's breathing increased as he became aroused. "Yeah! That's it. Now suck the tip." When she moved too slowly, Judson flicked her tongue with the knife.

Amber closed her mouth, pretending to savor the blood on her tongue. "Mmmm," she purred. "You're nasty, but I wouldn't have you any other way."

"You're damned right I'm nasty, baby. I'm the evilest son of a bitch you'll ever meet."

Her laugh was low and sexy, and she said, "Bring that knife back, so I can kiss it."

Judson did, and she took it deep into her mouth and sucked the blade, moaning all the while. His eyes grew wide, and he murmured, "That's terrific, baby. Oh, you know how to do it just right!"

"That's nothing," she whispered, her eyes half-closed and dreamy. "Let me show you how a real woman makes love to a man." She reached for Judson's penis, and he grabbed her arm.

"No, you don't! I call the shots here," he reminded her, moving the knife to her throat. "Let's see how good you are with the rest of your body." Judson trailed the knife slowly down her torso, putting enough pressure on the blade to cause a shallow cut.

Amber gritted her teeth to keep from screaming as the blade cut into her flesh.

Suddenly, a loud commotion in the hall caused Judson to glare at her. "What's that?" he demanded.

"I don't know."

Excited voices echoed from the first floor, then heavy footsteps clumped up the stairs, and someone knocked on her door. One of the bartender's duties was to note the time when a woman went upstairs with a man. This policy not only provided an extra measure of safety for the girls, but also alerted the tavern if someone was trying to cheat them out of some money. Amber was gone for quite a while, and the bartender wondered if the fellow falling down the stairs might suggest there was trouble. "Amber, are you okay in there?" a man's deep voice asked.

When Judson lifted the knife from her stomach, Amber punched him hard between the legs, bucking him off her onto the floor. "No, I'm not!" she screamed. "Some madman with a knife is trying to kill me!"

The door exploded under the bartender's enormous weight. Like a man possessed, he flew to where Judson was writhing in pain, and boomed, "Get up, you piece of shit!" As he snatched the naked man off the floor a flash of silver struck him in the chest. The bartender backed away in surprise, the knife sticking out of him.

While Amber rushed to help the mortally injured man, Judson grabbed his clothes and dashed out the door.

Judson knew he could not go back to his room because the police might come there to arrest him. He recalled Peter Reynolds had said to meet him at 9 P.M. on River Road. Since the area was heavily wooded, Judson thought that would be the perfect place for him to hide until it was time to go to Fort Fisher.

As he rode down Water Street, Judson saw no one of any consequence who might report him leaving town at 2:30 in the morning. The streets at this hour were taken over by drunken toughs who had invaded Wilmington when the blockade-running trade began. Carousing and fighting had become the natural order of business along the waterfront, and no one stopped their pursuits long enough to notice him.

At the appointed spot, the tree-lined river bank sloped down to the flowing black water. Judson unsaddled his horse and hobbled him nearby with a leather thong, then went to sleep under a bald cypress tree.

When Judson awoke, his clothes were damp, and he was chilled to the bone. The day before was unusually warm for January, and when the temperature dropped into the lower fifties last evening a heavy dew had formed. Judson checked to see if his horse was still where he had left him, then gathered wood for a fire.

Although the roaring campfire chased the chill away and dried his clothes, Judson was hungry. As he sat there contemplating his situation, the murmuring of the Cape Fear River drew him to it. Before its waters came into view, he could tell it was low tide. The powerful aroma of the sea filled his nostrils and reminded him of his youth in the tidewater of Virginia. As he came through the trees, he saw the water had receded from the shoreline about ten feet, and the mud was littered with empty clam shells and siphon holes. A great blue heron, wading in the shallow water and startled by the sudden intrusion, took flight on great expansive wings. Judson picked up a clam shell and began digging at a hole until he found a clam and scooped it up. Using his knife, Judson pried the shell open, cut the meat loose and sucked it down. Hundreds of siphon holes dotted the mud around him, and Judson continued to dig until he had thrown a dozen of the clams on shore.

Back at his camp, he cut off a long piece of thread from his saddle blanket. After prying open another clam, he cut out the meat and tied the thread around the middle. When Judson was a boy, he would take bits of whatever meat his parents had on hand and go crabbing. Because of their aggressive and tenacious nature, it was possible to catch blue crabs without a hook. They would cling to the bait even when the line was pulled from the water. The minute his line dropped into the water, he had a bite. He withdrew the string, then whooped with joy when he found two agitated crabs clinging to the piece of meat.

In a short while, Judson stoked the campfire with more wood and placed large flat rocks among the glowing charcoal. When the rocks were hot, he placed five crabs and fifteen clams on top of them, then wet the saddle blanket and threw it over the shellfish so they could steam.

After he had eaten his fill, Judson found a long piece of oak and began to whittle. He had no idea what he intended to create. As he carved, the idea of what this piece of wood should be came to him.

The stick had an odd shape. It was long and thin, but widened slightly in the middle, so Judson began to fashion a blockade runner.

Some time later, he heard hoofbeats and glanced to the road. A rider in a Confederate uniform approached at a leisurely pace, his bandaged head swinging from side to side, scanning the trees. Despite his attire, Judson recognized Peter Reynolds and walked out to meet him. "What happened to your head?" Judson asked, grinning. "Don't tell me the battle's started without me?"

Reynolds shook his head, swinging down from his horse. "No. I fell down some stairs."

"That's a shame. Couldn't hold yore likker, huh?"

Tying the horse's reins to a bush, he said, "I guess I had a little more than I'm accustomed to."

Judson gazed at Reynolds' uniform. "I didn't know you're a colonel."

"That's because I never mentioned it. I served a year in Richmond, doing clerical work mostly, until I became an advisor." Reynolds didn't like to discuss his military service and changed the subject. "I heard someone got killed at the Green Parrot the other night. For a minute there, I thought it might have been you."

Waving a hand of dismissal, Judson said, "Ain't no need to fret. This ol' boy knows how to take care of hisself."

"Good, because things will get dangerous from here on."

"I can handle whatever comes my way," Judson assured him.

"See that you do. Now saddle up. We've got a lot of work ahead of us."

Judson got his horse, and the two men rode south toward Fort Fisher.

Upon reaching the half mile clearing in front of the fort, Reynolds dismounted, tying his horse to a scrub oak. He unfastened the bed roll from behind his saddle, then spread it on the ground. A large knife and two shovels were inside the blanket.

"Grab a shovel and follow me."

The two men scurried forward using the depressions in the sand to conceal their movements. They halted at the palisade fence, fifty yards in front of the fort.

"This here's a mighty big fort," Judson said, gazing in awe at the mammoth fortification. "How you gonna find two bitty wires in all this sand?"

Reynolds smirked and said, "I know where they are, and you'll never guess who told me."

Judson shook his head he did not know.

"I went to the fort when General Bragg made his inspection in January, and Colonel Lamb was kind enough to show us how they had laid out the minefield."

"You're jokin'."

"Uh-uh." Reynolds nodded toward the fort. "You see that main wall in front of us?"

"Yeah."

"Well, a sally port tunnels through the middle of that wall so the defenders can rush out to man this fence in case of a land assault. It also allows them to wheel out some cannons for added firepower. This opening acts as a perfect conduit for the wires. It's twenty-five feet across, so all we need to do is dig a slit trench, find the wires and cut them."

Judson grinned. "Sounds easy."

"There's a problem I haven't mentioned, though. They will likely guard the sally port. That's why I wore my uniform today. Maybe I can create a diversion which will allow us enough time to cut the wires."

The men crawled through the palisade fence just as a cavalry patrol went out the gate. When the soldiers rode out of sight, Judson and Reynolds made a dash for the sally port. They climbed the raised platform and hid behind two cannons, then peeked into the tunnel entrance. The soft glow of a lantern illuminated an officer who was reprimanding a private.

"If I catch you sleeping on your post one more time you'll be put on report and court-martialed."

"But I wasn't sleepin', sir."

The Confederate officer folded his arms. "Oh, you weren't? Then why did I find you sitting on the ground with your eyes closed?"

"I was prayin', sir."

"You were what?"

"Prayin', sir. I figure since the Yankees got all those men, an' they're aimin' to take this fort, then we could use all the help we can get."

"We sure can, but it won't help us by closing your eyes on guard duty."

Shaking his head in resignation, the officer said, "I don't know whether you were praying or sleeping. But whatever you were doing, don't do it on my watch. I'm going to forget I saw anything this time. However, don't let it happen again."

"Thank you, sir."

"All right then. You've got a big post to cover. Don't spend all of your time hiding in here."

The soldier came to attention and saluted. "Yes, sir."

Reynolds and Judson ducked out of sight to discuss their plans. "You were right about the guard," Judson whispered. "What're we gonna do?"

Reynolds didn't answer and peeked into the sally port. He saw the shadowy figures of the soldiers fade into the darkness outside. "They're gone. I'll dig for the wires while you watch for the guard."

The two men rushed into the tunnel. Reynolds began to dig where the tunnel narrowed slightly in the middle, placing the sand alongside the hole. He was aware once he had found the wires and cut them, he'd have to replace the sand exactly as it had been to keep from arousing suspicion.

"The guard's comin' back," Judson whispered.

"Let me know when he's fifty feet away."

"Fifty feet? I can't even see that far in this darkness!"

"Well, buy me some time, damn it!"

Judson drew his knife, hiding it out of sight in his sleeve, then walked toward the guard.

The Confederate soldier raised his musket, "Halt! Who goes there?"

"It's Sergeant Thompson, 23rd North Carolina," Judson said, plucking a regiment's name from his imagination. "We jest arrived today an' I was explorin' the fort."

The Confederate soldier squinted in the darkness, lowering his musket. "23rd North Carolina? How come I ain't heard nuthin' about you boys comin' to Fort Fisher?"

Judson shrugged his bony shoulders. "I reckon 'cause we come through the back door. A steamer let us off at Battery Buchanan 'bout an hour ago, then we lit out for the main fort."

The guard hesitated, unsure. "If you're a sergeant, how come you ain't wearin' a uniform?"

"'Cause I'm a scout. Wouldn't do if I tol' the Yankees who I was, would it?"

"Reckon not."

"Who are you talking to, Sergeant?" Peter Reynolds asked, stepping out of the darkness.

"A guard, sir. He thinks I'm the enemy."

The guard nervously shifted his gaze to the officer. "Who are you, an' how come I ain't seen you before?"

"I'm Lieutenant Colonel Reynolds, and the reason you haven't seen me before is because I'm assigned to General Bragg's staff."

"That so? Then you won't mind if I call the captain of the guard."

Reynolds walked toward the soldier. "Why don't you do that, private? I'd like to ask him why his guards don't salute officers or address them as 'sir'."

The man's superior tone made the guard uneasy, convincing him he was an officer. "I'm sorry, sir, but I didn't know who you were."

Reynolds went up to the soldier, his dark eyes flashing their displeasure. The guard snapped to attention, looking straight ahead. "Private, call the captain of the guard. I would like to speak with him."

The soldier had just gotten chewed out for sleeping, and he didn't want any more complaints made against him. "Do we need to bother him, sir? This was all a big mistake."

Reynolds pretended to deliberate for a moment. "Very well, we'll just keep this between us. However, let this be a lesson to you, private. The next time you show disrespect to an officer, I'll see you're court-martialed."

The guard saluted and Reynolds returned it.

When the soldier resumed his patrol, Reynolds growled to Judson, "Follow me, sergeant."

After they had walked out of earshot, Judson asked, "Did you cut the wires?"

"Yes, I did." Reynolds turned to him and said, "Remember what we discussed. I'm going back to Wilmington to make sure General Bragg doesn't interfere, while you stay inside the fort. If anybody asks who you are, just tell them you're a scout for the General."

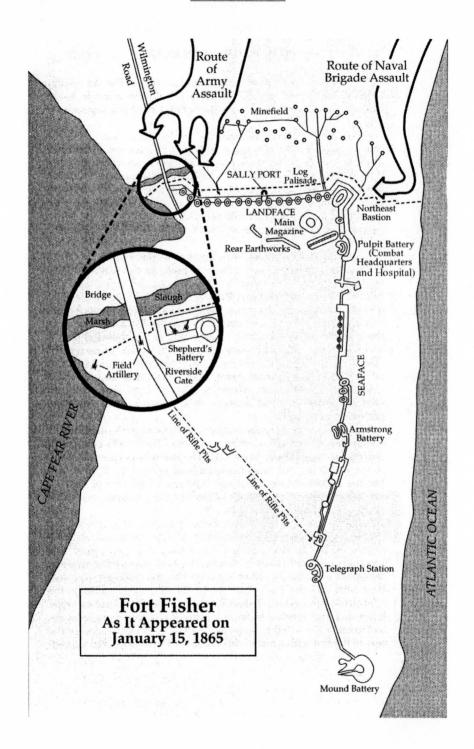

Fort Fisher
As It Appeared on
January 15, 1865

CHAPTER 15

Ripples from The War Between the States spread far beyond North America's borders. While Europe was adversely affected by shortages of Southern cotton; it enjoyed the enormous profits to be had in selling goods and munitions to the South. However, nowhere did the war have a more profound impact than in Nassau.

Beginning in 1861, the blockade-running trade brought a whirlwind of activity to the tiny Caribbean island. Shipmasters, pilots, blockade-running crews, dock workers and speculators prowled the waterfront on a daily basis--loading and unloading vessels and buying and selling goods or their services. Crafts of every description choked the harbor and dock space was at a premium. By January of 1865 the Federal blockade captured or destroyed one in three blockade-runners. With fewer Confederate ships arriving, the Bahamian Government had scaled back operations and a cloud of dread hung over the waterfront.

Swarms of workmen paused in their tasks, staring in wonder at the battered blockade-runner steaming into Nassau harbor. The *Atlantis* was missing half her forward funnel, the windows in the bridge were shattered, and what was left of her deck load of cotton was charred black along with a good portion of the planking on her deck. The crippled sidewheeler edged up to the wharf, wheezing and panting in distress while scores of dock workers rushed to assist her landing.

As soon as the deck hands heaved the ship's cables ashore, McKay came out of the bridge and leaned over the railing. "Fetch a surgeon quickly!" he called to the men on the wharf. "We've got wounded aboard!"

A Negro stevedore with a wide-brimmed straw hat looked up and shouted, "Yassuh, Capt'n!" before rushing off.

McKay walked aft to the engine room companionway and went below for a word with the chief engineer. A hiss of escaping steam and the distinctive odor of warm machine oil greeted him as he climbed down the ladder. "How does the engine look, Mr. Reichman?"

The sweaty engineer had just finished opening several relief valves and glanced at the captain. "I won't know until I shut everything down and have a look, sir. Lord knows we've been mighty rough on her--first the explosion, then running at full steam for two days. Judging from the sounds I've been hearing all morning, I'd say the main bearing needs to be looked at. And then there's the problem about the forward funnel, sir. Half of it's gone, and the rest is so mangled the furnace can't get the draft she needs. The whole thing should be replaced, but I'll see if I can repair it."

"Do what you think is best, Chief. If you can get the parts, replace it. I don't want anything to compromise our speed. That's about the only thing we have going for us."

The engineer shook his head, wiping his hands on an oily rag. "No, sir. We've got something much better than that."

"What's that?"

"We've got the best damned skipper who ever piloted a blockade-runner, sir. I'd sail through hell with him if he asked me to."

"Thank you, Mr. Reichman." McKay paused, then added, "You may have to before this is all over."

"No problem, sir. I meant every word."

An awkward moment came over McKay as he searched for something to say. He never handled these types of situations well, especially when it involved his crew. All he could think of was the question he'd had when he went below. "Do you think all the repairs can be made in forty-eight hours?"

The engineer scratched his head. "I don't know, sir. It depends on what I find when I inspect that bearing."

"Okay. Keep me posted." McKay turned to go, then hesitated, looking back. "By the way, Chief, you did a heck of a job bringing us in."

The engineer smiled and looked around. "Don't thank me, sir. The *Atlantis* did it all by herself."

"Nevertheless, you kept her going," McKay pointed out.

"I just understand her is all." The engineer thought a moment, smiling. "She's like a wife. You're with her so much you get to know her as no other man does. Like any woman, she needs constant attention. There's always something which needs to be done. Yet in the end, it's the little things that count most."

The engineer fell silent, then continued, "I hear things in that engine no one else does. She lets me know when something is wrong by making an odd noise. A ticking here, a whine there. I tend to her with a little grease, or by bleeding off some steam, and everything becomes quiet again."

McKay grinned. "Well, whatever you do, Chief, just keep doing it."

The engineer nodded, turning fondly to his machinery. The compliment was appreciated, but it wasn't necessary. The Captain's smile was all the praise he needed.

McKay went to the offices of Burgess & Linden and thrust the list of items Colonel Lamb had requested under the startled agent's nose.

"What's this?" the man asked, eyeing the sea captain before him.

"That's a list of supplies Fort Fisher needs desperately."

The thin-faced agent took a pair of spectacles from his pocket and hooked them over his ears. He examined the paper, shaking his head. "I can't grant this. I have your manifest right here, and it doesn't contain any of these items."

"I know it doesn't," McKay admitted, handing the man an envelope. "But I have a letter from General Whiting commandeering the *Atlantis* so we can bring those supplies through the blockade. The fort can't withstand another Yankee attack if it doesn't get them."

The agent read the letter, then folded his hands on the desk. "I don't care what this letter says. You have a contract with Burgess and Linden, and you are required by law to honor it."

McKay had enough of the man's condescending attitude. He leaned forward, jabbing a determined finger at the agent. "Look, you little pipsqueak, can't you understand if Fort Fisher falls to the Yankees, there'll be nowhere to take your damned cargos."

The man considered this. "I suppose you're right, Captain. However, we can't begin loading the *Atlantis* for five or six days. Three ships are ahead of you."

"I don't give a damn about those ships," McKay rumbled. "Those supplies are a lot more important than someone else's champagne and cigars."

"Nevertheless, Captain, there's nothing I can do."

"Yes there is. You can put the *Atlantis* at the top of your list."

The man shuffled the papers on his desk, nervously. "That's impossible, Captain. Now, if you'll excuse me, I have work to do."

McKay charged around the desk, hauling the man out of his chair by the lapels. The agent's face was pale, and his eyes were wide with fright.

"Look, I've got a ship which was nearly blown to hell, two men dead, and a score who were injured because the Yankees wanted to stop me from bringing in those supplies. If I survived that, there's no way in hell I'm going to let a little paper-pusher like you stop me."

The man quivered so hard it was difficult for him to get the words out fast enough. "Your--your ship will begin loading immediately, Captain."

McKay dropped the agent into his chair. "That's more like it. Don't you feel better now you've done something to help win the war?"

The nervous man, his spectacles askew, forced a smile and nodded weakly.

* * * * *

The Ladies' Soldiers' Aid Society left Wilmington aboard the steamer *Flora MacDonald* and put in at the dock near Battery Buchanan just after 9:30 A.M.. Groups of surprised men gathered to greet the ship and help unload the crates of food and equipment.

The first thing which came to mind when Brooke saw Fort Fisher after the December battle was that it resembled a huge pumpkin patch. Thousands of rusting cannonballs, and fragments from them, dotted the landscape with orange and made it appear strangely gay. Brooke hadn't expected to accompany the Ladies' Soldiers' Aid Society when they traveled to Fort Fisher to serve the soldiers a warm meal. But early that morning Virginia had come to Brooke's house and explained her mother had taken ill during the night, and begged Brooke to go in her place. Brooke went because she wanted to support the men who fought so valiantly in defending of their homeland. She also wanted to reunite Howard with his puppy, Rascal, and this provided the perfect opportunity.

After the battle during Christmas, the soldiers had found their quarters burned to the ground. The rows of fire-blackened brick chimneys, like ominous tombstones predicting their death, outraged the men so much they started rebuilding at once. Constructing new shelters became a matter of pride to the men, and they applied themselves tirelessly to the task. With finished lumber scarce, work parties went into the woods north of the fort to chop down trees. Others finished and dressed the logs, then sent them to the fort where they were used to assemble the new barracks.

Colonel Lamb was speaking with Captain Braddy at the barracks construction site when news of the women's arrival reached him. He excused himself and rode to Battery Buchanan. A dozen soldiers were setting up the huge tent the ladies had brought. Colonel Lamb swung down from his horse and walked over to the women, his scarlet-lined greatcoat billowing in the breeze. "How pleasant to see you again, Mrs. DeRosset."

The president of the Ladies' Soldiers' Aid Society smiled, extending her hand to the officer. "Thank you, Colonel. The ladies

255

and I have come to show our appreciation for what the soldiers have done by serving them a wonderful meal."

He smiled, bent at the waist to kiss her hand. "It seems the Ladies' Soldiers' Aid Society has done what the enemy failed to do."

Mrs. DeRossett became puzzled. "Oh? What's that, Colonel?"

"The ladies have surprised the garrison and taken the fort by storm!"

She smiled at the compliment. "You're a gentleman to say that, Colonel, but we sent a telegram announcing our arrival. Didn't you receive it?"

"Unfortunately no. We just got the telegraph line to Wilmington repaired yesterday afternoon."

Mrs. DeRosset's smile drained from her face. "Oh dear. You must think me the perfect fool."

"On the contrary. I think you're a genius. The men need a break from their duties, and you've found an excellent way to provide it."

The woman blushed in the warm glow of his praise. "Thank you, Colonel. You're most gracious."

"No, thank *you*. The men have been feeling a little down and this is certain to cheer them up. The euphoria of their victory has worn off," he explained, "and now they realize the enemy will be coming back. To make matters worse, our garrison hasn't received any supplies or reinforcements yet."

Mrs. DeRosset drew in a shocked breath. "That's terrible. What can we do?"

"Just what you're doing, ma'am. I wrote to President Davis, but he says he needs the army to protect Richmond and to attack General Sherman before he invades South Carolina." Colonel Lamb shook his head, continuing, "It seems our success may be our downfall. I'm afraid there's a widespread belief since we beat off the first attack we don't need any more troops."

Mrs. DeRosset appeared shocked. "Don't they understand if Fort Fisher falls, Wilmington will be closed to blockade-running?"

"I'm sure they do. They'd be fools if they didn't."

"Sometimes I wonder if fools are running this war," she mused.

Colonel Lamb smiled. "Well, enough about my troubles. Is there anything I can do to help?"

She tried to shake the dismal thoughts from her mind, considering what needed to be done. "Let's see. The tent is nearly up, and we prepared most of the food last night, so it only needs to be warmed. I guess you could begin sending the soldiers to our tent in about an hour."

"Splendid, ma'am. I'll see to it immediately."

Cradling Rascal to her bosom, Brooke wandered around searching for Howard Dutton. The dog's keen eyes spied the big man helping with the tent, and leaped from her arms.

When Howard heard the excited barking and saw Rascal, he dropped his hammer to the ground, whooping for joy. He scooped the animal up and held him close while the puppy happily licked his face.

Howard grinned. "Glory be! This must be my lucky day. All of my friends have come to see me. I seen Judd this morning and now you and Rascal."

"You saw Judson?" Brooke asked.

"Uh-huh. He came to the fort las' night."

"Oh dear. The police are searching for him," Brooke said, looking around.

"They are?"

"Yes. Two policemen came to our office this morning and asked if anyone had seen him. They said a bartender from the Green Parrot was stabbed to death, and a woman was badly slashed with a knife. One officer seemed to think Judson may be involved in several other murders."

Howard's eyebrows rose in a question. "Why would they believe that?"

"The woman who was attacked at the Green Parrot identified Judson. I believe they said her name is Amber."

As the long line of men drew closer to the Ladies' Soldiers' Aid Society tent, the tantalizing aroma of beef stew, biscuits and coffee caused excitement. Most of the soldiers had not seen a woman in months, and the sight of dozens of pretty women serving them food was nothing short of heaven. The women had brought blankets for the men to sit on, but the soldiers, used to doing without and improvising, sat wherever they could. Mrs. DeRosset and Colonel Lamb moved between them, chatting with the veterans as they ate.

A courier galloped up to the tent, hopping off his mount near a group of officers. The soldier spoke to an officer, who pointed to where Colonel Lamb was talking with several people.

Colonel Lamb tipped his hat to Mrs. DeRossett. "Will you excuse me, ma'am? I see I have a communication."

"Of course, Colonel," she said and left to see if they had enough food to go around.

The courier stepped forward, saluting. "Major Saunders' compliments, sir. He regrets to inform the Colonel at least fifty-eight Union warships have been seen on the horizon. They appear to be forming a line of battle."

Although Colonel Lamb knew this day was coming, he was not prepared for the feeling of surprise and regret which crept into his heart. "Very good. Have Major Rielly alert the garrison, and tell him I'll be along in a minute."

The colonel found Mrs. DeRossett behind a serving table, overseeing the distribution of the food. "Ma'am, Yankee warships have been sighted, and I must evacuate all civilians from the fort."

She drew in a sharp breath and paused to comprehend the situation. "I had no idea they'd come back so soon."

"None of us did."

The colonel hesitated, then asked, "Ma'am, would it be possible to leave the food here and let the men serve themselves? It may be a while before they get another warm meal."

"Of course, Colonel. Whatever you think is best."

"I'd appreciate that, ma'am."

She smiled, taking his hand and squeezing it. "Thank you for everything, Colonel. I'm certain our safety couldn't be in better hands."

Lamb nodded. "We'll do our best, ma'am."

Brooke had no intention of leaving Fort Fisher now that they needed her services. She turned to the young lieutenant escorting the women back to the sidewheel steamer, and asked, "Does the fort always refuse help when it's offered, or is it only because I'm a woman?"

"I'm just following orders, ma'am. Will you please come along?"

Folding her arms, Brooke said, "No, I won't. I want to volunteer."

Lieutenant Hurley looked around, his eyes pleading. He hoped no one would notice the difficulty he was having. "Please, ma'am. You're going to get me into a heap of trouble if you don't get on that ship."

"I'll be useful. I can tend the wounded which will free another soldier to defend the fort," Brooke pointed out.

"We have a surgeon to care for the injured men, ma'am. A good one, and he has a whole heap of assistants. We even got our own hospital."

"Good! Take me there."

"I can't do that, ma'am. You're going aboard that ship whether you like it or not."

She looked at this nice young man who looked like he wouldn't harm a soul. "And who's going to make me? You?"

"No, ma'am," he said, nodding behind him. "They will."

Two burly men trailed after them. One looked to be more animal than man because he had a face full of hair, and when he smiled Brooke saw he was missing two front teeth.

She turned to the Lieutenant. "You wouldn't dare. Where is your commanding officer? I would like to speak with him."

"He's busy right now, ma'am. Anyhow, I got orders from him to put all you ladies aboard that ship. And that's what I intend to do."

"But I need to warn him a murder suspect is hiding inside the fort." Brooke hadn't had an opportunity to report Judson yet, but she thought if she could speak with Colonel Lamb, he might give her a chance to help at the fort.

"The Colonel is mighty busy, ma'am. He doesn't have time to chase murderers."

Brooke's eyebrows were high arcs under her auburn hair. "But the man will get away."

"No, he won't. Give me his name, and I'll arrest him."

She folded her arms. "A lot of good that will do. He's not going to tell you who he really is." She thought a moment, then smiled. "However, if I go with you, I can identify him."

"I'm sorry, ma'am, but I can't take that responsibility. Only the colonel can give you permission to stay."

Glaring at him, Brooke said, "Fine. Then let's find him."

"I can't do that, ma'am. My orders are to get you on the ship and nothing else."

Brooke was growing weary of his attitude. "Come on, Lieutenant, we're not going to find him by standing here."

The lieutenant realized he was getting nowhere with the woman. He turned, motioning to the men behind them. "Take the women to the ship and make sure they get aboard. And tell the skipper not to leave until I give him the OK. I've got to take this lady to see the Colonel."

The men nodded, smiling at the group of women, who threw up their hands, aghast they were being left alone with such brutes.

Colonel Lamb was riding to the main part of the fort when Brooke and the lieutenant found him.

"Sir, I need to speak with you," the lieutenant called, rushing after him.

Colonel Lamb's horse wheeled about, tossing his head and snorting in protest.

"I'm sorry for the interruption, sir, but Miss Snow seems to think we have a murderer hiding inside the fort."

The colonel looked at Brooke. "Is that true, ma'am?"

"Yes, sir. The Wilmington police are searching for a murder suspect named Judson Bates. I'm certain I could help since I'm the only one here who can identify him."

The fort's commander placed a hand on his hip and straightened up in his saddle. "Ma'am, I assure you no one will escape from this fort while we're under attack. If you'll come back when the battle is over, I'll help you find him."

Brooke shook her head this was not good enough. "But I would like to stay here and help."

"I appreciate the offer, ma'am, but no civilians are allowed inside the fort. I'm sorry." Colonel Lamb motioned the junior officer over for a word in private. "Lieutenant Hurley, the clock is ticking. I want Miss Snow aboard that steamer in ten minutes. Don't disappoint me."

The lieutenant replied, "Yes, sir. Right away, sir."

Paddle wheels churned the dark water while Brooke clutched the steamer's railing, watching the gloomy faces of the soldiers on the wharf. What had begun as a glorious day was deteriorating into a nightmare.

A sudden flash of light above the fort caught her attention. Then a series of brilliant bursts followed in rapid succession, dotting the cloudless sky with puffs of gray smoke. The thunderous roar of the bombardment swept over the ship, terrifying everyone on board and driving them to the starboard railing to see what was happening. The men Brooke had been watching moments ago were scrambling for cover amid a barrage of smoke and flying iron.

A scraping beneath Brooke's feet startled her so much she jumped from fright. The ship had run ground with a gradual tilting of the deck, her steam whistle wailing plaintively.

*   *   *   *

Meanwhile, five miles north of Fort Fisher, Union Captain John Thomas leaned against the troop ship's brass railing and watched the line of Union warships pound the beach with their heavy guns. Every time a cannonball exploded on the Confederate shore, tons of sand and twirling pieces of maritime forest were tossed high into the air. In less than an hour 8,900 troops would assault the beach, and the Navy was determined to smash any bit of resistance the soldiers might encounter. This scene was all too familiar to the captain, who he had gone through the first landing in December. Major General Benjamin Butler was in charge then, and they'd had fewer men. Because he failed to capture the fort, Butler was relieved of command. Now the army had a bold new commander named General Alfred H. Terry.

As he watched the naval gunfire, Captain Thomas wondered if he had the courage needed to lead his men through the storm of shot and shell when they assaulted the fort. He had already seen the fort's formidable defenses during the last assault when he had crept within seventy-five yards of the walls. After a two-day bombardment by the Federal fleet, he still counted nineteen cannons on the land-face confronting the invasion route. Should he expect fewer this time?

Although the captain was a veteran of the bitter fighting in Virginia, those battles didn't instill in him the same sense of dread Fort Fisher did. In those conflicts he was unaware of the enemy's exact strength or position. Here he knew what his men would be up against. Twenty ten-inch columbiads on the land-face alone, two smaller artillery pieces near the front gate, two more near the sally-port, a palisade fence, a minefield and thirty foot high walls lined with rebel sharp shooters. In December, a Confederate division of 6,000 men had threatened the Federal rear. This time he expected even more troops to oppose them. Certainly the Confederates would reinforce now they had been alerted to the army's intentions.

At 11:45 A.M. the landing began. A dozen steam whistles shrieked, and the troop transports steamed closer to the beach. Soon the sea was covered with small boats of every kind, varying in size from small cutters to huge launches with twenty to thirty oars. Most of the men had gotten seasick one time or another during the long voyage and were relieved to be going ashore. Even if they had to fight for the beach, they'd rather be on land than sea. As the boats neared the coast, the Navy lifted their barrage so the troops could disembark. Cheer after cheer rang from the transports when the sailors saw the blue-coated soldiers splash ashore unopposed.

Peter Reynolds made sure he was at General Braxton Bragg's headquarters when the telegram about the Federal attack arrived. He was seated in the General's office giving him a report of how the increased pressure of the Federal blockade was affecting the military when Major Thorpe burst in.

"This telegram just arrived from Colonel Lamb, sir. I thought you would want to see it right away."

"Thank you, Major." The General opened the dispatch and read it. "My God! The Yankees have renewed their attack on Fort Fisher. They've landed thousands of soldiers north of the fort, and Colonel Lamb wants reinforcements to help repel the assault."

Peter Reynolds shook his head. "Sir, I know I'm only your advisor in matters regarding the blockade, but I must caution you against such a move. May I remind the General, Fort Fisher has already proven it can defend itself. Since the Federal Army's objective is to close the port of Wilmington, it would be a great mistake to take any troops away from the city and leave it undefended."

"But the Colonel's request?"

"Put yourself in the Yankees' place, General. If you were ordered to close the port of Wilmington, would you attack the enemy's strength by laying siege to Fort Fisher? Or would you go up the peninsula and attack the undefended port itself?"

"I would march on the city, of course."

"And that's exactly what the Yankees intend to do. They're guessing you'll send reinforcements to the fort, but don't be fooled, sir."

General Bragg still seemed unconvinced, so Reynolds added, "Remember when my scout Judson Bates reported to you last month?"

Bragg set the telegram on his desk, nodding.

"Well, sir, he told you about the December invasion, and didn't everything happen like he said it would? Weren't the Yankees driven back?"

"Yes, they were," General Bragg answered.

"That's because you maintained your defense of Wilmington. If you'd have rushed troops to the fort, like the Yankees wanted, they would have attacked the city and closed the port right then."

General Bragg walked to a wall map showing the peninsula from Wilmington to Fort Fisher. "Where do you think would be the best place to set up a defensive line?"

Peter Reynolds pointed to an area on the map. "Here, sir. About twelve miles south of Wilmington."

"Don't you think I should move closer to the fort in case Colonel Lamb does need my assistance?"

"No, sir. If you do, the men will be bombarded by the Navy. You've got good ground in this area. There's a large hill near the river and a swampy area which will make it difficult for your position to be flanked."

The General rubbed his graying whiskers, nodding. He picked up a pen and issued orders for a defensive line to be built twelve miles south of Wilmington.

When Brooke found out the ship was merely aground on a sandbar and not in danger of sinking, she was relieved. Her ease was short lived, however, as the gravity of their situation dawned upon her. Brooke slapped the railing in anger, walking over to the other women. "Well, isn't this just fine? Here we sit, no good to anybody, while the Yankees blow up Fort Fisher."

"What can we do?" a woman in a green cape asked.

"We can go back to the fort and help out."

"You can go if you want to, but don't expect me to be behind you," the woman declared, shaking her head. "People are getting killed over there."

Brooke nodded. "Yes. People are getting killed, but not all of them have to die. Not if we go back and help the surgeon care for the wounded."

"But there's nothing we can do. We're stuck on this sandbar."

"So? Are you going to let a little thing like this defeat you?" Brooke asked, glancing at the others. Every face was intent on hers. "We're intelligent women. I'm sure we can think of something."

"Not all of us want to follow you blindly," one of the older women said. "I have a family to think about."

Brooke nodded with understanding. "I know some of you have obligations. And those who do are free to go. Who'll come with me?"

A woman with fear-widened eyes spoke up. "I wouldn't go near Fort Fisher now. I've heard the Yankees rape every woman they capture."

Gasps of shock filled the air. When they subsided, Brooke asked, "Where did you hear that?"

"Well, I have a lady friend who said when the Yankees met resistance in Atlanta, they made the city pay by raping every woman they captured," she explained.

"I wouldn't believe such gossip for a minute," Brooke said, with a dismissive wave of her hand. "Besides, the newspaper reports I've read said they treated the civilians well."

"The newspapers will say anything to avoid a panic," the woman countered.

"And you'd believe the word of some woman who wasn't there over the newspaper."

"Of course I would. What reason would she have to lie?"

Brooke looked at her. "How can you call yourself a Christian and not help those men? How can any of us? I thought the women of Wilmington created the Ladies' Soldiers' Aid Society to support our fighting men. I guess I must have been mistaken," she said.

A silence fell over the group, then a woman stepped forward, and said, "You can count on my help. My husband's in that fort."

Another woman said, "Me too. I'll come with you. I'm tired of letting others fight this war for me."

Several others joined the women standing next to Brooke.

"That's the spirit! Let's show the Yankees they'll never defeat the South if Southern women have anything to say about it."

Brooke turned thoughtful. "Now we have to figure out a way to get back to the fort." She brightened when she saw two row boats coming from the fort. "Ladies, I think our prayers have been answered."

265

When Colonel Lamb heard the *Flora McDonald's* distress whistle and saw the steamer aground on a sandbar, he dispatched Lieutenant Hurley with two boats and orders to ferry the ladies to Smithville, across the river. The seaworthiness of their vessel wasn't his only concern, he was also worried about the cannonballs which overshot the fort and splashed into the water dangerously close to their ship.

Crewmen on the *Flora McDonald* threw a rope ladder over the steamer's side, and Lieutenant Hurley climbed aboard. The bearded captain extended his hand and asked, "Lieutenant, is it possible to get another steamer to pull my ship free?"

"There are none to be had, sir. I did a quick inspection of your hull when we approached, and it appears sound. Maybe you can float free on the next high tide."

"Yes," the captain agreed. "Perhaps if you take off some of our coal, it'll lighten the ship."

The young army officer's gaze softened, but his voice remained firm. "My orders weren't to help you get off the sandbar, sir. Colonel Lamb instructed me to take the ladies to Smithville."

While he was talking to the captain, the lieutenant was scanning the deck for Miss Snow. It was difficult to keep his eyes from seeking out such an attractive woman. Spotting her, he noticed she had gathered the other ladies and was speaking to them.

"If you want me to, Captain," Lieutenant Hurley offered, "I'll ask the Colonel if I can come back to assist you."

A cannonball screamed into the river, raising a tremendous geyser of white water not more than sixty feet from where they were standing. Both men ducked as the spray rained down on them. When the captain recovered, he said, "Thank you, lieutenant. I would appreciate getting out of here as soon as possible." He nodded his thanks, gesturing to the women behind him. "It appears the ladies are waiting for you."

Lieutenant Hurley walked over to the women, raising his hands, and said, "Ladies, may I have your attention please."

The women stopped talking and looked at the young officer.

"My name is Lieutenant Hurley. I've been instructed by Colonel Lamb to take you to Smithville."

"But we don't want to go to Smithville," one woman protested, shaking her head. "We want to go back to the fort and help tend the wounded."

"That's admirable, ma'am, but it's quite impossible while the fort is under attack."

The woman frowned. "Why? We aren't afraid."

"It's not a question of being afraid, ma'am. It's a matter of right and wrong. Women have no place in a combat situation where they could be killed or captured. I have orders to ferry all ladies from the Soldiers Aid Society to Smithville, and that's where we're going."

Brooke winked to the other women. "All right, lieutenant. We'll go to Smithville, if that's what you want."

The lieutenant went to the railing then motioned to the soldiers. The men clambered out of the launches and aboard the steamer, to escort the women to the boats.

Brooke got into a boat and most of the others followed her. Several women sniffed in contempt while walking away.

"Give me the oars to your boat," Brooke whispered to a woman in the launch next to hers.

After the woman slipped her several oars, Brooke pushed off from the steamer, rowing for Fort Fisher.

Lieutenant Hurley rushed to the railing when he saw what was happening, and shouted, "Come back here, Miss Snow!"

"I can't," Brooke cried over the din of the bombardment. "I've got business at Fort Fisher."

Lieutenant Hurley climbed into the other boat and discovered the oars were missing.

"You've taken my oars. How can I get the rest of the women to Smithville?"

"I'll send them back when we get to the fort," she called.

The lieutenant was already in trouble because of this stubborn woman, and he was not about to let her return to Fort Fisher and cause more. He estimated the boat couldn't be more than fifty feet away from the steamer. In a last ditch effort to stop her, he stripped off his hat and pistol belt, and dove into the water.

His actions surprised Brooke, and she craned her neck to watch him. "It's not going to do you any good to swim after me, Lieutenant. This boat is much too fast for you to catch."

At first the lieutenant appeared to be doing well. His strong arms broke the surface of the water and propelled his body forward. After several minutes, his progress slowed, and he began drifting downstream. The river's swift current, was too strong for him to swim against.

Brooke feared he would be swept out to sea, but knew if she picked him up he would demand she return to the ship. Her mind was made up in an instant. "Stop rowing toward the fort," she snapped. "The lieutenant will drown unless we save him."

After turning the boat around, the five women put their backs into the oars. The fifty-degree water sapped the man's strength. He floundered around a bit, then disappeared beneath the waves.

"Come on! We've got to hurry!" Brooke said, pleading. When the boat got to where he had vanished, there was no sign of him.

Suddenly, Lieutenant Hurley flailed to the surface.

Brooke was relieved to see him. "Can you swim over and pull yourself aboard?"

He shook his head faintly, his head bobbing low in the water. It was an effort for him to speak. "I. . .I don't think I have the strength."

"All right, hold on. We'll come to you."

When the boat pulled alongside him, Brooke said, "Give us your arms, Lieutenant! On the count of three, I want you to try and crawl aboard while we pull. Okay?"

He nodded, trembling from the cold.

"One--two--you gotta help us now," she reminded him.

He raised his arms and the women scrambled to grab them.

"Three!"

The women pulled for all they were worth, causing the boat to dip near to the water's surface. Gallons of cold river water flowed over the side as he began to slide aboard. Brooke grabbed the edge of his trousers and yanked, all the while leaning back. The man was too heavy, but she refused to let go. Ever so slowly she was being dragged to the edge of the boat and into the river. Soon her upper body splashed into the cold water, but still she wouldn't let go. Half in and half out of the boat, she screamed for the other women to help her. The ladies clustered about, grabbing her legs and pulling, until they halted her slide. Brooke turned her attention to the soldier.

"You've got to help me, Lieutenant! I can't do this all by myself," she said breathlessly. "We're going to try again, but this time, kick yourself up in the water. Time your kick so when I count three, you'll be rising out of the water. Okay?"

He nodded, shivering.

"All right! One--two--now kick--three!"

The women pulled the lieutenant and he tumbled into the launch, shivering. Brooke borrowed a cape to cover him, rubbing the man's hands and arms to increase his circulation. A woman came over and helped Brooke off with her wet cloak and replaced it with her own.

Finally, the boat got underway again. Lieutenant Hurley's muscles were numb, but when he regained control of his jaw muscles enough to speak, he thanked the women and asked, "Where are we going?"

"Back to the ship, where you'll be warm," she replied, kneading his left arm.

He considered what she had said. "I think I'd feel better if I were in the fort, wouldn't you?"

Brooke smiled and rubbed harder.

CHAPTER 16

Even before the bombardment began, Judson Bates was searching for a safe place to hide. Where could a stranger go and not be asked a lot of questions? The answer came to him as he was walking past the Pulpit Battery. The gigantic mound of sand had a deep cut down the center, and the crescent-shaped hospital was carved into one side of that cut. Huge timbers supported the planked roof and walls against tons of sand which served as a protective barrier. Opposite the opening, a wooden retaining wall backed by more sand acted as a buffer against exploding cannonballs. The hospital was a perfect bombproof since a shell would have to make a direct hit on the narrow opening to do any damage. In a little while, it would be so busy with wounded men, Judson knew nobody would notice him.

The monitors unleashed their fifteen inch cannonballs, opening the bombardment. The heavens above were virtually ripped apart by the terrible bursts of the monstrous shells. A huge cannonball exploded above one of the gun chambers, shattering the cannon's carriage and mortally wounding its crew. Judson witnessed the explosion and dove into a large shell crater for protection. When the sand and debris stopped raining down, he rushed up the mound. The gun chamber reeked of burnt sulphur, and Judson found it difficult to breathe. Shattered, smoking pieces of the cannon and body parts were strewn everywhere. As Judson studied the smoldering wreckage, a moan caught his attention. A wounded soldier sat on

270

the ground, propped up against an ammunition box. Purplish, rope-like intestines bulged from his blood soaked shirt, and he raised a feeble arm to get Judson's attention.

Judson went over, kneeling beside him.

The man's sweating face was black with powder burns, and a bloody hand clutched his stomach. He licked his lips dryly. "Thank God you're here," he rasped with difficulty. "Can you help me get to the hospital?"

Blood oozed around the man's hand to the sand beneath him. Incredible sadness crept into his face when Judson leaned forward to pull the bright red shirt aside for a closer look at the wound. "There ain't nothin' you can do for me, Mister, 'cept help me to the hospital," the wounded man said.

Judson pursed his lips. "You'll never make it that far. You're gut shot." He brought his hand away from the wound and looked at the blood on it as an idea began to take shape. He removed his hat, smearing the blood in his hair.

An explosion in the next gun chamber slammed Judson to the ground. Tons of sand fell from the sky like wind-driven sleet, covering everything in a thick blanket. As Judson crawled out of his premature grave, he noticed another soldier sprawled face down across a splintered gun carriage. He turned him over and gasped when he saw the soldier's face. The man's skin was blown off, and his whole head became an oozing wound. Blood gurgled around a smashed jaw bone containing several yellow teeth as he tried to speak. Judson paid no attention to the man's suffering and tore a strip of material from the gunner's linen shirt, then wrapped it around his own head and knotted it.

The soldier with the stomach wound was coughing up blood. He gasped with bright trembling lips, "Mister, ain't you gonna to help me?"

"Yeah, I nearly forgot." Judson drew his bone-handled knife from its sheath, grabbed the man by the hair and snapped his head back to expose his throat.

The wounded man fought against him, but he was so weak his struggle was merely token resistance.

Judson pressed the silver blade against the soldier's windpipe, and said, "I'm fixin' to do you a big favor, pal. You're gut shot--clean through. Which means you're already dead." Judson smiled at the irony of it. The man's bad luck was his good fortune because it fit his plans perfectly. Now he could truly look the part of a wounded soldier. Judson slit the soldier's throat with no more thought than someone would give to carving a piece of fruit, then moved around front, and basked in the warm crimson spray.

When the five women from the Ladies Soldiers Aid Society came ashore at Battery Buchanan, they accompanied Lieutenant Hurley into the fortification where Brooke and he were given dry clothing and steaming cups of "Confederate coffee". Coffee beans were scarce due to the blockade, so the soldiers brewed a substitute from parched peanuts with a bit of dried apple. Grateful for anything warm, the Lieutenant wrapped his hands around the tin cup, then winced as he took a sip of the dark fluid.

Brooke sat and considered her options while rolling up the sleeves of the big, woolen shirt the soldiers had given her. "I don't want to get you into any more trouble, Lieutenant. Just point us in the direction of the hospital, and we'll find our way."

The officer lowered the cup, his eyes amused. "Ma'am, I hope you don't take this the wrong way, but I'm in trouble no matter what you do. Still," he said, considering, "I'd be worse off if I let you women go there by yourself."

"Why, Lieutenant," Brooke said, and her mouth curved in a faint smile, "does that mean you'll come with us?"

"I suppose it does. Besides," he admitted, pouring the remaining liquid onto the pine floor, "I've about had it with this burnt goober-pea coffee anyway." He banged his cup on the table to get the women's attention. "Listen up, ladies."

The women stopped talking and turned to him.

"I noticed an artillery supply wagon outside which will get us to the hospital. It's not covered, but it's all we have. If you stay down in the bed, the sides will help shield you. I'll also spread several tarps over you."

He paused to consider the terrain they would have to cross, then continued, "The hospital is in the northeast corner of the fort, under the Pulpit Battery. The bank of the river slopes a little," he explained, "so it'll provide some shelter. I'm going to follow the river to the main gate, then I'll turn east. From that point on the wagon will be exposed to whatever the Yankees throw at us, so I guess we'll have a wild ride for about a mile. Anybody have any questions?"

He waited long enough to allow everyone to give his words careful thought. The muffled percussion of heavy guns penetrated the bombproof's walls.

When no one spoke, he continued, "If any of you have changed your mind, now is the time to tell me. Once we leave here, there'll be no turning back."

One woman, who was nervously gazing down at her folded hands the whole time, looked up. "I'm sorry, but I can't go," she said, glancing at the concerned faces around her. "I'm terribly sorry! Lord knows I tried, but I just can't do it." Her eyes became moist, and she hung her head in despair.

Brooke smiled, squeezing her hand to comfort her.

"That's all right, ma'am," the Lieutenant said. "We'll have some men take you to Smithville."

"If she's going, then I'm coming too," another woman spoke up. "Sitting here and hearing those guns have helped me come to my senses."

Knowing two women wanted to leave saddened Brooke, but the fact the others were still willing to go to the hospital heartened her. She smiled at the women. "Thank you both for your courage. Most women wouldn't have come this far. No one will think any less of you for not going."

The others nodded in agreement.

"If there's nothing else," Lieutenant Hurley said, "I'll go check on the wagon."

A bearded soldier with red sergeant stripes handed him a stack of tarpaulins and wished him luck.

Outside Battery Buchanan cannonballs hammered the sky with their explosions and filled the air with smoke and spinning shrapnel.

The supply wagon's two horses would have bolted long ago had it not been for the vehicle's brake. Braving the storm of screaming iron and choking fumes, Lieutenant Hurley rushed outside and grabbed the horses' bridles to pat their necks and settle them down. When there was a brief lull in the shelling, he motioned for the ladies to run to the wagon. Two of them scrambled into the rear of the wagon, while Brooke went to help Lieutenant Hurley spread the tarpaulins.

The soldier glared at her. "Miss Snow, get into that wagon and keep your head down."

"That's not practical, Lieutenant. Who'll drive if you get hurt?"

Lieutenant Hurley admired her spirit and was tempted to smile. "Thank you for sharing your belief that some great misfortune will befall me, but either you get into the back of that wagon right now, or I'm going to carry you."

Crossing her arms, Brooke said, "Then you'd better start carrying, Lieutenant, because I'm not moving."

Brooke cried out in shock when the soldier scooped her up, then dumped her in the back of the wagon.

"Now stay down, damn it!"

She huffed angrily, smoothing her ruffled petticoats along with her dignity.

Lieutenant Hurley threw two tarpaulins over the women before climbing onto the driver's seat. He eased the brake lever forward, releasing it, then cracked the reins while the sky above them blossomed with explosions.

The land close to the river was marshy, but Lieutenant Hurley needed to drive over the sandy, oyster shell mud to take advantage of any protection the bank offered. The wagon careened down the narrow embankment and raced alongside the winter-brown marsh grass lining the waterway. The women were holding onto the sides of the wagon to keep from being bucked out. Sandy mud flew from the horses hooves, splattering against the dashboard as the driver hunched forward, cracking the reins.

White smoke drifted across the path in front of them, concealing what lay beyond. Although it unnerved Lieutenant Hurley to drive into the haze without seeing where he was going, he had no choice and urged the horses on. In seconds the smoke thinned, and he saw a field of brown marsh grass where the riverbank should have been. He jerked the reins to the right, slamming on the brakes. The right front wheel locked, and the wagon skidded out of control into the marsh. Great sheets of water shot into the air as the wagon slid sideways, threatening to flip over and spill its cargo into the murky water.

When the wagon came to a stop, Lieutenant Hurley swung around in his seat to see if everyone was all right. Water cascaded off the tarpaulin as three pale faces propped it up. "Is everyone okay?"

"Yes! We are! What happened, Lieutenant?" Brooke asked.

"We ran off the road because of all the smoke, ma'am. You ladies keep down while I get us out of here."

Lieutenant Hurley swung forward in his seat, cracking the reins. The wagon creaked ahead a few feet, then became bogged down in the mud.

A shell shrieked overhead. It exploded in the marsh, hurling up huge chunks of earth, grass and a towering mist of water. The horses panicked, pulling the wagon free of the sucking mud as debris splashed into the water around them. Lieutenant Hurley turned right at the main gate and was overwhelmed by the damage.

The Union fleet of fifty-eight warships mounting 627 guns concentrated their fire on the gun chambers lining the fort's land face. Through the smoke and haze of battle he could vaguely see the fearless gunners, in red kepis doggedly loading and firing their cannons. A few brave soldiers were helping the wounded while others were buried in partial graves dug by the shells which killed them. To the wagon's right, dozens of barracks were burning fiercely, the smoke being carried away by a southeast wind to further obscure the land-face.

As the wagon raced on, a shell screamed into a gun chamber to their left, exploding. Twirling pieces of timber and tons of sand were hurled high into the air. A wounded Confederate soldier crawled out of this hell, then tumbled down the earthen wall.

Slamming on the brakes, Lieutenant Hurley hopped to the ground and sprinted over to the man.

Blood spurted to the sand from the ragged stump of his left arm, and his eyes were staring in shock. Lieutenant Hurley whipped off his belt, picked up a splinter of wood and applied a tourniquet above the man's elbow. In a moment, Brooke was at his side.

"I think I've got the bleeding stopped," he said.

"Let's move him to the wagon," She suggested.

Both of them helped the barely conscious man to the wagon. Lieutenant Hurley hopped into the back, dragging the man aboard by the shoulders. He scrambled into the driver's seat, cracking the reins while yelling, "Haaa!"

Carnage was everywhere and it seemed to get worse the farther they went. Shattered timbers, unexploded cannonballs and iron fragments littered the sand. The bright red and white garrison flag of the Pulpit Battery fluttered amid the bursting shells in the distant haze. Housed below it was the hospital. The vision of safety spurred the little wagon onward, until it reached the sloping mound of sand which marked their destination.

The lieutenant drove the wagon into the narrow passage that separated the hospital from a retaining wall on the other side.

He hopped to the ground, dragged the unconscious man from the back of the wagon, then threw him over his shoulder then hurried into the hospital.

Glowing lanterns hung from huge rough-sawn beams in the ceiling and spilled their yellow light on a bloody-aproned surgeon as he sawed through a soldier's gleaming thigh bone. The sweat-drenched man on the operating table was thrashing his head in agony and clenching a minié ball in his teeth while being held down by two husky assistants. The floor was packed with stretchers containing dozens of wounded men. Chaplain Luther McKinnon and several white coated orderlies were administering bandages, water, and prayers.

The Lieutenant carefully set the wounded man down where an orderly had suggested. As the attendant knelt to examine him,

Brooke came over and whispered in Hurley's ear, "Lieutenant, Judson Bates is here."

Hurley swung around. "Where?"

"He's in that corner, leaning on a crutch," Brooke said, nodding over her shoulder.

Hurley scanned the room and saw the man she was referring to. "Stay here. I'll handle this."

Brooke caught his arm as he began to leave. "Aren't you going to draw your gun?"

"I don't think that's necessary, do you?"

Brooke gazed at him as if he were crazy. "Yes, I do. Bates is dangerous."

The Lieutenant looked at the crippled man with the blood soaked bandage around his head. "He doesn't look dangerous to me."

"Well, he is. Don't let that crutch fool you," she warned.

"I won't. But I'm not going to cause a big scene by pulling out my gun. These men are scared enough without some fool waving a gun around."

Brooke shrugged her slender shoulders in resignation. "Okay. Do what you want."

The Lieutenant walked across the room and addressed the man Brooke had identified. "Judson Bates?"

The man looked up, leaning on his crutch. "Uh-uh. You got the wrong man, Lieutenant."

"Someone identified you, Bates."

"Who might that be?" Judson said, eyeing the room suspiciously.

"It doesn't matter."

"Oh, but it does. It matters a heap to me." He paused, then asked, "Why do you want this feller, Lieutenant?"

"He's wanted for murder."

"Murder?" Judson chuckled, shaking his head in amazement. "Well, it sure ain't me, by God. I've been in this here fort for the last six months."

The Lieutenant had only been at Fort Fisher a few months, so he tried to flush Bates out with a bluff. "That's funny. I've been here two years. Why haven't I noticed you before?"

"Don't know, Lieutenant. Reckon I'm not the kind of man folks take notice of."

"Perhaps. Then you won't object to coming with me so we can straighten this out."

"Won't mind a'tall, sir. I'll do jus' that," he said limping past the Lieutenant on his crutch. Suddenly Bates whirled and sliced the air with the wooden staff, striking the officer in the head and sending him crashing into the wall.

Hurley staggered under the blow, then pursued the man as he ran from the hospital bombproof.

Bates disappear around the corner of the mound, so the lieutenant drew his Navy revolver, sprinting after him as bursting shells lit the sky like newborn stars.

The two men raced through drifting smoke until Bates stumbled, falling into a bomb crater. While, scrambling to get out of the hole, he heard the revolver's hammer click and froze.

"Hold it right there, Bates," Hurley ordered.

Bates turned around in time to see a cannonball arc in the sky behind the Lieutenant. "Okay, it looks like you've got me."

The cannonball's blinding explosion slammed the officer to the ground. The revolver flew out of his hand and slid down the crater to Bates' feet. A darkening stain spread below the torn jacket near Lieutenant Hurley's right shoulder.

Bates picked up the gun, grinning. "Well-well, Lieutenant. Looky here. I got me this fine pistol while you got yourself wounded. Reckon I'm goin' to have to put you out of your misery."

Bates aimed at the officer's head, and pulled the trigger. The revolver was damaged in the explosion and clicked harmlessly.

A musket cracked from the direction of the hospital, and a minié ball hissed within inches of Judson's head. A Confederate soldier lowered a musket from his shoulder, then took a paper cartridge from the leather box slung across his shoulder and tore it open with his teeth. Several more soldiers were coming up behind him.

"Looks like you lucked out, Lieutenant, but I ain't through with you yet," Bates promised before dashing off.

Seeing Lieutenant Hurley chasing Bates from the hospital, Brooke stopped two soldiers carrying a litter with a wounded man, and told them what was happening. They set the stretcher down and ran after them. Brooke heard several shots fired, then went to the door and peeked out. She saw one of those men helping the lieutenant back and noticed there was blood on his uniform near the right shoulder. "You're hurt, Lieutenant!"

He glanced at the wound, nodding. "It's nothing serious. I'll be fine if I rest for a minute."

"This is no time for heroics," Brooke snapped. "Sit down so I can look at your shoulder."

The Lieutenant sat on the pine floor and unbuttoned his jacket, and held it open. A small cannonball fragment had entered the back of his right shoulder and tore a two-inch exit wound just below his collarbone.

Brooke snatched several cotton compresses from an orderly and held one on the wound to stem the flow of blood. "You never did tell me your first name, Lieutenant."

"It's William, ma'am."

"Mine's Brooke," she told him.

"So you think it's that bad?" he asked.

Brooke was surprised. "Not at all. Why would you ask that?"

"Because people become overly friendly when someone's badly hurt."

She smiled. "Oh, I see. Well, that's not why I asked at all. I just felt we know each other well enough to be on a first name basis," she explained adding another compress to the one already soaked with blood.

Smiling weakly, he settled back against the planked wall.

"William, can you hold this while I get some help?"

Brooke stepped around dozens of stretchers containing wounded men as she made her way to where the surgeon was working. A soldier was stretched out on the operating table, and the physician was using a forceps to explore a wound in the man's lower abdomen.

The veteran's pants were low enough to expose his genitals, but this did not deter Brooke. She looked straight at the surgeon, and asked, "Doctor, can you look at Lieutenant Hurley? He's been hit in the shoulder by a shell fragment."

"What size is the wound? Is there an entrance and exit?" Surgeon Spiers Singleton asked, glancing at her briefly, then turning back to continue probing the soldier's wound.

"He has two holes in his shoulder. A smaller one in back and a larger one in front. About two inches in diameter, I think."

"How is the blood flow? Is it spurting or merely seeping from the wound?"

"It's seeping. Although," she observed with a note of concern, "it appears he's lost a fair amount."

"All right, Miss. I assume you ladies came here to work, so here's what you do," Singleton said extracting a half-inch chunk of jagged iron from the soldier's abdomen with his forceps. "Get yourself a bucket of water and a bar of soap. Clean his wound and have an orderly bandage it for you." Sensing her concern, he added, "He'll be fine, Miss. I'll check on him as soon as I can."

Brooke found a bucket of water which contained a wash cloth and a brown bar of soap and brought them over to where the Lieutenant sat. "Help me get your jacket and shirt off so I can clean your wound."

He had trouble pulling them off his broad shoulders.

"Let me help," Brooke offered and carefully removed the garments, setting them on the pine floor next to him.

She scrubbed the bar of soap with the washcloth, producing a thick lather. Lieutenant Hurley lowered the bloody cotton when she was ready. "The Surgeon says you're lucky," she observed, gently washing around the wound. "The fragment passed through your body without doing much damage."

He wanted to laugh, but grimaced instead. "Somehow I don't feel so lucky."

The orderly Hurley had spoken to when they first arrived knelt beside her, setting down a tray of bandages. "How are we doing, ma'am?"

"Fine, I just finished washing his wound."

"That's great. Looks like you've done a wonderful job," he said, inspecting the wound.

"Thank you."

"You're welcome. I'm glad you ladies are here. We have more work than we can handle," he said, removing a roll of cotton bandages from the tray. "I'll put on a temporary bandage until the surgeon has a chance to look at the wound. He'll decide what to do later."

She nodded, watching while he placed several layers of bandages over the dressing and the right shoulder. Then he wrapped the remainder around the Lieutenant's chest several times, knotting the ends.

When he was through, the orderly gathered the women together, and said, "I want to thank you ladies for volunteering. Your duty is to make the men as comfortable as possible. Bring them water, wet their bandages, even just talking to them will help. A woman's voice can be soothing to a wounded man."

"Why should we wet the bandages?" one woman asked.

"We've found fresh wounds will heal faster when they're kept wet," he explained. "You'll see buckets of water for that purpose scattered throughout the hospital."

"It's so cold in here," Brooke observed. "Wouldn't the men be more comfortable if we lit the fireplaces?"

"I'd like nothing better, ma'am, but we can't chance having the fire get out of control if we suffered a direct hit. The only reason we have lanterns burning is so the surgeon can see to operate."

Brooke went from litter to litter with water, asking the men if they needed anything. Most welcomed the opportunity for a drink and a chance to tell her about the battle and how they were wounded. The more seriously injured gave her their names and urged her to write their families about what had happened to them. Brooke kept a list of all the men, but as the list grew longer, she found it more difficult to maintain her composure. She wanted to hide somewhere and weep, but as the battle progressed, more wounded arrived. Everywhere she looked, men were writhing in pain. Seeing their horribly mangled bodies and hearing their suffering made her forget about herself. There was too much to do.

When the incoming wounded slowed to a trickle that evening, Brooke sat, exhausted, keeping an eye on the injured men and listening to the bombardment. Every time a cannonball exploded on the hospital mound, she would stare at the ceiling as the sand fell from the cracks in between the beams, wondering how long it would be before the whole thing came crashing on top of them. About three o'clock in the morning, cold and weary from lack of sleep and overwork, she ceased her vigil, and closed her eyes.

*   *   *   *

While Brooke sat gazing at the hospital ceiling in Fort Fisher, Captain McKay walked out on deck beneath the starlit Nassau sky. A full moon shown down on the *Atlantis*, illuminating her hull and superstructure with its silvery-white light. Although McKay had never attempted to run the blockade during a full moon, the precious cargo in the hold changed all that. Those supplies meant life to Fort Fisher. If the fort was allowed to fall, then the Confederacy would soon follow. Colonel Lamb had told him the Federal invasion fleet was being assembled at Hampton Roads, so there wasn't a moment to lose. He had to get through the blockade tonight. The bright moon would make it difficult, but he had devised a plan.

The increased activity of the Federal cruisers off Nassau did not surprise Captain McKay. As the War Between the States progressed, so too did the strength of the blockade. The Federal Navy had begun turning out ships at a phenomenal rate. McKay was aware for every blockade-runner successfully running the blockade, three others were either captured or destroyed, and the Union was converting some swifter captured vessels into warships. Now every run through the blockade was more difficult than the one before.

*   *   *   *

Peter Reynolds had reported to the Union Navy the *Atlantis* was sailing for Nassau to pick up a cargo of munitions for Fort Fisher. Because the Navy wanted nothing to interfere with the assault on the fort, they laid a trap for the blockade-runner. If the *Atlantis'* cargo: ten tons of gunpowder, five thousand cannonballs, ten thousand rifles, twenty-five thousand cartridges and medicine was delivered, it could swing the battle in the Confederates' favor.

According to the Federal plan, most Union warships would sail far enough out to sea so they could not be spotted by anyone on the island. When the blockade-runner was at least ten miles off the harbor entrance, the warships would close in from all sides and capture her. In case the *Atlantis* slipped away, the Navy had also sent their fastest ship to the area to hunt her down. The *USS Black Prince* had a long list of captured blockade-runners to her credit, and her captain hoped to add the elusive *Atlantis* to that list.

*   *   *   *

The crew set about preparing the *Atlantis* to run the blockade. Lookouts wearing dark clothing and instructed to communicate with hand signals were posted in the mast tops and at various places around the deck. The binnacle was shrouded so no light from the oil lamp would escape, giving away the ship's position. Anything shiny enough to reflect moonlight was removed from the deck. The paddle wheel boxes were fitted with canvas skirts to help muffle noise. Both funnels were replaced with the new telescoping type which contained special screens to filter out sparks. The engine bearings were packed in grease to keep them running smoothly during the difficult voyage ahead.

McKay related his plan to his boatswain while the *Atlantis* glided out of Nassau Harbor. "We'll run the blockade as we normally would. If everything goes well, we'll continue to Fort Fisher and deliver our cargo the day after tomorrow. However, if we discover too many Federal warships to outrun, we'll turn around and head for the shoal area south of the harbor entrance."

The boatswain looked at Captain McKay as if he had gone mad. "But, sir, it's hard enough to navigate those coral reefs during the day. How are we going to do it at night?"

"Ah, that's where my plan comes in. A Bahamian pilot and I went out yesterday in a small fishing boat and marked a channel through the reef with buoys."

"So you propose to follow these buoys while the Yankees run aground?"

"Yes. What do you think?"

"It might work, Captain," the boatswain agreed. "Still, I have my doubts if the Federal ships will follow us. Those cruisers respect the five-mile limit, and that reef is only two miles off the island."

"You have a point, Mr. Gallagher. That's why I've asked the Governor to black out the lighthouse, so the Federal cruisers won't know how far offshore they are. I think it's safe to assume when those warships are chasing the *Atlantis* through the darkness, they'll be watching us and not where they're going."

The lookout in the *Atlantis'* forward mast lowered his telescope, waving an arm above his head to signal the sentry posted outside the bridge. He pointed to starboard and held up three fingers. The sentry, who was watching the lookout through a telescope, poked his head inside the bridge saying, "Captain, the lookout in the forward mast has sighted a Yankee warship three points to starboard."

"Very good. Let's hope he hasn't seen us," McKay said, his voice taking on a faint edge. "Helmsman, steer forty-five degrees to port."

McKay snatched a telescope from its leather case mounted above the chart table and climbed the stairs on the starboard paddle wheel box. Scanning the sea to starboard, he found the warship. Her moonlit rigging and gleaming bow wave gave the ship away. McKay heard his boatswain stir beside him and spoke without lowering the glass. "The warship must not have seen us yet, Mr. Gallagher. She is maintaining her course."

"Excellent, sir. Maybe our luck will hold."

"Perhaps." McKay fell silent for a minute, studying his enemy. "This ship appears to be of a newer design. Small, close to the water. She's a steamer, with funnels fore and aft of the bridge, and a battery of six pivot guns."

"Sounds like she's built for speed, sir."

McKay lowered the telescope, offering it to the boatswain. Gallagher took the glass from the Captain and searched the moonlit sea for the ship. A signal rocket zoomed off the warship's deck, trailing golden sparks and making her easy to find. Burning embers cycloned from the warship's funnels as the firemen stoked the furnaces. The knife-edged bow sliced through the water as the vessel, her paddles wheels whirling faster, swung around to intercept the blockade-runner.

The need for stealth was gone. Rushing into the bridge, McKay bellowed into the copper speaking tube, "Mr. Riechman, all ahead flank!"

A shudder ran through the *Atlantis* as her machinery leaped to life. The great paddles of her sidewheels slapped the ocean with a desperate rhythm, churning the water into a white froth.

The unmistakable sound of gunfire rolled along the water as the Federal cruiser brought her bow cannon to bear.

A shell shrieked overhead, then exploded just beyond the *Atlantis*. Its shrapnel kicked up a dozen geysers of water. The flash exposed a second Federal warship about two miles in front of the blockade-runner.

"Quartermaster, steer as close to that ship as you can," McKay ordered.

The boatswain looked at the Captain, shaking his head. "Maybe we shouldn't do that, sir. Remember what happened the last time we maneuvered under a ship's guns?"

"Yes, but this time we're prepared for them and can fight back."

The boatswain appeared confused. "How, sir?"

"Have you seen the fire hoses laid out on the deck, Mr. Gallagher?"

"Yes, sir. And I approve."

"Well, those hoses aren't for fighting fires. They're hooked up to the boilers. The idea is when we pass by that Federal cruiser, we'll spray the gunners with boiling water to prevent them from firing."

The boatswain gave Captain McKay a swift smile.

"I also had the carpenters install wooden shutters on the bridge we can close in case of danger. The one in the center has a small crack for the pilot to look through."

The boatswain walked over to the shutters and examined them. "That's a terrific idea. I can't count the number of times those windows were broken."

"We've replaced both funnels with a new design which telescopes into itself," McKay continued, gesturing at several deckhands cranking a winch to lower the forward smokestack. "The cannon blast that injured you also destroyed one of the funnels and reduced our speed. These new ones can be taken down. They also give the *Atlantis* a lower profile so she'll be more difficult to spot."

Half a dozen men stationed themselves around the fire hose, slaking it out. The warship in front commenced firing. Shells screamed in, tossing water high into the air.

"Ship broad on the starboard beam!" the lookout called from his perch in the forward mast, pointing off into the darkness.

"Just what we need! Another damned Yankee," McKay muttered, turning his attention to the new threat.

The Federal ship was another steamer, but she was too far away to tell much else. Orange flame flickered from her bow and seconds later a shell exploded in midair, its shrapnel hissing overhead and crashing through the *Atlantis'* rigging. One man on deck slammed into the bulkhead behind him, clutching his chest. Two men ran to his aid and carried him into the galley.

When the lookout called out another ship to port, the boatswain said, "This doesn't look good, Captain. Perhaps we should turn around while we still have the chance."

McKay shook his head. "It's too late. In a few more minutes we'll be close enough to that ship ahead the others will hold their fire."

"I agree, sir, but that ship will have a direct shot at close range."

"Well, there isn't much we can do about that," McKay admitted. "In our situation any maneuver has its risks. But the Yankees should have only one, maybe two, shots before we get too close. Once we get under her guns she won't be able to drop the elevation enough to hit us, and hopefully a douse of boiling water will keep the gunners away from their guns."

"But, sir, taking hot water away from our boilers will reduce our speed."

"I know it will, but we ought to be close to the reef by then. Any warships chasing us will run aground if everything goes according to plan."

Wearing thick leather gloves to protect their hands from the heat, the seamen with the fire hose moved toward the bow so they could begin spraying the warship before she could bring any of her guns to bear.

The Federal cruiser's cannon boomed again, and her bow disappeared behind its own bank of gun smoke. The shot shrieked through the night sky, plowing into the sea fifty yards before the *Atlantis*.

"Steady, men! That was only a warning shot," McKay called out.

As the Federal warship drew closer it was possible to see the Yankee sailors scramble to their stations. A bearded officer in a long blue coat adorned with two rows of brass buttons stepped from the bridge, raised a brass speaking trumpet to his lips and hailed the blockade-runner. "Ahoy *Atlantis*, heave to immediately or we will fire on your ship!"

The Federal captain watched the other ship, then shook his head in dismay. Not only did the darkened blockade-runner pay no heed to his warning, but Confederate sailors had gathered on deck to taunt him. He angrily ordered the gun crew to open fire. The cannon roared smoke and flame, hurling a shell into the bow of the *Atlantis*. A shower of wooden splinters exploded from the deck, knocking down some of the men holding the fire hose.

McKay rushed forward through the drifting smoke. Three men were down, squirming amid the wreckage. The others had dropped the fire hose and were trying to help their comrades.

"Get back to your stations, men!" McKay ordered.

A frightened man, bleeding from a gash on his forehead and squatting beside one of the wounded, looked up. "But, Capt'n, these men need help."

"We'll all need help if that Federal warship gives us a broadside at close range. Now back to your stations so we can give the Yankees a welcome they'll never forget."

McKay snatched a pair of gloves from an injured man lying on the deck, pulled them on, then picked up the hose. "Open the boiler's valve!" he shouted over his shoulder.

Seeing their determined captain clutching the fire hose by himself convinced the men to help him.

A brash Federal lieutenant dashed to the warship's railing, leveled a revolver at the men on the blockade-runner's bow and began firing. Water pressure shot through the fire hose, forcing the slack out. McKay spun the brass nozzle open as bullets smacked into the deck around him, splintering wood. A steaming jet of water arced from one ship to the other, sweeping over the Federal lieutenant, who was knocked off his feet by the force of the blast, screaming in agony. The forward gun crew, loading their cannon for another shot, heard the lieutenant's cries and felt the burning mist as it drifted toward them. They had no idea what evil liquid the Confederates were squirting at them and quickly retreated.

McKay searched for another target. He saw a Yankee officer strutting behind the cannons on the main deck of the warship, bellowing orders to his gunners. McKay bowled him over with the scalding spray, then turned the hose toward the gunners, driving them away from their guns, howling.

In seconds the Federal warship was cleared of sailors and slipped astern of the *Atlantis*. Men aboard the blockade-runner dropped the hose to aid the wounded and clear the wreckage.

"Buoy one hundred yards off the starboard bow!" the lookout called from the forward mast.

McKay ran to the railing. It had the familiar red and white markings of the large wooden buoys he had put out the day before. He grabbed a passing deck hand, and said, "Tell the quartermaster to steer to starboard so we pass alongside that buoy. I'm going to haul it aboard."

McKay grabbed a boat hook from its rack below the railing, and called, "Thompson, lend a hand."

The seaman hurried beside him and McKay said, "When I get the buoy aboard, take your knife and cut the line, then I'll toss it back. Maybe those Yankees will spot the ones we've cut loose and run aground on the reef."

McKay snagged the first buoy and brought it aboard where the line was cut, then threw it back. While he was snagging the second, the Federal cruiser they had sprayed turned around, firing at the blockade-runner. A cannonball plunged into the sea forty yards from the bow of the *Atlantis*. The next shell exploded in the air, peppering the bow with fragments. Men scooped up the hot shrapnel with their leather gloves, hurling them overboard so they wouldn't start a fire. Every man remained where he was, helping their captain or tending the wounded, even though the shells were falling closer.

When the Federal warship made her turn to intercept the *Atlantis*, the current carried her away from the narrow channel of safe water. She crashed into the reef, ripping a twenty foot hole in her hull.

The piercing scream of a steam whistle caught McKay's attention. The warship chasing the *Atlantis* was listing heavily to port. Another Federal gunboat had dropped out of the pursuit to lend assistance to the stricken vessel and approached the sinking ship cautiously, afraid to come too close.

The *Atlantis* steamed deeper into the reef, while her crew cut more buoys free and cast them into the sea. The rest of the Federal warships had slowed and soon were left behind.

*   *   *   *   *

The blockade hunter *USS Black Prince* had veered sharply to starboard to skirt the reef where another warship had gone aground. Because of this maneuver his quarry disappeared into the midnight sea, but Captain Travis wasn't worried. With his ship's lightning speed he would pick up the *Atlantis'* trail again and finish her rebellious blockade-running forever. "Quartermaster, steer three-five-zero," the Federal captain with the fierce blue eyes and an iron-colored beard ordered. "The *Atlantis* is making her run for Wilmington and so are we."

CHAPTER 17

Major General Alfred H. Terry did not earn his reputation as a successful Federal commander by being timid. However, once the thirty-eight-year-old veteran saw how strong Fort Fisher was, he carefully planned his assault. Terry had seen drawings of the massive Confederate earthwork, but those pictures failed to capture the sheer magnitude of the place. The fort, which rose from the low sandy peninsula like a sprawling medieval castle, had thirty-foot high walls which bristled with heavy seacoast artillery pieces. Every hundred feet or so the cannons' cavernous muzzles protruded from their gun chambers and commanded a deadly, uninterrupted field of fire for at least half a mile. Four smaller field pieces guarded the fort's gate and sally-port and added to the overwhelming firepower.

Terry gazed upon the fort with dubious optimism. Before his men could even think about storming the fort's walls, they would have to charge across half a mile of open terrain, get over a narrow bridge spanning a swamp, then somehow find their way through a nine-foot high palisade fence all while being exposed to hostile fire from an elevated, fortified position. In his mind's eye the general could see his men trying to negotiate these obstacles while they were being decimated by heavy artillery and small-arms fire, but he saw the flags more clearly than anything. He envisioned the bright Federal banners waving and leading the charge, then being reduced to shreds amid heavy fire, and finally being blown to bits.

From inside an abandoned Confederate earthwork several miles north of the fort, General Terry lowered his telescope, shaking his head. The Navy would have to do better. The fleet had bombarded the fort all day and, except for a few dismounted guns, it appeared relatively unscathed. Admiral Porter needed to concentrate the Naval gunfire on the land-face and smash that artillery before he would commit his men to such an assault.

General Terry realized the precarious position his army was in. They were in enemy territory and could not move in any direction. During the landing, he had set up a defensive perimeter in the woods, and his pickets had encountered the advance guard of a strong Confederate division to his north. Fort Fisher was to the south, to the west was the Cape Fear River, and behind him lay the Atlantic Ocean. Where could he retreat if the Confederates launched a full scale attack? Terry knew the best defense was a good offense and realized speed was essential to his success. If he could capture Fort Fisher before the Confederates attacked his army, then he could probably hold on until he was reinforced. Terry's greatest fear was once he launched his attack on the fort and his army was fully committed, General Hoke's division would slam into his rear. If that happened, he would be caught between two strong Confederate forces with no chance to escape.

Time was critical if General Terry's plan was to succeed. To create the false impression his army had remained on the beach for the night, he ordered a brigade to build hundreds of campfires around the fortified landing site, then took the bulk of his force south toward Fort Fisher.

The Federal army fanned out and made their way through the maritime forest with its dense underbrush. When the army was about two miles north of the fort, it stopped and dug a line of entrenchments which stretched across the peninsula from the Cape Fear River to the ocean. All night the Federal soldiers labored, digging trenches, cutting trees, then dragging the logs to their lines to build breastworks.

The Federal Navy did not want the Army to get all of the glory when the fort was captured, so they sent a force of two thousand sailors and marines ashore. The plan was for the Navy to storm the Northeast corner of Fort Fisher while the Army assaulted the Northwest side.

Inside Fort Fisher, Colonel Lamb telegraphed General Bragg about the Federal landing, asking for reinforcements. Hours later, when the Colonel had not received a reply and he saw General Whiting inside the fort, he thought maybe his friend had brought him news from Bragg. He had, but the news was not good.

General Whiting's diminutive stature quickly gave way to his formidable military bearing. His graying hair and well-trimmed moustache suggested wisdom and order. He was a man who presented himself with imposing dignity and grandeur, but as he climbed the Pulpit Battery and joined Colonel Lamb in his headquarters, he greeted his friend with somber news. "Lamb, my boy, I have come to share your fate. You and your garrison are to be sacrificed."

"Don't say so, General," the Colonel protested. "We shall certainly whip the Yankees again."

"If we do, it will be without General Bragg's help. The last thing I heard him say was to point out a line to fall back upon when Fort Fisher fell."

Whiting told Lamb the whole story, how General Bragg had refused to attack the Federal army north of Fort Fisher, and would send no reinforcements.

Colonel Lamb was appalled. He and General Whiting had worked so hard to build this fort from nothing, and now this commander, with a dreadful string of defeats, was allowing the fort to slip away without trying to help.

Lamb had suspected President Davis had made a mistake when he sent General Bragg to Wilmington last November. Now, there was no longer any doubt. He believed the man was so badly shaken by his military defeats he had taken the President's orders to defend Wilmington literally. He was trying so hard not to lose anything he could not see what an incredible opportunity this was: a large Federal army, supported only by the Navy, was surrounded and had no where to maneuver or retreat. Between the fort's garrison and

General Hoke's division, they had as many troops as the Federals did. If Bragg needed more soldiers, extra men from General Lee in Virginia were only two or three days away by rail. The Yankees had no reinforcements that close. Any help was weeks away and could only be brought in by steamer. Lamb knew his plan was daring, but desperate circumstances required bold action. If he and General Bragg coordinated their attacks, they could not only defend Fort Fisher, but also capture the Federal army and gain a stunning victory.

Sunday afternoon Federal Lieutenant Colonel Francis Meyer was ordered to advance with the 117th New York and reconnoiter Fort Fisher. Captain John Thomas summoned the men in his company closer with a wave of his arm. "Gather around, men."

The soldiers fell out and formed a half-circle around their commanding officer.

Captain Thomas clasped his hands behind his back and waited until he had everyone's attention. "Gentlemen, I think if we lose this fight, we lose more than just a battle. We also lose our self-respect."

The captain shook his head with distaste. "I don't know about you, but I wouldn't want that blemish on my record. I don't want any man to say to me, 'You weren't good enough. That's why you were defeated at Fort Fisher.'"

Captain Thomas gazed at the faces around him before continuing. "Since the expedition's failure last December, our reputation has taken a terrible beating. Now we have a new commander. I hear General Terry is a real scrapper. He's the type of man this army needs. Today we have been given an opportunity few men get. We can redeem ourselves by capturing Fort Fisher and placing our flag on the fort's ramparts."

He took off his dark blue cap with the brass bugle emblem, holding it aloft for everyone to see. "This kepi will be alongside our flag on the fort's walls. Who will join me?"

The men cheered, waving their hats and muskets in the air.

Captain Thomas smiled and placed the kepi on his head. "Fall in, men, and let's show the whole world the 117th New York will never settle for anything less than victory!"

The men formed a line of battle. Officers went to the head of their companies and ordered a line of skirmishers forward. In a few minutes, the regiment followed, moving through the dense forest of scrub oak and pine. The noise of the bombardment swelled, and an odor of burnt sulfur filtered through the trees as they crept nearer to the fort. Captain Thomas halted his company when he came to a clearing. "Sergeant Murphy, I'm going to have the men double quick to their new position. I want you to hang back and see there are no stragglers."

Murphy moved a wad of chewing tobacco from one cheek to the other. "Yes, sir. I'll boot 'em in the ass so hard they'll be happy to face the Rebs."

Lieutenant Colonel Meyer turned around and faced the regiment. "Color bearers forward!"

Three men unfurled the standards from their cases and marched to the front. One was the familiar United States flag, another denoted the first brigade of the Second Division of the 24th Corps, and lastly the blue and gold banner of the 117th New York. Behind them fluttered the company guidons.

When everyone was in place, Lieutenant Colonel Meyer drew his sword, and called above the din of battle, "Men of the 117th New York, forward at the double quick--march!" He whirled around, pointing his sword at the fort and stepping off smartly.

Scattered musket fire came from the fort as the blue-clad soldiers emerged from the tree line. The intense Naval shelling kept most of the Confederate riflemen away from the walls and in the bombproofs, but a few men remained outside to watch for any Federal movement. Others heard the gunfire, and rushed to the parapets to repel the invaders.

At first the 117th New York was hardly bothered by the bullets whizzing around them, but soon the firing increased and men began to fall. The cannon at the fort's gate joined in, belching grape and canister and tearing holes in the oncoming line. Lieutenant Colonel

Meyer saw his men could not continue taking such a beating and spun around. He pointed out a line with his sword and called, "Dig your entrenchments here, men!"

The soldiers hurled themselves onto the ground, scooping out rifle pits in the soft sand with their hands and bayonets. Some men feverishly hollowed out depressions with the butts of their muskets, then piled the sand in front of themselves to make crude breastworks.

Colonel Meyer sought shelter in a hole with Captain Thomas and several enlisted men and opened the leather binocular case he had slung over his shoulder. He raised the field glasses to his eyes and cautiously peered over the lip of the pit.

The fort was so misted with the smoke of battle it was difficult to ascertain what damage had been done. Bomb bursts flashed in the sky and exploded on the walls, throwing tons of sand into the air and gouging out huge craters. Through the drifting veil of smoke Colonel Meyer could make out bits and pieces of the fort. He saw the muzzle flash of only one heavy artillery piece and surmised the bombardment must have destroyed the rest. "Captain Thomas, send a dispatch to General Terry, with my compliments. Tell him all but one of the heavy artillery pieces have been destroyed, but we're receiving fire from several hundred infantry and four small cannons."

"Yes, sir." The captain scrawled the message in his notebook, then tore off the page. "Corporal Block, take this to General Terry right away."

The soldier, who was scooping handfuls of sand and throwing them over the edge of the pit, took the message and ran for the tree line.

The news was what General Terry had been waiting for. He sent word to Lieutenant Commander Randolph Breeze, the officer in charge of the naval brigade, and suggested they launch a coordinated attack immediately. Breeze agreed to lead an assault against the northeast corner of the fort, while the army stormed the northwest gate. Using signal flags, General Terry instructed Admiral Porter to shift the bombardment away from the land-face and the Federal attack.

At 3:25 p.m. the whistles of the fleet sounded, signaling the redirection of fire to the fort's sea-face and the beginning of the ground assault. While Lieutenant Commander Breeze led 2,200 sailors and marines down the beach, General Terry attacked Fort Fisher's northwestern corner with the first brigade of the twenty-fourth Army Corps. The 117th New York spearheaded the charge.

Inside Fort Fisher, Lieutenant William Hurley was growing uneasy. The bombardment had not ceased for two days, and the constant stream of dying and wounded men being carried into the hospital suggested the garrison was taking a horrible beating. Although he was wounded two days earlier, and had every right to be there, the Lieutenant was uncomfortable sitting in the bombproof while other men were being killed.

Suddenly, dozens of steam whistles began wailing in the distance. The bombardment ceased, and moments later a tremendous volley of rifle fire brought Lieutenant Hurley to his feet. He grabbed an Enfield rifle and ran for the door. Those soldiers who could still walk pulled themselves up from their stetchers by leaning on their muskets and joined the lieutenant. Most of the men appeared relieved the long-awaited land battle had finally begun. For two days they had sat helplessly as Yankee cannonballs ravaged the fort. Now it was their turn to show the Northern soldiers some hot Confederate lead.

Brooke was cleaning a soldier's wound when she heard the gunfire. She watched in sadness as the men got up to leave. When the lieutenant looked in her direction, she gave him a smile of encouragement which vanished as soon as he went out the door.

The men from the hospital climbed the Northeast Bastion and found hundreds of Confederate rifleman lining the walls and pouring a murderous fire down onto the Northern sailors. Through the thick rifle smoke General Whiting could be seen scaling the parapet. He boldly stood on top of the wall with his sword raised, pointing at the Yankees and urging his men to fire. Ramrods rattled and scraped in hot rifle barrels as soldiers ducked down to reload, then raised up to fire again. The refugees from the hospital rushed to the walls and either found a place to join the fight or loaded the empty muskets which were thrust into their hands. Lieutenant Hurley nudged between a soldier dressed in butternut-brown and wearing a battered felt hat, and another in a dirty, gray uniform.

Brandishing cutlasses and revolvers and cheering, the dark mass of Federal seamen surged forward, heading for a point near the water's edge where the palisade fence ended and low tide had exposed a narrow opening between the fence and the surf. With swords aloft, the officers led the charge through the deep sand.

Lieutenant Hurley aimed his Enfield rifle at the first naval officer to rush through the opening in the fence and squeezed off a shot. The bullet knocked the soldier off his feet, hurling him the sand. More men followed and fell to the ground dead or wounded within seconds. The blue horde continued to push through the opening in the fence in such numbers that stopping them all was impossible. Confederate riflemen fired, reloaded and fired again. The sally-port cannons and the lone land-face Columbiad spewed grapeshot and canister at the approaching swarm as fast as the gun crews could work their guns. Colonel Lamb ordered the explosive charges near the beach fired-but nothing happened when the switch was closed.

The fury of shot and shell forced the seamen to seek refuge wherever they could. Some sought out bomb craters for protection. Others hid behind the dead bodies of their fallen comrades, while still others rushed back through the fence and up the beach. What had begun as a determined assault, suddenly turned into a rout. Hundreds of sailors got up and ran for the rear as hard as they could. Federal officers urged them to come back and resume the attack, but their pleas were ignored. Reluctantly they sheathed their swords and followed their men out of rifle range.

On Fort Fisher's parapets, the Confederate soldiers stood up and jeered the fleeing seamen. But as the shouting subsided, a distant swell of gunfire could be heard to the west. Throngs of howling wild men surged down the Northeast Bastion and toward the sound of battle.

The men, flushed with the taste of victory, swept along the fort land-face. Within minutes, they swarmed over the mound and gun chamber nearest the river. They had arrived just in time. A mob of Union soldiers had stormed through the palisade fence and was rushing up the western mound.

Confederate gun smoke rolled off the parapet in a thick haze as the soldiers poured a concentrated fire into their foe. The blue and gold banner of the 117th New York went down, was snatched up again to be carried a few feet farther before another soldier crumpled to the ground. Captain Thomas seized the fallen colors. With a sword in one hand and the flag in the other, he raced up the steep earthen wall, shouting for the soldiers to follow him.

For a minute, Captain Thomas appeared to lead a charmed life as he climbed the slope through the hail of gunfire. Bullets plucked at his coat and kicked up the sand around him, but none found their mark. On he went, intent on reaching the top of the wall with his regimental flag. The Federal soldiers running behind him began to cheer. When the Union captain reached the crest of the parapet, his luck ran out. A well-aimed bullet slammed into Captain Thomas' chest. He dropped to his knees. His sword fell from one hand, but he held fast to the precious flag with his other. The flagstaff teetered for a second before it was snatched by another Union soldier, who rammed the regimental colors into the sand. When the trooper turned to resume the attack, he too was struck down. By this time, dozens of screaming blue-coated soldiers had gained the summit, spilling into the gun chamber and fighting like wildcats.

This was the moment the Confederate defenders were waiting for, when the enemy came close enough for their gunfire to have maximum effect. The men in brown and gray unleashed a murderous volley, then rushed forward to meet the Yankee charge, filling the air with their earsplitting Rebel yell.

The battle became a wild free-for-all. Men were shooting at each other point-blank, slashing with bayonets or Bowie knives and swinging their muskets like clubs. A Confederate gunner had managed to reload an artillery piece and was about to fire with the rammer still in the barrel when a Yankee colonel struck him down with a sword. Lieutenant Hurley smashed a Northern sergeant in the jaw with his rifle, then swung the weapon back again, crushing his skull with the brass plated butt. A Federal soldier charged at him with his bayonet out front. The Lieutenant leaped over the fallen sergeant, and parried the man's rifle aside. With the same motion, he swung the stock of his musket up, clubbing the Yankee in the face. The man reeled back, dropping his weapon. Hurley tossed his rifle away and grabbed the soldier's blood-spattered rifle with a bayonet. He rammed the dagger-like blade into the Yankee's chest, twisted it out, then thrust at another blue coated soldier.

One by one the Confederate ranks were being thinned as more men fell dead and wounded. When the battle began 1,500 Confederate troops were scattered throughout Fort Fisher. Now there were less than 1,200. With so few men available, there was no one to replace those who had fallen. Such was not the case for the Union army. For every Northern soldier killed, it seemed two appeared to take his place. The Confederate defenders were pushed back by the overwhelming blue tide, fighting desperately for every foot of ground they gave up.

While the men in the gun chamber were fighting for their lives, hundreds of Union troops stormed the palisade gate. Confederate sharpshooters knelt behind the sandbagged timbers, firing their muskets to hold back the screaming horde. Two Southern cannons opened fire, hurling crowds of attackers back in a mist of blood and smoke. The canister obliterated whole files of Federal soldiers, but still more men in blue came surging up the road, yelling as they charged. The outnumbered Confederate defenders were paying dearly for such stubborn resistance, as brigade after brigade charged the fort.

Soon Union soldiers seized control of the first traverse and directed a plunging fire down at the Rebels manning the cannons at the palisade gate. The Confederate artillerymen saw they were being flanked, but they could do little about it. They stayed at their guns, firing at the Federals attempting to force their way through the gate, while Southern sharpshooters tried to clear the Yankees off the traverse. Suddenly, Union troops who had trudged through the marsh came storming around the riverside end of the tall fence, flanking the defenders and catching them in a deadly crossfire. In less than ten minutes, all the rebels had fallen beside their guns while the unchecked Federal advance burst through the palisade gate.

Union soldiers swept around the rear of the first gun chamber and charged up the walls. The embattled Confederates were now being attacked from three sides and a determined squad of Northern soldiers was threatening to surround them and cut off any avenue of escape. They had no choice but to fall back to the next gun chamber and continue the fight there.

Standing atop the Northeast Bastion, General Whiting could see the Federal flag on the fort's parapet and blue-uniformed troops surging up the westernmost mound. He and several other officers searched the bombproofs and gun chambers for soldiers so they could launch a counterattack. They assembled about 500 men. With Whiting leading the way, they ran down the fort land-face, slamming into the Federals at the fourth gun chamber. The fighting was savage hand-to-hand combat. Troops were firing, jabbing bayonets, swinging muskets and grappling with each other. Mangled bodies littered the floor of the gun chamber, making it difficult to move. Men stumbled over them, slipping in the blood and gore.

Initially the Union troops had pushed the Confederates back several hundred feet because they were able to throw in fresh men while the Rebels had none. Now, with the Confederate ranks swelled by 500 men, the Federal soldiers were at last giving up ground.

General Whiting grabbed for the Federal flag atop the traverse and was confronted by a crowd of Union soldiers.

"Surrender!" they demanded.

"Go to hell, you Yankee bastards!" he shouted back, raising his sword.

They fired and the Confederate officer fell, severely wounded with two bullets in the right thigh. Some of his men saw him go down and came rushing to his aid. They fiercely attacked the Yankees on the traverse, pulling their commanding general to safety.

The Confederate counterattack had retaken the fourth gun chamber, but now the assault had stalled. Colonel Lamb suspected one more attack might dislodge the Yankees and save the fort. He assembled the remaining few men and led them to a line of earthworks near the third traverse. Here the soldiers halted and prepared for a bayonet charge.

Lamb looked confidently at the men, drew his sword, shouting, "Charge, bayonets!"

A furious volley of Yankee gunfire ripped into the men as they came running over the breastworks. The unexpected Federal attack shattered the formation. A bullet struck Colonel Lamb in the left hip, spinning him to the sand. Confederate soldiers were kneeling and firing, while wounded men limped and crawled away. A second Northern volley broke what little resolve the Rebels had left, and the men edged backward to the earthwork, shooting as they went. A fresh Federal brigade had turned the tide of battle once more.

In the hospital bombproof, Brooke was terrified, but inspired by the tremendous volume of gunfire. Maybe the defenders would save the fort after all. However, when several soldiers brought in General Whiting and Colonel Lamb on stretchers, she began to lose hope. The situation was becoming worse. The hospital was filled to overflowing, and everywhere she looked were dying and wounded men. Fortunately, the bombardment was shifted away from the land-face, and they were able to lay the wounded on the ground outside. The stretcher bearers were instructed to bring in only the most serious cases.

His face pale under the grime and sweat of battle, Lieutenant Hurley rushed into the hospital to report to General Whiting. He found the general on a stretcher with a thick, blood-soaked bandage around his right thigh.

The lieutenant, his jacket torn and bloody, gave Whiting a weak salute. "I have word from Major Reilly, sir," he said, out of breath. "He's been unable to halt the Yankee advance and respectfully suggests the hospital be evacuated to Battery Buchanan."

Whiting exchanged worried glances with Colonel Lamb on the next litter. "Have things gotten that bad?" he asked Lieutenant Hurley.

"I'm afraid so, sir. The garrison . . . it's putting up a hell of a fight, but the men are outnumbered, and they're being driven back. About half the land-face has already fallen."

"Very well," the General said with a weary sigh. "Tell Major Reilly to hold out as long as he can. We need time to evacuate and set up a second line of defense at Battery Buchanan."

"Yes, sir." Lieutenant Hurley raised his hand in a feeble salute, then collapsed to the floor.

"Nurse!" General Whiting called to Brooke. She was helping a wounded soldier onto a litter and eased him down. Two days in Fort Fisher's hospital had left Brooke physically and emotionally drained. She had seen too much suffering and death and no longer resembled the attractive woman who had volunteered so quickly. Her apron was dirty and blood spattered and her auburn hair was unkempt and straggly. Dark worry lines appeared beneath her weary eyes, but she performed her duties with stoic resolve.

Brooke rushed over and knelt beside the fallen lieutenant. His face was ashen and his breathing so shallow she had to lean close and listen carefully to see if he was still alive. She saw the blood soaked jacket and looked around for assistance. "Orderly, help me get this man on a stretcher!"

A tall, thin, bespectacled man in a blood-encrusted coat looked up from the soldier he was bandaging. "I'll be right there," he called, giving the man's chest another wrap and knotting the ends of the cotton dressing.

The orderly checked Lieutenant Hurley's vital signs, then summoned a soldier to bring a stretcher. The canvas of the litter was saturated with a sticky red stain from its previous occupant. Brooke watched in sadness as the men picked up the Lieutenant and set him on another man's soiled death bed.

He took Brooke aside and said, "He needs plenty of fluids and rest. I know that's virtually impossible under these conditions, but do the best you can."

She nodded, geting a cup of water and some bandages. While the Lieutenant sipped from the cup, she cleaned his wound and put on a fresh dressing. By the time Brooke had finished, a steady procession of walking wounded and stretcher bearers were streaming out of the hospital, trudging a mile and a half through the gathering darkness to Battery Buchanan.

Judson Bates spread panic and defeat wherever he could. When he ran from the hospital, he stopped in every bombproof on his way to Battery Buchanan and told his lies. The soldiers who were isolated since the bombardment began were eager for news of the battle, and Bates was only too happy to accommodate them. He told them wild exaggerations of enemy strength and deeds. Instead of a 9,000 man army, the Federals had landed 35,000. When asked if General Bragg would reinforce them, Bates announced the Northern army had already defeated him, so they could expect no help. The horrible lies, like a deadly virus, spread from man to man. Officers tried to calm the men by telling them not to believe these rumors. Yet panic raged like a wildfire out of control.

Bates had saved his best performance for last. He arrived at Battery Buchanan sweating and out of breath. The soldiers saw the bandage around his head and his blood-spattered uniform, and figured he had just come from the front and could tell them what was happening. Bates staggered to a chair. "It's horrible," he told Captain Chapman, the battery's commander. "The Yankees are slaughterin' our men mercilessly. The dead were heaped in piles two and three deep in the gun chambers. So far the bastards have pushed our boys back and have almost captured the land-face."

The captain was appalled. "How did they get inside the fort? What about the mine field?"

"It didn't go off. Some of the explosions must've cut the wires."

"Surely General Bragg will strike the Federal rear at any moment and together we can retake the fort," the Captain suggested.

Bates put an exhausted hand to his forehead, as if he were in great pain. "Don't expect any help from Bragg. He's already been defeated."

"What? How do you know?"

"I'm one of Bragg's scouts. The General sent me and two other men to reconnoiter the Federal position. We hid in the scrub oaks and watched the whole landing. The first thing the Yankees did was to take half their force and advance on Wilmington. We reported this to Bragg, and he entrenched his men south of the city."

"How many men did the Yankees land?"

Bates scratched his chin. "We counted the number of flags on the beach 'n figured there were at least 35,000 troops."

"What happened then?"

"The Yankees attacked the center of our line and broke it. Then they rushed through that gap and drove the men from their trenches. Our losses were horrible."

Captain Chapman tried to make sense of what this man was telling him. "If you were with Bragg, what on earth are you doing here?"

Bates had practiced this story with Peter Reynolds time and again and did not miss a beat. "After we warned the General of the Yankees comin', he sent us to Fort Fisher to tell Colonel Lamb. On our way here, we heard awful gunfire from Bragg's position an' doubled back to see what was happenin'. "We saw our boys being licked an' rode here as fast as we could. The main attack hit jus' as we got to the fort."

Captain Chapman eyed Bates suspiciously. "If what you say is true, why haven't we received word about this from Smithville? It's just across the river, and we still have communication with signal flags."

"I don't know," Bates admitted, shrugging his bony shoulders. "It could be they don't know nothin' yet. Hell, all this just happened."

Captain Chapman nodded. "Wait here." He called Major William Saunders over.

The major did not believe things were as bad as Bates had said they were, so he went to the fort to check for himself. He arrived in time to see the blue-coated soldiers overrun the final traverse of the land-face and drive the Confederate defenders back to the Northeast Bastion. Major Saunders was stunned. How could this have happened? Where was General Bragg's army? Only one answer made sense: Judson Bates had told the truth. The Federal army had defeated Bragg, was about to capture Fort Fisher, and Battery Buchanan was the next target.

Minutes after Major Saunders hurried away with the news the fort was lost, the hospital began its evacuation. The bombardment had destroyed the wagons and killed most of the horses, so stretcher bearers carried litter after litter through the deep sand. One of the assistant surgeons and Brooke Snow remained behind with the more seriously wounded.

When the procession from the hospital arrived at Battery Buchanan, they found the soldiers at the fort in utter chaos. Demoralized men milled about, most without weapons or ammunition. The gun crews had panicked and abandoned the fort by commandeering the boats docked at the landing. Before they left, they had spiked the four heavy artillery pieces by driving hardened steel nails into the vent holes, so the enemy could not fire them.

Now the defenders had no cannons to keep the Yankees at a safe distance while they evacuated the fort. But it no longer mattered. Without any boats, there could be no escape. Only surrender.

CHAPTER 18

It began as a faint line above the eastern horizon. So faint in fact McKay suspected it might be just his imagination. He trained his telescope on the object, then adjusted the focus until he saw a smudge of black smoke against the pale sky.

"What do you make of that smoke trail, Mr. Gallagher?" he said, pointing to the sea behind them and handing the glass to his boatswain. "It's about two points off the port quarter, near the horizon."

The seaman raised the telescope, scanning the water where his Captain had suggested. "It appears a steamer has crossed our path, sir. Judging by all the smoke, I'd say she's a Yankee."

McKay nodded with concern. "My thoughts exactly. I hope she hasn't spotted us."

The boatswain gazed at the wispy, gray smoke coming from the *Atlantis'* funnels. "I don't think she has, sir. That ship would need to be five miles closer before she could see anything."

An hour later, the cruiser could be seen without a telescope.

McKay rushed into the bridge, checking their speed for the fifth time. Sixteen knots, and still the ship was gaining on them. He snatched the copper speaking tube from its holder, calling down to the engine room, "Mr. Reichman, can you raise more steam? A Federal warship is overtaking us."

"I can give you another ten pounds, Captain. Will that do?"

"For the moment, yes."

McKay left the bridge and went back on top of the paddle wheel box. The boatswain lowered his telescope when the Captain approached. "I believe that's the same warship we encountered outside Nassau, sir."

"The small fast one?"

"Yes, sir. I've been studying her superstructure, and I'm sure it's the same ship. She's the only one I've seen which is painted all black."

McKay glanced at the boatswain, puzzled. "Don't you think that's peculiar? Running into the same Federal warship off Nassau and now here. Usually they patrol a particular area."

"Now that you mention it, I guess it does seem peculiar."

McKay considered this for a moment. "You don't suppose the Yankees have assigned a special ship to hunt us, do you?"

"I imagine it's possible, sir," the boatswain said, then brightened. "Makes me feel good in a way. Lets me know what we're doing is hurting the Yankees enough for them to single us out."

"Yes, but I'd rather not have their attention."

Mr. Gallagher fished his watch from an inner pocket and clicked open the lid. It was ten in the morning. "I hope we make Fort Fisher soon. That warship is getting a little too close for comfort."

"We should. The *Atlantis* is only a few hours sail from there now." McKay paused, then said, "You know, this will be the first time we'll be running the blockade in daylight," he pointed out. This departure from accepted blockade-running procedure had been bothering McKay for a while, and he felt now was the appropriate time to discuss it with his boatswain.

"Yes, sir. I've thought about that. A bit risky, isn't it?"

"Yes, it is, but we have no choice. If I am any judge in such matters, pretty soon that Federal warship will be joined by some ships from the blocking fleet off Fort Fisher."

"What do you propose to do, sir?"

"Well, a direct approach might work because of our speed. However, if the blockading squadron closes off the entrance to the river, we'll turn south toward Frying Pan Shoals and go in Old Inlet.

The Confederate forts guarding the entrance will drive off any ships pursuing us."

"The shoals can be dangerous, Captain. Those sandbars move around constantly."

McKay nodded. "The pilot has assured me he knows a safe passage through that area."

The boatswain looked doubtful.

"Don't worry, Mr. Gallagher. I'll post plenty of lookouts. Our light draft and crossing during broad daylight, so we can watch for shallow water, will allow us to come through just fine."

The junior officer nodded.

McKay thought he had handled that well. It was important for the captain of a ship to be confident and not show any fear or indecision when under pressure. The truth was, he also had doubts about their landing at Fort Fisher.

A puff of white smoke rose from the Federal warship. Moments later a cannonball fell into the sea well astern of the *Atlantis*. These were sporadic probing shots, trying to gauge the distance to the blockade-runner.

An hour later, the lookout in the *Atlantis'* forward mast sang out, "Smoke on the starboard bow!" A sudden column of water erupted along the port side and an explosion rocked the ship. The steamship rolled to starboard, her deck wet and slippery from the driving spray. McKay grabbed the rail in front of him to keep from falling, then fought to the wheel house, pulling himself through the door. "Quartermaster, three points to starboard!" he barked.

After five minutes, long enough to see a puff of smoke erupt from the pursuing Federal cruiser, he shouted, "Hard aport, now!"

The quartermaster spun the spoked wheel, while shells exploded all about the wildly careening blockade-runner, sending towering spumes of water high into the air.

Three Federal warships from the blockade steamed to intercept the *Atlantis*, their guns thundering angrily and adding to the barrage.

McKay could see Fort Fisher in the distance. "Why isn't the Mound Battery firing to drive off those ships?"

"I know why, sir," the boatswain said in a grim voice, lowering his telescope. "A Federal flag is flying over the battery. Fort Fisher has fallen."

The news struck McKay like a sledgehammer. He was too late! All the planning, the hazardous voyage to Nassau, running the blockade, his crew being killed and injured, had been for nothing. For a dreadful moment everything seemed lost, but then he realized he still had a mission to fulfill. The Confederacy still needed the *Atlantis'* cargo of guns and medicine.

McKay turned to the helm, and said, "Quartermaster, we're sailing to Frying Pan Shoals, and we're going to enter Old Inlet. I want you to continue to zigzag, but steer a general course of one nine zero."

An angry sea boiled about the blockade-runner, stirred up by the fall of shells from the four Federal warships. Seconds later an explosion rocked the ship, knocking men off their feet. The quartermaster was down and bleeding, so McKay scrambled to take the helm. Desperately he twisted the wheel back and forth, while the *Atlantis* snaked in and out among the columns of water. "Mr. Gallagher!"

The boatswain pulled himself up from the floor and stood beside the Captain.

"Go forward and see what our damage is. Hurry now!"

The man dashed from the wheel house. The rolling deck was practically a sea itself. Water sloshed about and ran for the scuppers as the steamship heeled heavily into her turns.

A jagged twenty-foot hole was all which was left of the hatch where they had stowed her cargo. Mr. Gallagher looked down into the smoking cavern and saw crates of rifles were smashed open. The explosion had tossed muskets and parts of muskets everywhere-- even up on the main deck.

"There's a twenty-foot hole where a shell hit us," the boatswain reported to McKay in a rush. "It must have pierced the deck, then exploded inside the hold. Fortunately the crates of rifles absorbed the blast and protected the hull."

"How about dead and injured?"

"I didn't see any, Captain."

A shell shrieked overhead, exploding into the sea ten yards to port. The men ducked as a huge wave of white water crashed onto the bridge. Seawater flooded through the doors and broken windows and swamped the men while they struggled to grab onto anything to keep from being swept away.

McKay recovered and gazed through the window frame. The lookout in the forward mast was gone--perhaps blown off his perch by the explosion. "We're nearing the shoals, Mr. Gallagher, but we've lost our lookout. Climb the forward mast and watch for shallow water."

McKay turned to the pilot and said, "Mr. Burriss, you know these waters better than I do. Why don't you take the helm?"

"Of course, Capt'n." The man with the broad felt hat and drooping mustache stepped forward, grabbing the spoked wheel.

A shell ripped through the rigging and exploded. White-hot shrapnel peppered the roof of the bridge and several heavy lines thumped to the deck.

Boatswain Gallagher, carrying a coil of line over his shoulder so he could lash himself to the mast, was climbing the rigging when the shell burst. The concussion shook the ship, squeezing the air from the seaman's chest. A blast of hot air threatened to tear him from the shroud, and he desperately wrapped his arms around the lines.

McKay ran on deck to check the damage.

The boatswain released one hand from the rigging and pointed to the sea behind them. "Look, sir! Three of the warships are turning away!"

The Captain swung around to look, and sure enough, three ships were dropping out of the chase. "It's because of the shoals!" he hollered.

But the small black cruiser that had chased them for so long was still plowing through the seas in hot pursuit. Plumes of smoke and flame stabbed from the cannon on her foredeck, to be followed moments later by the rumble of gunfire and the fall of shot.

McKay knew the Federal warship intended to stalk the *Atlantis* until she sank her. "Mr. Gallagher, bring that line here."

"But sir, the shoals."

"Forget the shoals." McKay glanced about and saw half a dozen men on deck watching the retreating warships. "You men are lookouts!" he ordered. "Go forward and watch for shallow water. Peterson, climb up to the lookout platform."

The men hurried toward the bow. The boatswain descended the rope ladder to the deck.

Columns of water exploded into the sky astern, tossing the two men to the deck and scattering spray across the blockade-runner. Both men looked around as they got up, dripping wet.

"That was close," the boatswain said in a worried tone, wiping the seawater from his eyes.

McKay nodded agreement. "Here's what we'll do. You and I will mix several cases of percussion caps into two barrels of gunpowder, then we'll tie a barrel to each end of that line. We'll throw both barrels overboard along with some empty crates. The Yankees shouldn't suspect a thing. They'll imagine we're trying to lighten our load so we can get away."

A shell exploded in the sea nearby, and both men glanced at the rising plume of water mixed with gray smoke.

McKay turned to the boatswain and continued, "Those barrels have to be spread apart, so we'll release them from either side of the deck. After the cruiser snags the line, and the barrels of gunpowder are drawn against her hull, we'll explode them with rifle fire."

"Great idea, Captain, but won't the gunpowder get wet?"

"I don't think it will. The barrels are lined with pitch to keep moisture out, and they won't be in the water long."

The boatswain nodded. "Sounds like it might work, let's give it a try."

While the men mixed the percussion caps with the gun powder and tied a harness around each barrel, the crew unloaded crates of muskets and carried the empty boxes to the stern.

"All right, men," the Captain ordered, grabbing a crate marked *Enfield Rifled Muskets*. "Let's heave these overboard."

A rumble of gunfire and the wail of shot alerted the crew to a near hit. They dove for cover as the rear deck house disintegrated in a brilliant flash. One moment it was there; in the blink of an eye, it ceased to exist. The smouldering deck was strewn with dead and wounded men and scarlet splashes of blood. Dazed survivors moved among the burning wreckage, moaning.

McKay raised up on his elbows, blood streaming down his face, and yelled to anyone who would listen. "Get some water on that fire! Quickly!"

The boatswain was an unmoving heap upon the deck. McKay crawled over and cradled him in his arms. John Gallagher's eyes were half-closed, and blood seeped from a dozen shrapnel wounds. When he recognized McKay, his labored breathing seemed to relax in an attempt to put his friend at ease. "Captain, promise me you'll get the supplies through to Fort Fisher," he said in a whisper.

McKay nodded. "I promise. Just lie still and rest."

Gallagher coughed weakly, shaking his head. "No, Captain. I need to tell you this while I still can. I don't regret a single thing I've done. I want you to know that." He closed his eyes, grimacing with pain. "Would . . . Would you tell my family what happened to me?"

"Of course, John. I'll go see them myself."

Gallagher smiled peacefully, then closed his eyes for the last time.

McKay clutched the man to his chest, fondly remembering all the things his boatswain had done for him in the past. John Gallagher had always been there when it counted, whether the trouble concerned running the blockade, or handling things of a private nature between himself and Brooke.

McKay eased his friend down to the deck. He rolled one of the heavy barrels of gunpowder to the stern, then heaved it into the blockade-runner's bubbling wake. McKay crossed to the port side and threw that barrel in also. He grabbed the rifle they had brought on deck to ignite the gunpowder, then fumbled in the leather cartridge box for a bullet. McKay bit a paper cartridge open and poured powder down the barrel, then pushed in a bullet with his thumb, ramming it down hard. He pulled the hammer back to half cock and pressed a copper percussion cap onto the nipple.

Another cannonball screamed toward the stern, but McKay didn't pay any attention. He had one thing on his mind--to shoot the barrels of gunpowder when they came alongside the black Federal warship.

A column of water boiled from the sea, sweeping the deck with its spray, but none of this existed for McKay. His whole world consisted of the black death ship behind him. He knelt trance-like at the gunnel, resting the Enfield rifle's long barrel on top. He tucked the rifle into his shoulder and followed the casks of gunpowder as the erratic waves tossed them about, all the while saying a silent prayer his aim would be true.

"A little closer. Come on, just a little closer," McKay said aloud, watching intently. He could see the gray bearded Federal commander pointing to the *Atlantis* and urging his men to destroy the blockade-runner.

Suddenly, the black pursuing warship tacked to starboard to expose her port guns. The shift in course took her away from the path of the barrels of gunpowder.

"Damn it!" McKay cursed in disbelief.

The black warship's port side erupted in a sheet of smoke and flame which hurled cannonball after cannonball at the defiant blockade-runner. One of the shells slammed into the *Atlantis'* starboard paddle wheel box. A man was standing on top when it exploded into a brilliant ball of flame and kindling. When the smoke cleared, the black skeletal wheel continued to rotate, missing more than half a dozen paddles.

Unexpectedly, the black warship veered back to port so her starboard cannons could fire. When she did this, her bow snagged the line and the barrels blazed a trail of sparkling water to the ship.

McKay pulled the rifle's hammer back to full cock, following the barrel's path. The instant they reached the hull, he fired his rifle. At the same moment, the enemy cannons unleashed their salvo. What began as the normal smoke and flame of gunfire spread to envelop the whole Union ship. Orange-yellow flame blossomed from the waterline to rise a hundred feet or more in the air. Blackened debris rocketed across the smoke filled sky, splashing up to a half-mile away.

McKay leaped to his feet, shook his rifle, whooping like a wild man. Slowly, men came out on deck. Some were limping, trailing blood. Others had the half-scared, half-savage look of men pushed to the edge of endurance. The battered men gathered around their Captain to take up his triumphant cry.

Suddenly, the sea exploded and tall spouts of water leaped into the air only fifty feet from the *Atlantis'* bow. Two Federal warships guarding Old Inlet were steaming to cut off the blockade-runner. The men, who moments before had let their guard down to give thanks for their deliverance, became rugged seamen again, rushing to meet this new challenge.

McKay threw down his rifle and burst into the bridge. "Mr. Burriss, stay close to shore. I want to keep as little water as possible under our keel. Mr. Johnston, come here."

A deckhand with a black bush of a mustache rushed over.

"Check our depth with a lead line. Don't let it get under ten feet."

The man nodded, hurrying away.

"Mr. Reichman," McKay bellowed down the speaking tube, "our starboard wheel has lost some paddles and we're losing speed. Can you raise more steam?"

"With coal alone, no sir. But there's a beautiful hundred pound slab of bacon in the cold storage locker that Cookie's been trying to hide from me. It'd make a wonderful fire, Capt'n, and get you the pressure you need."

McKay smiled. "Well, go get it then."

"With pleasure, sir."

Soon, the *Atlantis* increased her speed, cutting through the seas beneath a long plume of black smoke. An avalanche of shells wailed around the blockade-runner. The pilot had his hands full, trying to hug the shore and take evasive action at the same time.

A puff of white smoke erupted from the cannon on the bow of the starboard ship, which was instantly followed by another from the port vessel.

The salvo straddled the *Atlantis* and buried her in a blinding storm of spray.

"Hard aport, Mr. Burriss!" McKay shouted.

The ship heeled into her turn, while enemy shells burst behind her, obliterating the swirl of water her turn generated.

A series of explosions from shore grabbed McKay's attention. Ragged clouds of smoke rose from three Confederate forts protecting Old Inlet. Fort Caswell, a large masonry fortification which was built before the war, led the barrage, then was followed by Fort Campbell and Fort Holmes. McKay's hunch had proved correct. Old Inlet was still in Confederate hands.

Southern cannonballs screamed high above the *Atlantis*. Seconds later geysers of water erupted around the leading Federal ship. One of the shells struck high on her mizzenmast, bringing it crashing down in a tangle of rigging and canvas. Federal sailors swarmed over the deck while the ship reduced speed and turned out to sea.

The other Federal warship continued to close on the blockade-runner, her guns blazing. She soon came under a torrent of fire as spouts of white water rose all about her. An explosion rocked the warship and smoke and flame erupted from the port side. A list developed, and she ran aground on a sandbar to keep from sinking.

As the *Atlantis* steamed into the inlet, the crew danced in excitement on deck, waving their hats in the air to salute the Confederate forts.

Since Old Inlet lay seven miles south of Fort Fisher, no one there was aware of the exact nature of the fighting to the south. The soldiers saw some activity out at sea, and heard the distant rumble of cannon fire, but they suspected it was somebody else's battle which didn't concern them.

With a full head of steam, the *Atlantis* sped up the Cape Fear River toward Fort Fisher. When the blockade-runner approached the fort, the startled Federal soldiers could only fire a few muskets as she passed by.

McKay was shocked when he saw the once mighty fort. The cannons and the earthen walls were torn and shattered. Shell craters pockmarked the fort's interior, and the two dozen whitewashed buildings McKay had seen when he left for Nassau were smoking ruins.

Throngs of curious people began to gather when they glimpsed the battle-scarred *Atlantis* steaming up the river to Wilmington. Small boys raced the blockade-runner to her berth, thinking she may sink at any moment. The shattered hulk did indeed appear to be making her last voyage. Her engines were panting and wheezing, the bow smashed, the starboard paddle wheel box missing, along with the after part of her deck house. Haggard, grim-faced men lined her deck, many of them wounded. General Bragg, followed by four of his staff, rushed across the gang plank when it was set in place. "Captain McKay, I'm amazed to see you! I didn't think anyone could get through the blockade since Fort Fisher had fallen."

McKay wondered what Bragg was doing here, instead of fighting Yankees. He motioned to the injured men, and said, "We need a doctor, General. We've got wounded aboard."

"Of course." General Bragg turned to one of his aides, and said, "Major Block, have someone send for several surgeons." To McKay he asked, "How many men did you lose?"

"Nearly half our crew. Seven dead, and sixteen wounded."

"I'm sorry to hear that, Captain. Is there anything I can do?"

McKay thought a moment. "Yes, there is. We need men and wagons to unload our cargo, and I'd like someone to tell me what in the hell happened at Fort Fisher."

"The men have already been sent for. Since we no longer need the munitions here, I'm sending them north by rail to General Lee in Virginia." Bragg paused, uneasy. "As for telling you what occurred at the fort, being the commanding general, I suppose I can give you the best account."

McKay nodded. "All right. Let's talk."

Bragg looked around at the wrecked ship. "If we could find somewhere to speak privately, I'll tell you what I know."

"How about my cabin?"

"No offense intended, Captain, but this ship may be sinking."

McKay saw the *Atlantis* was losing her list. "We'll be okay. The pumps are running, and they're keeping ahead of the water."

Bragg nodded. "Very well then."

McKay led the way to his cabin.

General Bragg told the truth to McKay as he imagined it to be, which conveniently placed him in a better light. "You see," he explained, "President Davis sent me to protect Wilmington because it is the last port open in the Confederacy. I've succeeded in doing that. General Hoke's division is entrenched near Sugar Loaf to keep the Yankees from marching up the peninsula."

"How many men did Hoke lose defending Fort Fisher?" McKay asked.

General Bragg's stare turned cold. "None. I told you, Captain. My mission is to protect Wilmington, which I've done to the best of my ability. Fort Fisher was lost through gross mismanagement and drunkenness in the face of the enemy."

McKay could not believe what he was hearing. "Drunkenness?"

"Yes. I know what was going on. I sent General Colquitt to Battery Buchanan so he could take command of the fort. When he returned, he told me the garrison had thrown away their weapons and was blind drunk."

McKay shook his head in disgust. Bragg was a coward. He had done nothing to help the brave men in Fort Fisher. And now, since the soldiers were either dead or had been captured and were unable to defend themselves, this despicable little man was trying to diminish what they had done by saying the fort had fallen because the soldiers were drunk.

McKay shot out of his seat, signaling the end of their conversation. "I will not sit here and listen to these lies. I know the fort's commander. Colonel Lamb is a fine soldier, and he would never let such things happen." With eyes narrowed, McKay leaned across the table to speak his words more forcibly. "Yes. I am convinced Fort Fisher was lost because of cowardice. Your damned cowardice, General Bragg! Not the soldiers!"

Bragg's eyes widened with shock. "How dare you say that to me! I'll have you court-martialed."

"I'm not in your army, General. I thank God for that, because I couldn't stand by and do nothing while brave men die."

General Bragg opened his mouth to protest, then he stopped and suddenly became afraid of the angry man before him. He scowled, shoved his chair back roughly to show such talk did not intimidate him, and stalked from the cabin.

CHAPTER 19

After the cargo was unloaded and McKay had moved the Atlantis to Cassidey's shipyard for repairs, he took a carriage through the panic filled streets to Brooke's house. Droves of people were leaving town because they expected Wilmington to be looted and burned by the Yankee army just like Atlanta and Columbia. Men grabbed their wives and daughters so the marauding soldiers would not rape them, packed a few belongings on a wagon and fled to North Carolina's interior.

Nettie, the Negro maid, answered the door when McKay pulled the brass doorbell at Brooke's house. The maid said, "Brooke's not here, Capt'n. Lemme get Mrs. Snow for you."

McKay thought this odd, but said, "Okay."

In a minute Brooke's mother came to the door, her eyes red from crying. "Brooke isn't here, Captain," Mrs. Snow said, weeping. "She was in Fort Fisher when it fell."

"I don't understand. How could that happen?" McKay said, shocked.

"It's all Virginia's fault," she snapped, dabbing at her eyes with the corner of a handkerchief. "That dreadful woman came here the morning of the attack and asked Brooke to take her place at a dinner the Ladies Soldier's Aid Society was giving at the fort. She said her mother had taken ill during the night, and she couldn't go. Brooke said yes, of course."

McKay put a reassuring arm around the old woman and nodded in understanding. Although he too was reeling with the news, McKay was careful not to appear alarmed and upset the woman more.

Mrs. Snow blew her nose, and said, "The next day, when I went to church to pray for Brooke and the boys in the fort, who should I see but Virginia's mother. She looked healthy to me, so I asked how she was. She looked at me surprised and said, 'Fine. Why do you ask?' Well, I told her about what Virginia said. About how we thought she was on her death bed."

McKay led the frail woman to a green velvet armchair in the parlor. She sat and her thin hands clutched her handkerchief nervously. "Mrs. Drake said it must have been a mistake, she was sure Virginia would never do such a thing. I asked her where Virginia was, so I could speak to her, but she said her daughter had gone to the Aid Society to roll bandages. 'The soldiers need bandages more than they need our prayers,' the witch told her mother. Can you imagine that?"

McKay wondered if Virginia could have known anything about the attack. Although the chances were remote, he still needed to find out.

McKay remained with Mrs. Snow for a short while, listening to her litany of complaints against the girl she held responsible for her daughter's capture, and pondered his next move.

McKay walked the block and a half to where Virginia lived while considering the events of the last two days. His world was crumbling around him. Half his crew was dead or wounded, his ship was damaged, Fort Fisher had fallen. Now, the Yankees had taken prisoner the woman he loved. Who knew what her fate would be? For the first time in his life McKay felt powerless. He could do nothing, but wait and hope for the best.

McKay opened the wrought iron gate and crossed the front yard to the wide porch. He was about to ring the bell, when he heard Virginia behind him, "Oh, Wade, I'm so glad to see you. I thought I'd never see you again when I learned Fort Fisher had fallen."

He turned around, removing his cap. "Hello, Virginia. This isn't a social call. I came to find out why you lied to Brooke about your mother being sick."

She crossed the porch, slipping a hand under McKay's arm and looking up at him. "I'm dreadfully sorry she got captured, Wade, but I had no idea anything would happen. The truth is, I met a soldier at the hospital the day before, and he asked me to go on a picnic the afternoon of the dinner."

"So you went on a picnic, instead?"

"Yes, I did. I didn't tell my mother about it because she wouldn't approve. You know her. She thinks there's nothing more important than doing for the soldiers. But then I thought to myself, this man is a soldier. He's been wounded. He's lonely and away from his family and friends. Why not brighten his day by going?"

McKay was beginning to feel foolish for suspecting she might have known about the attack. He knew Virginia was man-crazy and this would fit in perfectly with what he had already seen. "I spoke with Brooke's mother, and she suspects you had knowledge of the attack. That's why you asked her daughter to go in your place."

Virginia batted her eyes, smiling. "Now isn't that the silliest thing you ever heard? How would I know anything about the Yankee's plans?"

The blonde woman's charming manner and naive questions completely disarmed McKay, and he returned her smile. "It is far fetched, I agree."

"My Lord, yes. What would I know about military matters, for heaven's sake?"

"I'm sorry, Virginia, but I needed to ask. You can see that, can't you?"

"Of course I can. Why don't we go for a walk and you can tell me about your brave dash through the blockade? I understand it was thrilling," she said, clutching his arm and steering him toward the sidewalk.

"To say the least. Practically the whole Yankee fleet was waiting for us when we left Nassau."

"Oh my," she said, gasping in horror. "Whatever did you do?"

"Well, we slipped through the blockade," McKay announced, demonstrating the movement of his ship with his hands. "Then, when a Yankee ship came close enough, we sprayed them with scalding water from our boilers."

"Oh, how clever of you," she cried with wonder, clapping her hands with delight. "Please tell me more."

That evening, McKay went to the Green Parrot to see his friend Amber. He found her talking to a customer at the bar and nodded a greeting. In a few minutes, she came over to the table where he was sitting, giving him a hug.

"Am I glad to see you! I was attacked, and one of the bartenders was killed when he tried to help me."

McKay's jaw dropped. "What happened?"

"Well, I had a customer who wanted to tie me up and pulled out a knife. Well, before I know what's happening he starts to carve up my chest. Fortunately for me the bartender noticed I was gone for a while and came upstairs. He knocked on the door and asked if I was all right. I screamed, and he broke down the door and grabbed Judson."

"Judson? You mean Judson Bates?"

Amber nodded with obvious distaste. "Yeah. That's him. The dirty bastard stabbed Will and killed him."

"Did they catch Judson?"

"No. The little shit got away."

McKay's face hardened. "Damn! I knew he was nothing but trouble when he was aboard the *Atlantis*."

"Yes," she agreed. "I don't understand why they didn't just keep him in jail when he killed that Negro family."

McKay ordered a beer, then told Amber about Brooke being captured at Fort Fisher. He also mentioned talking to her mother, then going to see Virginia.

"Virginia told me she wanted to get out of the dinner so she could go on a picnic with a man she had just met. She figured telling everyone her mother was ill would do the trick."

Amber nodded. "That sounds like something Virginia would do."

"I thought the same thing. So I guess, Brooke being captured in the fort wasn't so suspicious after all."

"It's possible, but I wouldn't take Virginia's word for it. She lies too well."

McKay shook his head. "I still can't believe she knew anything about the attack."

"You'd make a wonderful husband," Amber observed.

"Me? Why's that?"

Amber smiled. "Because you can't imagine a woman ever doing anything wrong. Let me tell you, Wade, when it comes to being conniving and ruthless, women can be a thousand-times worse than men."

"I don't think Virginia's the spy type."

Amber looked at him, surprised. "Are you kidding? Women make the best spies, Wade. They're natural born actresses, and what is spying but good acting. As little girls, they learn how to manipulate their daddies to get what they want. When they're grown, women do some acting practically every day of their life to keep their husbands and boyfriends in line."

McKay considered this. "All right, let's say I agree with you. How would I go about proving she knew anything?"

"That's easy. Let me talk to her."

"I don't know, Amber."

"If you're worried about upsetting that delicate flower, forget it. That woman is tougher than you think, believe me."

"Maybe, but I don't want to give anyone a hard time. Especially now. I feel bad enough about what happened as it is." McKay downed his beer and motioned to the bartender for another. "Tell me this. How do you expect to get any information from her?"

"I'll just ask her in a nice way," Amber assured him. "Because I'm a woman, her cutesy shit won't work on me."

"Thanks for offering, Amber. But I'll talk to her again," he said. "I have experience in these matters. As a captain, I have to know how to judge people and get the truth."

"What ever you say," Amber said, smiling to herself as he walked away.

The next morning, Amber went to Virginia's house and pulled the brass doorbell. She had to know the truth, for her friend's sake. When Virginia saw who it was, she quietly slipped onto the porch so her mother would not hear.

"Hello, Virginia. Wade told me what happened to Brooke, but I thought I'd come over and hear the story from you. I figured maybe you left something out."

Virginia cocked her head to one side and thrust her hands onto her hips. "I don't know what business it is of yours, but I'll tell you the same thing I told him. I needed to get out of the dinner at the fort so I could go out with a man. It's as simple as that."

Amber nodded. "I'm curious about that. Who is this man? Where can I find him?"

Seeing Amber was trying to trap her, Virginia's mind searched for an answer. "He was a soldier at the hospital where I work, but alas, the poor man died two days ago," she said, lowering her eyes.

"How convenient. What's his name?"

Virginia hesitated, thinking. "Nate, Nate Bridger, but I don't see where it's any concern of yours."

Amber narrowed her eyes, and said, "Whatever concerns Wade, concerns me. There are a half-dozen hospitals in Wilmington, which one do you work at?"

"Certainly you're not going to check on me?" Virginia asked, appalled.

Amber folded her arms and nodded with satisfaction. "That's exactly what I intend to do. So which hospital is it?"

Virginia stiffened, her face cold. "As I said before, it's none of your business. Now get off my porch."

"Yeah? Or you'll do what?"

Virginia turned for the door in a huff, and Amber grabbed her by the arm. "Not so fast, sweetie. I haven't finished with you--"

Virginia whirled around, slapping Amber in the face.

Amber shrugged off the blow, slamming the other woman against the door frame. With her hand raised, she yelled, "Did you know the Yankees would attack?"

"No! Let go of me!" Virginia shrieked with rage.

"I don't believe you!"

Virginia became a screaming wildcat, kicking and clawing. Amber had no choice but to return the slap. Virginia's head snapped back into the white painted door jamb. The force of the blow sent her reeling into a potted fern, which crashed to the floor.

Amber scrambled over the prostrate woman, when suddenly Mrs. Drake appeared at the door. "Virginia, are you all right?"

Amber helped Virginia up, whispering in her ear, "If you don't want your mother to find out about this, then tell her you're okay."

"I'm all right, Mama. I was chatting with my friend and tripped over that darned fern near the door."

"Good heavens, you didn't hurt yourself, did you?"

"No, Mama. I'm fine."

"All right. I'll have Wallace clean up the mess."

When she had gone, Amber said, "That was smart. Now you can do something else that's smart. If you admit you had knowledge of the attack, I won't tell anyone. If you don't, I'll go to the authorities and report it."

Virginia laughed. "Who would believe a prostitute, for heaven's sake."

"It won't be just me. Wade and Mrs. Snow will come, too."

Virginia stared at Amber for a moment, thinking. "This will be just between you and me? You won't tell anyone else?"

Amber nodded she could keep a secret.

Virginia glanced at the door to make sure they were alone. "All right. I knew the attack would happen."

"How did you find out?"

"Peter Reynolds came into the hospital drunk one night, about two days before the attack. He had cut himself, and I cleaned him up and bandaged him."

Amber nodded. "Yes. Go on."

"Well, Peter passed out, and I found this dispatch in his wallet." She reached under her skirt and removed a piece of paper from a secret pouch near the hem of her petticoat, then handed it to the other woman. "It gives information about the Federal attack."

Amber read the message, shaking her head with disgust.

"I couldn't go to the dinner knowing what I did," Virginia explained, "so I asked Brooke to take my place."

"You little bitch!" Amber growled and shook the blonde woman. "How could you do such a thing?"

Virginia's eyes became moist. "I'll admit what I did was wrong, but I had no idea the fort would fall."

Amber glanced at her incredulously. "You think that makes it all right?"

"No, I don't. I'm terribly sorry. I never meant to hurt Brooke."

"Forget Brooke for a second. How about the others you've hurt? If the soldiers at Fort Fisher had some warning of the attack, they could have been ready and things might have ended differently. And, Peter Reynolds is also a spy and needs to be reported."

Virginia began to weep and Amber said, "Don't waste those tears on me. Save them for someone who cares."

The stern words made Virginia cry harder. A middle-aged Negro servant stepped onto the porch with a broom and shovel and noticed Virginia was crying. "You awright, Miss Virginia?"

"She's okay," Amber said. "Miss Virginia's just upset about her fern."

He nodded, then began sweeping up the mess while Amber hurried down the stairs, clutching the dispatch.

Amber thrust the dispatch into McKay's hands before he could scold her for confronting Virginia. When she told McKay what Peter and Virginia had done, he bolted from the table, storming out of the tavern. She ran after him and caught him in the street. "Where are you going?"

McKay stopped and faced her. "To beat the hell out of Peter Reynolds."

"Don't you think you should let the soldiers handle this? If he sees you, he'll have a chance to run."

McKay considered this. "You're right. I should beat the shit out of him first, then drag him to jail."

"And what good would that do? It won't help Brooke."

McKay frowned. "No, but I'll feel better."

Amber knew spying was a deadly business, and thought Peter Reynolds would not hesitate to shoot anyone who came after him. "Wade, calm down and think about this. You know what they say. Knowledge is power. We know Peter is a spy, but maybe we could use this information ourselves."

"How?"

"I don't know. Let's just stop and think about it. Okay? If we don't come up with anything, then you can tell the soldiers and maybe go with them when they arrest Peter."

What Amber said made sense, and McKay let her take him by the arm into the Green Parrot where they sat at a table.

After a while, McKay said, "I have an idea. The Yankees will be sending some ships to Fort Fisher soon to take the prisoners north. If we could disguise the Atlantis and another ship to look like naval transports, perhaps we could fool the Federal commander into turning over his prisoners to us." McKay grinned, and added, "To make it more believable, we'll have Peter Reynolds find out when the ships are coming and what their names are. Maybe we can even find out who the naval commander is."

"Why would a Yankee spy help us?" Amber asked.

"He'll be executed unless he helps."

Amber nodded, impressed. "You might have something there. Where do we start?"

McKay pushed back his chair and stood. "By seeing General Bragg."

McKay and Amber sat at Confederate headquarters all afternoon, waiting to see General Bragg. The longer he waited, the angrier McKay became. "Sitting here all day is ridiculous," he said. "I should have pounded Peter into the ground when I wanted to and rescued Brooke myself."

Amber had accompanied Wade to keep him from doing anything foolish and getting himself killed. "Just be patient, Wade. The General will see us soon."

"But we've been waiting for three hours! I refuse to sit here any longer and do nothing."

A colonel passing by overheard their conversation and noticed how upset McKay was. He stopped, and said, "I'm Colonel Bennett. May I help you?"

"Yes," McKay said, irritated. "Could you remind General Bragg we've been waiting all afternoon to see him?"

"I'm sorry, but the General is busy. Is there something I could do for you?"

McKay explained the nature of his problem, and the Colonel ushered them into his office.

"We don't like to discuss such matters where others may hear. Now, you say you have knowledge of a spy?"

"Yes, sir. A man by the name of Peter Reynolds."

The Colonel shook his head. "These are serious charges, Captain. Peter Reynolds is an advisor to General Bragg. What proof do you have of his guilt?"

McKay pulled a piece of paper from his pocket, and handed it to Colonel Bennett. "A nurse found this Federal dispatch in his possession, Colonel. It came into my hands this morning, otherwise I would have reported it sooner," he explained. "You'll find it contains vital information about the attack on Fort Fisher."

The Colonel read the dispatch, nodding. "Peter Reynolds needs to be arrested immediately."

"I agree, Colonel. I also have a plan to rescue the prisoners at Fort Fisher. We might need Peter Reynolds to help our mission succeed."

"I don't understand, Captain. How could he do that?"

"If we bargain with him, he may be able to provide the information we need."

The Colonel's face hardened. "He's a spy, sir! The Confederacy does not bargain with Yankee spies."

"Colonel, we may jeopardize the rescue mission unless we get his cooperation."

"All right, Captain, you seem to have all the answers. What do you propose?"

McKay leaned forward in his chair, anxious to reveal his plan. "Well, sir, if we arrest him, but give him enough freedom to get the information we need, we could maybe reduce his sentence from death to life in prison."

"What sort of information do we need?"

"If we could find out the names of the transports coming to take the prisoners North, we might disguise some ships to fool the Yankees. We also need the names of their commanders and when they're due to arrive."

The Colonel furrowed his brow. "I see, Captain. Let me take your proposal to the commanding general. If Reynolds helps us, perhaps he can talk to President Davis and get the man's sentence commuted."

McKay suspected the reason he was unable to see Bragg stemmed from their argument the day before. "Colonel, would you tell him Captain Wade McKay would consider it a personal favor if he grants my request?"

"I'll tell him that, Captain."

Within a few minutes, the Colonel reappeared followed by a major and two lieutenants. "The General has agreed to speak to the President about the matter, Captain. Meanwhile, he has instructed these officers to arrest Peter Reynolds."

McKay showed the officers to the rooming house where Peter Reynolds lived. Peter wasn't home, so the men staked out his room and waited.

When Reynolds mounted the stairs to the rooming house and opened the door, he was suddenly surrounded by Confederate officers.

"What's this about?" he asked surprised.

"You're under arrest for spying," the Major announced.

Peter whirled around to escape, slamming into McKay's fist. He fell to the ground, with blood from his broken nose seeping through his fingers.

"You didn't need to hit me," Peter shouted.

McKay beamed with satisfaction. "Oh yes, I did. That was for Brooke and also for being a dirty yellow traitor."

"I'm not a traitor! This is all a mistake!" Peter shouted, as the two lieutenants grabbed him by the arms, hauling him away.

"Virginia told us everything," McKay said to Peter Reynolds. The men were seated at a long table in the jailhouse with Peter on one side and McKay and the major on the other.

"Virginia? Who's she?" Peter wanted to know, holding a bloody handkerchief to his nose.

"She took care of you at the hospital when you got drunk and cut your head. A dispatch from Union General Terry giving information about the attack was found in your wallet," McKay said, pointing to the paper.

Peter shook his head. "That isn't mine! I don't know how Virginia came up with such a ridiculous story. Perhaps the dispatch belongs to her."

"When you tried to run from us, that was an admission of your guilt," the major pointed out.

"If you're innocent like you claim, why did you attempt to run?" McKay asked.

Peter put his hand to his forehead, his eyes growing moist. "Because I'm sick with worry about my family. I'm having a nervous breakdown, and I didn't want anyone to see me like this."

McKay had seen enough of Reynold's theatrics. "Cut the crap, Peter. I saw the fear in your eyes. If I hadn't been there to stop you, you'd be out of the county by now."

The sound of hammering drifted through the window on the breeze.

McKay gestured to the window. "Hear that, Peter? It's your gallows being built."

Peter became worried. "You can't hang me. You don't have enough proof."

"This is all the proof we need," McKay said, holding up the paper.

"Does that message have my name on it?" Peter asked.

"No," McKay admitted.

"Then you have nothing."

"We have enough to hang you. Besides, Peter, this is war. The army doesn't need much of a reason to put a man to death," McKay reminded him. "It already shoots deserters, so hanging an accused spy will be easy."

"However," the major said, "if you admit your guilt, and help us rescue the prisoners from Fort Fisher, we may be willing to commute your sentence to life in prison."

Peter considered the offer. The war was nearly over, so he would not be in a Confederate prison long. Right now the most important thing was to stay alive. "All right," he admitted, "I helped the Yankees capture Fort Fisher. I only did it because I want this damned war to end. Too many people have been hurt already. You see, my family was in Atlanta when it was captured and burned."

"If you expect me to feel sorry for you, I don't," McKay said. "I have no sympathy for yellow-bellied traitors."

Peter nodded. "I understand. What can I do to help?"

McKay leaned forward in his chair and revealed his plan to Peter. "The Yankees will be sending some ships to Fort Fisher soon to take the prisoners north. If we could disguise the Atlantis and another ship to look like naval transports, perhaps we could fool the Federal commander into turning over his prisoners to us. What I want you to do, is to find out when the ships are coming and what their names are. We also have to know who the naval commander is. If the Yankees at the fort are expecting us to take the prisoners north, our appearance shouldn't arouse any suspicion."

Peter nodded. "Finding out that information shouldn't be difficult. Things like that are rarely kept secret." He thought a moment. "What about Fort Anderson? You'll have to sail right past it."

"That's not a problem. I intend to sail down the river at night and out into the ocean. When it's morning, we'll turn around and go to Fort Fisher. The Federals won't be expecting a rescue attempt to come from the sea. We will notify the commander at Fort Anderson that although our ships will be disguised as Northern transports, he'll be able to recognize us because we'll hoist Confederate flags when we leave Fort Fisher."

The major waited until Captain McKay was through, then asked, "Reynolds, who were your accomplices?"

"The only man I know in Wilmington is Judson Bates. He helped me cut the wires to the minefield, then stayed inside the fort to spread panic."

"Where is he now?"

Peter shrugged his shoulders. "Inside the fort, I suppose."

"The police want him for a string of murders and attacking that woman in Paddy's Hollow," McKay told the major. "He's also the one who killed that black family last summer."

"Those charges were dropped, weren't they?" the Major asked.

"Yes. Bates got off because of a technicality, but I swear he won't be so lucky this time."

The Confederate Government commandeered the Atlantis, along with another blockade-runner, to be converted for the rescue mission and put Captain McKay in charge of the work. McKay instructed the foreman at Cassidey's shipyard to build the superstructures higher on the two ships and paint them, so they resembled naval transports.

A few days later, McKay was inspecting the main cabin on the Atlantis when he received word Peter Reynolds wanted to see him. He reminded the foreman the work had to be finished in less than a week, and went to the jailhouse.

"I think I've found the best way to get the information you need," Reynolds said to McKay from his cell. "If I use the network of agents, it may be quite some time before we receive an answer. However, if Mrs. Lamb and several other women go to the fort under a flag of truce and ask to see their husbands, she can probably find out everything you need to know in a single day. The beauty of this plan is it won't arouse suspicion. What's more natural than a wife wanting to know the fate of her husband or being concerned about his welfare?"

"That sounds like a terrific idea," McKay agreed. "So we don't need you after all."

Peter held up his hands, worried. "Oh no, I would still go along to make sure the women don't run into any snags. Don't forget, I've spoken to a few of the Federal officers, and they recognize me."

"Why should I trust you?" the major asked. "Once you're inside the fort, you might tell the Yankees everything and stay there."

Peter nodded. "Yes, I could. But if I did, then you could simply abort the rescue mission."

"That'd do us a lot of good," said the Major. "We'd still be in the same situation and also lose a Yankee spy."

Grinning, Peter said, "That's the chance you'll have to take."

"No," McKay said shaking his head. "I don't like the odds. You're staying here where we can keep an eye on you."

Two days later, Mrs. Lamb and twenty-three women approached Fort Fisher under a flag of truce. A Confederate colonel accompanied them to speak with the officer of the guard. He explained the women had come to find out what happened to their husbands. The Federal captain nodded and went to see what could be done. When he returned, he told the colonel the army would allow only the women inside the fort, but not any soldiers. The colonel agreed to wait outside, while the Federal captain took the women to see General Terry.

"Who is the spokeswoman for this group?" the dark-haired Union General with a Van Dyke beard and mustache asked.

Daisy Lamb stepped forward. "I am, sir. I'm Mrs. William Lamb. My husband was the commander of Fort Fisher."

"What can I do for you, madam?"

Gesturing to the other women, Mrs. Lamb said, "The ladies and I have come to see our husbands. It's been nearly a week since the battle, and we have heard nothing. We have no idea whether our men are alive or dead."

"I understand completely, Mrs. Lamb. I have personal knowledge of your husband, and am happy to report he is alive, although seriously wounded. As for the others," Terry said, rummaging through the papers on his desk until he found the ones he was searching for. "I have a roster here with the names of all the prisoners taken inside the fort. If a man's name doesn't appear on this list, it means he was either killed during the battle or escaped."

Mrs. Lamb was relieved to know William was alive. She took the papers and passed them to the woman behind her. There was a rustle of petticoats as the ladies rushed forward for a glimpse at the list.

"May I see my husband?" Mrs. Lamb asked.

"Of course, madam. You all shall, if it's possible."

"Before I see him, General, tell me what will happen to William now?"

General Terry considered the question. "He, along with the other prisoners, will be taken north and imprisoned."

Mrs. Lamb shuddered, and asked, "When will this be?"

"Two troop transports will arrive before the end of the month, madam. The voyage will take about a week and, depending if the men are officers or enlisted personnel, they will be sent to various prisons."

Mrs. Lamb remembered she was instructed to find out the names of the ships and their commander. "You said they will be taken on transports. How comfortable are these ships? My husband has been gravely wounded, and he needs special care."

General Terry smiled. "I understand your concern, Mrs. Lamb. From what I've heard the *USS California* and the *North Point* are some of the finest ships the Navy has."

She nodded. "And the man in charge, is he a Christian gentleman?"

"Of course, madam. Commander Bishop is one of the most competent and charitable officers we have."

"Then you know him personally?"

"No, Mrs. Lamb. I do not, but I have heard many fine things about him."

She smiled at how easy it was to get the information she needed. "Thank you for putting my fears to rest, General Terry. I think I would like to see my husband now."

"Of course, madam." Terry hesitated, then added, "For security reasons, the visits will be limited to ten minutes, and only three ladies will be allowed to see their husbands at one time. An armed guard will stay with them."

Daisy Lamb smiled, and said with sarcasm, "I understand your need to protect this powerful fort from twenty-four ladies, General. After all, we could have guns concealed beneath our petticoats."

General Terry laughed. "I'm sure you don't, madam, but we have rules, and they must be obeyed."

"Of course, General. We wouldn't want to do anything to upset the army."

"Believe me, Mrs. Lamb, nothing you could do would upset us."

"Thank you, General Terry. I would like to see my husband now."

"Of course, Captain Dawson will see to your wishes."

Mrs. Lamb offered her hand to the General. "You've been most gracious, General."

General Terry bowed, taking her hand in his, then kissing it. "I'm glad I could be of service, Mrs. Lamb."

The evening McKay was to leave for Fort Fisher, he went to Virginia's house.

Virginia smiled when she saw who it was. "Wade, what a pleasant surprise. Why don't you come in?"

McKay shook his head. "No, I can't. It's a lovely night, and I thought maybe you would like to go for a walk."

Although Virginia wondered if Wade held her responsible for what happened to Brooke, she realized with her rival out of the way she had a clear shot at the man she wanted. Her plan was working perfectly because here he was on her doorstep. "Of course I would, Wade. Let me get my shawl."

A moment later, Virginia stepped onto the porch, slipping a hand around McKay's arm. The sweet aroma of freshly sprinkled lilac water filled the cool night air. "Where should we go?" she asked, gazing up at him with admiring eyes.

"Let's go by the riverfront. There's something I need to check on the *Atlantis* before we leave."

"You're leaving so soon?"

"Yes, I am. It's been nearly two weeks since the fall of Fort Fisher and everything is ready. The timing is perfect, too. Two Yankee troop transports are due to arrive at Fort Fisher soon, so we must move now."

When the couple got to the *Atlantis*, they crossed the gangplank and went to McKay's cabin. Virginia was thrilled he was inviting her into his room. She was positive now she had done the right thing by getting rid of Brooke. To her surprise, inside the cabin stood a heavily muscled seaman who was well over six feet. He had a tough bearded face, and a smouldering cigar was clamped between his teeth.

"Virginia, I want you to meet Luke. He's going to help tie you up."

Pulling away from McKay, she snapped, "Oh no he's not!"

McKay folded his arms, blocking her escape route. "Amber told me what you did to Brooke, and I intend to even the score."

As the bell at St. James tolled midnight, two ships steamed from the dock with the *Atlantis* taking the lead. McKay stood near the helm and watched as the buildings of Wilmington, their tiny windows dimly lit with candlelight, slipped by. He wore the uniform of a Federal naval commander, and his crew had put on the Yankee uniforms supplied to them by the Confederate raider *Florida*.

Two miles north of Fort Fisher, the steamships stopped their paddle wheels and let the current carry them down river. The darkened vessels silently drifted past the fort and slipped out to sea, where they hoisted Federal flags and waited for dawn.

CHAPTER 20

Brooke was in the hospital helping a man with one arm eat his breakfast, when a gruff voice demanded, "Madam, get your belongings and come with me."

She looked up, and was astonished to see Wade standing there in a Federal naval officer's uniform. She was also amazed his Northern accent sounded so real. Sensing the need to play along, Brooke complained, "Why should I? I'm sick of jumping every time one of you damn Yankees says jump!"

"I'll have no trouble, miss. Come along peacefully, or I'll have some armed guards escort you aboard my ship."

"You'd better get your guards then, Admiral or Commander, or whoever you are, because I'm not going."

McKay turned around, nodding to the two men disguised as Federal sailors. "Escort this woman aboard the *California* and put her in the cabin behind the bridge. Post a guard outside her door."

The sailors grabbed Brooke by either arm, pulled her out of the chair, and dragged her from the hospital, screaming. A white-coated surgeon, his mouth agape, halted in his examination of a patient.

"She'll be all right," McKay assured the man. "These Rebel women can be real wildcats when they get angry."

The surgeon nodded. "So I see, Commander. It's odd she never displayed that kind of temperament before."

"She was never being sent to prison before," McKay pointed out. "I'll send some men to round up the rest of the prisoners. Could you have them ready to go and maybe have someone gather her belongings?"

"Of course, Commander," he said, hastening to add, "Some men have been severely wounded and require further treatment. Do you have adequate medical supplies?"

"We have some, Doctor. However, we would be grateful for anything you can spare."

"That's what I suspected. I'll send along what I can."

The latest turn of events amazed McKay as he returned to his ship. The Yankees were not only providing him with the Confederate prisoners, but giving him medicine to care for them as well. But what he saw next erased any sense of joy he felt. Federal soldiers were leading a line of haggard prisoners from a tent compound to the dock more than half a mile away. The bearded Confederates wore shabby gray and brown clothing and were being prodded along by Federal troops carrying bayoneted muskets. Some men limped along slowly, while others dropped back to help their crippled friends catch up. This slowed the procession, angering the guards. A Federal soldier charged among the prisoners and hit a sluggish man with his rifle butt, yelling for the fallen man to move along. Unable to quell the rage inside him, McKay stormed over, snatching the weapon out of the startled trooper's hands.

"Don't ever let me see you hitting a prisoner again, or I'll use this rifle butt on you!" McKay promised the guard, his face flushed with anger.

Visibly shaken, the soldier snapped to attention. "Yes sir. It won't happen again."

"Capt'n? Capt'n McKay, it's me, Howard," a voice called.

Out of the corner of his eye, McKay saw Howard Dutton waving one hand to get his attention and supporting a wounded Confederate soldier with the other. He ignored the big man and quickly thrust the weapon into the trooper's hands. "Here's your rifle back, soldier. Be careful how you handle prisoners in the future."

The soldier snapped to attention, saluting. McKay returned the salute, then walked toward the *Atlantis* hoping nobody had paid any attention to what Howard had said.

As the line of prisoners got closer to the dock, Howard spotted Judson standing close to the line of march.

"Hey, Judd, it's me, Howard!"

Bates turned, saw Howard waving to him, and walked over. "Hey, partner."

"Hey, Judd. How ya been?" Howard asked, smiling. The big man was supporting a gaunt Confederate soldier who was trembling with fever.

"I'm doin' fine," Judson said. "The Yankees made me an actin' trustee. Which means I help em with the prisoners. How 'bout you?"

"Okay, I reckon. Hey, guess who I seen jest a minute ago?"

Bates wasn't in the mood for guessing games. He had an important job to do, watching the prisoners and making sure none of them snuck out of the line. "I don't know. Who?"

"Capt'n McKay! He's capt'n of the *Atlantis*. 'Remember?"

"McKay's here? Are you sure?" Bates asked, scanning the crowd, his eyes widening with surprise.

"Yeah. 'Cept he's wearin' a Yankee uniform, an' he was hollerin' at one of the guards."

"Where's he now?" Bates demanded. "D'ya see him?"

Howard craned his neck, looking toward the dock. "Yeah, that's him yonder."

Bates looked to where Howard was pointing. The man he had sworn to kill for having him arrested was boarding one of the ships. "It's him all right. But the reason he's wearin' a Yankee uniform is 'cause he's a spy."

Howard appeared confused. "Say what?"

"The man's a damned spy, Howard!"

Howard shook his head, smiling. "He don't look like a spy to me, Judd. When I look at him, I just see Capt'n McKay."

"Study on this, Howard. The man's wearin' a Yankee uniform, an' he's fixin' to carry us to a Yankee prison. What else could he be?"

Scratching his head, Howard said, "Well, since you put it that way, it don't seem quite right."

"Course, it don't. We gotta figger a way to stop him."

"Yeah," Howard agreed, then his face grew puzzled. "How we gonna do that, Judd?"

Bates glanced around and spotted a guard he recognized. "I got me an idea," he said, then left.

Bates took the guard aside, pointing to Howard and spoke quietly. "Hey, Ethan, see the large man yonder? The one with the fool grin an' holdin' up that prisoner?"

"Yeah. Is he plannin' to escape?"

"Naw. He ain't, but he learnt the prisoners are gonna try to take over that ship. Can you tell the officer in charge what's happenin' while I go aboard an' try to stop 'em?"

"Sure, Judd. You need help?"

"Yeah. Round up as many men as you can git, an' meet me outside the *California's* wheelhouse."

"Sure thing," the man said, rushing off.

Judson rejoined Howard, and said, "Get rid of the fella you're totin' an' come with me."

"All right, Judd." Howard passed the man to another soldier, leaving the line of prisoners to go with his friend. "Where we goin'?"

"Aboard Capt'n McKay's ship."

When the two men got on board, they acted like part of the crew, coiling lines, so no one would notice them waiting for the Federal soldiers to join them. While Judson was appearing to be busy, he saw a sailor carry a puppy and a carpet bag aboard, then knock on a cabin door. Brooke opened the door, crying with delight when she saw the man had brought her pet and belongings.

"Judd, that's Rascal," Howard said, starting toward the cabin.

Judson grabbed his arm, and snapped, "Howard, we can't let anybody know we're aboard yet."

The big man turned back, nodding glumly.

A few minutes later, Ethan appeared with a dozen armed men. "This is all I could get, but I notified the officer in charge about the escape plan. He said he'd round up some men and join us in a few minutes."

"Good," Judson said. "Let's take over the bridge."

The men cautiously moved forward, and Judson peered inside the wheelhouse doorway. The bridge was deserted except for the quartermaster. Judson waved the soldiers back. He did not want to act until he knew where McKay was.

Being recognized by Howard caught McKay completely off guard. Although he had instructed his men to put the prisoners into the hold, which meant Howard would soon be down there and out of the way, he still needed to be careful until just before the ship left the dock. McKay desperately wanted to see Brooke, so he went to her cabin by going through the rear door in the bridge.

When McKay opened the door to his cabin, Brooke flew into his arms, kissing him. "Oh, Wade!' she cried with tears of joy streaming down her face. "You don't know how I prayed for this nightmare to end. I had lost all hope. Then, my handsome protector appeared," she said, hugging him tighter.

Stroking her back, McKay said, "I promised you when we went to Thalian Hall if the Yankees ever came, I'd take you on my ship and sail away. Remember? Well, I'm going to keep that promise. In another fifteen minutes, we'll leave the dock and all our troubles will be behind us."

Wade grew serious. "Brooke, your friend Virginia set you up to be captured."

Brooke's mouth opened in shocked. "No! That can't be true."

"Yes it is. It seems Virginia had knowledge of the Federal attack. She faked her mother being ill, then asked you to go in her place. She wanted you to be inside the fort during the attack."

Brooke clenched her fists. "That bitch!"

"I also have her tied to a chair in the next cabin," McKay said.

Brooke appeared confused. "Why did you bring her here?"

"Well, I needed an appropriate punishment for her."

"Oh? What do you intend to do?"

Smiling, Wade said, "I'll show you in a minute, but first I have to see if the prisoners are finished boarding yet." McKay peered out the door. He saw Judson and Howard with a dozen armed Federal soldiers, and closed it before they had a chance to notice him.

"Are the prisoners on board?" she asked.

"Yes. They've finished loading. I also saw Judson Bates and some Yankee soldiers about fifty feet away, near the forward hatch. I think they know this is a trick." Wade opened a desk drawer and handed a Colt revolver to Brooke. "Take this pistol for protection and stay here."

Brooke was always afraid of guns and placed it on the desk. "What are you going to do?"

"Untie Virginia."

"Why on earth would you do that?"

"You'll see," McKay said, opening the door to the corridor which joined the two rooms. Wade went next door to where Virginia was. He untied her from the chair, but left the gag in her mouth.

Virginia's eyes widened with fright when she saw Brooke glare at her.

"I hope you've got a good punishment for her," Brooke said with contempt. "Because if you don't, you could leave us alone for ten minutes."

"You two? Not a chance," McKay said with a hint of amusement. "The way I have it planned, I'll release Virginia on shore right before we leave. The Yankees will think she helped the prisoners to escape, and arrest her."

"Not bad," Brooke said, smiling.

"Thank you. When I give the signal, open the door, and I'll shove her out."

In a moment, McKay nodded and the door swung open. He pushed Virginia out on deck, then steered her down to the end of the gangplank, where he removed her gag and the rope from her wrists. "I hope you like Yankees, Virginia, because they're really going to love you!" he said, shoving her ashore.

Virginia fell on the dock, glaring up at him. "You bastard, Wade! I hope you rot in hell for this!"

"You stand a better chance than me, Virginia!" McKay called, running up the gangplank. When he got aboard, the sailors on deck heaved the mooring lines into the water. McKay hurried to the engine room skylight, yelling through the hatch, "Mr. Reichman, all ahead full!"

There was a rumble from below as the engines thumped to life, then fountains of sparks whirled from the two tall stacks as the steamship accelerated.

Several deckhands were rushing to remove the gangplank.

"Leave it, men. We've no time to lose," McKay said, pointing to the mob of blue-coated soldiers running on the dock toward the *Atlantis*. "Come with me. We've got Yankees aboard!" he said, drawing his pistol, then charging the soldiers outside the bridge.

When the ship began to move, the startled Federal soldiers aboard the *Atlantis* glanced around to see what was happening. They saw men running toward them, but these men were wearing Federal naval uniforms, so they didn't shoot.

Leveling his revolver at the sailors and firing, Judson shouted, "Shoot 'em, boys! They're Confederates!"

The rest of the men with Judson opened fire. Bullets whistled through the air, smacking into the deck, splintering wood.

A minié ball whipped past McKay's head, thumping into another man's chest. The round knocked the sailor off his feet, and he tumbled to the deck. McKay had just six bullets, so he fired his revolver only when he was sure of a target. He drew a bead on a soldier, who was ramming a bullet down the smoking barrel of his musket, then squeezed off a shot. The man was snatched backward, his rifle flying in one direction and the ramrod in another.

Two of Bates' men took up positions around the forward hatch, so they could fire at anyone climbing the ladder from the engine room.

The soldiers on shore made the situation more dangerous by shooting at anyone aboard the ship. When the firing became heaviest, Bates scurried for the protection of the bridge. The quartermaster looked at him in surprise, then snatched a pistol from beside the wheel. This was all the persuading Bates needed. Whirling around, he raced out the door, then hid behind the fire hose box just outside the bridge.

One of McKay's men screamed as a bullet hit him in the face. Another staggered to where the railing should be, but the steel gangplank had ripped it from the deck and tore off the front of the paddle wheel box when the ship left the dock. His blood-stained hands were clutching his belly, and he plunged to the water below.

A rifle bullet smashed into McKay's left thigh with the force of a mule kick, slamming him to the deck. While minié balls whistled and cracked scant inches above his head, McKay rolled onto his stomach. He took advantage of his stable prone position, emptying his revolver at the Federals.

A screaming Yankee charged the Confederates, a pistol blazing in either hand. Shot after shot plucked at the blue coat he wore, but nothing seemed to stop him. He finally flopped to the deck a few feet from McKay, twitching as blood spurted from his chest.

The gunfire became sporadic, then trailed off as more men fell. When the shooting sputtered to a stop, Bates stared out across the deck. No one remained standing. Only dead and wounded littered the ship. Thinking it was safe, he emerged from behind the fire hose box and crept forward. Bates walked down the deck, shooting each wounded Confederate soldier in the head. When Bates pointed his pistol at McKay, he heard Howard calling behind him.

"Hey, Judd, you're alive!"

"Yeah. Looky who I got here," he announced to Howard, as the big man came alongside him. "I got me a Yankee spy."

McKay struggled to get up, but his wounded left leg buckled under him, and he collapsed back to the wooden deck. "Howard, you've got to help me," McKay pleaded. "I'm not a spy, but Judson is. He helped the Yankees capture Fort Fisher. Now, he's trying to take us to prison."

"Don't pay him no mind," Bates snapped. "You can see for yoursef that lyin' dog's wearin' a Yankee uniform."

"Yes. I am," McKay admitted to Howard. "But I was pretending, so I could help you escape."

While the men were arguing, Brooke peered out of the cabin's window. She took the revolver Wade had given her, then slipped through the rear door to the bridge. She did not know Rascal had followed her. Brooke snuck up behind Judson and Howard, cocking the revolver, and said, "Don't anyone move or I'll shoot."

Bates turned around, grinning. "Well, what do we have here? A little lady with a big gun."

Brooke held the heavy Colt revolver in her trembling hands, praying she would not have to use it. "Wade's right, Howard. Judson is a spy," she said with an edge of fear in her voice. "He's also a murderer."

"She's a damned liar," Bates said, "but I got me a way to deal with traitors like her."

As Bates leveled his revolver at Brooke, Rascal ran from the bridge. Terrified to see his puppy so close to the line of fire, Howard grabbed Judson's gun hand, yelling, "Don't shoot, Judd!"

The revolver fired when Bates tried to wrestle it away, but the shot went through the fleshy part of Howard's right arm and did little damage.

The men grappled for the gun, while Brooke ran closer so she would not shoot Howard. Unfortunately she came too near, and Bates backhanded her. She flew across the deck, falling to the river below.

McKay screamed in horror, pulling himself toward the edge of the ship.

Rascal joined the fray, growling and tugging on Bates' pant leg. Judson kicked the dog to free his leg, and Rascal yelped in pain.

Judson had gone too far. Howard may have been able to forgive his friend for shooting him, but not for hurling Brooke into the river and hurting his puppy. The big man picked Judson up and carried him to the edge of the deck, then hurled the screaming man into the paddle wheel. Judson's clothing became tangled in the iron framework, and he was dragged underwater with every revolution.

Each time he surfaced, his screams were a little more feeble, and his face was paler.

Brooke appeared in the bubbling wake behind the *Atlantis*. McKay watched hopefully for any sign of life, but there was none. Finally, because of the swirling black water and the distance involved, she drifted from his sight.

Three Federal gunboats steamed around the bend in the river, firing at the fleeing blockade-runners.

Unable to go to the bridge because of his wound, McKay cried, "Howard, tell the quartermaster to turn around! We have to go back and save Brooke."

Howard faced McKay, his cheeks glistening from his tears. The Yankee cannons thundering in the background. "Brooke's gone, Capt'n. I saw her body floatin' behind us, then it disappeared."

"No!" McKay shook his head, screaming. "She's still alive. Turn this ship around."

Cannonballs shrieked through the air, plunging into the river fifty feet astern.

Howard helped the injured man to his cabin. "It's too late, Capt'n," he said, easing McKay onto the bed.

McKay knew he must put the safety of his ship and men before his own concerns. If they turned around, more men would die. Every minute that went by carried Brooke farther downstream, closer to the enemy. He held his head in his hands, and said, "The Yankees will be turning around soon. Their ships will be in range of Fort Anderson's guns any minute now."

No sooner had he finished speaking, then he heard the heavy rumble of big Confederate guns. McKay lay back on his bed, listening to the artillery duel, wishing he had died with Brooke.

When the *Atlantis* docked in Wilmington, the spirited strains of *Dixie* filtered in the window of McKay's cabin. He listened to the music, but he could find no joy in it. Sure, he had released hundreds of Confederate prisoners, but in doing so, he had lost Brooke and many of his crew. He also heard the excited voices of a crowd waiting to see their new hero. McKay could not disappoint them.

"Howard, give me a hand. I'd like to go outside."

Howard, holding his puppy and staring out the window, turned to help McKay out of bed. Surgeon Singleton had given McKay a crutch to help him get around. Howard grabbed it, helping Wade to his feet.

However, it was not McKay the crowd had come to see. Most of the people stood near the gangplank to get a better look at the shabby, dirty faced Confederate soldiers as they unloaded from the ship. Hundreds of hopeful eyes searched every face that appeared. Some came away delighted when they saw a loved one. Others became increasingly nervous as man after man walked by them, and still there was no sign of a husband or sweetheart. A few individuals were cheering. Their jubilant voices seemed odd at first. Then McKay understood. These people had nothing but bad news for more than a year. Sherman, who had burned a path of destruction through Georgia and South Carolina, was now threatening to invade North Carolina. General Grant, whom Robert E. Lee had fought to a standstill in Virginia, was finally gaining the upper hand because his army was being supplied with more men and material than the South could provide. Fort Fisher had fallen two weeks ago, and 10,000 Yankees were only 25 miles away. It was merely a question of time until they smashed through the thin Confederate defenses and captured the city. But now there was good news for a change, and these people seized it with all the enthusiasm they could muster.

McKay glanced at the band and grew even more sad. It was made up of old men and boys. Practically all Wilmington had to offer.

Farther down the wharf, the blockade-runner disguised as the *USS North Point* was unloading more Confederate soldiers. A seaman in a loose fitting uniform ran ashore, fighting through the crowd to the *Atlantis*. The sailor pushed past the men coming down the gangplank and burst onto the deck.

The buzz of excited voices drew McKay to see what the commotion was about. Suddenly, he saw Brooke emerge from the throng of prisoners wearing a baggy sailor's uniform. She rushed McKay's arms. Brooke lifted her face to his, and he kissed her passionately. When the kiss broke, McKay looked at Brooke and said, "I thought you were dead."

She smiled, slipping her arms around his neck. "So did I when I fell in front of that paddle wheel," she said. "Oh, Wade, I was so frightened. I dove down in the water, but the wheel pushed me to the bottom. My dress got caught in the branches of a sunken tree. So I tore it off and swam to the surface. There was so much shooting all around."

"Your dress!" McKay cried. "That's what Howard saw."

"Yes. But I was able to swim to the North Point, and a sailor jumped in to get me," she said, tears filling her eyes. Unable to say more, Brooke kissed the man she loved.

The End

ABOUT THE AUTHOR

Originally from Chicago, Illinois, Richard Triebe is a freelance writer living in Wilmington, North Carolina. He has an Associate in Applied Science degree in Marine Technology and much of his writing concerns the sea and underwater activities. His hobbies include the Civil War and scuba diving and underwater photography.